Praise for *Lit Life*

"Gossipy enough to keep you turning the pages at a steady clip."
—*USA Today*

"A once-promising novelist battling writer's block hooks up with his literary hero; together, they're mercilessly lampooned in this hilarious debut novel about the publishing world."   —*People*

"[An] adroit comic novel . . . This biting sendup of New York's literary scene cruises along, establishing the kind of perfect momentum those eastbound weekenders on the Long Island Expressway can only dream about."   —*Los Angeles Times Book Review*

"An entertaining guide for any[one] still toying with that great-American-novel idea."   —*GQ*

"A wicked sendup of the writing life."
—*The Atlanta Journal-Constitution*

"Wenzel has an insider's knowledge and cautionary sympathy for the pitfalls and queasy pratfalls of the writing life, as well as a sly affinity for embellishment, portraiture and blistering caricature and a well-tuned ear for the expertly aimed zinger."
—*The Miami Herald*

"Wenzel marches us in so heedlessly that we dig his chutzpah and enjoy the ride. . . . The novel moves, too, with limber prose cantering just behind the galloping plot." —*San Francisco Chronicle*

"Among its many accomplishments, *Lit Life* . . . reveals the excess and dishonor in the literary culture without dismissing the moral potential within it. . . . It proves both entertaining and thought-provoking."   —*St. Louis Post-Dispatch*

Photo: © Sebastian Piras

Lit Life is KURT WENZEL's first novel. In addition to writing fiction, he is a contributing editor at Privymagazine.com. He and his wife live in New York City and East Hampton, New York. For more information about Kurt Wenzel or *Lit Life* visit www.kurtwenzel.com.

Lit Life

Lit Life

A NOVEL

KURT WENZEL

RANDOM HOUSE TRADE PAPERBACKS
NEW YORK

2002 Random House Trade Paperback Edition

Copyright © 2001 by Kurt Wenzel

This work was originally published in hardcover by Random House, Inc., in 2001.

Grateful acknowledgment is made to Alfred A. Knopf, a division of Random House, Inc., for permission to reprint excerpts from *The Journals of John Cheever* by John Cheever. Copyright © 1990 by Mary Cheever, Susan Cheever, Benjamin Cheever, and Federico Cheever. Reprinted by permission of Alfred A. Knopf, a division of Random House, Inc.

Library of Congress Cataloging-in-Publication Data

Wenzel, Kurt.
Lit life : a novel / Kurt Wenzel.
p. cm.
ISBN 0-375-76031-8
1. Manhattan (New York, N.Y.)—Fiction. 2. Hamptons (N.Y.)—Fiction. 3. Male friendship—Fiction. 4. Authorship—Fiction. 5. Novelists—Fiction. I. Title.
PS3573.E573 L58 2001
813'.6—dc21   00-051832

Random House website address: www.atrandom.com
Printed in the United States of America
2 4 6 8 9 7 5 3 1

To anyone who ever doubted me,

and to my mother, who never did.

Phyllis Wenzel 1942–1997

ACKNOWLEDGMENTS

To my father, for unflagging support in everything, always. To my beloved wife, Ty, for believing before there was a reason to. To Doug and Pamela, for plucking me from the abyss of obscurity. To my aunt Sida, and again, my father, for the financial assistance that allowed me to write the first half of this book without spirit-deadening employment. To Guillermo and Francis, for friendship and for pretending the early stuff was good.

Lit Life

Morning. All was quiet. The bombardment had ended. The swirling tidal pools washed away, the great fissures open, still gaping from the catastrophe. Along the concave, the rubble lay in ruinous pile after ruinous pile, dust hanging inert, sparkling in the light.

Goddamn. What went on last night?

Without lifting his battered skull, the young man opened his eyes, taking prostrate reconnaissance of his surroundings. Just below, at eye level, black and white tile, cool, soothing against a grit-covered cheek. Above, the hip swell of baby-blue porcelain, the voluptuous contours fouled by rivulets of a greenish brown glaze.

All in all, a somewhat discouraging topography.

Not to mention the odor, which was not quite urine but more distilled spirits, impossibly various, turned sour-sweet. At least the bathroom was his own, he was pleased to discover. Yes, beloved Jesus, at least there was that.

He propped himself up on a dirt-spiked elbow, testing the waters.

Choppy to say the least. Then, suddenly, another tidal pool began to swirl, demanding a place to break . . .

Ah, I love you, Porcelain God. I kiss your big fat Buddha belly. Hug it, plump and welcoming. It understands my weakness. Want is suffering, yes, you are right. One day I will renounce these desires. One day.

The survivors were silent, a soft moan from under the rubble. Only they knew, only they could speak of it.

Lord of fucking God, what went on last night?

PART 1

Charmed Life

1

A dark New York noon, the sky a gray silhouette. A storm is blanketing the city. Ten inches of the stuff, and still the subways are on schedule, the *Times* stacked high in the newsstands. From midtown on down, the offices are full, the windows glowing above with ambitious, amber light. Even the corner vendor is there for you, Fagin-like, fingerless gloves spearing kabobs, boilers billowing smoke like cauldrons.

The Northeast is on its knees, says the weatherman. But the city is impervious, defending its dreamers like a castle.

Downtown, meanwhile, one such dreamer sits, feet on desk, laptop glowing empty before him, searching eyes drifting out a tenement window. Seven aspirin float half dissolved in his belly, helpless dinghies on the Sea of Bacchanal. The morning's mission? Simple. To do something. *Anything.* To get his shit together.

Today will be the day, Kyle Clayton announced in his head. Today's the day when I start again.

The screen glows with naked urgency.

Minutes later a number is dialed, a phone is picked up.

"What," a voice quickly answered, its brusqueness suggesting interruption, irritation, fury.

"Don't tell me you're working."

"Goddamn, Clayton," came the response, punctuated with a sigh. "I shoulda known. Whaddaya want?"

"Just checking up on my rival. Making sure writing's getting done, that the commonweal of literature's still turning, so to speak, on this most gorgeous of afternoons."

"Blow it out your ass."

"When'd you get started?"

"Dawn."

Bastard, Kyle whispered to himself.

"What?"

"Me too."

Kyle could just picture it, the prolific Devon Schiff, at his desk by seven in Gap jammies, cup of Wakeuptime tea next to him. The worker bee. A disciplined son of a bitch, he had to admit. Had everything down to the minute, this guy: designated times for lunch, phone calls, jerking off—all of it strictly observed. Didn't even own a television set. The Mennonite of young writers.

And every year a book. A nice, well-crafted, Go-ahead-bore-the-shit-out-of-me-see-if-I-care book. A friggin' machine.

"Sure, Kyle. Hundred bucks says you're staring at an empty screen, that you haven't touched a key."

Kyle keystroked the letter *a,* just to rebuke him.

"All right," Kyle said resignedly, "so maybe I'm off to a slow start today. But haven't you looked outside? It's a snow day."

"A *what?*"

"Snow day," he repeated. "How can you work when it's snowing out?"

"I don't even know what that means."

In the background Kyle heard the sound of typing. Fucker's working right over me.

"Don't you remember being a kid? A snow day, schmucko. No work."

"I'm thirty-two years old."

The typing was gaining speed, a cacophony of productivity.

" 'Be true to the dreams of your youth.' Herman Melville. Ever hear of him?"

"All your heroes were failures, Clayton. Think about it. What does that make you?"

A conspicuous pause. The typing continued.

"I haven't failed," Kyle said finally, the wound audible in his voice. "I just haven't tried lately."

Devon's typing stopped now, the break suggesting a rare surge of regret. The failure comment was out of line. And not even true. Devon knew—hell, *everybody* knew—that Kyle Clayton had tasted the kind of success he could only dream of. Some years ago now, granted. But nevertheless, a stunning, improbable, infinitely enviable success.

"I'm not saying you're a failure, Clay. I just want to see you working again. Everybody does." A few last clicks on Devon's keyboard. Nails in a coffin. "Anyway, I'm going. I'll see you at the party tonight."

"Whoa, whoa, whoa, hold on," Kyle urged. "Some punks over on Broadway threw snowballs at me when I went for my coffee. Whaddaya say we go retaliate?"

Schiff offered up another sigh, this one full of weary sanctimony. "I have no time for snowballs, Kyle. And neither do you."

"What's wrong with snowballs?"

"You should be working, that's what. It's what you're always talking about, isn't it? Working. You keep *calling* me to *tell* me how you should be working. Clayton, your talent . . . it's immense. But you refuse to use it."

Not a word.

"When was the last time you put in a full day? I'll bet it's been months. What're you doing, Clay? This is what everybody wants to know."

Silence.

"Clay?"

"Lunch then," Kyle said suddenly. "There's this new bistro just opened up down the street."

Devon laughed. "Oh, man. You *are* insane."

"C'mon. We'll order an irresponsible bottle of wine and watch the snow come down and talk about how you'll never be as good as me despite all your tenacious dedication."

"I'm hanging up now."

"All right, all right. But let me leave you with one nagging thought, if I may."

"Not interested."

"It's about your work."

There was no response, but Kyle could picture it: Devon staring at the receiver, clearly smelling the blood on the trap—too weak not to have a taste. Like most world-class fuckups, Kyle Clayton possessed a keen sense of the flaws in others. Devon had been impressed with his opinions of fellow writers, the peccadillos in their craft, the dead spots in their character that manifested themselves on the page. If he was giving out free critiques this morning, Kyle thought, Devon Schiff would not resist.

Kyle said, "I'm worried about you."

"Oh, really?"

"Yes. There's something that's tormenting you lately."

Schiff sniggered into the phone.

"I know the signs, believe me. You've met so many of your ambitions—God knows you're ambitious—but there are still nights when you can't sleep, when you have nightmares."

"This is funny, Clay. Really. Top-shelf stuff."

"We both know what it is, don't we?"

There was no answer, though Kyle imagined his rival's heart thumping.

"You're worried that deep down inside—and I'm not talking about your ego here, that's impenetrable—I'm speaking now about in the depths of your heart, in your *gut*—"

"Go on."

"Yes, deep down in your gut you're worried that you're mediocre."

Devon delivered a scoffing laugh that fell short. "Go back to bed, Clay. You're still drunk. I can smell your breath over the phone."

"Now, granted," Kyle continued, "in the under-thirty-five club you're seen as top dog. But you know this means nothing. You're worried that it's by default. That maybe the fact that you're gay has given you a leg up in these timid times."

"*Fuck* you."

"When you go back and read your books you see things in your writing, things that make you wince. Clearly it's good work, but it lacks something. Some magic."

"Your work lacks something too, Kyle. It's called ink—"

"And so I've become worried about you, because I think you may be right."

"Lazy piece of shit."

"And I think I know why. In fact I've just realized this now. Do you want to know what it is?"

"You has-been," Schiff murmured.

Kyle waited for the hang-up. It didn't come.

"Because anybody who could shut his curtains and dribble his fingers across a keyboard during a snowstorm like this has no romantic spirit. No reckless spontaneity in the face of beauty. And if you don't have those things, my friend, you are *lost* as a writer. Utterly lost. I pity you."

"You need help, Clayton. You're off the deep end."

"Look at the storm, Devon. As your friend, I demand it. Open your blinds right now and look at it. It's beautiful! LOOK AT THE STORM, YOU FUCKING MACHINE—"

Click.

KYLE SAT in the half-bedroom he used as his study, watching the snow. His head was getting worse, the brain cells reduced to cinders. There would be no work again today, he knew. Today would be another in a line of lost days. Lost years. At least this morning's excuse would leave him with a little less than the usual mind-numbing guilt. There'd been a holocaust in his head. How could he be expected to perform? That this devastation had been his own doing, of course, was not a detail to be looked at too closely.

Plus, hell, it was a snow day.

Then there was Schiff's comment about failure. Much of this, Kyle knew, came from jealousy. Not that he wasn't used to it by now. At twenty-five Clayton had published an absurdly successful first novel, *Charmed Life,* and had quickly became a literary star, the supernova of young authors. Just four years out of college, a dropout no less, and suddenly his life had begun manifesting all the perverse clichés of a certain kind of American fame. His name, for example, appearing in bold type in bad newspapers. Various Hollywood agents—that impulsively nurturing bunch—started calling him at home, just curious to see "how he was doing." At parties so many women would slip their number into his pocket, one friend began calling him the "human lotto drawing." *And the winner is . . . Surprise! We have a three-way tie!*

But something had happened. A full two years after the book hit, there was still no new fiction from Kyle Clayton. No previously unpublishable short stories, no hastily written novellas punched out to capitalize on his success. All to the great disappointment of his agent, Larry Wabzug. "Their tongues are out, my friend," Wabzug had told him. "It's time to stoke this fire."

Larry was old-school. Honorable but realistic. He warned Kyle to keep the buzz going, reminded him that his good fortune was unprecedented and needed tending.

Six months later Wabzug began to plead. "Give me something old, then, if you're not going to work," he said. "They'll take anything. Something you did in high school, for chrissakes."

When still nothing new came, he reverted to threats. "They'll forget you, Clayton. You don't think they will? Shit, you're *already* half forgotten."

As of this snowy afternoon, it had been seven years since *Charmed Life*. Except for a few limpid celebrity profiles (all of them, suspiciously, with young actresses) and a few harsh reviews of some of his contemporaries' books, nothing of Kyle Clayton's authorship had appeared in print. Offers of writing assignments had disappeared; his name had faded from the tabloids.

He had not spoken to Larry Wabzug in almost two years.

Wandering to the kitchen, Kyle discovered a note, the handwriting scraggy, hasty: *Just had to say that you are the most repulsive, most disgusting man I have ever met. Seriously. I mean barring NONE. Fuck you, creep!*

What went on last night? Always best not to know.

2

Early in the morning that same day, a two-and-a-half-hour drive east of the city in the town of Sag Harbor, Long Island, Richard Whitehurst rose from his bed for the twenty-three thousand three hundred seventy-sixth time. Or so he had calculated.

His limbs creaked, lungs labored. The old heave-ho of waking. In his stomach, the nausea of an aging man. The detritus and bilge of old organs, decaying in the night.

Why get up at all? he'd been asking himself these days. Give me one good reason.

Answer: What the bloody hell's the alternative?

Behind him, his wife stirred. "Come back to bed," she murmured. "It's so *cold*."

The room was enveloped with a bone-snapping chill, as the house always seemed to be in winter. Why? Richard wanted to know. He'd never asked the question before, yet suddenly it demanded an answer. How had it come to this?

Their house, Whitehurst knew, had never exactly been the envy of the East End. It was an old sea captain's house, built in the 1830s, and although in this way it was not so different from the other homes on John Street, it was, in practicality, nothing like its brothers. The grounds, for one, were a mess. The roof sagged like a hammock. The interior was badly in need of renovation. As for the heat, or lack of it, Richard could not remember ever checking the insulation of the old house in the twenty-one years he and his wife had lived here. To be honest, he wondered if he knew what proper insulation should even *look* like.

Previously, this was not a fault that Whitehurst had ever concerned himself with. If he was not Mr. Handyman, the kind of fellow to be found with the wail of a bandsaw screeching from his garage on a Saturday morning, so much the better. If he never looked at a checkbook, if he never knew how the VCR worked, if he was confounded by a simple train schedule, well, so what? Wasn't that all part of the cruel compromise that made life so bittersweet? "The more you are one thing," his father used to say, "the less you are another." What he *could* do was write. He was a creator of aesthetic pleasure, an artist (though he shuddered to call himself that). Word for word, it had been said, one of the best writers in America. His sentences shimmered, cut and polished like diamonds. His contemporaries swooned at his talent, worshipped him like a god, a genius. Did anyone really give a green turd if he didn't know how to work the steam iron?

He was no longer sure. He was no longer sure about anything, really, for Richard Whitehurst had recently been taking a severe look at himself. The kind of self-laceration people subject themselves to after a bad love affair, say, or the tragic death of a loved one, though Richard could not claim either of these as an excuse. It was a kind of reassessment. One that had been slowly under way now for the better part of a year. The kind of reassessment that had prompted an aging writer disinclined to numbers to take out a calculator one unproductive morning a few weeks earlier and multiply the sixty-four years of his life times 365, of course adding in sixteen leap years. Just for kicks.

He'd written the digits down in large numerals on the yellow, legal-sized paper usually reserved for his painstaking prose:

23,376

At first the figure seemed quite large to him. Over twenty thousand mornings! An optimistic number, was it not? Full of the proof of a generous God who granted us an endless stretch of time, relatively speaking. Time in which to make mistakes, recover, fail again, and finally get our act together, if we had any brains at all. Plenty of time to get it right.

But the longer he looked at it, the more paltry a figure it seemed to become. Twenty thousand? That's *it*? You call that a *life*? The figure could probably have been doubled or tripled and it still wouldn't have mattered. In his state of mind, it was the number's simple existence, the very fact of life's finiteness, that enraged him.

So then on this morning, as he watched his sleeping wife exhale plumes of vapor from bluish lips, the lack of heat in their house was no longer the charming eccentricity of a literary genius. How could he pretend anymore? Just a year ago he had given them his best, his magnum opus, a book ten years in the making, his blood and guts, only to see it disappear without a trace. No, he was not a literary genius— he'd decided that once and for all. He was simply a fragile old man, lonely to his bones, a disgrace as a father, a failed artist who couldn't even provide his dear young wife with proper warmth in winter.

Come back to bed, darling. It's so cold.

The words lanced his heart. Throwing on his robe, he rummaged through the closet and found an old afghan blanket, which he added on top of the others—layer number four. He thought for a moment of rejoining her in bed, to use his body to keep hers warm, but by the time he rearranged the covers, pulling them up to her chin, she was fast asleep again. This eased just enough guilt for him to head downstairs, to begin the journey, the Monday-morning ritual that led to yet another week of work.

I'm a writer, hear the caffeine coursing through my veins. See the pile of fingernails under my desk. I am writer, hear me groan.

The ritual had been the same for fifteen years now. Every Monday morning at seven sharp, regardless of season or weather, Whitehurst hauled his bag of bones out to his Ford Bronco—in winter he stoked the engine for five minutes or so—and then drove forty minutes to Montauk, to a small secluded road almost near the Point. There he took down the chain with the NO TRESPASSING sign attached, parked his truck under a hovel of pines, and began walking, for almost a mile, back through a path walled by high sea grass. He had been walking here since back when the property was state land, and he was pleased that its current owners—an aging pop star and wife number four—didn't seem to mind his presence, despite their obvious lust for privacy.

A few minutes' walk past the house, Whitehurst would reach the ocean, atop severe cliffs that dropped off hundreds of feet down. It was almost like a stage, this vantage point, before him the diorama of a burly sea, unforgiving, heroic. Here, at one of the end points of America, he found his escape from the insularity of writing. Once a week without fail he came here to gain perspective, inspiration. Despite the years of struggle, his Monday mornings were a lifeblood, reviving him. The Atlantic urged him with a message: Push on, friend. It can be done. An illusion, probably, but nevertheless, to him Monday morning said, *possibility*. To miss the ritual was *im*possible.

In the kitchen, he parted the curtains. The dawn looked ominous. A low, punishing wind was whipping off the bay, shaking the barren trees, the cold seeming to have washed all color from the earth. The thought of venturing out into that stark scene was daunting, crushing to the spirit. He squinted; were those snowflakes he was seeing, whirling in the wind like bits of fine sugar? A storm was coming in today, he remembered. Meryl had warned him of it, had urged him not to go today. Just this once.

But he would go, Richard knew. He would whine and curse and bitch and moan, then zipper his coat and remove the keys from the little hook above the sink. Just as he had always done. Genius or no genius, he would forge ahead.

What in bloody hell was the alternative?

3

The Plaza Hotel had never looked more inviting, Clayton decided, shielding his eyes from the snow as he exited the subway at the corner of the park. He grinned at the memory, nine years earlier, of an afternoon whiled away in one of the larger suites. He was new to the city and had gotten lucky with a very rich girl on a theater date the night before. She was not a great beauty, if he remembered correctly, but then, that wasn't really the point. The point was that here was a poor Jersey boy, a recent college dropout whose formative years had been spent in the cement hell of a "garden" apartment complex, now strolling naked through a room at the Plaza Hotel, empty bottles of champagne strewn across the floor like expended grenades. Through the dusting of icy snow on the windows you could see people getting into horse carriages near the fountain, and out at the far expanse of the park the great sea of lightly dandruffed trees. He'd decided that afternoon that he liked New York very much, oh, yes. Very much indeed. Decided you could do some serious damage here. Decided, like many an optimistic young man before him, that he would stay and make it his.

But unlike those millions of other mad dreamers, Kyle Clayton had somehow made it happen. In fact, it was that very same day that he'd begun his great success, *Charmed Life*. Just sat down that night with a legal pad and a six-pack and banged it out—or so said his much compromised powers of recollection. The indisputable part of the tale was that eighteen months later he'd become that most endangered of species, the literary celebrity. Yes, for one shining moment Kyle Clayton had seized the great city by its wide trunk and had held on. Forget that he was slipping now. That was no matter. He'd done it once and would damn well do it again. He was sure of it.

"Martini," Kyle said, barely through the revolving doors of his destination.

Ordinarily Harry Cipriani's would be bursting at this hour. The heavy cocktail crowd, the power-lunch bunch. Today, though, the storm had lopped its inhabitants in half. There were just a few diners in back, and the bar was empty. Kyle had no problem finding a seat.

"Hey, Joe," Kyle said as the barman wiped down the space in front of him.

Joe was old-time, a sturdy-looking fellow somewhere in his late fifties. He wore a plaid bow tie and had a face like a horse's saddle, formed in a time when life was still interesting enough to forge people's features into something worth a look. He was known to make the best martini in the city. And Kyle was a loyal disciple.

Joe's secret, Kyle had discovered, was simple. It entailed three essentials: temperature, temperature, temperature. And despite the afternoon's frigid inclemency, today, apparently, would be no different. Clayton watched avidly as the bartender turned to his freezer, removed shaker, glasses, gin, vermouth, *and* olives, and set them in front of the young man. Seeing those heavenly elements so close, Kyle

felt his cheeks pinch, taste glands rev up like engines; he forced himself to sit patiently as Joe combined the ingredients and shook them
with his powerful wrists. Soon a frost developed on the outside of the
closed chalice, a finger-numbing, eighty-proof sleet.

"Watch the frostbite," Kyle quipped, nearly mad now with anticipation.

Finally Joe began to strain the liquid into the Y-shaped glass. Kyle
could do little but shake his head, awed by the purity that was emerg-
ing. Not even a drink, really. More a potation, a frothy, heavenly
quicksilver, a glacial sublimity that could, as one restaurant critic put
it, "numb the lips of a polar bear."

"Class in a glass," Joe said, shaking out the last of it. It was what
he always said.

He stepped back and watched Kyle's hand quiver ever so slightly
as he brought the glass to his mouth. Although the glass was vibrat-
ing perceptibly, and filled to the very top, Joe watched, impressed, as
not a drop of the steely liquid left the rim before he brought it to port.
Then Kyle's eyes closed, as if in relief.

The consummate professional, thought Joe, who'd seen quite a
few. A true prodigy.

"You *wastrel*," announced a voice suddenly from behind Kyle's
bar stool. "You pathetic son of a bitch."

Kyle turned and was startled almost out of his seat by the familiar
figure poised there in accusatory gaze, awkward and Chaplinesque. It
was his agent, Larry Wabzug.

Clayton smiled meekly, trying to move his martini out of sight.

"Nice, Kyle," Wabzug continued, looking down at his watch.
"Lovely. It's what, a quarter to one? In the old days you'd at least
start with Bloody Marys."

Joe quietly moved to the other side of the bar.

"How are you?" Kyle said, fixing his eyes on his old friend. He was the same as ever—short with thick glasses, black blazer too large for him, the nasally voice, yet altogether somehow dignified. Kyle wondered if Larry had turned seventy yet.

"Been a long time."

"Has it, Larry?"

"Close to two years."

Kyle suddenly recalled their first meeting. Many years ago now, but how could he forget? He'd submitted his novel through a friend, and Larry Wabzug, a legend among literary agents, had wanted to speak to him about it. The walls of the waiting room were lined with framed covers of books penned by writers Wabzug represented, writers Kyle had worshipped for years. Finally he was called in. He could still remember, syllable for syllable, those first immortal words as he sat there sweating in the old man's office:

Young man—Wabzug had taken his glasses off then, rubbing his eyes as if in disbelief—*I can barely express to you how excited I am, having read your manuscript for the first time last evening.*

It was the moment of Kyle's life.

"I've been working again, Larry," he said now.

Wabzug gestured to his drink. "I can see."

"No, I mean it. Something special. I . . . I don't know what it is. The stuff just *flows*."

The agent groaned cynically, letting Kyle know he'd heard it all before, that he didn't believe a goddamned word.

"Who you here with?" Kyle asked, looking back to scan the dining room. Wabzug never was and never would be a Cipriani's kind of guy. His idea of lunch was beef tongue on rye and a salty pickle.

Larry hesitated. Suddenly he seemed uncomfortable.

"A new client," he said finally.

At that moment an extremely tall, almost beautiful woman in her early thirties stood up from her table in the back of the restaurant and made a beeline for the bar.

"Oh, you've got to be kidding," Kyle said under his breath.

As she approached, the woman held out her hand, eyes bulging.

"Lorrie darling," Larry said, lacking some enthusiasm, "have you met—"

"Kyle *Clayton,* oh my *Gawd*!"

Clayton smiled back laboriously, then extended a limpid group of fingers.

"Forgive me," Lorrie said, holding her chest in mild hyperventilation, "I'm a little starstruck. I must have read *Charmed Life* a dozen times."

Lorrie Terell wrote what could loosely be called short stories, mostly about heavily sexed young women and their adventures in the big bad city. Once a year she collected them in a very slim hardcover with large type and a photo of her on the book jacket, clad in bra, garters, and high heels, sprawled come-hither on the unkempt bed of some downtown loft. Her last addition to the literary canon was titled *Bone in My Throat.*

"I just want to thank you," she said to Kyle.

"For what?"

"For paving the way for me and so many others."

Though he didn't like it much, Lorrie was probably right. After the success of his novel, publishers were relentless in their search for the next wunderkind, the next Kyle Clayton. And so by the end of the eighties it seemed that every twenty-something with a number-two pencil had a book deal. The results were dubious: a shelf-choking litany of Gen-X books, handsome-young-actors-trying-their-hand-at-fiction novels, and people like Lorrie Terell.

"I don't know what you're talking about," he said.

"C'mon, Kyle," she pleaded, squeezing his leg as if testing a melon, "don't be so modest. You know that without you, artists like me would never have been able to publish a book."

Clayton delivered a rather large ironic grin. "Well, when you put it *that* way," he said, "almost makes me wish I never—"

The retort was cut short by the pain of a crushed big toe, compliments of Larry Wabzug's scuffed Florsheim.

"I hope we're going to see something new from you soon," she said. "Everybody's wondering."

"Actually," Clayton began, turning to Wabzug for emphasis, "there's a new novel coming in the fall. Right, Larry?"

"Better get started then," Wabzug answered, without missing a beat. "Speaking of which, Lorrie, could you give Kyle and me a minute or two alone?"

She smiled, slipping Kyle a wink. Of course she could. Clayton's eyes followed her as she shimmied back to her table.

"Geez, Larry, I didn't know you represented pornographers now."

"She *produces*, Kyle. *She* has a career."

"I told you, I'm working again."

Wabzug shook his head. "It's too late."

"No, listen, this thing I got going, it's the best thing—"

"No, no, you don't understand, Kyle. It's too late. I mean it's *really* too late." Wabzug sighed, suddenly looking grim. "I hate to spring this on you here, but you haven't returned my calls."

The young man sat forward. "What're you talking about?"

Wabzug's voice was careful, hesitant. "Brownstone and Company. They contacted me."

"That Trevor guy?" Kyle asked, hoping he was wrong.

Wabzug nodded, and Clayton wondered where the hell he'd put his drink.

David Trevor was the new president of Brownstone, Clayton's

publisher. Brownstone was a small imprint, the subsidiary of a much larger house, and was known to publish only literary fiction, therefore garnering a reputation for nobility—and, of course, for being a perennial money loser. For nearly a half century this had been just fine with the stockholders. When shameful best-sellers brought in millions, they could still straighten their bow ties at Park Avenue dinner parties and say, *Yes, but you know we do also have this little thing called Brownstone . . .*

But then just this past January, when the conglomerate that owned the larger house landed in the red for the first time in decades, the stockholders had gone ballistic. Heads rolled. "Boutique" imprints like Brownstone and Company were suddenly viewed as corporate waste, and David Trevor—previously the publisher of a London tabloid and notorious shitkicker—had been brought in to turn things around.

"They want their money, Kyle," Wabzug began. "They want you to return the advance for your second book."

Clayton shook his head; he wasn't hearing this right. "You're not serious?" he said.

"It's no joke, son."

"C'mon, Larry," he said, laughing without humor, "authors are late on books all the time. He knows that."

Now it was Wabzug's turn to laugh. "We signed a two-book deal, my friend. We guaranteed them a second book in two years. That was almost *six* years ago. Six! That's a four-year wait. Who do you think you are, Norman Mailer? This crackdown is *real*. Everything's changing. This guy Trevor won't be reasoned with. I tried, believe me."

Kyle looked up with a glimmer of affection.

"Yeah, I went to bat for you. I kissed ass a little, tried to buy you some more time."

"What'd he say?" Kyle asked.

"Told me to go fuck myself."

"To *you*?" Nobody talked to Larry Wabzug that way, Kyle thought. "Who the hell does he think he is?"

"He's also a big fan of yours, Clayton."

"What's he got against me?"

"To begin with, he thinks that you're lazy and spoiled."

"And what did you say?" Kyle asked.

"I told him he was probably right."

"Thank you, Larry."

"I also told him you happened to be very talented, and that if he lost you, he'd regret it. He told me to go fuck myself again."

Clayton slumped in his chair and downed nearly half his martini in one gulp.

"How much did they give you for the second book?" Wabzug asked. "I can't even remember, it's been so long."

"Seventy-five," Kyle answered gloomily.

The old man nodded, considering the sum. "That's not so bad."

"Plus another thirty against royalties."

"Oh, Jesus. When?"

"Two years ago. You don't remember? You helped put it through."

Wabzug shook his head. This was bad. Very bad.

"What am I gonna do, Larry? I don't have it. If they sue me, it'll ruin my career."

Wabzug nodded, trying to be sympathetic. It actually occurred to him to lend Kyle the money himself, maybe ten or twenty thousand, just enough to appease Trevor till he finished something—and then the bartender placed another birdbath of gin in front of him. Doesn't even have to order, Larry thought. He's got them *trained*. He looked on helplessly as Kyle lifted the glass to his mouth, the rim bobbing in tight, diminutive reverberations. Any thoughts of generosity quickly dissolved.

Maybe this is how it should happen, he thought. Maybe the kid has to bottom out. Be damned if I'll stick around for it, though. He gestured to his table in the dining room, then patted Kyle on the back.

"I gotta get back to work," Wabzug said. "Give me a call. We've gotta get this straightened out. Don't be such a stranger, huh?"

The young man kept his head down, nodding despairingly into his glass.

Reluctantly, Wabzug started away, his walk still the Chaplin-like waddle, arms dangling out behind him. Kyle finally looked up, watching after him fondly.

"Larry," he called out from the bar.

The old man turned.

"Where do we stand now?" Kyle asked, his voice tinged with bittersweetness. "You and me. You think we can work together again?"

The agent scratched his head and looked out on the snowy afternoon. He had not seen Kyle for so long it was as if he'd gained some new perspective now, was seeing him whole for the first time in ages—the most talented, most troubled young writer he had ever met. And the biggest pain in the ass. Damned if he knew why, but he liked him.

"It's up to you," Wabzug said, shrugging. "Finish that damn book you keep talking about. No more bullshit. It's the only chance you've got."

Kyle grinned, his eyes betraying a watery sparkle. "Oh, it's going to happen, Larry," he said, his voice suddenly charged with excitement. "Wait till you see." He raised his martini in emphasis. Then, realizing his faux pas, he quickly brought it down.

"Be good, my son," Wabzug said. Then he waddled back to Lorrie Terell.

4

Curled like a cat on the old couch, Meryl Whitehurst wallowed in
the delicious languor of a snowy morning, the silence broken only by
the occasional crackle of the fireplace. In her hands was a copy of *The
Journals of John Cheever,* a book her husband greatly admired. Now
she could see why. Within its covers was a complete picture of the
contemporary writer's inner life: paranoia, elation, heartbreaking
loneliness, secret desires. And the day-by-day chronicle of a marriage,
Cheever's mostly loveless, sexless alliance with his wife, Mary. Meryl
inspected its pages ravenously, like a detective looking for clues:

> *I have thought of taking a mistress, but they are not easy to come
> by, and I am timid. I claim that my timidity is exacerbated by the
> situation. After a particularly bitter quarrel twenty years ago I
> stood in the garage, sobbing for love . . . I don't divorce because I
> am afraid to—afraid of loneliness, alcoholism, suicide . . .*

Though over the years she had certainly entertained fantasies about infidelity (as her husband had, no doubt), it was this allusion to grief that had gotten to her, gripped her by the throat. Just a few months ago something similar had happened with Richard.

It was a glorious late afternoon in fall. Beams of sunlight streamed through the trees, the first leaves coming down. There was a barn in back of the property, an old dilapidated thing, collapsing like an accordion. Meryl had come there innocently, looking for the tiller. She had spent most of the morning working in the garden, so she was not surprised to find the door slightly ajar. When she stepped in, there was her husband sitting on one of the old snowmobiles, his back to her, crying vigorously.

He held his face in his hands as he wept; he had no idea of her presence. Her first impulse was to call out to him, to offer him comfort, but then she thought better of it. If it was comfort that he wanted, would he be here, hiding in the barn? Not knowing what to do, Meryl stood there frozen, fascinated by the strange scene. Here was her husband, a man almost twenty years her senior, crying like a schoolboy. Through the sobs came a collection of choked, jagged exclamations, filled with self-loathing. He was scolding himself, she realized, a certain phrase repeated over and over, the words muffled by the tears and sniffles. After a few moments she was able to understand:

"Failure," he was saying, shoulders jerking from the sobs. "Fu-cking f-f-fail-ure."

She quietly backed her way out and returned to the house. The incident was never mentioned, though it had haunted Meryl ever since. How frustrating it was that his sorrow was out of her control, something she was powerless to prevent or soothe. It would be useless to reassure him of her love, she knew. He was not "sobbing for love" in the Cheever sense. No, this was a different kind of love that her husband longed for. The kind that had eluded him his whole life and that seemed now like it would never come.

Sag Harbor Sonata was the title of Richard Whitehurst's latest novel. The one he had been sure would change everything. He had labored on it for nearly a decade. It was his last shot, he felt, his final chance to make a splash. He was sick to death of the niche the literary world had created for him. The "neglected author," they called him; the "most underrated writer in America." Well, *screw you,* he thought. It was the kind of thing he'd been hearing since his first book, been hearing it so long he'd begun to wonder if it wasn't a self-fulfilling prophecy. Enough already! His whole life Whitehurst had watched passively as novelists of much lesser talent garnered award after award, huge sums of money, fame—all the while pretending he was above it all. Now, in his mid-sixties, he could no longer say he did not covet these things. It was perhaps not the things themselves that he desired so much as what they represented—the spoils of recognition. Some tangible proof of his worth. Certainly he had the respect of other writers, good reviews, and a small but intense following. But his overall impact, he knew, had been marginal. And it was getting late. He was in danger, he believed, of becoming a footnote to the literary history of his time.

That *Sonata* would be the answer to Richard's problems, Meryl hadn't been so sure. Not that it wasn't a breathtaking achievement. She remembered the day he had finally showed it to her. It was morning, she was in the kitchen making coffee, concerned that her husband hadn't made it to bed the previous evening. Finally he came down the stairs from his studio, eyes puffy, exhausted from working through the night. Still he managed to smile. "Better put on a full pot," he said, plopping the manuscript down in front of her. "I'm done."

And so she canceled her plans for the day and sat down to read the 635 pages of her husband's decade-long dream.

Richard, too nervous to sleep and somehow energized by the marathon finish, went for a walk. He walked for hours, mile after mile. Down into Bridgehampton, to the beach at Sagaponack, walking, walking. His eyes were glazed. He saw everything, registered nothing. People pointed as he passed, honked their horn as he walked in front of their cars. He looked like a zombie, they said, and in a sense they were right. He was a man lost in some unreachable zone, a kind of aftershock of concentration and struggle. And now that he'd finally let the novel go, doubts began to torture him. Ten years of labor, but was it any good? Was it even really *done*? He kept on walking, too frightened to recognize his fatigue. Finally, at dusk, he returned.

His timing was perfect. As he came in through the back door, hand shaking as he turned the knob, he saw his beloved wife sitting just as he'd left her at the kitchen table, the huge pile of manuscript pages turned facedown. There were tears streaming down her face. Yet she was smiling triumphantly.

She stood up and they embraced. "Oh, Richard" was all she could manage to say.

And yet, for all her joy, in her heart she could not believe that this would be the book that would secure her husband's dreams. For all its grand beauty, *Sag Harbor Sonata* did not have the elements that captured the public's imagination. The book was not au courant in any respect. As ever, Whitehurst was stubbornly obsessed with the eternal, the universal. There was no gossip, no juicy self-revelation. Like its author, it had no political perspective. It was beauty for beauty's sake, and this, perhaps, was its flaw. Cynicism was in. Irony was in. Beauty, most definitely, was *out*.

"This is the one, isn't it?" Richard said as they stood in the kitchen, hugging and crying. "They can't ignore me any longer."

"Let's hope so, darling," she said carefully.

The next evening they went into town to celebrate. Her husband always experienced a rush when he finished a book, but Meryl had never seen anything quite like this night. He was giddy with energy. His voice boomed. On the way to the restaurant he couldn't keep his hands off her, fondling her breasts like a teenager. At dinner, over a two-hundred-dollar bottle of Echezeaux that they could ill afford, he spoke of the literary prizes he would be nominated for. When Meryl reminded him that he had always scoffed at prizes, he seemed undaunted.

"Let them give me a few," he said. "It'll be like a peace offering. Show how they were wrong about me all along."

It got worse. Draining the last of the wine, of which he'd drank all but a glass, he announced that he would even consider doing TV "when they ask me." Meryl could only shudder. She tried to picture it: her severe, sad-faced husband on some silly morning show, his hair combed all wrong as usual. He would wear his old tweed jacket, frayed at the cuffs, answering banal, breakfast-friendly questions with a schoolmaster's condescension. A *disaster*.

But Meryl never had to worry. The TV offers never came, and in the following months they watched numbly as the book was met with what Richard later referred to as "phenomenal indifference." Once again the reviews were laudatory. Once again Richard Whitehurst had failed to capture the public's interest. The book failed to sell out even its modest first printing. To Whitehurst, the unthinkable had happened: He had published his masterpiece, and the world had yawned.

After this, of course, he crashed.

The following summer had been dreadful, almost more than Meryl could bear. He still wrote every day, but they rarely went out. In the evenings they sat in the living room reading, though most of the time Richard's book was facedown on his lap as he stared blankly out the window. Then, in the fall, there was that fateful day in the barn.

And several weeks ago there'd been another incident. It was Christmas Eve, and, as they did every year, Richard and another writer friend, Arthur Trebelaine, had gone into town to do their last-minute shopping. It was a kind of tradition—the two absentminded writers mustering up a season's worth of gifts in three hours. Only this year something went terribly wrong. The pair returned home an hour later, empty-handed, Richard's face ashen.

"You're home early," Meryl remarked, surprised, but with not so much as a glance as Richard marched right past his wife and made an immediate beeline up to his study. Arthur called her into the living room. Speaking softly, he explained what had happened. He described the good mood Richard had seemed to be in at first, how they'd gone to the American Hotel for some drinks and then made their first stop at the bookstore just a few doors down. It was there Whitehurst had discovered some hardcover copies of *Sag Harbor Sonata* stacked in the remainder bins, a fluorescent $2.99 sticker brightly displayed on each cover. He was so shaken up, Arthur said, he'd almost had to carry him out of the store.

Meryl leaned forward, burying her head in Arthur's shoulder. When would it end? It had been over a year since *Sonata* had done its belly flop, but her husband had only grown more depressed. For years people had remarked how handsome Richard had gotten, how well he had aged, but lately he looked old, she could see, beaten up. There was a defeat in his eyes that was breaking her heart. "When will it end?" she said out loud into Arthur's shoulder, his sweater growing damp with tears. "I'm so worried."

Now the fireplace popped and hissed. She was grateful for it. It had taken her this long, she realized, to finally get the chill out of her bones from last night. Two hours out of bed. The *house,* she thought, trying to muffle her anger. On top of everything else, the goddamned house.

She turned another page of Cheever's *Journals*.

I have written to myself imaginary letters of praise from Auden, Bellow, Trilling . . . I have also imagined opportunities from Holly-wood and Broadway. In fact I have received one letter from a man in a rest home.

I cannot accept the degree of dependence upon the tastes of others and in general my lack of success.

The serenity of Meryl's morning was soon interrupted by the soft purr of an engine coming down John Street. Gliding on the banks of snow, the Whitehursts' jeep pulled into the driveway.

Resignedly she closed the book and, with a strange touch of guilt, returned it to its exact place on the shelf. Then she went to meet Richard at the front door.

"Good morning, darling," Meryl said as her husband stepped into the foyer. Although his face had held a grim countenance lately, he managed a modest smile. At least he's trying, she thought. "I was worried about you," she said, knocking some flakes off his shoulders. After helping him remove his coat, she knelt down to take off his boots.

"Did you go all the way to Montauk?"

"Oh, yes," he said. "It was gorgeous. Like being on the moon, everything so quiet and white."

"Here, hold your leg still."

On her knees, pulling the boot as in a tug-of-war, Meryl was reminded of many similar scenes with her daughter, years ago. Of course Kerry had left home at seventeen, finishing high school a semester early to spite her father. Meryl had always felt a little cheated when she thought of Kerry. Her only child, bolting out the door as soon as she had the chance. She'd barely had an opportunity to be a mother. Ah, but there was always Richard, wasn't there? *Here, darling, let me get this for you. Oh, no, darling, let me do that for you.* Feckless Richard, she mused, and only getting worse with age.

"I was thinking of asking you to come," Richard said, "but you looked so . . ."

Cold, she sensed he was going to say, before he'd snatched it from his lips.

"Exhausted," she said, rescuing him. "God, yes. I wish I knew why."

"You were up late again last night."

"Was I?" Meryl tugged mightily at the boot. Damn it, she thought, if he'd just hold still.

"I saw the light on. It must have been after one."

"I didn't realize it was so late. I was reading."

"Anything in particular?"

"This and that," she said. "I've had a little insomnia lately. Winter blues I think. Hold *still.*" Meryl groaned as the boot finally passed the heel and slid off.

"How would you like to do something different tonight?" he asked. Meryl looked up, trying to read his tone. She was surprised to find his eyes holding the sparkle of something mischievous. Richard had always had a boyishness about him, but this was an old look, something she hadn't seen in years. "I was going to see if you wanted to go into the city tonight."

"The city?" she said. "You mean *New York* City?"

"Why not? There's a literary party I was invited to. I thought we might go."

Meryl looked to see if he was kidding. Then she laughed. "Richard, there's a blizzard outside."

"That's why we have four-wheel drive," he said, undaunted.

Well, wasn't this remarkable? she thought. She couldn't remember the last time they'd done anything social. For six months they hadn't even been to dinner with another couple, never mind a party. Not that she wanted to discourage him. It was a good sign after all, wanting to be around people again. But *tonight*?

"Do you really think it's wise? You know how nervous you get driving in the city."

"The streets'll be empty," he said.

It was just then, after she'd pulled the second boot off and they'd both stood up, that the strange thing happened; Richard suddenly reached out and put his hands on her waist. It was an action so unexpected, so unfamiliar, she had to fight her initial urge to step back. My God, she thought, a man's putting his hands on me! Then, reminding herself that it was her husband, she let herself be drawn in, however tentatively.

"After the party . . . ," he said. Was his voice suddenly a bit hoarse? "Well, I was thinking."

She was further amazed now as his hands moved down to the slender part of her back.

She cleared her throat. "Yes?"

"I thought we could get a room somewhere near the park, one of the big hotels. Could be very romantic." He leaned over and ran the tip of his nose along the tight cords of her neck, smelling her. "What do you say?"

What could she say? She was stunned, and a little suspicious. What was this? Had he finished something new without telling her, another masterpiece that was going to "change everything"? Was he once again walking up that great mountain of expectation, only to be thrown off again in a few months, hopes dashed on the rocks?

But there was something else going on inside her too, something warm and electrical. She'd be forty-seven this year, still beautiful (so she'd been told), but she couldn't remember the last time she'd been held like a woman. "Be like a little adventure," he said, now pressing his lips against her neck.

"You'll drive slow?"

He promised he would.

"Where should we stay?" She began to enjoy this, thinking of all the hotels that were available, the restaurants.

Richard suggested The Four Seasons, knowing it was her favorite. Still, she seemed to hedge.

"Can we really afford it?"

"Who cares?" Richard said, almost purring in her ear. "You smell delicious, by the way. Like peonies."

He reached down between her legs, squeezing at her there through her jeans, and just as she thought he might escort her up to the bedroom, or even better, gloriously attack her right there on the staircase—something he hadn't done in years—she saw him looking over her shoulder, distracted by something high above them. Then, as abruptly and inexplicably as he had taken her into his arms, his hands dropped.

He had seen the clock at the end of the foyer.

"Getting late," he said. "I should get some work in if we're going to go." He kissed the top of her head, as if this was an appropriate ending to what he had so hastily started, and then headed toward the stairs. "You'll make the arrangements?" he asked without turning.

Meryl didn't answer, and Richard didn't wait for her to. Who else, she thought. She leaned back against the door, trying to ease her quickened breath. She was disappointed, of course, confounded, and yet at the same time something inside her had lifted a little. Just when she was preparing to live without sex for the rest of her life (something, in her devotion to him, she had resigned herself to) he had surprised her. He had given her hope.

Her eyes followed him as he headed up the stairs. Her husband had changed suddenly, she realized. There he was again, the *writer*. The shoulders hunched, head hanging limp. A man on the way to the gallows. My God, what keeps you going? she wondered. All this fret and worry, the painstaking work. And for what? It was a question she had wanted to ask him for as long as she could remember.

She picked up the phone and called The Four Seasons. The concierge informed her that because of the weather there were suites available. She booked one way out of their price range, feeling she deserved it. Then, secure that her husband was engaged upstairs, she went back to the living room. Through the curtains she could see the snow, falling hard. The thought of driving anywhere this afternoon seemed ridiculous, but then the alternative—another night of book talk, staring at the fire, sexlessness—that seemed much worse.

She went to the bookcase and took down the Cheever. As she curled up once again on the couch she could hear the familiar sound from the attic, the faint wheeze of floorboards under soft worn shoes: Richard, pacing in his studio. He was at it again, forever the wanderer, in his desolate search for inspiration.

Loneliness I taste. The chair I sit in, the room, the house, none of this has substance. I think of Hemingway, what we remember of this work is not so much the color of the sky as it is the absolute taste of loneliness. Loneliness is not, I think, an absolute, but its taste is more powerful than any other. I think that endeavoring to be a serious writer is quite a dangerous career.

5

Around four that afternoon, Kyle Clayton lay waking in a bedroom twice the size of his apartment.

He sat up on his elbows, trying to determine exactly where he was. All around him the light swam in waves, the colors of aqua and burnt orange undulating softly in the dark room.

A few tumblers of mescal could sometimes send him hallucinating; had he partaken of the great agave today? He couldn't remember, and the headache was definitely saying gin. Then he looked up, eyes finally adjusting to the light, and saw the colossal tank embedded in the wall, the illumined fish casting their exotic colors across the room, and knew all at once where he was.

Oh, great, he thought. Wonderful.

There, splayed out regally next to him, was one Mrs. Dorothea Clementine.

Say this for sad Kyle: Dorothea was fifty-seven but looked fifteen years younger. A lifetime of mud baths, collagen implants, RNA cream, Palm Springs weekends, Eastern European masseuses, half-hearted yoga, and most recently BOTOX injections had given her skin a tautness and glow that defied natural laws. But sometimes even this wasn't enough. She was still, when all was said and done, well into her sixth decade, and sometimes Kyle would come over and really have to work his mind to get it going, close his eyes and tap into the most vivid recesses of his imagination to give that evidence of enjoyment Dorothea so desperately needed. Exhausting, really. And probably damaging to his work too, if one is to believe in the myth of Eros and creativity. Sometimes, on the melancholy subway ride home, he would joke to himself that Larry Wabzug ought to get a test tube over to her place pronto, that for the past year or so, whatever new fiction he had in him was being left on the perpetually tanned, freckled collarbone and silken sheets of Mrs. Clementine. Not just short stories, but whole novels. Magnum opuses. Bloody *trilogies*.

Dorothea liked to portray herself as a belle from the Deep South, but really she was from Virginia horse country. Her "husband," Zeddy, had made his fortune in medical insurance. So, if you wanted to know why your HMO was so goddamned expensive, and just where the hell all that money went to anyway, all you had to do was walk the balcony around the Clementines' apartment on Sixty-eighth and York and check out that view they had of the East River.

Though he had begun as an infrequent visitor, these days Kyle Clayton found himself at the Clementines' twice a week. Mondays and Thursdays. Like clockwork.

QUIETLY, KYLE SLID to the edge of the bed, lightly brushing Dorothea's knee. Ah, fuck, he thought.

"Where you goin', Honey Kyle?" she asked groggily. "You hardly been here but a minute."

Her voice, a thick syrup of faux-Southern coquettishness, irritated the shit out of Honey Kyle, and he was furious at himself for rousing her. Now they would actually have to talk.

"Got to get ready for tonight," he said, bending to put his socks on.

"Well, for goodness sakes, it doesn't start for another three whole hours." Carelessly, like an empress amusing herself, she began to trace the crack of his backside with a long red fingernail. At first touch Kyle seemed to flinch ever so slightly. "You gonna wear one of Zeddy's suits, aren't you? He's got a closet full of Armani he never touches."

"Little small for me, isn't he?"

"He buys them big," she said, still running her finger behind him. "I think one'd fit you fine. I think anything would fit you fine, Honey Kyle."

That evening Kyle was planning to attend a PEN party over on the West Side. Five years ago the parties were on the East Side, many of them in Zeddy and Dorothea Clementine's very apartment, but the finger waggers of the politically correct had put a stop to that. In a much publicized debate, a group of PEN members had complained that the rich were using writers to legitimize themselves, to gain respectable cachet. "A literary petting zoo" was how one writer described the events. Succumbing to the pressure rather passively, in Kyle's eyes, patrons like the Clementines were now banned from hosting any PEN entertainment, and of course now the parties weren't nearly as good. You had to wonder if some of the objectors hadn't secretly lived to regret it. The apartments were so much smaller now, after all. Everyone on top of one another, wafting away the clouds of billowing cigarette smoke under the low ceilings. Caviar had given way to chopped liver and a few Ritz crackers. No longer was there a handsome actor to serve top-shelf liquor; *real* writers, PEN had decreed, drank Chilean jug wine from plastic cups.

But Kyle remembered the old days—bottomless glasses of champagne and Bobby Short at the piano. Pretty interns from *The Paris Review,* junior editors from *The New Yorker* and *Vogue.* Grist for the mill, so to speak. As a party thrower, Dorothea Clementine was an artist, a virtuoso, and she always made sure to pepper her gatherings with young women, knowing, like all great entertainers, that sex gave a party its juice. "Why do people go to a party in the first place?" Dorothea would say when asked about the success of her soirées. "You want good conversation? Pick up a phone. No, honey, whether they know it or not, people come to a party to get *laid.*"

At her best bashes, the tension between the two major factions—literary-minded young women in their first overwhelming months in the big city and famous older writers not in the company of their wives—was downright combustible. As for younger guys like Kyle? "Shooting fish in a barrel" was how he remembered it, "with a shotgun." He always had had a natural glamour about him, a kind of aura. It was something everybody noticed, even before his novel had taken off like a rocket. Of course, he wasn't entirely unattractive, either. One interviewer had described him as Kennedyesque, an overused image but apt. He was tall with dark, wavy hair, his mouth usually arranged in a subtle sneer. And, perhaps even more important, he was heterosexual, which may not seem like much of an endorsement, but was actually in quite short supply these days in male writers under forty.

Kyle was always surrounded by admirers. Not just young women, but writers as well. Upstarts who wanted to feel the glow. Older guns who wanted to remember what it was like.

It wasn't until later that he and Dorothea had started their . . .

well, call it what you will. In fact, if you had asked anyone privy to their association in those first few years, none could've ever recalled them exchanging more than ten words in a given evening. They'd meant little to each other beyond the obvious: Dorothea invited Kyle for his celebrity, Kyle accepted because her parties were the best in town.

Then something happened. Stories began to circulate that Kyle Clayton had stopped writing, and pretty soon the crowds around him at the Clementines' began to thin. Hollywood called; the film version of *Charmed Life* had fallen through. Then the rumor came out that he was broke, and before you knew it his friendship with Mrs. Dorothea Clementine had begun to deepen.

"TELL THEM BLACK CHERRY," Kyle was saying now, spinning red wine around the sides of his glass in tight swirls. "Tell them anise."

"Anise," repeated Zeddy Clementine. He wrote this down in a large leather notebook he had in front of him, the cover of which said "Wine Dossier" in large gold lettering.

They were in the grand dining room, Kyle feeling slightly uncomfortable in Mr. Clementine's monogrammed silk robe. Zeddy wore the usual pinstripe suit and lemon ascot that was supposed to signify breeding but only served to highlight the baldness of his pate. In front of them sat three bottles of first-growth Bordeaux, two of the bottles sporting a vintage older than Château Clayton himself. As it turned out, Zeddy was giving a dinner tonight and, knowing nothing about wine, had sought out the advice of Kyle Clayton, who knew more about the subject than a young man should. His job was to supply key adjectives the old Philistine would repeat later that night.

"And a bit of leather," Kyle said.

The old man smacked his lips. "Well, of course leather," he said. "Obviously leather."

Kyle knew he could've said Cherry Garcia and Zeddy would've nodded like a marionette. Man, he thought, I could really fuck the old guy's night up good if I wanted to. Strawberry rhubarb, Zeddy. Syrian billygoat anus. No really, there, in the finish.

The two had really only warmed up to each other a few months ago. Not that there'd been any sort of animosity. Kyle had learned very quickly that his presence had not only been tolerated by Zeddy but downright encouraged. The Clementines had separate bedrooms, after all, and as far as Kyle had been told, they'd never had *that* kind of relationship.

"Sex with *Zeddy*?" Dorothea had said one day, laughing as if it were the most ridiculous question ever asked. "Oh, no, dear, not on my *life*."

This was during their first rendezvous. As they had talked, Kyle lay watching the sweat dry on her old limbs, thinking he could do this three, maybe four times tops. Just a little something to get his feet on the ground again financially. That had been two years ago.

"He did climb into bed with me one time," she'd continued. "I can't imagine what brought it on. I think he was soused to the gills. Anyway, he begged me to make love. He said that just for one night he wanted to feel like a man."

"What happened?" Kyle had asked.

"I told him to go call one of his Thai boys. But then he wouldn't stop touching me. So, naturally, I Maced him. That was the end of that."

Naturally, Kyle had thought.

Zeddy leaned over now and breathed deeply into a glass of '61 Lynch-Bages. "Mmmm. Nice bouquet," he said.

"Nose," Kyle countered, trying not to show his annoyance. "We talked about this the last time. Nobody says *bouquet* anymore, Zed. That's the nineteenth century. Now they say *nose*."

Christ, Kyle thought, get me out of here.

That moment, as if by divine dispatch, Dorothea came swishing out of the bedroom in a glorious peach-colored dress.

"That's quite enough now, Zeddy Doll," she scolded, fabric hissing against her thighs as she strode. "We don't want Kyle to be late for his party."

Zeddy nodded flaccidly—the boss had spoken. Then Dorothea reached over his shoulder and took a sip of the Lynch-Bages.

"Needs ice," she said, smacking her lips.

Just then the maid arrived, arms weighed down with a hirsute coat so sumptuous that only a nation of minks could have created it, a mink genocide. Dorothea slid her arms in and began checking the pockets.

"Ginny?" she said, still patting the sides in search of something. "Ginny, dear, where's my Mace?"

One evening a few years ago, on Lexington Avenue, Mrs. Clementine lost a fur coat to a PETA member with a spray can—and had been armed for battle ever since. Apparently she had misconstrued the directions on the back of her weapon, instructing her to "spray liberally," which Dorothea took to mean often. The victims had been piling up. So far they included one fur spitter, two Marymount coeds shouting "Murderer!" at the top of their lungs, and three plain dirty looks. Litigations were pending.

"I see you two conspiring," she said, looking from the maid to her husband. "Now hand it over."

With an apologetic look at Zeddy, Ginny handed her the small canister.

"Now, Kyle, you know you're welcome to take a shower," Dorothea announced without shame. "I had Ginny lay out one of Zeddy's suits for you in my room. Call me next week, okay?" She blew a kiss to her two men and headed out of the dining room.

As she left, gloom passed through Kyle's body like a shadow. There'd been something missing from her parting words, something rather important. The reason he came today, the reason he always came. And now she was going, and *shit*, there was that question he had to ask them.

"And oh, yes," she said, blowing back in, as if in afterthought. "Your envelope is on the mantel by the front door. Toodle-oo now."

"Dorothea," Kyle said, standing up.

"Yes?"

He hesitated. For a moment he thought of forgetting the whole thing. Some emissary of pride, long buried, had risen up and poked its head through the sand, demanding to be heard. He was better than this, the messenger told him. There were other solutions. It was a question of dignity.

But then, as he did with all the other couriers of good sense that approached him these days, he hit it over the head with a shovel.

"I have a favor to ask you."

He turned to see if Zeddy was listening. Kyle felt instinctively he would need the old man's support on this issue. But Zeddy had his nose deeply buried in the dossier.

Dorothea stood impatiently in her great coat, beads of sweat now dotting her forehead.

"Your, uh . . . gifts," Kyle began. "You know, your envelopes. They're always very generous."

"We think so." Lifting an arm of the mink, she wiped her brow.

"Well, I've kinda gotten into some trouble lately. You see, I, uh . . . I owe some money and . . . *Damn it,*" he said, stamping his foot. "This is so hard for me."

"How much?" Dorothea asked without hesitation. Her tone had in it all the matter-of-factness of people who spend their lives having others tell them how hard it is to ask them for money.

"I don't know exactly."

"Ballpark figure."

Kyle pulled his earlobe, scratched his nose, did everything but hem and haw, and then finally, thinking, Ah, what the fuck, said, "A hundred, a hundred thousand."

Dorothea wrapped two arms around her munificent coat and, with a great backward rocking, began to laugh.

"It could be like an advance," Kyle amended, but Dorothea was already in hysterics.

"Hey," Zeddy said, "what's so funny over there?"

Dorothea tried to gather herself. "Kyle here wants us to give him a hundred thousand dollars."

"That's not funny," Zeddy said, beginning to laugh, never lifting his chin up from his notes.

"You don't understand, it's my *career,*" Kyle began, but he was drowned out by the hilarity.

He had no choice now but to stand and take the humiliation, to try and give some kind of show of dignity. In his mind, though, he beat himself like a flagellant. Of course he should've known better. It was true that for people like the Clementines a hundred thousand dollars was the equivalent of Kyle buying a bagel for a hungry bum. But he also knew that in these rarefied financial heights, accumulation was akin to obsession. Had he not turned away at the sight of Dorothea kneeling down in the elevator to pick up change that was not hers? Had he not squirmed as Zeddy left a 3 percent tip one afternoon at "21," and sneaked back to rectify it? Even the "gifts" that

Clayton had come to rely on so much recently seemed proportionally meager. Just generous enough to survive on; just cheap enough to make him dependent.

Fuckers, he thought. The idea of going out in a blaze of glory began to pump in his blood. Smashing the cabinet of Czech crystal with a wine bottle, for example, or, better yet, having a go at the Modigliani with his pocketknife.

He decided against it. He was in enough trouble already.

"I guess I'll get dressed," Kyle announced, his voice hardly more than a whisper.

"Oh, I'm sorry, dear," Dorothea said, the laughter subsiding as she sensed injury in her lover. "That just struck me as so funny. Of course you know—despite appearances to the contrary—you know all our money *really is* tied up."

Kyle nodded, then in passing gave her a little jab of a smile, one that he hoped conveyed his knowledge of the real truth between them, the real motivation behind her laughter at his request: her fear that with that kind of "gift" he would never, *ever* come within a mile of that oversized bed of hers again. Not in a million fucking years.

As he disappeared into the great hall, he heard Mrs. Clementine's faux-Southern voice calling out after him: "Oh, Honey Kyle? Say hello to the old gang for me tonight, won't you?"

6

"This is insanity," Meryl was saying.

It was late afternoon on the Long Island Expressway, snow slashing horizontal and dense. The jeep's headlights were on, revealing only the scarcity of other vehicles on the road. Though Richard had been true to his promise so far, keeping the Bronco at about forty miles an hour, Meryl still had her fingernails dug into the dashboard like a climber's pick.

Suddenly the jeep swerved a few inches, sledding a bit into the other lane. Someone beeped. Richard slowed and righted the vehicle.

We're going to die, Meryl told herself, patting her heart. It had just occurred to her that she was being driven to New York in a blinding snowstorm by a man who, for the greater part of a year, had shown no particular interest in what the rest of the world called being alive.

"No point in turning back now," Richard said. He reached down and turned off the radio news report, which was barely audible but insistent in its doom.

"I don't understand this. Why are we doing this?"

"I told you, I've been feeling cooped up."

"I know, so have I. But why *tonight*? What's your obsession with this party, Richard?"

What indeed? When he'd first received the invitation a little over a month ago, he'd immediately thrown it in the garbage. Richard Whitehurst was probably PEN's most inactive, apathetic member. First of all, he was not particularly interested in the plight of writers in hostile countries, which had recently become the organization's primary focus. Screw them, Whitehurst thought. As he saw it, he had his *own* literary plight, his *own* country's hostility toward *himself* to contend with. Secondly, he was not much of a partygoer, never had been. He was painfully awkward in all but the tiniest of gatherings, and had an antipathy for small talk that people often mistook for arrogance.

So, why tonight? The answer was not something he was sure he could share with his wife. It was beyond odd, preposterously unlikely in fact. The truth being that Richard Whitehurst had in recent years become interested in what he had previously spent his life despising: that peculiar niche the media presented as the "literary life." This phenomenon had begun during the final drafts of *Sonata,* when Richard found himself doing the most extraordinarily uncharacteristic things. Scanning, for example, the bold type for the names of writers in the celebrity columns of the *New York Post;* buying glossy magazines for their profiles of famous authors; and then, most shameful of all, prodding writer friends for literary gossip. In the midst of all this, the name of one young man remained a constant, a name inspiring derision, envy, and delicious speculation. Much to Whitehurst's secret embarrassment, this gentleman had somehow captured a portion of his imagination, and though recently the rest of the world had tired of the young man, Richard found that his own fascination had not waned.

So yes, initially he had thrown out his invitation to the PEN party, but then his agent and dear friend, Larry Wabzug, had assured him that this certain writer would be in attendance.

"Are any of our friends going to be there at least?" Meryl asked.

"Larry said he'd try to come."

"Oh, good," said Meryl, who'd always been fond of the agent.

Then carefully—a man sticking his toe in the ocean—Richard said, "And there's this younger writer I'm interested in meeting."

"Who's that?"

"Kyle Clayton," he said, sneaking a glance at his wife.

"Clayton?" The name seemed to ring a bell.

"An interesting character, don't you think?"

"Clayton," she repeated, looking confused. Then her eyes narrowed. "You don't mean that jerky kid from a couple of years ago. What was that book?"

He reminded her.

"Right. One-book wonder. Why would you ever be interested in him? He's everything you can't stand. A total poseur."

"No, I don't believe he is."

"Have you read his book?"

"Yes, as a matter of fact." Actually, he'd read it three times. "Have you?"

"I wouldn't dare."

"Well, there you go," he said, throwing up a hand.

Here was a specialty of his wife's that never failed to drive him crazy: her opinions of writers she'd never read.

"Who wants to read about some young cad picking up girls in college?"

"That's what they said about *This Side of Paradise*."

"Oh, *please*. You're not going to compare him to Fitzgerald now."

Her voice, Richard was surprised to realize, was becoming hostile.

You see? he told himself. He's even got my wife riled up. He was suddenly jealous of Clayton's power to provoke.

"You didn't read the book, Meryl."

"You're saying it was a great book?"

"I didn't say that."

"Well, what is it you're saying exactly?"

Richard remembered the evening he read Clayton's novel. Three or so years ago, after the kid's big run. *Charmed Life* and its writer had become a symbol for something insipid, the names synonymous with eighties excess and brash youth. It was unfair of course, but nevertheless the book was now a despised text, a joke, and for that reason Richard had been intrigued by it. His own work, after all, had never provoked that kind of reaction. There must be a power in it somewhere.

The story was not much. A college romance, beautiful young woman and the ne'er-do-well, full of bawdy humor. Not exactly a Whitehurst kind of book. And yet the writing was astonishing. The language had a lushness, a voluptuousness Richard hadn't seen in a young writer for quite some time. He finished it in a single sitting and was left feeling stunned, beaten up. He understood the backlash completely—so young and so much talent. And a good-looking fellow to boot.

Kill the bastard, was his first thought.

Then he read it again the next night, just to make sure. It was even better the second time. The whole thing was a put-on, he'd discovered. A finely tuned satire, sly and nimble as a cat.

"What I thought," Richard began, fighting to keep focused on the road, "is that it was a very good book with greatness *in* it. And the fact that he's young and happens to be attractive—"

"Ugh," Meryl exclaimed, as if nauseated. "Not to me."

"Well, fine, but I'm telling you, this happens every time a young writer shows some talent. It's a blood sport in this country. They throw him up in the air for a year or two, then drop him on his head and step on his face. So the fellow likes to go to parties, so what? Hell, I wish I'd gone to more parties. It's just jealousy, pure and simple."

For the first time since they'd been on the road, Meryl forgot about the snow and turned to her husband. She hadn't heard this kind of vigor in his voice in over a year. She hoped it boded well for tonight. Back when they were still having sex—when dinosaurs ruled the earth—a heated argument usually led to a night of intense fucking.

However, she didn't want to be too optimistic.

"You really wish you'd gone to more parties?"

"Yes," he said matter-of-factly. "I feel like I've missed out on a lot of fun these last few years. I've spent too much time away from people." Richard suddenly reached out and took his wife's hand. "I'm afraid I've made our life a bit insular, haven't I?"

Yes, darling, as a matter of fact you have.

"I have my friends," she said instead.

Darkness was falling. In the headlights the flakes were large now, like ripped-up pieces of paper. Meryl stared at them, trying to escape the intimacy of her husband's revelation. She resented it in a way, she realized. What about *her* regrets, *her* disappointments? Good Lord, if she'd ever really got talking, it would devastate him. He worshipped her, she knew. A few bits of honesty and Richard would crumble.

Forget it, she thought. Save it for the shrink.

"You know, I've never told you this," he said, his tone still confessional, "but I've been a bit lonely in our life. It's been my fault, no doubt. Absolutely self-imposed. But nevertheless . . . *very* lonely at times." He looked over at her again, searchingly. "Have you?"

A myriad of responses were considered. Finally, she decided on just a pinch of the truth. "I suppose I have a bit, yes," she said. "Sometimes."

Looking up she found him nodding to himself, as if he had known it all along. She thought she heard a slight groan.

"I thought as much," he said.

Now it was time, Meryl knew, to assuage the damage. "I think that's true of every marriage, though, don't you? There's this certain amount of loneliness. It's a given."

"No," he said flatly, looking out into the treacherous dusk. "Not like ours."

AN HOUR LATER the Bronco was approaching a snow-slicked entrance ramp, below them the empty streets of a waterside Brooklyn neighborhood. Richard looked on with near shock at the bleakness, the aesthetic holocaust of the place, noticeable even in the graceful snowfall. Treeless avenues, buildings faceless except for a snarl. And home to his daughter.

Kerry Whitehurst was now twenty, or so Richard approximated. Meryl had told him that she currently resided in the DUMBO section of Brooklyn—short for Down Under the Manhattan Bridge Overpass—along with many other struggling artists. She was a budding sculptor and "installationist"; the last they'd heard, she was sleeping illegally in her studio in what used to be an old textile factory. There, apparently, she had two thousand square feet, a futon, and a hot plate. Nobody had any idea what she did for money. Her sculptures barely sold enough to cover her art supplies, and so far she'd refused to cash any of the checks that Meryl had sent. There was no word of a boyfriend, although she'd hinted to her mother that she was promiscuous, a suggestion designed to stir the cauldron of anxiety and guilt.

Kerry blamed everything on Richard, had a raging, mouth-frothing hatred of him. Unlike her mother, she'd been very vocal with him about his patriarchal failures. The accusations focused primarily on his selfishness, which, she claimed, had led to the great distance that had come between them over the years, and her insistence, twenty years running now, that he must've "fucking wanted a boy." The bottom line was he'd never really been a father to her and that any mishaps she'd incurred over the years—drugs, drugs, and more drugs—as well as any future screwups could be attributed directly to dear old Dad.

Richard, though, wasn't buying it. He didn't go in for this non-mea-culpa shit. Not to say he didn't have regrets. Certainly he'd always been absorbed in his work. He'd never had a driving desire to be a father anyway; he'd made that clear to Meryl. The child was what *she'd* wanted. Giving her Kerry was one of the few unselfish things he'd ever done in their marriage. And yet, it wasn't like the fathering hadn't gone past biology. He *had* tried, God knows, especially when Kerry was a girl. There were the school plays he never missed, Little League—that curveball he'd taught her. Nasty, nasty pitch.

"What's so funny?" Meryl asked now.

"I was thinking about Kerry."

"And this you find a cheery subject?"

He winced. He wouldn't fight with Meryl about their daughter; it was a battle he could never win.

"I was just thinking fondly of her, that's all."

"Mmm-hmm," Meryl murmured.

Fondness didn't last long, not with Kerry. He remembered now when puberty struck, how things had suddenly broken down. Along with the bra and the monthly periods came the end of their communication. She became wild, an angry young woman. She had a rage that frightened him. By the time she was fifteen Richard was suddenly in over his head.

By his own admission, he was not much help during these years.

Richard was in his most extreme working phase then, spending ten, sometimes twelve hours a day in his studio. Downstairs, Meryl struggled to keep things together. A single mother, essentially, with an M-80 for a daughter. Soon there were the heavy drugs and skirmishes with the law. Shouting matches echoed down their quiet street. Kerry was unreachable.

Eventually, her belligerence became too much. In the fall of her freshman year at Rutgers, she was "excused" for a combination of drugs and "brawling"—the latter of which Richard found especially disconcerting. That night she showed up on their doorstep with a black eye, high as a kite and pissed off at the world. Richard was incensed. At least she might show a little goddamned humility, he thought, on the eve of her expulsion—what with a year's worth of tuition down the drain—but no, that night they had a terrible argument at the dinner table, about nothing of course, and Kerry suddenly popped up, snatched the aluminum baseball bat from the umbrella stand, and went running up the stairs fast as she could.

Husband and wife stared at each other, until Richard jumped up and ran after her, suddenly realizing what was about to happen.

He took the stairs two at a time, yelling after her—but he was too late. Kerry was already at it, pounding on his most prized material possession: a 1938 Olivetti typewriter, the one he couldn't do without. Her fury was horrifying. *Wham, wham, wham!* Gears and letters flying in the air. He didn't dare try to stop her. He stood in the doorway, too stunned to move.

When she was finally done, flailed to the point of exhaustion, she raised the bat and pointed it at the disfigured clump, trying to catch her breath.

"You like metaphors, right?" Kerry shouted. "Well, there," she said, pointing her finger at the typewriter, "there's a fucking metaphor for you. We'll call it childhood. How's that?"

Despite his fear, Richard snickered—he couldn't help himself. Oh, come off it, he thought. What rubbish!

With this absurd bit of melodrama, though, it was over; Richard had had enough. He asked her to leave that night, immediately. Meryl wept bitterly but Richard insisted, and in no less than an hour Kerry Whitehurst, not yet having had a chance to unpack from the college that had tossed her out—and still a little stoned—simply revved up the beat-up Impala they'd given her and left for New York City, vowing never, ever to return.

Should he be ashamed now to admit that a part of him was relieved? That their lives had been better now without her?

As they approached the bridge, a digital sign warned of closed lanes, minor delays. Suddenly a crazy impulse came over Richard.

"You don't happen to have her address with you, do you?"

"What? Whose?" It took Meryl a moment to realize what he meant. *"Kerry's?"* she said, doing a double take. "She would never actually *see you*, Richard. You must know that." This was said with the utmost distaste, as if he'd completely forgotten his daughter's loathing for him, forgotten how justified it was. In the house, Meryl had always defended him against Kerry's tirades, but in private, he knew, they had banded against him.

"Anyway, I couldn't bear to see that place of hers again," Meryl said. "Once is enough."

Still, he missed her. He thought of her every day, especially on those Montauk jaunts, and not all of his thoughts were marred by anger or regret. Some days, shuffling as he did through the high reeds and black-peppered sand, he managed to smile at the irony of her life. How determinedly Kerry had rebelled against him, how hard she'd tried to piss him off, to shame him. And yet he was *proud* of her in a way. He did not share his wife's concerns over Kerry's unsettled lifestyle. Was it really so terrible that she hadn't finished college, that she wasn't now sitting in a cubicle all day with one of those awful New York "careers"? She was an artist, or at least trying to be. She was creating, making love to whomever she chose, experimenting with life. She was out there taking her lumps in the greatest city on earth. Bravo, my dear.

How surprised she'd be, Richard thought now with a smirk, how supremely *pissed,* if she knew how her father really felt, how much he admired her, albeit from afar.

Meryl was not convinced. "I just wish she wasn't so completely screwed up." She said this with a sidelong glance, the implication clear.

"Hey, give her some credit," Richard said. Giving up on the idea of dropping in on Kerry, he committed the Bronco to the bridge exit. "She doesn't want to be some yuppie."

His wife glowered at him. "That's a very cavalier attitude, Richard."

"Is it?"

"I've been to her apartment, remember? I've seen the way she lives. I'm telling you, it's murderers' row down there. In *DUMBO!* Can you imagine? People ask me where my daughter lives, and I have to keep my face together and tell them DUMBO."

"It's actually very chic, from what I've read."

Meryl gave a start. "Not for a girl living alone. Goddamn it, Richard, don't try and justify it."

On the bridge then the Bronco was suddenly lifted skyward, the cityscape looming into view. It was beautiful enough to put a muzzle on their bickering.

His blood gave a little rush—he was *back.* New York, city of exaggerations. Place of Herculean ascensions and perilous falls. His home for ten years. The happiest time of his life.

7

A short time later, in a smoky journalist's apartment on Manhattan's Upper West Side, the PEN party was under way; Jimmy Scott on an old stereo, drinks flowing, tweed jackets bunched shoulder to shoulder, the best minds in the world coming together, exchanging ideas.

"Fifty bucks says I fuck that girl in two hours."

"One hour."

A pause. "You're on."

Kyle and his friend Patrick McCreary watched the fiery-haired girl put herring on a Ritz cracker, trying to assess the promiscuity quotient. She was too far for them to get a good look, but Kyle's overwhelming buzz had him feeling invincible.

"One hour," he said. "But then I get two-to-one odds."

"No mentioning *Charmed Life*."

Kyle crossed himself. "Scout's honor."

The young man stuck a fifty in Kyle's jacket.

"Fuck that girl," he said.

McCreary was an old friend, an Irish playwright who'd somehow failed to make a big splash in the States despite exemplary reviews and a press kit that included such toutings as "the next Brendan Behan" and "the new voice of Ireland." Kyle had found all this talk incredibly ironic ever since the drunken evening when McCreary admitted he'd actually grown up in the South Side of London and had never really set foot in his "homeland." His accent was something imitated from his grandparents, he confessed, and he'd decided to set his plays in Ireland only after seeing such films as *The Quiet Man* and *My Left Foot,* which he thought terribly charming, and keenly observing the dearth of Irish plays on the market.

This tiny detail was of no concern to Kyle. He was a good buddy, plain and simple, and, more important, one who could be counted on, with the shortest of notice, to join him in his various nighttime adventures. McCreary had spent the last few minutes regaling Kyle with the exciting, life-changing news that had been his recent good fortune: After years of struggling Off-Broadway with great reviews and little money, McCreary was now making a "fuggin' mint, mate," working in Hollywood, and there was plenty of opportunity for an "arse-wipe Yank" like Kyle to get some of it.

Though in the past Kyle would've immediately sloughed off such a proposition, this evening he sipped his drink and listened with interest.

"How you doin' with money these days anyway?"

"Pecuniary difficulties," Kyle replied with Dickensian intonation.

"You're fuggin' broke."

"Worse."

"What's worse than that?"

"I *owe,* man. Big time."

It was just nine o'clock, and already the tiny rooms were starting to fill up. Because it was nobody's business, and because writers were, of course, the cattiest, most vile gossips this side of a beauty parlor, Kyle escorted Pat to a neutral corner, where he whispered sweet troubles into his ear. He offered tidings of Brownstone and Company; of its new evil wizard, David Trevor; of the certain toilet flush of whatever was left of his career should the bastard sue him for breach of contract; of the whole shotgunned mess he called his professional and financial life.

"Fuggin' Hollywood," Pat countered. "Made seventy-five thousand pounds last year."

Kyle did the math. "Get out."

"True."

"You wrote a script?"

Pat, who, Kyle realized, was even more lit than he was, bellowed in outrage, "What, you think I'm some kinda *whore*!"

Kyle told him that he certainly did not.

"I polish, mate."

"Polish?"

"That's right," Pat said proudly.

"Meaning what, exactly?"

"Basically, I clean up bad dialogue. It's easy. And the *money*. Phew!"

Hol-ly-wood. Clayton let his mind float along the soft, sirenlike consonants.

"Thing is, Pat, I don't like the movies."

"Me neither. Hate 'em. *Hate* the fuggers. So what?"

"Well, personally, I don't know if I'd want to contribute—"

Pat was already shaking his head. "Whoa, whoa, whoa, wait a minute. Hold on a second here. What do you mean, 'contribute'? Who said anything about *contributing*?"

Kyle looked a little confused.

"Look," Pat explained, wrapping an arm around his friend's shoulder, "writing for a studio's not at all like what we do. You're on the assembly line out there, man. That's the fuggin' beauty of it. For example, let's say I get a script, spend two, maybe three weeks cleaning up the piece of shit; *my* version then gets passed on to another guy, see, and he does his thing, totally changing what I did, and then probably some woman takes a shot at *his* work, and so on and so on, until the director gets disgusted with the lot of us and goes with the original first draft, or gives it to his nephew, or finishes the goddamned thing himself. Nobody said anything about *contribution*. Oh, no, no. Don't you worry, as a writer in Hollywood you'll never be *contributing* to anything. You think a line of your stuff would ever make it past a test audience?" He squeezed Kyle's shoulder even harder, leaning in for additional privacy. "Let me tell you, Clay, I pride myself on the fact that having worked on at least twenty movies, not one word of mine has ever made it to the screen. Not a fuggin' *word*. That's the day I quit—when I see my shameful labor come to fruition."

Kyle stared at his friend, thinking, You sick bastard, and, simultaneously, I'm *in*.

"C'mon," Pat urged, then took a hefty slug of his wine. It was his turn to whisper in Kyle's ear now. "Can you imagine you and me out there, in sunny L.A., with *money*?"

Kyle could, actually. The thought instantly revived his hangover.

"What about your plays?"

"Still write 'em."

"When's the next one?"

"Don't know," Pat said, shrugging. "Just signed a new contract with Universal though. Hundred thousand pounds."

"Polishing," Kyle said.

"Fuggin' aye, mate."

They touched glasses, then Kyle excused himself. He had a bet to deliver on.

She was over by the bar, pouring herself a Third World red.

Kyle came up behind her, soaking up the scent of her hair.

"Hi. My name's Kyle. Kyle Clayton."

The woman didn't turn.

Kyle looked around, making sure McCreary was out of earshot before he fired round number two.

"Ever hear of a book called—"

"Oh, you've *got* to be kidding me!" the woman hissed in a voice somehow familiar. When she finally turned, her profile hit Clayton like a bullet.

"Charlene?"

"I was going to leave when I saw you, but then I thought, No, damn it, let *him* leave." Her voice was thin and strained, slightly hysterical.

"No, Char. Don't go."

"Two years we live together, and you don't even recognize me."

Clayton stood in silent awe, taking in her face. Here it was, in the flesh (albeit a little blurry), the very features he had tried to put together a thousand times in his mind and failed. The red hair, softly bobbed, the large, soft eyes, hidden behind a pair of horn-rimmed glasses she was pretty enough to render unchaste. The X.

Actually she was wrong, Kyle noted; they'd lived together two years and three months. The first half in domestic bliss, a connubial euphoria, at least by Kyle's estimation. His one success in love, his one victory in a long campaign that, since she'd left, had gone into a weary, humiliating retreat.

"Sorry, I'm a lit-tle . . . bit . . . *Shit*." He stopped then, furious with himself that his buzz was slowing the flow of words.

"You're not a little anything, Kyle," she said knowingly. "You've never been a little anything in your life."

She looked up at him searchingly, as if she too had spent nights trying to picture his face and was amazed that it actually existed.

"You look . . . different," she said, trying to be polite.

Excited as he was, a wave of fatigue was falling over him and his lids began to dreamily descend, as if ready for sleep. The day had finally caught up with him. He'd been early for the party and had stopped around the corner at the Blarney Stone to kill some time, though now it seemed that time was coming out on top.

"Give me this," she said scoldingly, taking the drink from him. Where others had failed, she'd always known how to keep him temperate. Her method was simple—just take it away. How was it his so-called friends could never understand this? Ah, but then they'd miss the show, wouldn't they?

Carefully, they moved a few feet down to the coffee urn, where she fixed him a tall one, black with two sugars. Kyle found this touching. *Yes, black, exactly. She still remembers.* He stood there, sipping his coffee and nodding as she talked, growing a little steadier each minute. She was still in graduate school studying English, she explained, still writing poems nobody wanted. She'd snuck into the party with her roommate, who worked as a secretary for PEN American. Of course she'd realized there was a chance she'd see him here, but then she'd wanted to come so badly and figured the snow would keep most people away.

"Why'd you leave me?" he suddenly blurted out.

She looked around self-consciously. "You can't ask me that here, Kyle," she whispered sharply. "Not now."

After Kyle's book, they could rarely have a private conversation at a party. Someone was always listening in—the rabid fan, the malevolent gossip columnist. Snippets of their bickering would appear the next day in the *Post* or *Daily News*. It had been devastating to their relationship.

Tonight, though, nobody was paying attention. Tonight nobody seemed to care.

"I think you know perfectly well why," she whispered.

"Char, if you knew the temptations—"

"Oh, poor baby," she said, irony brandished like a sword. "The rigors of keeping your cock in your pocket."

"I'm different now. That's not me anymore."

"You just tried to *hit* on me!"

"C'mon," he said, nudging her. "I knew it was you."

She folded her arms like a sentry. She'd swallowed it for a while, choked on it, and now she was done.

But Kyle couldn't help himself. He put his hand on her arm, needing to touch her. Surprisingly, she let it stay.

"I'm sorry, Char. I wish someday you could forgive me. You don't know how many times I've thought of that."

She turned her face up to him again, making Kyle wish he'd never broached the subject at all, for he knew that her response would be without malice—though certainly it was what he deserved—and that it would remind him all over again of the decency and goodness he had squandered.

"I have forgiven you," she said.

He pulled the dagger out of his chest and laid it on the table.

"Seeing anyone?"

"None of your damn business," she said. "But no."

"Me neither."

She examined his face. "You don't look good, Kyle. I'm sorry to tell you this, but you don't. People have been saying things; I think maybe they're right. I'm worried about you."

He felt an irrational pang of hope. Was it drunken sentimentality, or was he seeing something in those big brown eyes of hers, a softening, an opening up? She was worried about him! When she reached out her hand and cupped his face in her long fingers, he felt like weeping, or whooping with joy, thinking there might just be another chance here.

It was all destroyed by the sounds of a mawkish, sickly sweet voice that dropped Kyle's heart ten stories to the sidewalk below.

"Oh, *Honey Kyle.*"

They turned to see a bejeweled Dorothea Clementine suddenly standing before them, two huge shopping bags in each hand.

"Well, don't just stand there, Kyle," she said. "Help me with this."

Horrified but not knowing what else to do, Kyle pushed aside the chopped liver and deviled eggs and lifted the bags to the table. Wasting no time, Dorothea began to unpack. From the first bag she removed ten tins of Osetra caviar and a large sack of toast points, and from the other, four bottles of Krug champagne, the heroic '85 vintage (pillaged from Zeddy's cellar, no doubt). The presentation was dramatic enough to incite a smattering of applause. The party's host suddenly scurried up behind her like a servant, a half dozen champagne flutes stuck in his fingers. His face held the subtle grimace of someone feeling upstaged but having to act like it was all for the best.

"I won't stay long," Dorothea assured the group, some of whom were already opening the caviar tins and scooping out the eggs with their fingers. "I just wanted to drop off some goodies for all my old artist friends. To help you through the long haul."

A bottle of champagne was popped. She handed Kyle the first glass.

"And I wanted to apologize to *you,*" she said, at the same volume, "for our little misunderstanding this afternoon."

Kyle snuck a glance at a confounded Charlene. Tongue-tied, he raced around his mind searching for a reply, and then all interaction was cut off by the sudden rush of bodies as the artists clamored for the champagne.

"We need more glasses!" a panicked voice called out. There were rude murmurs echoing through the apartment now, sharp retorts. "Don't *push* me," one sophisticate yelled. The air had suddenly become tense.

Mrs. Clementine turned to Kyle and the X. "Isn't it wonderful?" she proclaimed. "They love it!"

Another surge pushed Kyle right up against Dorothea. *"Well,"* she said in delight, and in her great swell of pride she took the opportunity to kiss him flush on the lips.

Oh, this was bad, Clayton fretted, instantly pulling away. So very, *very* bad. Though she was usually discreet in public, every once in a while Dorothea got into one of those frisky moods where she just couldn't help letting the room know that Honey Kyle was indeed her beau. The timing couldn't be worse, and yet, how dare I be surprised, he thought, on this most lucky of days?

Dorothea narrowed her eyes at the X. "And who are you, exactly?"

"A good friend," Kyle quickly interjected, reaching behind him to remove Dorothea's arm from his waist.

"Well, I'm leaving," Charlene suddenly announced.

"No."

"Bye," said Dorothea.

Kyle reached out for Charlene. "Please, don't go," he pleaded, only to be pulled back a step by Dorothea, disengaging him from the X.

"No, please *do*," Dorothea chirped.

Kyle turned to her with a fiery anger. "Can you just once," he growled through gritted teeth, the words louder than he had hoped, "just *once* in your life, SHUT THE FUCK *UP*."

Licking black eggs from their fingers, a few nearby partygoers leveled a scrutinous gaze at Kyle, incredulous about this hostility toward their wonderful benefactor.

"Here here, young man," a proper English voice called out. A white-haired, dignified-looking octogenarian stepped forward from the cluster.

Clayton, unfocused though he was, recognized him as a famous poet, a Nobel laureate. *Sir* Something-or-Other.

"I daresay," the man continued in pitch-perfect Oxfordese, "that's no way to speak to a lady." Nearby, all eyes turned toward Clayton as the poet walked to a spot directly in front of the younger man. He stood there expectantly, the very image of fading chivalry, waiting for the inevitable apology to their benevolent Mrs. Claus.

The voices near them grew quiet in anticipation.

"Well?"

"Blow me, Pops," Kyle replied.

Amid a cantata of gasps, he pushed firmly past the old man, sending him nearly to the floor, if not for the rescuing arms of his cohorts.

Clayton looked around. The X was gone. He got on his toes and scanned the crowd, sighting her by the front door. Though coatless, she was hurrying through a hasty good-bye to her roommate.

Elbows tucked, he forced himself through the thickening crowd.

As he gained on his target, Devon Schiff suddenly stepped forward, dapperly dressed with a rather pissed-off look, blocking Kyle's path with folded arms.

"We've got to talk," he said. "It's about this morning."

"Later, Shit," Kyle replied, reviving an old nickname.

"No, *now*."

Clayton sighed, pretending to relent, then barreled a shoulder into

Devon, knocking his sparkling water to the carpet. There were more gasps. Finally getting the hint, the crowd parted for wild-eyed Clayton, allowing him a clear path to the door.

Out in the hallway, the elevator was already on its way down. He took the stairs two at a time. In the lobby he was a blur to the doorman, driving through the revolving doors like a fullback. Through the frosty glass he caught a glimpse of her on the sidewalk, hand waving furiously for a taxi.

"Charlene!" he called out, his voice entombed by the rotating vestibule. She looked back anxiously, hopping on her toes. Before the doors could spit him out she was on the run again. A cab was pulling up across the street.

He raced into the snowy evening, out from under the building's canopy—*Charlene!*—she was still without a coat, he realized, red hair bobbing. He was gaining on her rapidly now, within ten feet. He could almost reach out and grab her.

Instead he slipped on some ice, his legs splaying out under him like they'd been lopped off, his body airborne. He descended onto the very edge of the curb and into *the* butt-crunching fall of a lifetime. His howl echoed down the street as if he'd been shot. It was a new level of pain, a threshold unto itself.

"I BROKE MY FUCKIN' ASS!" he screamed.

He sat half-dead in the street, his body immobilized, littered with gutter snow. He watched helplessly as the X jumped into a cab, the still-rolling vehicle like a getaway car, her good-bye an uncharacteristic middle finger sticking up at him from the backseat window.

His angel, his true savior, gone into the night, signing off with an unholy and long overdue *Fuck you.*

8

In a suite at The Four Seasons, Meryl was smiling mischievously.

"I just had a déjà vu," she said.

"About what?"

"About the night we met."

She was stamping her feet into new shoes, something more appropriate for the party. Dinner downstairs had taken longer than expected, and now they were running behind.

"Something about being back in the city brought it on, or maybe it was the snow. I'd forgotten it was snowing that night. Do you remember?"

Yes, she was right, of course. The party at Arthur's, that amazing apartment overlooking Gramercy Park. A miserable night. 1969, he guessed. His second novel due out the following month. He skied along the sidewalks in his one good pair of shoes, icy snow striking his face. Forgetting the number, Richard looked up at the building's façade, hoping for a miracle. On the second floor he found it: golden light from the large windows, brilliant profiles, the sparkling beads of a chandelier.

"I'd forgotten about the weather," he said now.

"Oh, it was a terrible night. I almost stayed home. Did I ever tell you that?"

"Yes," he said with a wan grin, "many times."

"Isn't that funny?" She went over to the mirror and began brushing her hair in long, luxuriant strokes. "The crazy chances in life."

Richard sat down on the bed. This was going to be a while.

"What do you remember about that night?" she asked.

"We're very late, Meryl."

"I'm hurrying," she said, brushing her hair vigorously. "Tell me something. An image, anything."

He lay back on the bed, looking up at the ceiling as if to invoke recollection.

"Your breasts," he said.

She turned and narrowed her eyes at him.

"Oh, come on."

"What?" he said, sitting up slightly. "They were magnificent. The whole room changed because of them."

"That's absurd."

Richard lay back down, summoning his flagging memory. *Remembrance of Breasts Past*. Gorgeous, he thought now, their coming into view, a very monument of beauty. They were the focus of the party, the absolute center of the universe. How was it possible she didn't know? He didn't believe her.

"I'm telling you. Everybody was sneaking looks. Women too. There was a sense of awe in the room. You had that really deep-cut dress on, even though it was November. And your skin—I couldn't believe how moist it was. It looked like—Jesus, it looked as if your breasts were *basting*."

"Basting!"

He laughed. "It's true. I remember telling Arthur that."

"Bastards," she said, only half displeased. "What did Arthur say?"

"He said, 'I'm writing that one down.' He said he was going to steal it. And as a matter of fact he did, the son of a bitch."

Richard sat up, invigorated. Meryl had unzipped the back of her dress, and now he could see down to the top of her buttocks where the soft white flesh clashed with the nut-brown remnants of a faded summer tan.

He looked at his watch.

"I thought we were supposed to be getting dressed, Meryl, not un-dressed."

"I'm almost done," she said, brush cutting rapidly through her hair with a staticky *phhhhit*. How long was she going to brush her goddamned hair? She looked perfect. Almost good enough to eat, in fact—if he were so inclined. Which these days he was not.

"So that's what you remember, huh? My tits."

"I remember a lot of things."

"Such as?"

Richard leaned back, letting out a soft, audible sigh. It was clear they weren't going anywhere until he indulged her in this memory game.

"All right, let's see . . ." He covered his mouth, suppressing the urge to laugh—the breasts were still hovering in his mind's eye. "Okay, I got it."

"Go on," she said impatiently.

"I remember when we sat down to dinner, how we positioned our-selves right across from one another, even though we hadn't spoken yet."

"Yes." She smiled, pleased.

"Then during dinner we played that game, the one where someone recites a first line and you have to guess the writer. I believe you won on Ford Madox Ford."

"This is the saddest story I have ever heard," she chimed in.

"An easy one."

"Oh, *please.*"

"Impressive nonetheless, darling. Quite impressive. Definitely got me in the nuts."

"What else?" she said excitedly.

"I remember kissing you on the corner afterward with that hail coming down on us—we were supposed to be looking for a cab—and how your lips tasted like white wine and cigarettes. I remember pleading with you to come back to my apartment with me."

"Begging."

"Oh, I don't doubt it," he said, grinning. "Begging, yes. Absolutely."

She came over and sat next to him on the bed, dress hanging off her shoulders. Richard caught a whiff of perfume, the combination of violets and a woman's groin at the end of a long, unchaste evening.

Almost enough to get an old man riled up.

"So I'd just go back to your apartment and screw your brains out, is that what you thought?"

"No," he said, noticing his wife's momentary satisfaction. "But I didn't think a blow job was completely out of the question."

Meryl whacked him on the shoulder with her hairbrush, laughing in mock outrage. "What, you were so irresistible? In your frumpy tweed jacket."

"If you'll recall, you had a taste for writers back then."

"Well, if *you* remember," she said proudly, "you didn't get a thing that night."

His face turned dark suddenly. "Yes, darling," he said, his tone following his countenance, "your ruse of chastity was well played."

He instantly regretted the comment. Here was an old wound that had never quite healed.

That icy evening, as Meryl Smith disengaged herself from his arms and slipped into a cab, Whitehurst decided he was in love. Knew it as firmly as he had known anything in his life. He returned immediately to Arthur's apartment, the guests all gone now, under the auspices of helping with the cleanup—but really to pick his friend's brains about his newly beloved, to extract every known detail, and to exact an opinion as to how long he thought it would take to marry her.

The answer was not what he expected. Her dewy innocence, as it turned out, was a fraud. Richard remembered how his heart sank (and secretly throbbed with excitement) as his friend explained how Ms. Smith was the owner of what was then known as a "rep." She was from a wealthy Hudson Valley family, Arthur explained, worked part time at *Esquire,* and had a "notorious" sexual appetite, especially for writers. They were her whimsy, her obsession. Knock off a few lines of Shakespeare, word had it, and Ms. Smith's panties were the Great Lakes. Show published work and you were *in.* When Richard balked at this, Arthur told him about two other men at that evening's party, also writers, who had known her biblically, and, with great prodding, he admitted to receiving oral sex himself one night in her West Village apartment.

"Wonderfully skilled" was his friend's verdict, oblivious to the sudden depths of Richard's feelings.

Thus came the first personal intellectual dilemma of Whitehurst's life.

His first novel, *Heart's Crest,* was considered an erotic classic, and he'd always prided himself on his libertine ideals. In certain literary circles, in fact, his name had become synonymous with sensuality. Yet on their dinner date the following evening at P. J. Clarke's, after several martinis and nearly two bottles of wine, Richard hit the roof when busty Meryl Smith freely confessed to "roughly" fifty sexual partners.

"Fifty?" he whispered in disbelief.

"More or less," she said, casually chewing her steak.

Whitehurst shifted in his seat, as much agitated by the enticing way she looked as by the number of lovers she'd divulged. She looked ripe and ready tonight: blouse buttoned one notch too low, white pearls a bridge over the swelling ravine. Though the number astounded him, he would have to be discreet in his outrage, since what he really wanted on this evening, more than anything else on earth, was to be number fifty-one.

"Wait a second now," Richard said, blinking as if to solve a riddle, "let me get this straight." He leaned over the table, taking a quick peek at the bridge of pearls, and lowered his voice to a whisper. "I just want to make sure you understand the question. I'm not talking about kissing, now."

She shook her head and shrugged, sipping her wine.

"So you—*Jesus,*" he said. "So you mean to say you've . . . you've . . ." He couldn't bring himself to use the word. "*Fifty* guys?"

Her eyes widened in surprised recognition. "Oh, no!" she said with a dismissive laugh. "Oh, heavens no, I think you've misunderstood me."

His face was impassive, though inside he was suddenly overcome with a joyous, cosmic relief. Of course he was wrong! He sat back, slumping with the release of nervous energy. A simple misunderstanding, he thought. Well, how wonderful, how very human. All was right with the world.

"There are a few women in there too," she said.

Richard gulped.

"You don't have a problem with that, do you?" she asked innocently, slicing another piece of steak. "I knew I could tell you this because I just finished reading your book this afternoon—which I loved, by the way! It's so rare to read a male author who *really* understands women, but I think you do. The way you defend their sexuality, for example."

Richard stared at her, flabbergasted. *It's a fucking book!* he wanted to scream; it's not real. I want my *heroines* horny, not my future *wife*!

He looked down again at the pearls. Ah, fuck it, he thought.

They went back to her apartment that night, a Friday, and, with the exception of a few food runs, stayed there until Monday morning. In all his years of female seduction (at which he'd only been moderately skilled), and for all the sexual audacity of his writing, he had never experienced anything like that weekend. Had never experienced such a low-down, tongue-shredding, dick-blistering, joyous, and sometimes even tender sexual apocalypse in all his life. Their good-bye was sealed with whispers of infatuation, and Whitehurst thus found himself that Monday morning faced with the most pressing intellectual question of his life:

Could one, or should one, fall in love with a woman who gave so freely of herself? A woman who by twenty-two had fucked the lights out of enough men to fill a professional football roster—no, make that *two* teams: home *and* away; whose lust had extended to the same sex; who had, let's admit it, blown more than the mind of one of your closest friends?

Richard Whitehurst had somehow hit the motherlode with the gorgeous, intelligent Meryl Smith, but as he rode the train downtown from her apartment that morning, a part of him was unreconciled. *She's goddamned perfect—except, of course . . .* Except *what*? What was her crime exactly? Lust? What a *coward* he was. He could rail at hypocrisy in his writing, but his real life was a contradiction: He wanted depravity *and* purity. He wanted a highly skilled lover but with no experience. The origin of this problem was evident, of course. The Connecticut Presbyterian at odds with the New York intellectual; the sixties man-about-town, reared in the values of the forties. But even this knowledge was unsatisfying, irrelevant. His heart remained divided.

Perhaps it always had been. A few months went by, and he finally came to his senses. They were married in Millbrook in the late summer. But even now, decades later, there were moments where he wasn't sure he'd completely gotten over it. A feeling lingered, however irrational, that a part of her had been overused—like an old coin, passed through too many hands. Something forever tarnished.

"Who were the famous writers you had sex with?" Richard asked now at the hotel. He made the question sound casual, irreverent.

"What?"

"Your literary lovers. You know, way back when."

Meryl sat forward on the bed and began to apply a deep red lipstick.

"Give me one name," he said.

"Richard, you've been asking me this for twenty-five years. You know there's no way I'm going to tell you."

"Come on, I'm an old man," he said with a shrug, a strained apathy in his voice. Like all writers, he was a pitiful actor. "What does it matter now?"

"Please, you're trying to manipulate me."

"How?"

"It *does* matter to you. Of course it does."

"It does not," he said, laughing. "Christ, not *now*." He'd momentarily forgotten about the party—now that an old obsession had suddenly returned. "Don't be silly," he said, "it was more than twenty-five years ago. Who cares?"

"Then why are you asking me?"

He shrugged. "I'm just curious, that's all. It's fun."

"There are at least a hundred reasons why I won't."

"A hundred?"

"That's not what I mean. It's just that . . . Okay, for example. Let's say I did give you a name, and it turned out that the writer was more famous than you. How would that make you feel?"

"Meryl, *all* writers are more famous than me, by definition. I am, without question, the least-known living writer."

"That's not true and you know it."

"Wait a minute," he said, suddenly excited. "That's a hint, isn't it? Somebody very famous. One of the top brass."

"No."

"Saul Bellow," he suddenly blurted out.

"Oh, *God.*"

"He was in New York back then, wasn't he? That horny toad. And we all know how much you liked the Jews."

Meryl was shaking her head, humored by this game. Should she give him a name or two to stir things up? Jealousy had once been his great aphrodisiac, after all.

"Updike," he accused.

"With that beak?" she said. "Forget it. He did make a pass at me though. Some *New Yorker* party, I think."

"Fucking lecher," Richard grumbled.

Meryl shook her head, but her spirit was brightening. She enjoyed the tone of his response, the primitive competitiveness of it. She could almost feel him growing warm with envious desire.

"I'm a better writer than him anyway. Don't you think?"

"Of course you are," she said. She put her head on his shoulder and ran her hand up his thigh. Her breath was in his ear now, lips tickling the folds with the lightest of touches.

Richard was looking straight ahead though, lost in thought. "That

Brazil book of his was a disaster. Unreadable. I'd put *Sonata* up against that any day."

"I'll tell you this much," she went on, trying to bring back the heat, "you can tell from a man's writing how he'll perform in bed."

"Really?" Richard asked. "How?" He sat up completely straight. "In what way?"

"Well, let's see . . . The more sensual a writer, for example, the more attentive you know he'll be."

"Really?" he repeated, fascinated. "What else?"

"Well, poets tend to fuck more intensely, but for a shorter length of time. Novelists, of course, usually have more stamina. It's a very symbiotic relationship. Someone should really do a study."

"And me?" he asked.

"You? You I would describe as a . . ." She thought for a moment. "A cunning linguist."

But suddenly he wasn't listening. His eyes were large again.

"Roth!" he announced triumphantly.

Meryl pulled her head away.

"That cocksucker—it *had* to be him. I'll bet you're the girl in *Portnoy*. The meshuggener cunt."

Abruptly, with that determined air of all or nothing, the kind born of twelve months of desperation, Meryl Whitehurst rose from the bed and stood before her husband. There was a hot fury in her eyes, something Richard hadn't seen in quite some time. He winced, frightened, ready to put his arms up in defense.

She's going to hit me, he thought.

"I was only quoting Roth," he said apologetically, but it was too late—the dress was already falling from her shoulders.

She stood above him, heels giving the impression of height, stomach slightly swollen with the years but still womanly. Her breasts were especially phenomenal tonight too, he thought, higher than he remembered, set up firm and bulging in her bra. Hey, he thought, just what in the hell's going on here?

An ambush, that's what it was! It all made sense now: the stilettos, the cocktail dress unzipped down to *here*. A sexual coup d'état, perpetrated on a helpless old man. Uniforms by Victoria's Secret.

"Meryl?"

She knelt down in front of him.

"Oh, Meryl, darling . . . Hel-lo?"

She unzipped his pants and took it out. It was not what she'd hoped for. Half mast, maybe less. Pink and blotchy, an uncooked sausage. She began to use her fingers.

"I'm afraid it's not much use," he said.

"Give me a shot." She started to use her tongue.

"You remember what the doctor told us."

She kept at it for close to a minute, desperate, using all the tricks; then she pulled her head up.

"I'm sorry, honey, but—"

"I know, I know, the *depression*," she said. She was still stroking it, still trying, though not knowing why.

"That's what *they* call it. Whereas I'm convinced . . ."

He stopped himself as she let the penis fall from her fingers. It was no use. She rocked back onto the floor with a faint thud, a defeated puff of air expelled from her lips. They sat silently for a moment, both embarrassed.

It was Richard finally who decided to break the ice, attempting a spot of humor.

"Well, I suppose by your theory my new writing will be rather limpid."

Not even a smile. She stared at the floor.

"What are we going to do, Richard? This is important."

"It's important to me too."

"Well?"

He reached down and grabbed at the mound between her legs. It was wet, a fact Richard found distressing rather than complimentary. "I'm still a cunning linguist, aren't I, after all these years?"

She shrugged, saying nothing.

"But sometimes you want more," he said, nodding grimly to himself. He let go of her. "Yes, that certainly is reasonable, isn't it?"

She stood up and began to put her dress back on. Richard watched her, cursing himself. She was stunning for a woman her age—for any age. He felt like an idiot.

"You're more gorgeous than ever, darling. You know I think that." When she didn't answer he added, "We'll try later. I promise."

"After a few drinks? Great." She smoothed her dress with short, aggressive strokes. "I'm sure we'll have no problem then."

"Meryl, please."

She took a step toward him, silky stockings hissing in the empty room, then spun around. Her back was still exposed, the crack of her rump inches from his face. It was a slight, he knew, a kind of provocation. *Here it is,* she was saying. *What man would turn this down? What kind of fool?*

She was dangerous, he suddenly realized, a lethal entity: a beautiful woman nearly at the end of her run, wondering if it might not all be going to waste.

"Zip me up," she said, "and let's go to this goddamned party."

9

"Literature is dead, my friends. Utterly irrelevant. Technology, that awful mammon, has finally destroyed it."

At the PEN party the Nobel laureate had taken center stage. The caviar was gone, the champagne all poured out. Now was the hour for pontifications, for the big literary guns, fawned over and feted, to deliver on their end of the deal.

Sir Peter Lawrence was his name, and a good forty people had gathered round him. The great man was almost ninety, with poems going back to before the Second World War, crimson sash of knighthood worn proudly across his chest. He was a Brit, of course, an ex-lover of Auden's, and the only living writer you could still find in an anthology like *Immortal Poems*. His mind was somewhat doddering now, his face red as a steamed lobster, but he was a walking piece of history nonetheless. The crowd listened with the same dutiful attention they gave to old ruins on their summer vacation, determined to understand, to be *moved*.

Dorothea, for example, stood next to him, gazing up into his face with the rapture of a lover. It was just the kind of old-fashioned sermon that she loved: Old = good/New = bad. Her head bobbed with every syllable.

"I shudder to think what this new generation of writing will be like, trying to compete with the Internet and high-definition TVs and specialized pornography." Sir Peter shook his head piously, the secular old preacher, the fin de siècle doomsayer. The crowd loved it, this cultural fire and brimstone. "I'm just lucky, I guess. I came about in a different era. I knew all of Shakespeare by the time I was fifteen, and there were great subjects to write about, world wars and love affairs—and yes, okay, a little sex." A smattering of polite laughter. "All the barriers were still there, all the old enemies still clear. Not at all like today. What more is there for a writer to discover? What taboos are there to transgress? Ah, but then, what do we expect, now that the computer and television have taken over our soul?"

The crowd nodded in assent. There were murmurings of *So true*, and *What I've been saying for years*—their public television hunches confirmed. Mrs. Clementine, whose apartment had a screening room the size of the Ziegfeld and who hadn't read a book since Harold Robbins died, patted him on the shoulder.

The poet took his praise with practiced humility, then licked what last patina of caviar still flourished on his pinky.

"NONSENSE," boomed a voice from the far corner of the room.

Doppler waves of horror rippled toward the source, heads turned in disbelief. Now just who was behind this disrespectful voice? they wanted to know. Who was foolish enough to disagree with such a man? Among the poet's friends there was the sinking feeling that the rude young man was at it again, for despite their protests he'd somehow been allowed to return. But no, this was a speaker of some age,

perhaps even of distinction. The voice had an authority, a noble reso-
nance that bellowed through them.

A path cleared to the poet's rival, who stepped forward. He was
an intelligent-looking gentleman in rumpled corduroy, with a bitter
glint in his eye and thin lips angled downward at a derisive pitch.
Though few knew his name, everyone recognized him—or, shall we
say, knew the type. It was the kid from the back of the class, the one
nobody liked, the smart, pimply boy who always had to say the contrary thing. The outcast.

"Excuse me?" replied the poet. The room was suddenly quiet;
somebody had turned the stereo off. A kind of literary *High Noon*.

"What you said, *sir*"—Richard Whitehurst's tone had more
than a hint of mockery in it—"I could not possibly disagree with
more."

"Well, I see." The poet looked right and left, smiling to his admirers as if to say, Now what do we have here? "And just where is it in
my thesis that I've gone wrong?"

"Everything," Richard brazenly countered. "That writing is somehow dead. I find that absurd, not to mention insulting and self-
serving."

The crowd bristled. Meryl grabbed her husband's hand. "Easy,
darling," she whispered.

Richard rejected her grip and stepped forward. "You address a
roomful of people, at least half of whom are writers, and you tell
them, 'Now that I'm done, there's nothing more to say. Now that I
leave this world, it's going to ruin.' Well, how convenient. But what
you fail to take into consideration, *sir,* is that the computer, maybe
technology itself—both of which, let me add, I am no great fan of—
could be the greatest thing that's happened for writers since the hor-
rid World War that launched your career."

The poet remained confident, still smiling at his disciples. "And just how would that be so, my friend?" he asked.

"A new enemy has presented itself," Richard asserted. He liked the comment and let it hover in the air for a moment before amending it. "As you yourself have just said, writers need enemies. Well then, what greater circumstance could there be for a novelist, say, than for the computer to become the god of the twenty-first century, as it appears it will? What clearer enemy could manifest itself? As a novelist myself, I envy these young writers. There is a new battle to be fought. Perhaps even more important than the ones waged by your generation."

An awful silence ensued. The crowd stared, waiting anxiously for the old poet to parry the blow, to show off and shine, but Sir Peter merely rolled his eyes and grinned. Richard had struck skillfully, and for a few seconds one could feel the room's momentum shift. Where was their knight, they wondered, their Nobel warrior? Who was this usurper? Hail the new king?

Whitehurst, though, was greedy. Instead of letting the silence build, to wait for the wound's blood to flow, he went in for the quick kill.

"Second, if you think your generation has answered all the questions, has plumbed the very depths of love, the mysteries of sex, of violence, of race, and so thoroughly that there is no more work left to be done, well, I say, *Sir* Peter"—his voice was rising now, lips quivering, losing control—"take the sash from your breast and lift up your head. Step out of your Academy-appointed limousine and into the street. You are sadly mistaken. Perhaps you've gotten a bit soft in your old age, eh? Perhaps too many glasses of wine over the years at backslapping Nobel functions, perhaps—"

"Oh, dear!" Dorothea Clementine interrupted in horror, the exclamation quickly followed by a burgeoning rumble of protest.

Whitehurst cut himself short. It was over. He'd been on a roll and in the next nanosecond had buried himself.

Immediately the crowd's emnity began to grow. Someone yelled something at him—he didn't know what—while others shook their heads, waving their hands in dismissal. He felt broken inside, humiliated.

He turned to Meryl. She looked at him with melancholy affection but without surprise. Her sad smile said it all.

You had to do it, didn't you?

The poet himself put on the finishing touches. "As I learned during my tenure on the Oxford debating team—of which, incidentally, I was captain for two years running—the man who engages in the ad hominem attack has something to hide, an axe to grind, and exchanging ideas with him is a pure waste of time. In this case, clearly that something is a romantic and, to my mind, utterly naïve point of view. So good luck to you, sir, whoever you are, and good riddance."

The music came back on; the duel was over. Richard seemed to limp back to his wife, head hung low, like a pitcher who'd just walked in the winning run. While the poet was immediately swarmed with nodding heads and shoulder pats, only one person was brave enough to cavort with the slain. Or perhaps, only one man in the room had so little left to lose.

"The old coot," remarked the young man. "He hasn't written a good poem in fifty years."

Richard smiled, grateful for the comment but feeling much too low to pick up his head.

"Kyle Clayton," the young man introduced himself. "A huge fan." He shook Richard's hand and then turned to his wife. "You're Meryl, I presume."

Husband and wife looked up. Here he was, presented with a stunning suddenness: the last literary celebrity, and subject of Richard's tacit obsession. He was taller than they'd expected, and not nearly as put together. His jacket hung askew on his shoulders; there was a rip in the pants' knee. His hair was a mess. He looked like he'd just been in a fight, and yet—even Meryl would later admit—the fabled charisma, that so-called magic quality, still emanated.

"How did you know my name?" she asked almost warily.

"I guess I read it somewhere," Kyle said with a grin. He pointed to Richard's glass. "I see you've managed to get some of the champagne. You're very lucky. I didn't think the vultures would leave a drop."

All around them was the evidence of disapproval, the sharp looks and under-the-breath whisperings. *Look*, Kyle felt them thinking, *the black sheep have found each other.*

"We share an agent, I believe," said the young man.

"Yes," Richard answered in a thin voice. He was doubly discomposed now. He'd not yet had a chance to recover from his tête-à-tête, and here he was thrust into the presence of his years-long curiosity. By way of deflection, he proceeded to squint over Clayton's shoulder, as if looking for someone. "He told me he was coming tonight."

"Larry's one of our dearest friends," Meryl added.

Richard smiled sadly. "We sure could use a few of those tonight, couldn't we, darling?"

His wife frowned.

Just then Dorothea Clementine slid past them, the ruffling of her dress mowing down everything in its path. She cut the three of them a hard look, saving the last barb for Clayton. Then she scurried on.

"I'm sorry, Kyle," Richard said, coming alive a bit for the first time. "I'm afraid any association with me this evening immediately marks you a pariah."

"Maybe we should leave," Meryl proposed.

"No, please don't," Kyle urged.

Richard raised his eyes, surprised by the younger man's conviction.

"If you go now," Kyle said, "it'll look like you're running. Don't worry about them. Let them worry about you."

Richard nodded vaguely. This seemed to make sense to him. His wife seemed less sure.

"Anyway, you just got here, right? What's the rush?"

"Please, young man," Richard said, "don't feel obligated to talk to us just because—"

Kyle shook his head vehemently. "Mr. Whitehurst, I've been waiting to talk to you for years. I could give a rat's ass what these people think." He made a flourish with his hand signifying that, if necessary, he was ready to take on the whole room for his hero. For the first time since he'd arrived, Richard smiled.

Meryl, though, was suddenly not so impressed.

She was looking at Kyle Clayton's eyes. They were thoroughly glazed, spiderwebbed with blood in the most amazing patterns. She realized then that he was dead drunk, absolutely out on his feet and probably holding on by a thread. Richard, of course, was oblivious.

"Why don't we go somewhere private?" Kyle suggested, and now Meryl thought she could hear a slight slurring in the young man's words. "I'm sure there's an open room in the back—if you wouldn't mind sparing a few minutes for me."

"I don't know, Richard, maybe we should think about—"

But before she knew it they were off, her husband tugging her along through the crowd, Kyle in the lead. The young man moved confidently enough, Meryl observed, with no stagger or slip, and with this she was quite impressed, till she caught him furtively running a hand along the moldings for support.

Then, as they approached the study, she observed something especially curious. An effete, rather handsome young man was leaning confidently against the bathroom door. Just as Kyle was about to pass by, it seemed the two young men locked eyes, the other mouthing something to Clayton. Though she couldn't make out what was said, she presumed it was hostile, since Kyle immediately reached out and clamped a hand down hard on the man's shoulder, squeezing violently enough to make him wince. Vise in place, he leaned in and quickly whispered something in the other man's ear, then released him and darted into the empty room.

The man was left standing there, his eyes wide with incredulity, and, to Meryl's perception, more than a little pissed.

Though she could not know it, the other man was Devon Schiff, and what Kyle had whispered to him were three simple words:

"Ten minutes, asshole."

10

Though Richard could never have guessed it, Kyle's obsession with him actually eclipsed the older man's fascination for Clayton. His novel of life in France, *Heart's Crest,* written the year Kyle was born (a detail that he, in his Whitehurst-mania, saw as significant), was a book he had read more times than any other in his life. Once a year since he was twenty, he'd taken Whitehurst's novel down from the shelf; with each reading the book provided him newer, fuller pleasures. Kyle always thought it strange that Whitehurst had never risen above minor cult status, that he had remained the kind of author one comes to only through the recommendation of others. But hadn't there always been something suspect, something common, about work that reached the masses? To him, Whitehurst's obscurity only made him more precious.

Via fame, half-assed charm, and an extraordinary surplus of free time, Kyle had managed to meet nearly every living writer he'd ever admired. But Whitehurst had remained elusive. Little was known about him, probably since so few cared. Kyle had hounded Wabzug for details, back when they were still talking, but Larry had been reticent. He didn't gossip about old friends, he said, failing to mention that Whitehurst had been asking about *him*. One could suppose that Wabzug had done this on purpose, that some instinct had told him that his two clients should not cross paths. Not now. Not ever.

Yet here they were.

The back room Clayton had led them to was the study of a midrange journalist. Lots of pressed wood and rusting file cabinets. Richard sat in the chair, which Kyle thought his due, while the younger man leaned near him on the desk.

Meryl stood across the room, arms crossed, silent. She'd had a lifetime of this sort of thing, of being the third wheel, and she'd turned the knack of keeping out of the way into an art form. Still, she was keeping a keen eye on Kyle Clayton.

The door was kept open. From time to time a guest would peer in, only to grimace somberly upon surveying the scene.

"So," Whitehurst began with a wry little smile, "how much of a disaster was it?"

Though the question was directed toward his wife, Kyle saw fit to interject. "Don't be ridiculous," he said, pulling a Daffy Duck pronunciation on the last syllable. Kyle had gone to a bar for a few more rounds before returning and he knew that by all rights he should probably be on the floor by now—but the proximity of his hero had buoyed his resolve. This revived buzz was a blessing in a way, he tried to tell himself. Could he have faced Whitehurst sober? Richard fucking Whitehurst!

"You got a little heated," Kyle continued. "So what? You were brilliant."

Richard seem to brighten. Maybe it wasn't as bad as he'd first imagined. "They got very angry though, didn't they?" he asked.

"They couldn't follow your argument," the young man contended. "You know what happens in those situations. People begin to feel stupid, left out, they get fru*th* . . . Excuse me." Kyle smiled self-deprecatingly and licked his lips. "They get frustrated."

Richard looked across the room to his wife, knowing that this was where true objectivity lay. Unfortunately, she was shaking her head.

"He's being polite, darling," she began. "The fact is you were making a terrific point out there, and then you had to get personal."

"I know," he said. "I know." He lowered his head resignedly, somberness returning. How had it happened? How could he have been so stupid? He'd seen the bitterness coming, had felt it rising in his blood like a tidal wave, but had been helpless to subdue it. The world's indifference to his work, breeding like a cancer for so long, coupled with the poet's vainglory, had churned in his gullet until he couldn't hold it another second.

"I just couldn't help it. That red sash. I mean, imagine it, coming to a party with a prize strapped to your chest! Why didn't he just dangle the goddamned Stockholm Medal from his dick."

Kyle laughed, but Meryl sighed deeply, echoing a profound dispirit, the weariness of advice given for twenty years and never taken.

"Darling, you have to understand, men like Peter Lawrence are why these people are here tonight. He's why the rich contribute to organizations like PEN in the first place. They want to at least be able to say they talked to a Nobel Prize winner, a poet-knight or whatever, have him be charming and witty. That's why they turned on you. By insulting him, you insult them."

"Tough shit," he couldn't help saying.

"For *you*, Richard. It's tough shit for *you*." She folded her arms, frowning again. "You know, it's curious, darling, because for all your brilliance, for all your talent, you've never really understood the way things work. Your vision of life is so narrow. I mean, you've always complained that the literary world is a game. Well, *hel-lo!*" she said with a scoffing laugh. "Of course it is! So is *everything*. What the hell did you expect? There is a kind of perverse logic to it all, you know."

"Not to me."

"Well, that's why you don't win any prizes."

"Don't want 'em."

She laughed again. "Oh, I don't believe that for a second."

"The Nobel's like the goody-two-shoes award these days," Kyle declared, trying to temper Meryl's criticism. "You have to be a minority or been in a gulag to get one of those."

"How true, Kyle," the older man said. "Literature's just another branch of politics now. Who was it that won the Pulitzer this year?"

"Oh, you mean the P-U?" Clayton responded.

Now, for perhaps the first time in months, Richard laughed heartily.

"The P-U," he repeated. He leaned back in his seat, holding his stomach with merriment. "*Very* funny . . ."

Encouraged, Kyle joined in the laughter.

Meryl wasn't buying it. She detected a tragic ring in the mirth. The truth was that Richard would have welcomed the Pulitzer without question, on his knees, with tears of joy. How desperately he'd wanted approval out there tonight, she thought. How badly he'd needed, after all the recent failures, for this crowd to finally love him. Instead, he'd gone and pulled his Coriolanus bit. Essentially, he'd been booed off the stage.

The laughter quickly ebbed, and Richard rubbed his brow grimly. "Ah, but I did some damage out there tonight," he said, nodding. "Yes, I'm afraid I did."

Meryl's heart suddenly ached for her husband, for their marriage. He'd come here for affirmation, and look what had happened.

Now it seemed nothing would get better. The downward spiral had picked up momentum.

"Here, drink this," she said, setting down her glass of champagne near him on the desk. "You'll feel better."

He waved it off, and then, to his wife's dismay, slid it across the desk toward Kyle.

"You have it," Richard said. Then he added with a knowing grin, "I hear you take a glass now and then."

Kyle looked at it for a moment, then shook it off. "That's a myth," he said. He looked at them straight-faced, with absolute sincerity. "Don't touch the stuff anymore. Doesn't agree with me."

Meryl tried to hide her distrust. Had she misheard him, she wondered, or was he simply a lying sack of shit?

Fearful he'd made another faux pas, Richard looked distraught.

"Oh, pardon me," he said, quickly pulling the flute back toward him—only to have the young man's hand swoop down, like a bird of prey, to intercept it.

"Ah, but what the hell," Kyle said. He winked broadly over the rim of the glass before bringing it to his lips. "Maybe just this one time."

It took a second, but then Richard fell instantly into another paroxysm of laughter, though Meryl failed to smile.

A HALF HOUR PASSED. The two authors heaped lavish compliments upon each other, Kyle confessing his hero worship for the older man, Whitehurst divulging his high regard for *Charmed Life,* how he thought Clayton the best young novelist to come around in twenty years. But where was the next one? Richard wanted to know. Sipping his champagne, trying desperately not to muff his words, Kyle went into an inebriated but inspired riff, telling the tale of a large, ambitious work-in-progress, a "Balzacian" overview of "end-of-the-century New York." There were no fewer than fifty characters, he said, various intersecting themes, and a roman à clef to boot. Still, he admitted, it was mostly still bits and scraps—he didn't know how it would all come together. At the moment, he admitted, his life had gotten away from him a bit.

Whitehurst was enraptured. How he would love to see a book like that, he said. He must finish it, he implored, absolutely *must*.

Meryl, meanwhile, told herself Kyle was full of shit. No such thing existed. Not from this drunk.

Finally, at Meryl's urging, the Whitehursts excused themselves. In a show of newfound friendship, Kyle insisted on helping them with their coats, which had conveniently been stored in the study. Then, despite intense protest, Kyle insisted he have the privilege of escorting them to the door. They would face the gauntlet together.

The living room hushed as they appeared. With nearly every eye on them, Kyle mistakenly guided his guests right past the exit and toward another door a few feet beyond. He swung the door open quite confidently, oblivious to the fact that it revealed nothing more than an overflowing wall of coats—he had mistakenly directed them to the closet. Then, as Meryl shook her head, Kyle gallantly put out a hand toward the erroneous opening, bidding his friends a sonorous good night.

The laughter that followed was almost without joy. These buffoons, it seemed, were too pitiful for humor. Richard, finally realizing the poor young man was skunked to the gills, kindly patted Kyle on the back, urging him to come with them for some coffee, perhaps back at their hotel. But before Kyle could answer, Richard was quickly drawn away by his wife. Without a word to anyone, or even a backward glance, the Whitehursts disappeared.

Kyle, meanwhile, was left to the lions. He turned to the crowd and smiled defiantly. Secretly, though, he was humiliated, and with his blood no longer charged with the presence of his hero, the day's cumulative vexation rose another notch.

His second wind was gone, along with the third and fourth. He was wobbling now, out on his feet, like a fighter who'd gone the distance with someone who could've knocked him out long ago but who wanted to see him suffer.

It was in this charming state of mind that Kyle went in search of Devon Schiff.

"Kyle!" a young woman's voice exclaimed after he'd taken a few tenuous steps.

He turned to the batting eyes of Lorrie Terell.

She had just arrived, delayed, apparently, by the application of a blood-red lipstick to the endless hectares of her pillow lips, and of the tiny, sparkling flakes that adorned her eyelids.

"Hel-lo!"

There was a party afterward, she whispered to him. Would he like to go with her?

Kyle undulated from one foot to the other, eyeing her woozily as he considered the offer. Embarrassed by the nakedness of his gaze, Lorrie took a step back and blushed. "Kyle, *please,*" she implored.

Unable to speak, Clayton spun his finger, directing her to turn around for him. When she failed to obey this romantic request, he reached down and flipped up the hem of her skirt.

"Hey!" she said, slapping his hand away. "What the hell?"

Kyle shrugged and headed off to find Schiff.

He discovered him by the bookcases, talking to a pale youth whom Kyle had been introduced to many times as Schiff's boyfriend but whom he failed to recognize now.

"Nice move with the Whitehursts," Devon said coolly as he approached. "Kind of ironic showing Richard to the closet, don't you think? Sort of a metaphor for his career." Schiff dropped his boyfriend's hand and stuck a finger in Clayton's chest. "You know, I didn't appreciate your little appraisal of me this morning." This outburst quickly drew the interest of some of the nearby crowd, and Schiff, ever inspired by attention, threw his voice up another few intervals. "And then, you nearly dislocate my shoulder tonight. Who the *fuck* do you think you are?"

Clayton's lips sifted, his tongue lolled; nothing came out. Words were beyond him now. He rocked on, back and forth, swaying to the music. Meryl's empty champagne flute hung upside down from his fingertips, a weather vane to his every bob and weave.

Schiff's finger jabbed like a hot poker. "I think you owe me an apology, asshole. In fact, I think you owe everyone here an apology."

Kyle's eyes closed completely.

"What a loser," Schiff said, taking a step back in disgust. "In fact, you're too pathetic to even—"

The blow was slow and deliberate, but poor Schiff had been lulled into complacency. The deadly violence of it shocked everyone in the room. High-pitched screams pierced the air. There was blood streaming down from Schiff's forehead, dripping off his nose.

Kyle had hit him with the champagne glass.

Schiff, who was by necessity a competent fighter, fell back against the bookcase, hands to his head, neutralized. His boyfriend instantly rushed to his defense, coming at Kyle with a flurry of slapping blows.

Clayton promptly sent him to the floor with a shot to the chin. *Wham!*

Then he turned to the crowd, looking for someone else to hit. He wanted them *all*. He would kill every last one of them, these serpents who had kissed his ass when he was on top and now rejected him.

"*Come on, you fuckers!*" he cried out.

The whole thing was over in the next moment as Dorothea Clementine walked up behind Clayton, calmly tapped him on the shoulder, and, as he turned, doused her erstwhile lover with enough Mace to take down an elephant.

Mayhem followed. There were more screams. Kyle was down on one knee, howling and holding his eyes. Lorrie Terell came up then and for good measure gave him a swift kick to the abdomen, sending him to the floor. There was a smattering of applause.

Clayton was just about done. He felt as if his eyes had been plucked out. His nostrils were on fire, and there was the taste of jalapeños and hot cinnamon on his tongue. Soon the vortex began spinning and the troops retreated, ducking for cover once again.

And then there was nothing at all.

11

Thirty-three. A kind of signpost for a man, is it not? The intermission, more or less. Thirty-three: Christ dies on the cross; Michelangelo begins the Sistine Chapel; Thomas Jefferson writes the Declaration of Independence; Melville publishes *Moby Dick,* Joyce begins *Ulysses.*

And Kyle Clayton awakes with a hangover for the fourteenth consecutive morning.

Yes, it was his birthday. February 8. Aquarius, the Water Bearer—you better believe it. Too tired to move, he'd let loose in his bed; the sheets had turned that fluorescent, multivitamin yellow.

What had gone on last night?

Answer: Everything.

He lay like a soldier from a routed army, left on the field to die: eyes burned (Mace), kidneys throbbing (booze), coccyx bruised (fall), stomach churning (don't even mention it). Remembering everything, he reflected on yesterday's campaign, a farrago of unpleasant doings: how he'd suddenly discovered his $100,000 debt, then alienated his benefactress and sole source of income; how he had lost the X for the second time; how he had pushed a ninety-year-old Nobel laureate at a public gathering; how he had committed assault with a deadly weapon (champagne glass); how he had consumed thirty or more drinks on yet another day when he had sworn to take it easy; and, finally, how he had permanently established himself as persona non grata on the New York literary scene, probably forever.

And, oh yes, lest we forget. He had broken his ass.

The hangover was the only comfort, a remembrance of better days—the days before yesterday. If people could only see him now, he thought, lying in his own piss. It would be useful in a way. *All you folks out there who hate me so, look at me now!* The perception (or misconception), the magazine idea of Kyle Clayton as "man about town," Bachelor of the Month, the guy who at twenty-five had some-how pulled a literary fast one and now had the life you'd always wanted—could he borrow a diaper?

I mean, where is it? he wanted to know. *Where is the charmed life?*

No one gave a shit about the real story. Nobody wanted explana-tions that required more than five seconds to comprehend. Oh, how he wished he could have an hour to explain himself to the world. To set the record straight. But would they have believed it, he won-dered. Would they have understood? Could they, in their left-to-right, binary-moving minds, comprehend Kyle Clayton's dirty little secret: that for all his ambition, his admitted love of the things one garnered through achievement, there was a part of him that was a little in love with failure. And could they fathom the idea that he would not write another book until he was good goddamned ready, until his heart was full to exploding with something to render, and that he would never become a literary corporation à la Devon Schiff and pump out books and articles like sausage links in order to fulfill his contract like a good little Condé Nast slut?

No, they wouldn't give him that hour to explain. Because, even as the X had noticed, nobody gave a shit anymore about Kyle Clayton. He had failed to write another "wild" book for them to read at their summer share, was no longer fun to bring drinks to at a party—he'd barf on your shoes now, or hit you with a glass. And his celebrity was no longer potent enough to want to fuck.

And so he lay there alone, urined thighs chafing, waiting for the sound of the sirens. There they were, he heard them in the street; the police were coming to take him away. In fact, he didn't understand why he wasn't in a jail cell this very minute. He'd smashed a glass in a man's face for crying out loud! His soul was sick and needed help. He was ready. "Yes, I'm here, come get me!" he called out to no one, the sirens wailing closer now. *Please, for the love of God. I'm so sick of this shit.*

The sirens caterwauled, whined, then faded to a distant moan.

He leaned over to the nightstand. It was 1:23. That would be P.M., judging from the intensity of hangover, which was roughly 5.7, Richter. His answering machine indicated six messages.

BEEP: *Kyle, dumb fugger, Pat McCreary here—that's Hollywood Pat to you. What a piss you had on last night! I had to carry you home on my back after the row, almost wouldn't let you in the cab. Listen, I know you're asleep right now, but a bloke from the* Post *called me this morning to get the scoop on your prizefight at the party last night. The headline they're planning is a hoot: "Literary Bloodbath!" With a picture of Schiff, blood running down his face. Call me, fugger, I gotta—*

BEEP: *Clayton, David Trevor here. Call me immediately at—*

BEEP: (Larry Wabzug's voice) *As of this moment, Kyle, our relationship is null and void. This saddens me, but what other solution is there? Don't call me again or contact me in any way. But please, get help. Immediately. You need it.*

BEEP: *Kyle, this is your father. What the hell went on last night? I wake up to some drunken, rambling message from you on my answering machine. Please call me immediately. Jesus, I'm worried about you. Listen, if you need a lawyer, don't forget Bloustein. Remember how well he did with that paternity thing of yours—*

BEEP: *David Trevor here again. Kyle, please, when you get—*

BEEP: *Clayton, Wabzug again. Uh, this is kind of awkward, but . . . call me, would you? Call me immediately. We could be back in business.*

Back in business? Had the old man gone insane? Kyle wondered. Didn't he realize that the only business Kyle Clayton would be conducting for the next few years was keeping his backside unperforated during his Rikers Island residency? You're losin' it, Larry.

And then, after going through all the messages, Kyle realized that no one remembered it was his birthday. Not even his father.

The phone rang, kick-starting his heart. This is *it*, he thought. He cleared his throat, practicing: *Yes, Officer, that's right, it was me. Mmmm-hmmm, apartment 3A. Door's open. I'll put some coffee on for the boys . . .*

"Hello?"

"Kyle!" There was relief in the British-accented voice. "About time. David Trevor, here, Brownstone and—"

"Ah, fuck off."

"Hey, come on now. Give me a chance over here. I know we got off on the wrong foot. Let's talk, huh? I think we might turn things around."

Turn things around?

Though he had never spoken to the infamous Mr. Trevor before, this certainly was a surprising start. The legendary shitkicker's voice was downright civil, the model of reason. Why? Kyle wondered. Not that he really gave a rat's ass anymore. He had nothing to lose; his head was already in the guillotine. Why not flip His Majesty the bird as the blade was falling?

"Hey, Trev, didn't you hear?" Clayton asked. "I'm *through*, man. Done. Toast. So really, go ahead and fuck off—"

"You're not done, Kyle."

"Oh, I'm not?"

"No. In fact, you're just beginning. And I think you know it."

Clayton laughed, a pig snort of rebuttal.

"You didn't hear about what happened last night, did you, Trev?"

"Oh, I heard first thing this morning. Thrilling news. The whole city's abuzz."

"Abuzz," Kyle mocked. "Listen, Trev, your *ass* is gonna be abuzz when I tell you what your chances are now of ever getting money back from—"

"Oh, the advance money?" Trevor said with a dismissive laugh. "Forget about that."

Kyle was struck silent.

"Keep it. It's yours. What you planned last night was brilliant. Exquisitely calculated, deftly played."

"Huh?"

"Come on, you *know*. The publicity stunt. That nearly-forgotten-writer-reestablishing-interest-with-a-single-blow thing. Ingenious, Kyle! Dastardly, my conscience says, but ingenious. You scare me, my boy, I get chills from you. The pure, Machiavellian orchestration of it—*that* frightens the living shit out of me!"

"Oh, no, no, no, no, no, no . . ." Kyle murmured. He was shocked, stunned at the implication. "You don't get it at all. I didn't orchestrate anything. I threw a champagne glass into another man's *face*. I've gone off the deep end over here, I'm going to *jail*."

"First of all, forget Schiff," Trevor said flatly. "I've spoken to his publishers. They've assured me that they're as excited about this thing as we are. And anyway, Schiff isn't that hurt. It was just a scratch really."

"A scratch?" Kyle remembered the blood seeping through Devon's fingers as he covered his face. "I'm a little lost here."

"Oh, please, this is getting tiring." Trevor sighed deeply. "But fine, I'll play along. I'll spell it out for you, if that's what you want. You're *hot,* my friend. Okay? H-O-T. So is Schiff. One writer hits another with a glass—it's awesome! You must understand, Clayton, the literary brawl is the greatest advertising weapon in all of publishing. Your new novel, which Larry has been telling me so much about, is going to *debut* on the best-seller list based on this incident alone!"

"Oh my God," Kyle murmured.

"Marvelous, isn't it? I . . . no, excuse me, Clayton, *we*—we are going to give Brownstone the first number-one best-seller in its shabby fifty-year history! How far are we, by the way, from a first draft? I have to tell you, I can't lie, our publishing spies have already learned that Schiff has promised to work round the clock to speed his new book to press . . . Anyhow, you probably want to know what the bottom line is. Fair enough. I'll tell you. Keep the advance. That's what this is about, Kyle. That's the kind of guy I am."

"And?"

"And I want a book in six months."

The phone slipped from Kyle's hand. He caught it by the antenna. *"Six months?"*

"The public has amnesia, Kyle. Anything beyond that and the whole thing'll have been forgotten. Six months, period."

"Impossible," Kyle said. "I can't do a book in six months."

"Why?"

"It'll be garbage. A piece of shit."

"So?"

"What if I say no?"

"If you say no?" Trevor answered, his tone now quietly ferocious. "If you say no, I bury any book you submit after six months; it does me no good after that, and by contract I've got your next one by the balls. If you say no, I tell all future houses what an unproductive pain in the ass you've been—a real chop job, so that by the time I'm done, *Kinko's* will view you as a publishing risk. If you say no, I'll have my lawyers pull a gang bang on your ass that'll have you howling like a banshee, not to mention in paralyzing debt until the third millennium. If you say no, Kyle, you drunken bastard, I will personally dedicate my life to tracking you down—even if I have to visit every bar in this city—and sink my shoe into your rotted cantaloupe of a head and laugh as you shit bicuspids and sip single-village mescal through a straw for the next fifty years. If you say no."

Kyle wandered into the kitchen, drawing a touch of interference on the cordless. He opened the fridge and removed a rather large tub of Absolut-spiked Jell-O. Otherwise known as breakfast.

"So?" Trevor asked. "What do you say?"

Kyle scooped out a large spoonful of the jiggling gelatin and then, hitting it with just a dash of Reddi-wip, swallowed it down without a single chew.

"Clayton? C'mon now. What do you say?"

"What do I say?" Kyle answered, smacking his lips. "I say call Larry Wabzug. I'm back in business."

There was a second of silence on the other end, the pause of triumph.

"Wise," Trevor said finally. "You're a good boy after all." He was calm again, ever so pleased. "And oh, by the way."

"Mmm?"

"Happy birthday, Clayton."

12

The deli that Wabzug had chosen to meet at was down on Houston, just east enough to make Richard Whitehurst nervous. Taking the cab down from his hotel, he'd left his wife on Broadway at the Soho Guggenheim and, getting a taste of the brilliant, poststorm sunshine, decided to walk. To take a stroll through the old neighborhood.

Unfortunately for Whitehurst, the old neighborhood had gone to hell.

Walking east along the still-snow-covered avenue, slipping and sliding, the long-forgotten smell of reefer in the air, Richard found himself trying to stifle the urge to be discouraged at what he saw. East of the Bowery, he tried to remind himself, had never been the apotheosis of New York beauty, but, dear Lord, entropy certainly *had* taken its toll.

On a lark, he took a detour down to his old apartment on Attorney Street, to the very tenement he'd lived in so many years ago. The building was condemned now, a fact Richard found highly ironic.

Noticing the elementary school across the street, he smiled, recalling those countless afternoons trying to work through the blare of schoolyard pandemonium.

Now the place had the feel of a minimum-security prison. The schoolyard was fenced in, barbed wire running along the top. Though the asphalt was covered with melting snow, it was obvious that all that remained now—where once had stood jungle gyms and tennis courts and tetherball poles—was a lone, severe-looking basketball court, the basket rim hanging loose and useless, the word CUNT sprayed on the backboard. The new generation, he thought. The new world.

A white man in dreadlocks appeared and stealthily approached one of the first-floor windows of the tenement. Though he was a good hundred feet away, the scabs on the man's face were quite visible. He looked at Whitehurst suspiciously, and then, perhaps deciding the writer was too old for police work, knocked loudly on the boarded-up window. Richard tried not to look as the plywood was quickly removed and a transaction committed so swiftly as to be almost by sleight of hand, the man disappearing around the corner as suddenly as he'd appeared.

So many dreams, Richard mused sadly, glancing up at the broken panes of his old fourth-floor window. So many years, typing, typing away . . . And for what? He'd had a conceit back then—it was almost embarrassing to think of it now—he had believed he was going to change the culture. Yes, he'd decided, his talent was undeniable, and with it he would create beauty that would make people weep, monumental works the world could not live without. A recognized genius leaving the world more human than he'd found it.

Ha, he thought now with a smirk, what a fool.

On perhaps the most irrational whim of his life, Richard suddenly began walking toward the tenement, heart beating fast. On the ground near the steps he discovered what he thought was a used crack pipe. Looking back and forth to make sure the street was empty, he picked it up and held it at eye level, examining it with naïve fascination. Instead of being frightened, the possibilities suddenly intrigued him. Might there not be some magic here? he wondered. Might this not be just the thing?

It was probably ridiculous, he thought, but then he also knew he desperately needed *something*. The new book was going poorly, with no relief in sight; it would probably be his last. He was stale, used up. He could feel it inside him, a deadness. He needed to shake things up, to do something daring and dangerous.

He slipped the pipe into his pocket.

Quickly, before reason could take over, he took a fifty out of his wallet and knocked on the boarded-up window. Instantly the flimsy plywood was removed. Though Whitehurst could see nothing inside except blackness, he stuck his hand in, waving the money invitingly. Then a pair of large, dark eyes appeared, regarding him suspiciously from the blackness within. The man shook his head, apparently distressed at the age of the countenance before him.

"It's a losing game, Pops," he said.

Thinking the man exactly right, a true sage, Whitehurst clenched the Ziploc bag with the six or so little rocks that was presented to him, stuffed it into the pocket of his blazer, and in an instant was gone faster than his sixty-four-year-old legs had taken him in a very long time.

13

"Big enough for you?" Larry Wabzug inquired with a prideful grin.

Richard looked intently at his half of pastrami, held precariously aloft, the meat blood-red between the slabs of rye.

"Shylock special," the writer replied, eliciting a hearty, Wabzugian laugh.

Though most of his younger clients now preferred their restaurants au courant—airy, open-spaced gymnasiums where they could see and be seen—Larry Wabzug had always preferred to conduct business at one of the city's many great local delicatessens. Anyplace where there were good pickles and hot coffee, he would say, these being his two favorite things in the world. Next, of course, to a big, juicy advance. Hold the mustard.

How lucky he was, then, to be dining here with Richard Whitehurst, great writer and equally good friend, and perhaps the last client he could count on to meet him under such a humble roof.

They'd known each other forever (since the late fifties), and

Whitehurst had always eschewed the pomp of the "literary lunch." Larry had long ago determined that this noble author, a man of class and humility, was simply above the ego rush some lesser scribes gleaned from squeezing an agent's budget at a fine restaurant. How calming not to have his gastritis aggravated by the young writer who immediately turns to the reserve side of the wine list, say, or nods to the waiter when the seven-course tasting menu is mentioned. As if this were some kind of grab-whatever-you-can free-for-all just because he or she had splayed some ink on a few pieces of paper. Take an oenophile like Kyle Clayton, for example, whose gross indulgences had nearly detoured Larry's second daughter from Brandeis to junior college. Bottle after bottle after bottle.

What Larry didn't realize, however, or had chosen not to see, was that in recent years Whitehurst had actually begun to resent the modesty of these meetings, even to the point of insult. Not that the wound was endured without understanding, of course. Richard knew his friend well enough to realize the forces at work here—not a stinginess exactly, but rather the momentum of a convenient habit. It was a tradition they'd begun years ago, when Larry's business was not yet profitable and Richard was just grateful for a meal whose options weren't sesame, salt, or poppyseed. In those first lean years, a brisket on rye was like chateaubriand to Whitehurst, and he could remember looking forward to those lunches with sometimes as much as two or three days of mouthwatering anticipation.

But that was almost forty years ago, and times had changed. Larry Wabzug had become one of the city's premier literary agents. And though it was true that his friend was the rare writer who failed to get a rush from sitting at a good table in the restaurant of the moment, it was also true that everybody needed a little stroking now and then, even Richard Whitehurst. Especially the Richard Whitehurst of late, whose last book was currently choking the remainder bins at bookstores nationwide. For some years now Richard had been wondering how fair it was that every young scrub with a pencil was dining out like a king on Wabzug's tab—young peachfuzzes throwing down magnums of boutique California wines, gnawing through steaks the size of doormats—while Larry's oldest client and dear friend, after four decades of loyalty and devotion, had to content himself with celery soda and a pastrami sandwich.

In the end, though, Richard had learned to swallow it. We're too damn old to argue about lunch, he'd decided. Over the long haul of time, he knew, there wasn't much to complain about as far as Larry Wabzug was concerned. For those four decades Larry had been not only a generous business partner but also his dearest friend and confidant, guiding him through many a literary disappointment and marital storm. He had all but rescued Richard from poverty back in the late fifties, placing his early stories in magazines, and ever since had patiently endured skimpy outputs, paltry advances, and the generally stubborn and unprofitable determination of his client to create art. Richard knew that in the end, in the balance sheet of their friendship, he had received far more than he'd given to Mr. Larry Wabzug.

"I heard you had quite an evening last night," Larry said.

"Actually, most of the fireworks happened after I left," Richard answered. "Unfortunate incident."

Kyle Clayton. Wabzug shook his head as he pondered the name. Well, something like that was bound to happen, wasn't it? You could see it coming. And yet the kid seemed to have nine lives.

"How's Meryl, by the way?" he asked. "I was expecting her."

Whitehurst shrugged noncommittally. "Left her at the Guggenheim," he said. Then, somewhat evasively, "Amazing what passes for art these days."

This was hardly a satisfying answer, Wabzug thought. She and Larry were old friends too. Usually Meryl would join them—if not

for friendship's sake, then at least to keep tabs on the business deal-
ings, in which Richard was either disinterested or completely inept,
depending on your perspective. In any event, her absence was conspicuous.

"Too bad," Larry said.

"She's not real happy with me right now."

"I see." *Now,* Larry thought, they were finally getting somewhere.

"Anyway, she says hello. She wants to have you and Elaine out to
the Island soon."

"Love to," Wabzug said. "So, how're . . . you know, *things*?"

Whitehurst looked pained. "What can I say, Larry? Same problem. It doesn't get any better."

The pickles arrived. Larry reached for one immediately.

"Well, I don't want to be a harborer of pessimism here, but it's sort
of to be expected, don't you think?" Larry looked up tentatively.
"This kind of thing."

"Expected?"

"What did I tell you twenty-five years ago when you said you were
going to marry Meryl? I said she's lovely, but she's too *young*. Eventually it becomes a problem. Take Elaine and I, for example. We're
the same age—too old. She's too old to want it, and I'm too old to do
it. It's a beautiful thing, really."

Wabzug got a refill on his coffee, the first of many, then glazed his
pickle with coffee before eating it—a lifelong habit Richard was as
disgusted by as he was now by New York delis.

"This, by the way, is as close as I get to dipping my pickle these
days," Wabzug confessed.

The attempt at levity masked a serious concern for Larry. He
didn't know what to make of his friend's marriage anymore. The
other problems they'd had through the years had always been work-
able, and he'd helped whenever he could. But this one worried him.

This one had been hanging on for a long time. He wondered what Meryl was thinking, how much she was willing to put up with. Richard was sixty-four, she was about to turn forty-seven. If she was going to make a move . . . Oh, God forbid, he thought. That would really put the poor guy under. That might just be the end of Richard Whitehurst.

"How about those Chinese herbs?" Larry asked. "I thought you said they helped."

"Yeah, they work. But . . ."

"But?"

"There are side effects, Larry. They give me indigestion. The next morning is a horror."

"So." He laughed a little. "What's the problem? So you have a little indigestion now and then."

"I can't write that way. Can't concentrate."

Larry was nonplussed, even a little angry. "Richard, for godsakes, take a morning off every once in a while, make love to your wife. This is still a young woman we're talking about here."

"You don't understand," Richard said, shaking his head.

"Well, it doesn't make sense. You've been complaining to me for the better part of a year that you can't perform, and now they have this stuff that can help you, and . . ."

"Look, Larry," Richard said, "I can't afford any days off, okay? I'm an old writer. There aren't that many days left."

"You're sixty-four years old. You've got time."

"How many writers do you know that did great work in their seventies?"

"Tolstoy," Larry shot back.

"Keep going."

Wabzug racked his brain. Richard let him flounder awhile before rescuing him. "Forget it," he said. "There aren't any. Let's face it, I've

got just a few good years left. I've got to make one last big push. I owe
this to myself."

"What about your wife?"

Richard sipped his celery soda. "She needs to be patient."

"She has been, seems to me."

"The sex thing'll take care of itself. It will."

"Oh, really? Just like that." Wabzug snapped his fingers.

"Yes. If I start writing well again, yes, it will." He looked hard into
his friend's eyes. "It's all about hope, Larry."

Wabzug dunked a fresh pickle, then watched the drops fall back
into his cup. How much can one tell a friend? he wondered. How
truthful can one be? He wanted desperately to explain to Richard
what a mistake he was making, wanted to grab and shake the idiot,
tell him he could not afford to alienate Meryl, not at this point in
his life. She did everything for him, literally; everything except go
to the bathroom and write for him. Banking, cooking, car maintenance, laundry—he hadn't touched these tasks in twenty-five years.
Six months ago, in fact, Larry had asked him how much a stamp was.
Richard laughed, implying it was ridiculous.

No, really, Larry had said. Tell me.

Richard suddenly looked lost.

"A dime?" he'd said meekly.

He was a child in many ways. A man-child. He'd seen Meryl put
Richard's *shoes* on for him. To lose her would be like cutting off his
hands.

There was another matter as well, an even stickier one: the issue
of money. Despite Richard's wild dreams of greatness over the years,
it was all Meryl's money, always had been. It was her inheritance
(and her maintenance of it) that had provided the Whitehursts with
their Bohemian country lifestyle and that had afforded Richard the
luxury to write unheeded. From his books, Wabzug knew, Richard

earned less than ten thousand dollars a year, and if it hadn't been for Miss Meryl Smith's Hudson Valley dowry—her grandfather having made a killing in Cornwall real estate at the turn of the century—the author would have spent a good deal of his studio time the last three decades wading through first-year creative-writing efforts at SUNY/Southampton. Sometimes Larry thought that would've actually been better for him. The writing life certainly hadn't done his friend much good as far as he could see. Whitehurst's whole career had been one of frustration, of nonfulfillment, and now, ever since his disappointment with *Sonata*, he'd watched the man go steadily downhill. There were stories from his friends out on the Island, wild rumors, the refrain always the same: *We're worried about Richard.* They complained of despondency, of dark moods. He would come to parties and not speak to anyone the entire evening. Arthur Trebelaine had called the week after Christmas, saying Richard had come to his door one morning at dawn, tears in his eyes, blubbering about how he'd lost one of the short stories he'd been working on. Arthur had laughed when Wabzug asked him why a writer shouldn't be upset about losing work.

"Larry," he'd said, "Richard hasn't written a short story in thirty years. Obviously he was out of his mind."

Meryl was especially worried, he knew, and her calls to Larry at his office were becoming more frequent. The house had become very sad lately, she'd confided, intolerably quiet. She'd caught him talking to himself a few times recently, as if he were hallucinating. She didn't know if she could stand it anymore.

"He thinks he's finished," she said. "He's given up."

And yet, here he was, Larry thought now, in the city, talking about a new book and looking better than he had in a while. It was like he was suddenly invigorated. For the first time in a year, the man had a little verve. What was up?

"You look better, Richard."

"Don't believe it," he said.

"You do, you look well. Of course, you do know you took that whole *Sonata* thing too hard. You wrote a great book. What else can you do?"

"It wasn't just the book," Richard said. He put down his sandwich, wiping his face with a napkin. "It was writing," he continued, "the work in general. The whole damn lifestyle."

Wabzug sipped his coffee and dunked his pickle, keeping his eyes on his friend.

"The loneliness, Larry. I think it's caught up with me." He shook his head, as if embarrassed. "Ah, shit, I know you've had to put up with this whining routine from writers your whole life. It's inexcusable in a way, I know. I mean here we are, making up stories for a living. Some of us are paid very well. But there are the other things too, Larry. Things nobody talks about."

Now Wabzug dipped his pickle again, feigning only casual interest. Rarely was his friend in such a confessional mood.

"I never realized this before, but writing is a very dangerous way to live, Larry. The most unhealthy occupation I can think of."

"There certainly are better ones," his friend said neutrally, wanting to hear more.

"I mean, just think of the writer's study for a moment. If I told you of a room where men and women go to be alone, to live solely in their imaginations, a place where they must not be disturbed so that they may hear the various voices in their head, eight, ten, twelve hours a day—what would you think I was describing? A padded cell? An insane asylum? It's craziness, this way of life. And the loneliness is enemy number one. I'm convinced now that the solitude is beginning to affect me. It's been five decades, Larry. I'm sick of it, finally. Sick to death. Do you know what my dreams are these days?"

Wabzug sat up, replying that he did not.

"Oh, you won't believe it," Richard said with a laugh. "They're not an old man's dreams at all. No, it's not about young women or prizes or my chances at Paradise—I've pretty much given up on those. No, what I dream of now is just walking into an office in the morning, an office full of voices, familiar faces. Can you imagine? *Me*, Larry. And I'm not kidding here at all. This is what I want now. To go into a room full of people every day, folks who know me a little, who respect me and my work and understand my place in the world. Simple things. I want to have a chat at the coffee machine, invite somebody to lunch. God, I used to *loathe* the idea of that kind of life, but now it seems like heaven. *People*, Larry, you know? Community. No, I think I've made a terrible mistake with my life. I've removed myself from all decent social interaction. I've denied myself the most basic human need. And now it's too late."

"Retire," Wabzug blurted out. He was quite serious; his friend's monologue had him slightly panicked. "Go to Florida," he continued. "The Carolinas. Pick up golf, eat the early-bird special. Fuck your wife. *Enjoy* something."

Richard shook his head. "Writers don't retire, Larry, you know that. It's not allowed. Anyway, I'm not ready for the bingo parlor yet."

"Well, *what* then?" Larry asked, concern rising to the surface. "You can't go on like this. It's not fair to your wife, Richard—or yourself, for that matter. As a friend, I have to tell you, this conversation is worrisome to me. It really is."

Perhaps touched by his friend's distress, Whitehurst offered a sly smile.

"Actually, I have a solution," he said. "At least I think I do."

This caught Wabzug off guard. Richard had never been one for solutions; that was the wife's department. Where the hell was Meryl anyway? So what if she was angry with him? She was *always* angry with him for something. It'd never stopped her from coming to lunch before.

"Well, let's hear it," Larry said.

"I've decided to invite another writer to live with me for a few months. Probably starting in the spring."

What? Larry thought. At first he was thrown, and then his eyes burst open wide—of course! It was perfect, and so obvious. Someone to talk to, someone to look after him. What could be better?

As if to prove his enthusiasm, Wabzug dunked and then munched a chunk of sweet pickle.

"I think that's the most wonderful idea you've had in years."

"I know," Richard said, quite pleased. "I don't know why I didn't think of it sooner. It's just the kick in the ass I need. The camaraderie, you know? Someone to have a drink with in the evenings. I mean Meryl is wonderful, but the house has become so quiet."

"Fantastic," Larry amended, rubbing his hands together with excitement. "Let's think about who you could ask. There isn't a writer alive who wouldn't jump at the chance—"

"Oh, no, no, no," Richard said, waving off the agent. "I've already invited somebody."

There was a surprised pause. "Oh?"

"Yes, and he's accepted. I just spoke to him on the phone, as a matter of fact. Just before you arrived."

"Well?" Wabzug said impatiently. "Who is it?"

Richard looked tentative. "Actually, you know him quite well. He's a client of yours."

The agent squinted, trying to think. He couldn't imagine who.

"Kyle Clayton," Richard said finally.

It took a second, and then Wabzug's body bolted backward in his chair, his eyes staring out dumbfoundedly. An indecipherable sound escaped from his lips.

"You okay, Larry?"

The agent searched the room with his eyes; he was in some kind of shock.

"You don't even know him," he said thinly.

"I met him last night. Nice fellow, actually. He told me he's had trouble working lately, the city's too much of a distraction. Of course, I can sympathize. He's quite a good writer, don't you think?"

"He's an alcoholic," Wabzug said, strength returning to his voice. "The worst kind. You know about what happened with him after you left."

"That was my fault, actually," Whitehurst said.

"*Your* fault?"

"I'm afraid I got him all riled up at everyone, then left him alone with the wolves. Turns out he's quite a fan of mine. Anyway, it's hard to explain. He was defending my honor in a sense. So what do you think?"

"Honestly? I think this is the most ridiculous thing I've ever heard."

"Why? I like him, Larry. He's a nice kid. He drinks too much, I understand that. The loneliness . . ."

"Ah, shit, Richard, don't romanticize everything all the time!" Wabzug took a deep breath, realizing he was on the verge of great anger. If he was going to stop this—and he absolutely *must* stop this—then he had to show some control. "Please, Richard," he implored, more subdued now, "I know this kid. I like him too, though I'm not entirely sure why. But listen, he's not someone you want in your house, okay? Trust me. What does Meryl have to say about all this?"

Richard looked away, and suddenly Wabzug realized why she wasn't here. There'd been a battle over this, a real blowout. Of course there'd been, he thought. Meryl was reasonable, Meryl was objective—she wouldn't stand for this sort of lunacy.

"Look," Richard said, "I don't give a shit what anybody thinks, all right? I mean, I can't figure out why the young man is so reviled, even by his own *agent*!"

"I don't hate him, Richard, I just told you that. What did Meryl say?"

Richard pushed his plate away, the sandwich half finished. He didn't answer.

"She's furious with you, isn't she? Yes, of course she is." Wabzug leaned forward. "Don't do this to her, Richard. She can't take much more."

"She'll come around," he said casually. "She always does."

Larry shook his head, wanting to laugh. He absolutely could not believe it. Kyle Clayton! Of all people. It was almost beyond absurd. *Clayton.* In *their* house. Like inviting a rhinoceros into Tiffany's. You dumb son of a bitch, he thought.

Wabzug stood up, tossing his half-eaten pickle on the table. Lunch was over.

"All right, Larry, come on. Sit down."

Wabzug signaled for the check.

"Larry . . ."

"Forget it," the agent said. "Do whatever you want."

"Larry, look at me. *Larry.*"

With disapproving eyes, Wabzug gazed down: There he saw an ashamed, almost frightened-looking old man.

"I just can't be alone anymore," he said flatly. "It's as simple as that." It was one of the most pitiable things Larry had ever heard anyone say.

Still, he thought, the bastard was selfish. Evil selfish.

"You're *not*, you fool," Wabzug said. "Don't you get it? You're not alone."

Then he threw down some bills and walked off.

A FEW MINUTES LATER, Richard was heading across Houston, back toward SoHo and his furious wife, Wabzug's scolding still ringing in his ears. That kind of day, he guessed. As he passed the Chrystie Street park off Bowery, he considered approaching the small flock of dealers he saw standing under the abandoned amphitheater, figuring twenty bucks would get him a lesson on how to use his new toy. But like the melting snow around his feet, the urge rapidly dissolved. Instead, he kept walking, and the itch to escape, to flee from the pain of this world, was soon crowded out by a stronger, though slightly unfamiliar, feeling. It was hope. For despite a half day of spirit-pounding rejection and castigation, the afternoon had turned unusually warm and he had somehow managed to detect the faintest hint of spring in the air.

Change was right around the corner.

PART 2

Sag Harbor Sonata

1

On close inspection, Long Island's South Fork, as it is called, does not really look like a fork at all. Even the most literate of imaginations can see that the thrust of land known as eastern Long Island resembles nothing so much as a lobster's left claw, the thicker one, turned upside down. These claws jut from the side of America quite dramatically, as if reaching out to snag something in their pincers—a testimony, perhaps, to the voracity of the inhabitants.

Though still on this south claw, the town of Sag Harbor rests some miles north of the more coveted oceanside properties, along the modest wakes of the bay, and therefore is a bit removed from the summer madness. The Whitehursts had discovered it by accident, back in the early seventies. Meryl's father had died and the Whitehursts' solvency was at its peak. Richard had had it with New York. The noise, the crime—the city was falling apart. His once-great paradise had begun to frighten him, and so they'd begun to look eastward for simplicity, for a new life.

It all made so much sense back then. Many of their Manhattan writer friends had already made the move. Everyone they knew, it seemed, had a place in Sagaponack or Bridgehampton. A kind of writers' belt, it was said, and they visited often. Every weekend in July and August, for example, the Trebelaines entertained at their "cottage" in Water Mill. There one could find Irwin Shaw flipping burgers, a cherubic Capote swinging in the hammock, Leonard Bernstein playing croquet on the front lawn. Along with the remarkable company, the Whitehursts fell in love with the landscape: the soft rolling farmland, the saltwater meadows, the white-sand beaches. An artist's paradise.

For the first time in their lives, money was plentiful. Besides Meryl's whopping inheritance, Richard was actually earning something close to a living. Never a best-seller, *Heart's Crest* had sold reasonably well (his one book to do so), and a Hollywood producer had given him fifteen thousand dollars for the film rights. But though they could afford to live anywhere they pleased, they would not settle oceanside near their friends—so Richard had decided. Even geographically, he would have to be contrary, on the outside. No matter that Meryl had fallen in love with a house in Wainscott that Patty Trebelaine had shown them. Patty was working part-time in real estate back then, just for fun, and had brought the Whitehursts to her pride and joy: a lovely cedar-shingled, two-story house, right on the beach. The steal of the season, Patty assured them. A sort of gift to her friends. She would even forgo her commission.

Meryl's heart jumped when she saw it. She hadn't really wanted to leave Manhattan in the first place, but this! She could hear the *whooosh* of the ocean through the back hedgerow. *This* she could handle. Now she could have the English garden she'd always dreamed of, not to mention a view that could make you tremble. It was perfect.

Holding hands in triumph that afternoon, the two women came

skipping around the side of the house like schoolgirls free for the summer, only to find Richard on the front lawn, looking grim, unimpressed.

Patty was flabbergasted. Meryl could almost see it coming.

"What's wrong?" she asked when they were alone in the car, already knowing it was over.

"Half of our friends live in Wainscott," he reminded her. "It's nothing but writers out here."

"So?"

"It's too obvious. I don't like joining little groups and cliques."

Meryl snickered. "Then what are we doing here every weekend, Richard? You're already a part of it. You're *dying* to be a part of it."

"It's different when we visit," he said.

And that was it. They rode in silence, tears welling in her eyes. What was the point of arguing? she thought. Her husband was the most intractable, least compromising man alive. For the first time in her life she thought she might actually like to kill him, to put her hands on his throat right there and squeeze. It would not be the last.

A week or two later, after another exasperating day of house hunting with Richard, Patty suggested lunch in Sag Harbor. Though it was nothing like the Hamptons, she assured them—not a place to go looking for a house—it was a charming little village nonetheless, and there was a lovely hotel in town that served a fine lunch. Well, Richard was hardly over the North Haven bridge, yachts of the harbor bobbing in the distance, when Meryl noticed his rather long neck beginning to crane, his eyes tapering to focus. Her heart dropped; she'd seen the look before. It was the look he'd had at Arthur's dinner party five years ago, when he'd decided within the first ten minutes of meeting her that she would be his wife; the way he looked when a novel was beginning to form itself in his head, when you couldn't talk to him for days. A certain furrowing of the brow that said, *This is it.*

WELCOME TO THE VILLAGE OF SAG HARBOR the sign read as they crossed the bridge. Well, look around, Meryl thought. Get used to it. Though they had yet to set foot in the town, she had chosen to love a man of impulsive and exasperating will. This, she knew, was to be her new home.

FOR RICHARD, the irresistible pull of Sag Harbor was, no doubt, due to its history as a whaling port. This took him back to his boyhood days on the Connecticut shore. Though he was born in New London, his indulgent—and therefore highly cherished—grandmother lived in nearby Mystic, just blocks away from the harbor and the whaling museums. At port there were two old whaling ships, restored for family tours. As an adolescent, Richard would sneak away from his grandmother Grace's house and haunt their decks till closing.

At night there were the stories. Tales of typhoons and rogue whales and errant ship captains. In fact, Grace said, the Whitehursts boasted a long line of Mystic seamen, and the stories she told so intoxicated young Richard that, even as he neared middle age, he still dreamed of writing a great seafaring novel.

It was for this reason he must settle in Sag Harbor, Richard announced to his wife on a summer's afternoon in 1974. They were still in Patty's car, hadn't even walked around town yet. Still, his mind was set. Whaling villages, he told her, the whole maritime life, was in his blood. It was his history.

"In your blood?" Meryl turned to him from the front seat.

"That's right."

"Richard, you haven't been on a boat in twenty years. You won't even let us take the ferry when we need to. You make us drive all the way around the Island to get to the other side."

"Phobias are not the point," he said. He was wide-eyed, looking around like he'd been dropped into Paradise. "It's in my *blood*, Meryl."

His wife looked over at Patty and threw up her hands.

Patty made a call to a broker friend, and in an hour they were strolling through a nineteenth-century sea captain's house on John Street, six bedrooms, a leviathan of a place. Meryl was pregnant, but still, *six bedrooms*? Why was the broker wasting their time? she wondered. Even Richard knew better.

Dust fell around him as he pulled at a piece of plywood hanging from the ceiling like an old Band-Aid. "I like it," he said, rubbing his eyes.

"You like it," she repeated, almost not surprised.

"It reminds me of Grace's, when I was a boy. It's a captain's house, Meryl."

"Oh for godsakes."

They went to lunch to talk it over, to argue over it. She'd tried to remind Richard what the broker had said, that it was a fixer-upper, a real project. Had she ever seen him so much as hammer a nail? Not to mention the six bedrooms. *Count 'em, Richard, six!* He was a compulsive, fanatical word-fixer. Did he really want to begin spending large chunks of his time maintaining a run-down mansion? Heaven knows she didn't—she was pregnant! A house like this house would become a full-time job.

Logic turned to pleading: It was the first house they'd seen in Sag Harbor; could they at least look around a little?

Meryl waited for the rebuttal, meanwhile allowing herself a momentary confidence. How could he talk around this kind of logic? Six bedrooms. A fixer-upper. The whole thing was ridiculous. But what was fiction writer Whitehurst if not a great fabricator, a master purveyor of elegant disinformation? He whipped up a counteroffensive that came at her sideways, at her unprotected flank—some nonsense about a fixer-upper being just the thing he'd been looking for, a foil to the sedentary life. About his need to "feel the physical side" of himself again. Of his longing to hold "organic materials in his hands" and get "back to the earth." A stew of inspired malarkey, seasoned with a pinch of Thoreauvian charm, designed to bulldoze her into this house that was too big for them. And for what? Because he had spent summers as a boy in Mystic reading too much damn Melville when he should have been out building a tree house, or asking girls to show him *theirs*? No, she said firmly. She wouldn't stand for it. Not when there was a perfectly lovely house in Wainscott on the goddamned beach! The sobs poured forth, rolling out like the heavy surf it seemed she would now have to live without.

"Fine, forget it," Richard said, melting under the tears. "You're right, darling. Stop crying. We'll go live in Wainscott."

The remarkable thing, the inexplicable thing, was that within a week she had caved. She didn't know how exactly, except to say that it was the very thing she had always wanted to change about herself but could not: ambivalence. The big *A,* her scarlet letter. The same ambivalence that had allowed her to give up her own writing as a young woman, the better to serve Richard the Great. Yes, she too had been writing stories when she first came to the city, Whitehurst knockoffs though they were. But she'd been easily discouraged. God knows Richard hadn't tried to help her. Oh, sure, he would read them, but then his gentle editorial comments were really just a way of dismissing her, weren't they? Polite condescension. *Hmm, not bad, all quite lovely, darling, now would you mind dropping off my new story to Wabzug on your way across town.* No, of course she wouldn't. It was Richard Whitehurst. And he said he was in love with her.

Ambivalence. Her Achilles heel. What had gotten her into bed with all those men back in her single days. With a lot of them she hadn't really wanted it to end up in sex, but then they were so insistent, so focused on it; finally it was easier to just *do* the damn thing. The word *no*—so easy, so simple. Why couldn't she use it? Later, she watched herself become what she had always sworn against, one of those women who are led by the nose through life, who yield to strong wills. Little Miss Accommodating, she thought, that's me. At every big turn she'd followed someone else's hunch. Where was *her* determination? *Her* desires? Life should've been whatever she'd wanted it to be, should've yielded easily to her desires. Instead, it was something that had simply happened to her, a force named Whitehurst.

But, hell, Richard wasn't really to blame. That was too easy. There were hidden fears, dire hopes, dichotomies galore. Just like with the Sag Harbor house. There had been something more than her husband's punishing will that had swayed her to sit down a few afternoons later and sign away $195,000 of inheritance on a crumbling nineteenth-century whaler's house, a fool's paradise forged from Richard's childish imagination. Underneath it all, it was the six bedrooms that got to her. Those empty rooms that had given her the hope—the dream, really—that now seemed so absurd in looking back. She thought that because Richard had been so understanding, so open about the "accident" currently residing in her womb (not thrilled, mind you, not joyous—but willing at least), he might then someday be open to more. The creative urges that she had so regretfully left behind were now being stimulated again by the soft kickings and rumblings of her lower abdomen. With this, Meryl realized, perhaps unconsciously, she could top even Richard Whitehurst. A baby! Try pulling *that* out of your typewriter, Mr. Genius. And anyway, what else would you do with six bedrooms?

Well, you fill them up, of course. She did the math in her head: one for husband and wife, the huge bedroom facing John Street; another for the little one on the way (Kevin or Kerry, they'd decided). And then what? A guest bedroom? Yes, of course, perhaps another turned into a writing studio. What, he preferred the attic? Fine then. That left three. Just sitting there, waiting . . . Perhaps it was in the back of his mind too, she'd thought.

But it wasn't to be. Kerry was a battler from the get-go, a firestorm of a child, more combustible with each passing year. Instead of pastoral bliss, it had been the Seventeen Years War, Kerry moving out as soon as she could. She'd worn her father out over those years, and as far as another child went, Richard was simply intractable, refusing even to talk about it. ("She cost me two books," Richard had always said about Kerry. "Two books at least.") As for the fixer-upper, it had never really gotten fixed, had it? The grand padrone had fallen to craven failure, and the bedrooms had for the most part stayed empty until now, twenty years since they'd bought the place, occupied again this spring finally; not with wonderful sons and daughters, mind you, to be followed a few seasons later by husbands and wives and friends, friends of friends, the varied tapestry of comings and goings, of normal life—not with *grandchildren,* goddamn it—but with a prodigal, a rogue, a human hazard in the back guest room.

The young cad named Kyle Clayton.

2

"Any more wine?" Kyle asked.

This of an early evening in May. Kyle and Richard had taken the short drive from Sag Harbor to Northsea and now faced a placid bay in a pair of bamboo chaises, just beyond the reach of a light surf.

Whitehurst had been coming to this obscure spot for years. These days he preferred the stillness of the bay to the rugged ocean. Now, in late spring, the temperatures were just about suitable for swimming, and he and Kyle were starting to make the Friday-evening dip something of a tradition—a reward for the week of hard work, followed by a half bottle of wine and a sunset. Tonight's sky offered exceptional pleasure, the celestial rays streaming down through ruddled clouds. A "biblical" sky, as Richard had commented, full of fury and blood.

"So sorry," said Whitehurst, noticing the empty glass. Kyle lowered his by the stem, and Richard began to pour the straw-colored liquid.

"Uh-uh," the younger man scolded after a few drops, "just a splash."

This time he meant it.

Yes, it was remarkable. If you'd had a million dollars, you would have wagered it all against him. But it was true. Despite Meryl's antipathy and Wabzug's prediction, flying in the face of all logic and common acumen, Kyle Clayton was, for all intents and purposes, sober.

Of course he hadn't been at the Whitehursts' quite five weeks, yet the transformation had been extraordinary. In bed by twelve or so, up by nine. Every morning a walk into town with Richard for the *Times*. At the desk by ten-thirty.

They'd knock off from writing at about five, at which point Meryl was usually making dinner (amazing how much the woman did for him, Kyle had noticed). At the meal one bottle of wine was shared by all. In the old days he'd have one bottle himself—an aperitif—and then start drinking.

In the evenings they read, or else they played cards, in which case the house was engulfed in the faded, static effusions of a transistor radio, meticulously tuned in to a station in Westport, Connecticut. This was the closest broadcast of the Boston Red Sox, one of Richard's many esoteric obsessions. And how could Kyle be surprised at this? The Red Sox, after all, were the tragic losers—not just of baseball but of all sports. Though he'd played quite a bit of ball himself, Kyle hadn't had much time for professional sports since he'd moved to New York. But he knew the Sox. You'd never have had to watch an inning of baseball in your life to know the Sox. The legacy was indelible: more stupid trades, more freakish career-ending injuries, more painful losses, more heartache than any team that ever played a game, anytime, anywhere, anyhow. These were the ultimate underdogs, the ones who not just lost but lost in style, with soul-crushing beauty, who couldn't just get trounced and walk away but had to rip your heart out and stamp on it, leaving it a bloody, smoking carcass.

The last time they'd won a World Series was 1918.

Night after night, they listened. Kyle didn't know how they'd kept at it all these years, Richard and Meryl. It was torture. It was *unhealthy.*

Abuse, that's what the Red Sox were about. Yet another ninth-inning collapse, and Richard would pound the dining room table with his fist, teaspoons doing double-gainers. He'd flick off the radio amid the boos of Fenway, Meryl closing her book with the snap of finality.

"For godsakes, Richard," she would exclaim, herself smarting from the defeat, "do we have to listen to this?" She loved that team too, if only by necessity. If you loved Richard, you loved the Sox; it was a package deal. But she was finally showing signs of fatigue. "I can't take this anymore, subjecting ourselves to this . . . this *cancer* every night."

Richard agreed, shaking his head in disgust, pain visible in his face. "Never again," he'd say. "You're right, it's not worth it. I'm done with them."

This scene, Kyle quickly surmised, had been repeated for years. For at nine the very next night, Richard—head buried deep in an after-dinner novel (*The Way of All Flesh, The Aspern Papers*), seemingly in a trance of language—would suddenly pop his head up and, folding the book over his left thigh, announce with utter casualness, "Anybody heard anything about the Sox?" This without any reference to the previous night's repudiation. And Meryl the accomplice. Within seconds she herself would flip on the power, station already cued from the night before, and the flagellation would begin all over again. Go Sox!

．   .   .   ．

ON THE BEACH, the heavens had returned to normal. Dusk was
falling, the mosquitoes starting to swirl. As often happened, the subject turned to celebrity. It was Richard's favorite.

"Tell me again how it felt to be famous."

Of all the topics they'd discussed over these weeks, this had to be
Kyle's least favorite. There was something prurient about Richard's interest, he felt, which was discomfiting coming from a man he held in
such high esteem. He much preferred to talk with Whitehurst about
writing, the craft itself. So far, Richard had been strangely reticent on
the matter. He seemed worn out on books, as if something had been
washed from his heart. In fact, Kyle could not help but notice something unforeseen and highly ironic about their mutual fascination: All
the famous man wanted to discuss was art; all the artist wanted to
talk about was fame.

"Like I've said," Kyle began, subtly reminding his interrogator
that they'd been over this before, "I was never really that well known.
I mean not in any major sort of way."

"But people recognized you on the street."

"Well, sure, sometimes they did. I guess it was from the talk
shows. Ugh, now there was a horror! Thank God you never had to do
that."

Whitehurst's crooked smile let him know he didn't agree. "They
never asked me," he said sadly.

Oh, how Kyle hated this. Here was a lose/lose situation if there
ever was one, and very masochistic on Richard's part. The more he
heard about Clayton's old life the more it vexed him; the more it
vexed him the more he wanted to hear. It was like he was punishing
himself for his standards, for being too good. He was like the jilted
lover, wanting every detail of an infidelity.

"What about on the street? They would stop you and then what? Shake your hand? Ask you for an autograph?"

"Mostly they would just point and whisper. Occasionally I'd overhear them. 'Hey, isn't that what's-his-name?' A lot of the time they couldn't place me. Or they'd recognize me and sneer. Not particularly inspiring, Richard, I promise you."

In the cool gray of dusk, Kyle could see the older man's eyes were closed, that he was in a kind of trance again tonight, a reverie of what might have been.

"But it must be something to walk into a party and hear that palpable hush. That spark of electricity. There is a certain charisma that you have, Kyle. You must realize that."

"I'm also quite despised," countered Clayton, who couldn't remember any hush. "They're calling for my head back in New York right now."

He was recalling now an episode from his first week out on the Island, one that he'd tried unsuccessfully to forget. It was just his second or third day at the Whitehursts'. As of yet, Kyle had shown no initiative for change: March back in the city had been an all-out debauch for him. He'd promised himself he'd do better once he was out in the country, but he'd spent the two-and-a-half-hour train ride nipping at a bootleg in his knapsack, and when Richard arrived a few minutes late to pick him up from the station in Southampton (Meryl had refused to come), he'd discovered the young man leaning over the platform, retching onto the empty tracks, Whitehurst thinking he was in for one hell of a summer.

For the first two days Kyle worked little and mostly slept at his desk, trying to adjust to the new hours and waiting anxiously till his hosts were in bed so he could sneak down to the kitchen to get at Meryl's cooking sherry (wisely, she had hidden the good stuff). Then, on the third day, he and Richard took their morning walk into town. As Whitehurst gathered the usual staples—eggs, milk, et cetera, the one job Meryl could actually count on him to do— a bleary-eyed Kyle wandered over to the magazine rack and took down a copy of *New York* magazine. It was one of his guilty pleasures, after all, and the title of this week's issue was deliciously malevolent: THE ONE HUNDRED MOST HATED NEW YORKERS. As his eyes scanned the list, he was half ashamed to find himself ripping into each name with true Gotham misanthropy. Most of the big guns were ever-familiar: number one, Donald Trump, a no-brainer; George Steinbrenner, a perennial at number three; number seven, Kathie Lee Gifford, still crazy after all these years; Al Sharpton, forever in your cracker face, at number nine. Grotesques one and all, he thought, serves them right, until he stumbled across Kyle Clayton, at thirty-six.

For a moment he failed to comprehend it. *Kyle Clayton?* What a coincidence. How unlikely that someone else would have the same— and then he suddenly understood. The thirty-sixth most *hated* New Yorker, *me?* It was outrageous, he thought; it was *wrong*. He felt a sickening tightness in his chest. His hands began to shake. He wanted to weep.

Whitehurst, on the other hand, thought it was marvelous.

"You've hit the big time, my boy," he said proudly, holding the magazine to his chest in beatitude. "What luck." With his free arm he embraced the young man, congratulating him as if he'd just won the PEN/Faulkner Award.

Kyle was not amused. Luck, you say? Then *fuck luck*. Intellectualize all you want, old man, but you don't know how it feels.

As Richard handed him back the magazine, Kyle flung it against the rack—a gauntlet thrown down. You'll never have me again, Kyle swore to himself, thinking of all those who had so suddenly turned against him. I'll sober up and show you, you two-faced fucks. *I'm back.*

But so far the work was coming slowly. Not that he wasn't dutiful. The hours were put in, his discipline rediscovered in sobriety. But that spark he'd had during the writing of *Charmed Life,* that hair-standing-up-on-the-back-of-the-neck kind of excitement, was decidedly absent. The chapters were there, but how did it all fit together? Where was the unifying theme?

After a while Kyle began to harvest severe doubts about himself. Maybe they're right, he'd started to think. Maybe I *am* done. A one-hit wonder. All washed up and nowhere to go.

And then here was this worn-out old tree stump, telling him how lucky he was.

"I wish I'd been despised," Richard reaffirmed now, setting his glass down in the sand. "They were indifferent to me. That's much worse."

"You have your fans."

"Oh, I suppose," he said dismissively. "Here and there."

"Plus, you're immensely respected. Your name carries weight. I'd trade my career for yours in a heartbeat."

Richard's face lit up at the thought. "Wouldn't that be nice," he said. "But no, Kyle. I wouldn't let you. This gift you have, to antagonize them, to get under their skin, it's too valuable. Believe me, there's nothing better than being hated."

Oh, for chrissakes, Kyle thought, not this again. He rose a little in his chaise, ire forming in his eyes. Enough was enough.

"Is that what you think?" he asked.

The older man cleared his throat, sensing a sudden irritation. "Well—"

"Because I gotta tell you, Richard," Kyle said hotly, "you keep mentioning how wonderful this is, how lucky I am, and all I can see it doing for me is destroying my confidence. I mean it doesn't make much sense, if you really think about it. Why the hell would any writer—any *person* for that matter—want to be hated?"

Now it was Whitehurst's turn to sit up in his chaise. Darkness was falling hard, and he wanted to get a better look at the young man's face. During the weeks he'd stayed with the Whitehursts, Clayton had been the epitome of graciousness and good behavior. Almost too nice, Richard had thought. Though they'd gotten on well, and the company was more than welcome, the union had been something of a bust as far as Richard was concerned. After all, Kyle had not been invited to Sag Harbor for iced tea and cards, for pliant hero worship. The plan had been stimulation. For the influx of young, buoyant energy, good or bad. Quite frankly, he'd expected more fire from Kyle Clayton.

So good then, he thought now, seeing the fervor in the young man's eyes. The kid has a pulse.

"Revenge," he answered finally.

Kyle didn't quite get it. "Revenge?"

"Or outrage, if you will. The single greatest muse there is."

Kyle let this rattle around in his brain for a second. "I don't quite follow."

"You've mentioned you're having some trouble with your New York book."

"It's dead," Kyle admitted. "There's some good things there, but it's murky, you know? I don't know how it fits together. There's no engine. It won't *breathe*."

Richard was nodding and smiling. "I know, I know," he said. "I've been there. I've been there a million times."

"What do you do?"

"What do I do?" He gave a painful grin. "I panic, that's what I do. I pace back and forth. Then, eventually, I get mad."

Kyle waved a mosquito from his face. The bugs were starting to converge.

"That's when I know things are about to turn around," White-hurst continued. "You see, I have to be mad to get anything done anyway, so I use this as a jumping-off point. I get mad that nothing's going well on the page, then turn that anger to something else. Something I hate, or some*body*. When my work's going well, I'm usually sort of sick with hatred."

"Revenge," Kyle repeated weakly.

"Look," Richard said, "you've been through some things lately, am I right?"

"I like to think so."

"Made some enemies along the way."

Kyle smiled. "Oh yes."

"Excellent. Now, why don't you begin with those things? With the things you hate most. People, if you must. Move your hero through this world. Get your revenge."

Hmmm, Kyle thought, now this was something. Maybe this was what his new book was missing, some of the old piss and vinegar of *Charmed Life*.

"Like what, though?" he asked. "There's so much to hate. Where's the focus?"

"Try this," Richard said. "Try thinking of an anti-Clayton reader. Your worst detractor. They despise everything you are, everything you stand for—everything they *think* you stand for. Then you start writing. Eventually a light goes off. You look at what you've just written and you say, 'Oh, no. I can't *possibly* do this. They're going to *crucify* me for this.' There, you see! Now you've got your book. Everything else you get rid of."

Kyle let out a strange sound, a kind of croak somewhere between a laugh and a grunt. A snort of recognition.

"Hey, that's not bad," he said, looking over Richard's shoulder out onto the bay. "That might actually be very helpful."

If his compliment seemed muted, his eyes distracted, it was only because his mind was spinning so, already glazed with ideas. Entire plotlines suddenly appeared, unifying passages. New York, Kyle thought, home of the ambitious ingrates, invidious betrayers. Take them down—that's what I'll do. Every one of them.

"Revenge," Kyle murmured.

Richard stood up, grinning contentedly as he replaced the glasses and empty bottle in a wicker picnic basket. Night was falling fast, the air thick with mosquitoes. It was time for dinner. Meryl would be waiting. Still, he could not resist adding a little more.

"Really let 'em have it, Kyle," he said. Richard's words pulsed with caustic verve. Listening closely, Kyle thought he could hear the toxins in his voice, the bitter hiss of old wounds. "Let the bastards have it like I never could."

3

In the past, the Whitehursts would entertain once every few months. It was something they had done for years, though Richard's recent moods had brought an abrupt halt to these get-togethers. But this spring the festivities had picked up again, much to their friends' delight. They were pleased to see Richard in such good spirits, were once more dazzled not only by Meryl's competence in the kitchen but by the aesthetic deftness that she brought to everything she touched. An almost painterly eye, it seemed, for underneath that sagging roof and rotting beams were rooms like something out of Bonnard. In fact, when an overwhelmed dinner guest once mentioned, half jokingly, that Meryl was the true artist in the family, Richard seemed to bristle for a moment before he remarked, somewhat ambiguously, "Well, she certainly has a wider audience than I do."

Although the crowd was a bit older than him, Kyle reveled in these gatherings. Saturday cocktails began around five. By six o'clock the bar in the front room was almost always packed with at least fifteen guests, three or four of these being among Kyle's favorite living writers. The encounters filled him with a great sense of pride and good fortune. Here was a milieu he never would have been exposed to had it not been for Whitehurst, especially now with his rather outré literary status. These were not the avaricious, backslapping vampires of the New York publishing scene, but a more rarefied group. And, remarkably, under the influence of flowing wine and a companionable atmosphere, they seemed to welcome Kyle's company, even to thrive on his youthful vigor, much as his host apparently had—Richard's newfound vitality being directly attributed to the young man. Drinking responsibly now, Kyle had the pleasure of interacting with some of the most interesting people of his time. Though the old "writers' belt" had dwindled in past years, having been replaced by what was referred to as "Hollywood East," what little was left of it could be found once every few months at the Whitehursts'.

Each faction has its nucleus, its rubbered center that provides its flight and trajectory. In this crowd it was Arthur and Patty Trebelaine. Like Richard, Arthur had been something of a late bloomer, literarily speaking. He was a former Air Force man who'd struck it big in his mid-thirties with a novel entitled *Lions in the Sky,* about fighter pilots in Korea. As a writer, he did not enjoy anything like Whitehurst's small but intense academic following, yet Richard most surely envied him. Each one of Arthur's novels had hit the *New York Times* bestseller list, and three of them had been made into successful Hollywood films, with a fourth in the works. He was as famous a serious writer as there was in America, a world-renowned figure, his tales of love and battle having a universal appeal that Whitehurst's work never would.

The Trebelaines lived in according grandness. They spent half the year in an apartment in the Passy section of Paris, the other half on the Atlantic, in the white-sand bluffs of Sagaponack. Both had a sort of glow, though Patty, now nearing sixty, was beginning to look somewhat overmatched by her husband. Now, at sixty-two, Arthur was better-looking than ever, his palpable virility tempered by a sort of European elegance, all of it culminating in a commanding yet graceful confidence. He was a man entirely at home in the world, at ease with the assurance that life had yielded, and would still yield, willingly to his powers. He was so seemingly complete, in fact, so flawless a creation, Kyle found himself in a kind of stuttering awe the first time they met.

It was the Whitehursts' first party of the season. The Trebelaines made a dashing entrance that day, albeit a tardy one. But even their lateness had a certain style. Kyle could see the guests nervously checking their watches before their arrival, and you could almost hear the collective sigh when they entered. Here they were, Beauty and Perfection! Perfection and Beauty! Patty had a neck of pearls and a perfect early tan, while Arthur came in looking as fit and solid as a man half his age, ready that very night, it seemed, for another tour of duty in the cockpit. His size surprised Clayton—he could not have guessed his height from the book jackets—six feet four, by his estimation. And powerful; the backslapping hugs of his old friends thumped hollow on Arthur's ribs, like punches to a steer's haunch.

Finally, when there was no one else for Arthur to greet, Whitehurst gestured for Kyle to step up and be introduced. The young man took a deep sip of wine for courage and put a tentative foot forward.

Arthur towered over him, his voice booming into Kyle's face: "Uh ho, so *here* he is!" His catcher's-mitt-sized hand swallowed Kyle's whole, then he gestured to the young man's wineglass. "Hey, Richard," he said, feigning a backward flinch, "your boy's not going to hit me with a glass now, is he?"

Wary of Clayton, the guests seemed to hold their breath for a moment. Believing the young man was some sort of sociopath, they wondered if perhaps Arthur had committed a deadly faux pas.

But Kyle just grinned, and then the room's initial hush of stupefaction gave way to a strange, spasmodic laughter. It was an explosion of relief. Any trepidation seemed to dissipate, all fear seemed absurd. Silence fell again as the guests waited for Kyle's response. Something witty was required, obviously. Arthur had set him up, he could see, had passed him the ball.

But Kyle was quietly choking. The man's presence was too upsetting. The fact that Arthur Trebelaine actually lived, was a breathing, corporeal being, overwhelmed him. His throat began to close. He couldn't speak. They waited, the moment built, until Clayton decided to just spit it out, to get the damn thing over with.

"We-hell, th-then," he stuttered, "y-yo-you better be nice to me."

What few chuckles spilled forth were born of mercy. Kyle was dying from embarrassment. He'd muffed it, and everybody knew it. Hell, he wasn't even dangerous.

It was later that evening, after dinner, that Arthur sealed Kyle's infatuation. Kyle had gone out onto the porch for some air—and, no doubt, to get ahold of himself in the wake of the disaster from which he was still reeling. Never shy in groups, Kyle had barely said a word through dinner. This only furthered his embarrassment. It was time to hide.

On the porch the air was cool. There was the smell of wet leaves and smoke from a neighbor's fireplace. More October than April. Kyle stood staring out on the dark street, trying to figure out what had happened. Was he not used to meeting famous people? Like he'd ever given a shit before. But then this was not some fatuous TV star, as per his interviewing days, or even Richard Whitehurst. This was the *big one*. If he'd worshipped Whitehurst's prose style above all others, studied it as a religion, then it was Arthur Trebelaine's life that he'd always admired, the man he'd actually wanted to *be,* in his most proleptic of daydreams.

Suddenly the former fighter pilot appeared in the doorway, brandy snifter in hand. As he approached, Kyle could hear the porch creak plaintively underneath him. He knew that many of the boards were rotting, and suddenly he began to wonder if this hulking form might break through the decaying platform. But then Trebelaine was at Kyle's side and without a word lit up the longest, darkest Havana cigar the young man had ever seen.

After a few puffs he reached out and put his large arm around Kyle's shoulders, speaking from the side of his mouth that his cigar was not occupying.

"Let me give you a little advice," he said, his voice a mixture of gravel and music. "Don't ever be intimidated by anybody. I mean *anybody.* You understand?"

Initially, Kyle thought of challenging that presumption, if only to save face. *Intimidated? Ha! Is that what you think?* Then he looked up at the statue standing over him and simply nodded. The older man gave Clayton's shoulders a powerful shake. "Now come back inside already, would you?" he urged. "It's like the friggin' geriatric ward in there."

4

I don't understand it at all. I say that I am a loving person, and she asks how can I be a loving person, since I never see anyone? There is a digression here on the loneliness of the novelist, but I do see people and go out to them directly and warmly. I ask—it seems to me one of the few aggressive points I make—if she is afraid of being dependent. "I am," she says, "completely independent of you." I say that as a provider I've given her whatever she wanted. She says I haven't . . . It is she, who has indicted me as venomous, emotionally ignorant, a bad provider, self-deceived, whom I desire.

Here she was, at it again. A regular Sherlock. She'd read through Cheever's journals twice and now was going back over the passages she'd marked. Obsessed? Maybe a little, but then all the clues were right there. So many similarities between Cheever and her own husband, she'd decided. Except for the drinking, obviously; Richard had no stomach for hard liquor. And, of course, young men. But then who really knew? Who really knew any damn thing about Richard White-hurst?

She closed the book and put down her wine. The afternoon nip was a new wrinkle in her life (very Claytonesque, she'd joked to herself). Never really one to drink much, she found, now that summer had come, that she liked to relax in the late afternoons with a glass or two of chilled white. Just something to cool down with after a few hours in the garden. Sometimes, like today, she would even launch a preemptive strike and indulge in a glass before gardening. And why not? she thought. It wasn't like there were any responsibilities to intrude on. Not like she had any *writing* to do. God knows there was no pregnancy to protect. Slightly buzzed, she let her mind run with this fantasia: If, by some miracle, she came in contact with a man's seed sometime before the millennium, however unlikely, could she still have a child? She would be forty-seven this summer and had already experienced a sort of mini-menopause last fall. But then she'd heard of women in their fifties having babies, and last year a woman in her sixties had had twins. Ah, but Richard would never stand for that, would he? And the last time she checked, you still had to get *laid* to get pregnant.

She retreated to the garden in the back of the house. There the sun fell hard around her floppy straw hat and onto her well-tanned hands and wrists. Despite the season's great sunshine the rhododendrons were a little off this year, not their usual deep lavender, and the petunias seemed a little dispirited. But then she didn't have the heart to prune. Meryl liked her garden unfettered, especially in back, not like those sterile crew-cut styles in the decorating magazines. She let her flowers grow where they may, gave them their freedom. It all worked out in the end anyway. Eventually the ones that wandered too far became entangled with their neighbors, the weaker ones overwhelmed, put down.

The garden hose lay curled and still, sunning itself in the too-high grass. Closing her thumb over the nozzle, she turned on the water and chirped out a short, sharp shriek as the first blast of hot water spurted forth.

"You all right down there?"

Up on her left, from one of the bedroom turrets of this fallen castle, Kyle Clayton poked his head out of an open window.

"I'm fine," Meryl said. She pulled the thumb out of her mouth and tried to shake out the sting. "I forgot to run the hose first. I didn't mean to disturb you."

"Don't be silly," he said, flashing his patented grin. "It's your house."

She'd been wrong about him; she had to admit it. He'd been a perfect gentleman since day one—minus a few shots of cooking sherry she'd found missing that first week. And though he and she weren't exactly close, she did enjoy having another person around the house. Certainly he'd been good for Richard. The aura of doom and gloom that had followed him for the past year or so had lifted. Friends had remarked on her husband's good spirits. Things had turned around.

There was, however, a new thorn. Kyle had been somewhat absent the past few weeks. He'd hit some stride in his work, apparently, spending ten, sometimes twelve hours a day up in Kerry's room, typing like a madman, then revising late into the evening. Richard's writing, on the other hand, was going more slowly than ever. In fact, walking by the two rooms as the men worked was interesting these days, hearing the snap of their respective keyboards, Kyle's like an Uzi, *radadadada . . . radadadada . . . radadadada,* Richard's like, well, a musket—*pop* . . . first the powder . . . then the ball . . . (long silence). Now to pack it all down . . . *pop*. The tortoise beginning the long race.

Also, Clayton had recently spent a few nights over at the Trebelaines'. Some sort of bond was developing between Kyle and Arthur, and she could see her husband suffering over it. She knew, deep down, that he did not approve of Arthur, that he was jealous, quite frankly, of his phenomenal success. Richard did not trust success; he was anti-success, a guru of failure in desperate need of followers. Kyle had, at first, seemed a willing apostle, having garnered success and then wasted it. That he was now choosing to spend time, even a few scattered nights, with Arthur really burned Richard up. It was a betrayal of sorts, a rejection of the Whitehurstian philosophy.

"Good," he would say on learning that Kyle had decided to have another dinner over at the Trebelaines'. "Maybe they can fuck each other."

Yet even this tension, Meryl felt, was preferable to the void that had come before it.

"Beautiful day," Kyle said now from his turret.

Meryl picked up the hose and began watering again.

"Yes," she said, not looking up.

"Wish I could enjoy it."

"Work going well?"

"Great. Unbelievable." He seemed very excited.

"About time," she said.

The comment was typical Meryl, half humor, half ballsy truth. Living full-time with the dreamy Richard, one learned to season one's words with a pinch of veracity.

An exaggerated laugh spilled down from Kyle's turret. "I suppose you're right," he said with another chuckle. "After six years, I guess it's time."

"Well, good luck."

Her segue, her unsubtle hint. She didn't like talking to Kyle privately for too long, for obvious reasons. Here was a sexual young man, after all, in her house, with no sign of a lover. And then there was that buzzing she felt in her lower abdomen when they were alone. It was a feeling that quite surprised her. She supposed Kyle was somewhat attractive after all, though nothing like his ridiculous book-stud reputation. Of course she'd contemplated adultery before, had dreamed of it daily now for the past few sexless years, had weighed the psychic damage it would inflict versus the pleasure and hadn't liked what she'd seen. Richard would take it badly, she knew. And say she *were* ever to begin something, it wouldn't be with the likes of Kyle Clayton.

Simple desperation, this little tickling down below. Nothing to do with the source.

"You know, I really want you to know how grateful I am for this opportunity," Kyle said. "I don't think I've gotten a chance to thank you."

Meryl felt obliged to answer, then tongue-tripped over the stinging appendage—her thumb was back in her mouth. Not cool, she thought, quickly pulling it out. Not the kind of energy you wanted to be putting out there, not with the likes of him in the house. Oh, he'd give her a stick if she asked for it, she could tell. A polite young man, yes. But deep down, the morals of a gopher.

"Well, you've made Richard very happy," she said in a tone of neutral detachment. Then she returned to her garden.

Kyle's head ducked quickly back into his cocoon, and now Meryl felt a tiny surge of self-reproach. She'd been a little brusque, she thought sadly. It was actually kind of sweet for him to have poked out his head when she'd yelped. Richard's narcissistic little noggin certainly hadn't shown itself.

Opportunities for love had been presenting themselves lately.

Some perhaps imagined, others not nearly so coy. This surprised her, thinking herself almost beyond a man's affection. What to do? She was a forty-seven-year-old woman, in her last bloom, she thought. The rhododendrons are faded this year, the petunias starting to droop.

Yet she loved him. Loved the bastard, and not simply from the long habit of years. Somehow, he still managed to astound her. His stubbornness, his creative will, were so inexorable you had to shake your head in admiration. There he was, upstairs again today, trying still. She could practically hear him pacing. Crazy bullheaded freak! He was still sexy too, even in his impotence. Not like this little boy living with them. Richard was a *man*. He had the aura of a holy failure, a tragic sage, doomed to exile. The world could not abide him. He'd never made peace with things and never would. Even marriage didn't fit. But she loved him.

Meryl turned the hose on a little higher and, without missing a beat with her watering, proceeded to recite from memory a passage from the Cheever journals that had been haunting her:

> *I suggest that we discuss a separation or a divorce. We will sell the house, divide the price etc. She can go live with her beloved sister in New Jersey. This is all preposterous and drunken, and, hearing the songbirds in the morning, I realize I don't have the guts, spine, vitality, whatever, to sell my house and start wandering. I don't know what to do. I must sleep with someone, and I am so hungry for love that I count on touching my younger son at breakfast as a kind of link, a means of staying alive.*

Cheever and Whitehurst? Not here, not really. In fact, she realized now that many of the passages she'd marked or committed to memory actually had very little of her husband in them. No, something else was afoot in these trenchant words of his. Something unexpected, almost sneaky, yet no less important.

The curtains of Kyle's room had been left parted, she noticed, revealing a figure looming in silhouette (elbow sliding slowly?), and she brought the burnt thumb back to her mouth, thinking, Fine, go on then. She was on her knees now, hose surging, wondering if it just might be someone else she'd been searching for in the journals all along.

5

Kyle took a pull of the cigar, letting the thick puffs of smoke engulf his face like a perfume. Ahhhhhhhh, coffee bean and sweet wood, chocolate and roasted nuts. Now here was a habit almost worthy of Bacchus. Kyle had Arthur to thank for this one. He hadn't thought there were any vices left, had been a little disappointed, frankly, to think he'd covered them all, and along comes Mr. Trebelaine to the rescue. Not a moment too soon, either. This sober lifestyle, this so-called healthy living, was killing him. He needed something new to ruin himself with.

The good news was that the work was flowing—no, make that exploding—out of his keyboard. Whitehurst's advice had sparked a fire. The bad news was that he'd forgotten how goddamned exhausting writing was, and there wasn't much R and R to be found at Chez Whitehurst. That's where the Trebelaines came in, what with the billiard room, deck pool, tiki bar, and walk-in humidor of his Starship *Enterprise*.

It sat on the bluffs above the beautiful lapping stink of Sag Pond, a benign flotilla of water lilies breathing softly down below, the hard blue of the Atlantic just off to the right, over a phalanx of trees. Their home was one of the original bêtes noires of East End architecture. "The Spaceship," it had been dubbed, a hubristic collaboration of Bauhaus, Frank Lloyd Wright, and little green men from the Virgo cluster. A miracle of pressed wood and corrugated steel. It always looked about to take off, and for some twenty-plus years the neighbors had been praying it would. They'd solicited the zoning commission to stop construction back in '72, but then that was a good year for Arthur Trebelaine. Hollywood money was flowing in like a river, and some of it blew away, spreading like garden seed. New laws sprouted; amendments were passed. They moved in the spring of '73.

Arthur and Patty seemed unaffected by the local criticism. Gaudy, you say? So's Versailles, Arthur would bellow back. Kiss my ass. A spaceship, you say? Well, money talks, brother, and out here it says, Too fuckin' bad.

Kyle had enjoyed being a regular guest at the Trebelaines'. The Whitehurst house had become a bit of a drag. He was intensely fond of Richard, but those daily interrogations on fame were a bit much. And then the Red Sox at night, Jesus Lord! They were in first place, tied with the hated Yankees, but not, of course, without their daily bloodletting: the bad-luck injury, the blown lead. Clayton found himself getting sucked in, knowing the lineup by heart now, suffering over painful losses. That was no way to live, he decided. Forget booze, drugs, and dangerous women—the Sox would get you before any of them.

But worst of all, there was a marriage falling apart in that house, right in front of his eyes. Or so Kyle hoped—hoped that Richard and Meryl hadn't always been so tense, so uncommunicative, so unsexual.

In the two and a half months that he'd been a guest he hadn't heard one sound of lovemaking in that quiet house. The air was getting a little thin on John Street these days, and Kyle felt in the way.

Arthur was making it very comfortable for him, almost courting him in a way. When he slept over he took the guest cottage, down in the dunes. Mornings were quiet, Zen-like. The only sounds were those of the waves and the occasional squawk of gulls. There were lunches on the deck, trips to great restaurants at night. All of this kept firmly hidden from Richard.

They were really hitting it off, he and Arthur. It was different from his friendship with Richard. Richard was like the stern father, the one you loved even though he was the world's biggest pain in the ass; Trebelaine was the fun uncle you wished your father could be more like.

Today Kyle peered over the railing of the Spaceship and saw Arthur down on the lawn, checking up on the roast pig. It hung on a spit in the large brick fireplace, dripping fat, a Delicious apple lodged under its snout. Arthur stood consulting with the chef, then glanced up and noticed Kyle gazing downward.

"It's the *New York Times* reviewer," he called out, piercing the swine with a long-tined fork. "Big of me to invite him, don't you think?"

This earned a hearty laugh from Kyle. Arthur was still smarting, he'd learned, over an especially bad review of his last novel in the *Times*. As usual, it was Trebelaine who'd had the last laugh, selling nearly three million copies worldwide. The film was set to start shooting this fall.

Kyle sat back in his deck chair and continued with the day's activity: scouting the grounds for beauties. It was the Fourth of July, the annual Trebelaine barbecue, and the girls were out in full force.

Hollywood girls, Clayton noticed. Much of the Hamptons' film contingent were now in town for the summer, and a number of them were here today. Richard, of course, was a no-show. In fact, of the old gang, only Meryl was here, downstairs helping Patty with the food.

There, over at the badminton court, were at least four love bunnies, their assets bouncing and shimmying like panna cotta in the hands of a nervous waiter. And there, at the tiki bar, sat another group of hopefuls, their smooth, slim legs swinging out in advertisement. What, then, was Kyle doing up on the deck of the Spaceship, tobacco phallus hanging out of his mouth? Why wasn't he down there, on the wide lawn, teaching the girl in the marigold bathing suit the correct way to grip a croquet mallet? Scooting up behind her, his arms wrapped around, hands intertwined on the stick, *Keep the head steady, my dear, that's it.* In fact, he hadn't had a tumble since he'd arrived! The problem, he realized, was courage. This was the sober summer after all, and Kyle was trying to remember how one talks to women without the glowing, protective shield of alcohol. The last time he had approached a female straight was when he was . . . Christ, *fourteen* was it? Sober now for the first time since, he remembered them as he did as an adolescent: barb-tongued, wily creatures, all-powerful Circes. Without his liquid armor now, rejection could be lethal as a dagger, an exploding bullet of pain. Plus, he wasn't exactly the hot ticket of the summer, Case in Point pulling up a deck chair near him at this very moment.

"What's with the cigar?" Ms. Point inquired. "Isn't that kind of, I don't know, passé?"

She'd come up from behind him, though he'd seen her circling. Brown, shiny shins, vacuous blue eyes, predatory nose. Kyle was game.

"Cuban tobacco is not of the moment, dear. It's eternal." This
from a man who'd been smoking cigars for two weeks.

"You look familiar. Movies?"

"Books," Kyle said.

This let quite a bit of the air out, he could see. He needed to rally.
Then she crossed her long, praying mantis legs, and Kyle's tongue
pulled up lame.

"It's not polite to stare," she said.

This lowered his confidence yet another notch. It was like home-
room all over again, he thought, minus the braces; Betty Something-
or-Other giving him the thumbs-down, the awful subsequent silence.
Suddenly his throat felt parched. He needed some octane in a hurry.
Some bottled charm.

"What's your name, anyway?" Ms. Point asked. "You do remember your name, I hope."

It occurred to him to lie. *Naton. Naton Lyle.*

Instead he fessed up.

She cocked her head, immediately alarmed. "You mean Kyle Clayton, the *writer*?"

He nodded sheepishly. Ms. Point sprang to her feet.

"I . . . gotta go. See you later."

Then a blur, the smear of a body across the atmosphere.

Kyle turned a deep crimson, then went back to sucking the cigar.
Better get used to it, he thought with a deep puff. Women are lost to
you forever.

Arthur, seeing him alone, came up to save him. The captain appeared on deck in khaki pants fit for a safari and an impeccable dark
blue shirt that matched the deep color of his eyes. He seemed hand-
somer than ever today, his face interesting, world-weathered, sharpened by success.

"The women kicked me out of my own kitchen, can you imagine? They guard that goddamned food with their life."

He took Case's spot in the chair next to Kyle.

"You and Meryl get along?" Kyle asked. It seemed like a reasonable question, but Arthur looked a little surprised, like he'd been snuck up on.

He paused, fidgeting a bit in his chair. "I'm sorry. I . . . it's just that we had a little fling some years ago, you know, before Richard."

"Really?" Kyle asked, thinking this quite amazing.

"Just before she and Richard met. Of course he never forgave me for it, even though I'm the one who introduced them. But then she and Patty became best friends. Now it's fine. Everything's been forgotten."

A waiter came by with a drink for Arthur. A double whiskey, neat. His usual.

"How 'bout you?" he said, taking a sip.

Kyle shrugged. "She tolerates me. I suppose she does it for Richard."

"Oh, what doesn't she do for him! Son of a bitch should be thanking his lucky stars. He couldn't survive without her, you know."

Kyle was surprised by the irritation in Arthur's voice. Still, he had to agree. "I don't know how she puts up with him sometimes."

"Let me tell you, more people shake their heads at that marriage," Arthur said, shaking his own head. Then he nudged Kyle with an elbow, saying in a lower voice, "What a set of cans though, huh? *Jesus*. Unbelievable."

Kyle politely smiled, then immediately regretted it. Not that Meryl didn't affect him in the same way. How many afternoons had he stood behind the curtains in Kerry's room, leering at her like some demented pervert while she worked in the garden? There was, in fact, a growing pile of discarded manuscript pages under his desk, stuck together like glue. But you didn't just come out and say something like that, not about your friend's wife.

"So anyway," Arthur said, after a beat, knowing exactly how to fill in the dead space, how long to wait to smooth it over. "What do you think, Kyle?" He gazed proudly around his compound, taking a deep, satisfied breath. "Not bad, huh? Not a bad fucking life."

"Not bad at all," Kyle said.

"Look at that ocean, Kyle. Look how blue it is."

Clayton agreed it was very blue.

"See that beach? That's the best freakin' beach in North America. Nobody goes on that beach except me. That's *my* beach."

Kyle nodded.

"You could live like this too, you know."

The young man looked at Arthur like he was crazy.

"Sure," Arthur said, sipping his drink, "why not? You have the talent. You could have all this and more."

Kyle grinned at the notion. He'd always dreamed of a house by the sea. Who the hell hadn't? He'd pass on the Trebelaines' architect, though.

"How's your book going?" Arthur asked. "You still optimistic?"

"Well, *I* like it." Clayton smiled mischievously. "It'll piss a few people off, though. I know that much."

This gave Arthur some pause. "Is that what you want?"

"Sure." He shrugged. "Why not? Fuck 'em, you know?"

He said it almost as a reflex; it was something Richard would have loved. Clayton saw Arthur looking at him skeptically.

"I guess that's what he tells you, huh? That it's okay. Tells you to go out there and mix it up, stir up trouble. Not that he ever had the guts to do it."

"I think he has," Kyle countered. "In his own way."

"Well, he's stubborn, I'll give you that."

"He never gave in to them," Kyle said. "I hope I'm as strong."

This provoked a nasty laugh from Arthur. "Never gave in to them . . ." He laughed again. "So, you bought that one too, huh?"

Clayton bristled. He was surprised how protective of Richard he was. Of course, he owed the man a tremendous debt. If the new book was good—and Kyle was sure now that it was—he had Whitehurst to thank. The man had rescued him, in a way. Though Arthur still intimidated him somewhat, Kyle wasn't about to let him run all over Whitehurst behind his back.

"Arthur, come on, you have to admit it. If there's one thing you can't criticize Whitehurst for, it's his integrity."

"Hey, listen, it's okay," Arthur said, a little defensive. "Obviously the man has you under his spell. Maybe it's a good thing, who knows? If you can't be romantic at your age, when can you be?"

Out of a glove-shaped pouch of Italian leather he pulled out another Havana, Arthur's third of the day; he clipped the end with a diamond-studded cutter. This contraption also doubled as a lighter, Kyle discovered—in this case a mini-blowtorch.

As for Kyle's stogie, he was content to let it go out. Perhaps he'd smoked too many recently; the last few puffs hadn't tasted very good.

Arthur, though, wasn't done. "Us versus Them, this is the whole Whitehurst schtick. I've been hearing it for years. Personally, I've never seen it. There is no Them, Kyle, it's just something he's manufactured from bitterness. It's a shield."

Kyle begged to differ. There *was* a Them. He'd seen Them, and they needed a good fuck-you. As Arthur's guest, he decided to keep the opinion to himself.

"Look, I love the guy too," Arthur continued, somewhat unconvincingly. "I suppose he *is* noble, in a way. But don't take that too seriously, Kyle. Don't let him pollute you with his disappointments.

There's an old saying: If you're not idealistic when you're young, you have no heart. If you're idealistic when you're old, you're a fool."

With his eyes closing in a kind of ecstasy, Arthur took a long, greedy drag of his cigar, fumes breathed back in like a French inhaler.

"You have this beautiful fluidity to your writing, Kyle. Let it loose. Don't be afraid to entertain, make some goddamned money." He leaned forward and wrapped one of his big bear arms around Kyle's shoulders, then swept his other hand out regally, as if to invoke the landscape. The pond, the ocean, the beach that was his.

"Life, my friend, is to be enjoyed."

SHAKE SHAKE SHAKE . . .

The bar of the Trebelaine living room was just over fifteen feet long, the prow of a Montauk whiting boat, ingeniously transformed. The beams had been heavily shellacked and urethaned, then finished a deep, shiny walnut, the better to offset the amber display of rare single malts and nineteenth-century Armagnacs. Manning it was the Trebelaines' full-time bartender—poached for the summer from the "21" Club—dressed in a captain's uniform of perfect white.

It was a rather inviting little skiff, Kyle had to admit. Every time he passed it, pools of saliva would form near his molars, throat constricting in desire. Alluring a scene as this was, he had thus far avoided boarding the S.S. *Shitfaced*. But today he was being summoned by a long-lost sailor friend, a shipwreck on the literary high seas.

"Pat?" Kyle asked, coming up alongside his old pal. He was at the bar, slumped on an old stool. Pat "Hollywood" McCreary lifted his head from the skiff.

"Kyle!" he exclaimed. "Kyle feggin' Clayton! What're you doing here?"

"I'm visiting," Kyle said, "writing my book. What're *you* doing here?"

"*Writing again,*" Pat repeated. His eyes drifted over to the ocean view. Kyle noticed dried tears on his cheeks. "Good for you," he said morosely.

"What's wrong? You look terrible."

Pat shook his head and downed a plug of Irish malt, spilling half of it, the overflow adding more streaks to his already grief-stained face. "Oh, Clay," he began, voice plummeting, "the most terrible thing's happened."

"What is it? What's wrong?" Kyle asked. "Did somebody die?"

"No, it's worse, Clay. Much worse than that! I *got it,* mate," he said finally.

Kyle stared at him, waiting. "You got what?"

"*Screen credit!*" Pat hissed.

His head sank back to the bar, arriving with a defeated thud.

"Screen credit," Kyle repeated.

"Yes," Pat said miserably.

Oh, wow, Kyle thought, understanding fully now. Oh, boy.

"How'd it happen?" he asked.

"How'd it happen? How do *I* know how it happened!"

"Well, there must be a reason."

Pat looked straight ahead, shaking his head. "I wrote something meaningless, you see, something inane, and they . . . they jumped all over it! They went with *my* version!"

Pat buried his head again, trying to stifle the sobs.

"I'm really sorry," Kyle said.

"*Now* look at me," the screenwriter rejoined, lifting his head just enough to speak. "I'm ruined. I've rented a house in East Hamp-

ton, just like every other Hollywood wanker. East Hampton, Clay!
The studio's leasing a Land Rover for me. Look at me, look at
me," he said, holding his arms up. "I have a *tan*. I'm Irish and I have
a tan."

"British," his friend reminded him.

"I should've known this would happen. I should've known I'd be
successful in Hollywood someday. Every studio wants me now.
They're throwing money at me left and right, Clay. Heaping it on.
Oh, I could just die."

"Maybe it'll flop," Kyle said, trying to be optimistic.

Pat's tears stopped suddenly. He wiped his face on his sleeve.

"You think?" he asked, his voice revealing a trace of hope.

"Sure, why not? It's not good, is it?"

"Good? It's terrible, Clay! It's inhuman."

"See? There you go," Kyle said with rising excitement. "Maybe
you've still got a chance, maybe you can—"

"But wait, they like terrible. Terrible is *good*, Clay," Pat said,
lowering his head again.

"Hey, c'mon now." Kyle began massaging his friend's shoulders.
"You never know," he said. "Things could change."

"No," Pat said. "I'm a screenwriter now. It's done."

Kyle stayed with him for quite a while, both sitting in silence.
Eventually, of course, the tears subsided. Once Pat had wiped his
eyes with his drink napkin, Kyle decided to leave him to his vices.

"Good luck," he said, squeezing Pat's shoulder. Kyle stood up to
leave. The bar was starting to give him the jitters. It felt so much like
home.

KYLE WANDERED through the cavernous living room, beveled windows stretching up from floor to ceiling. After a few lame attempts at

conversation with miscellaneous guests, he made for the kitchen. The
pig was taking forever, and his stomach was all agrumble. He was
hoping maybe he could sweet-talk his way into a preview of some of
Meryl's famous guacamole. Was he growing on her just a little these
past weeks? Maybe, he thought, but Patty might be better to approach for favors. She was a less prickly sort. She had accepted Kyle
immediately, with her forever grinning, hostess-with-the-mostest per-
sona. Not that he would compare her with Richard's wife. Though
pleasant enough, Patty Trebelaine was not a woman who weighed
heavily on a man's spirit—not like Meryl Whitehurst.

Conversationally, Patty's opinions tended toward paraphrased re-
productions of the *Times*'s op-ed page, or muted affectations of her
husband's more passionate displays. Her looks had faded to a sort
of remembrance of loveliness. Initially, Kyle secretly wondered how
Arthur could be satisfied with such a union. Then he began spending
time at the Trebelaines' and observing Patty in action. She ran events
like a field marshal, whispering stern reproaches to her servers in one
breath and in the next delivering a zinging compliment to a dowdy
dinner guest that had the recipient glowing the rest of the evening. She
organized croquet, introduced coy singles, cooked s'mores for the
kids. She was everywhere and nowhere. She *directed,* rarely touching
a thing. All this allowed Arthur to hang back, to bask in the glow of
good company and his Gentleman Jack.

Clayton's feeling was that whatever the Trebelaines' marriage
had once been, it was now one of those practical middle-aged part-
nerships. They were a corporation, a well-oiled machine of domes-
tication, unhindered by affection and deep feeling. To Kyle, the
Whitehursts' marriage was in many ways superior—if one measures
such things in terms of love. Richard and Meryl's life together was
one of frustration, buried resentments, severe melancholy—and now,
clearly, a manifest antagonism. All of which highlighted the simple

failure to realize their great love for each other. Miserable as the Whitehursts could be, at least they suffered over failed expectations. The Trebelaines, it seemed, just didn't care.

Was there infidelity? Clayton had his guesses here too. With Patty he doubted it, maybe a quick thing or two over the years, and nothing for quite a while. There was something a little sterile at the heart of her, he thought. Something a little too tightly wound.

As for Arthur, well, of course he was too discreet to ever talk about it, but one had only to hear the man on the phone to the butcher at Balducci's, ordering dry-aged sirloins for the grill ("Not too lean now, the fat is the flavor"), or to watch him smoke a cigar—the way he caressed and tongued it, the way he made *love* to it—to know that he'd had his share of mistresses. Clearly, Kyle had decided, this was a man who denied himself nothing from the sensual world.

Kyle entered the kitchen to find Meryl on the phone in a state of great agitation.

"What do you mean she doesn't look good?" she said. She was pacing back and forth across the Spanish tiles. "Is she okay?"

Patty stood nearby, face held in dutiful concern. She rolled her eyes at Kyle, letting him know something big was up.

"What's going on?"

Patty waved her hand at him to keep his voice down, then mouthed something to him—*Gary*, it sounded like—then raised her eyebrows. The name meant nothing to him.

"Okay, okay, I'll be right there." Meryl put the phone down next to a pile of avocado skins.

"Well?" Patty asked.

Meryl looked uneasy. "She's okay, I guess." She gathered her pocketbook and quickly extracted her keys. "Listen, I have a favor to ask," she said, turning to Kyle. "Can you stay here tonight?"

He shrugged and looked at Patty, who was already nodding. "Of course," she said. Then Meryl kissed Patty on the cheek, thanked them both, and hustled out the door.

"Good luck," Patty called after her.

"What happened?" Kyle asked as the door closed.

Patty stared straight ahead, her gaze intent and, somehow, a touch triumphant.

"Kerry's here," she said finally, voice touched with foreboding. "That crazy daughter of theirs is back."

6

Richard sat in the chair near the fireplace, massaging his temples like a man to whom trouble has come in the form of a nasty headache. He hadn't seen her for close to three years, but he'd quickly adopted the same look he always had when Kerry was around: tense, ill at ease, and more than slightly annoyed.

Christ, he thought to himself. I thought I was rid of this one.

She sat on the couch across from him, army duffel bag at her feet. Her hair was long and matted in places, as if it had been styled with lard. She wore a man's thermal top and a pair of thrift-store pants, dolloped with artist's paint. Her skin was pallid and blotchy. And she was thin. Bone thin. He could see the outline of her sunken rib cage, skeletal hands peeking out below the sleeves.

"So," she began in a weak, though slightly exultant, voice, "what do you think of Daddy's little girl now?"

Richard resisted the urge to roll his eyes. Oh, here we go, he thought, off and running. My charming daughter. Still, he stifled the impulse for instant conflict. He'd always been a little afraid of her, but today the apprehension was much worse. Today she looked to him like Death itself. He was convinced that she had come back to kill him.

The bell had rung and he'd answered it and there she was. If he'd known it was Kerry, he might have ignored it, waited till her mother returned, let *her* deal with it.

"You want to tell me what's happened to you?"

She slouched a little on the couch, looking tired and a little spacey.

"I'm fucked up."

"Obviously," he said. "How? On what?"

She raised a few bony fingers. "Little of this, little of that," she said with a shrug.

Richard sighed. They sat silent for a while, neither knowing what to say. Eventually Kerry stood up and began walking around the living room, looking and touching. She ran her fingers over paintings, inspected some of the books lying about. Finally she pulled the curtain back and looked at the side lawn where she used to play.

My God, she's thin, Richard thought. Her arms were like twigs.

"Mom's still with the shabby chic, huh? That's finally in, you know. She was ahead of her time."

"Well, that's your mother," he said.

Kerry moved over to the bookcase, head turning to inspect the titles. They were like two boxers, Richard thought, feeling each other out in the early rounds. What could he say? The tremendous chasm between the two of them—all the terrible things that occurred before she'd left—made anything but antagonism seem trite and embarrassing.

"How's your art going?" he said finally.

She laughed.

"Is that funny?"

She flopped back down on the couch, seeming to catch her breath.

"'How's your art going?'" she repeated, running her hand through her stringy hair. "Gee, what a trenchant query, Dad. Our communication is better than ever."

"You could try a little too, you know."

She took a few more deep breaths, trying to relax. He imagined this was as traumatic for her as it was for him. What was she doing here anyway? Hadn't she sworn to never come back? Kerry was nothing if not prideful; she must be in one hell of a state to come skulking home like this.

"My art," she said. "Well, let's see . . . Not great, Dad, to tell you the truth. Nope, not exactly taking off." Then she added, challengingly, "How's *yours*?"

"Mine?" he said. "Terrific. What, are you kidding? Number one in Cameroon, as we speak. In Central Africa I'm like a god."

She smiled, his humor catching her by surprise. Two points, Richard thought.

"What is it exactly you're doing?" he asked. "Sculpture, is it?"

"Installations," she said, annoyed again, looking away.

"Right, right," he answered. He was never exactly sure what that meant.

"*Brilliant, but a touch esoteric.* That's what the *Voice* said about my last show. Whatever that means."

"Ha, the *Voice*," Richard said, perhaps remembering an old slight. "That still around, is it?"

"It was actually a pretty good review." Shafts of sunlight were pouring in through the windows and onto the couch. Lowering her eyes now, Kerry began tracing the patterns on the cushions with one of her pencil-thin fingers. "I sent the article to Mom," she said, almost

in a whisper. "Did she ever show it to you?" Looking up, her eyes be-
lied a twinge of hopefulness. "I told her not to, but . . ."

Richard's face flushed. Meryl had showed him the piece. He remembered how he'd picked it up only to search for his *own* name,
some reference to himself: *Kerry Whitehurst, daughter of . . .* There'd
been nothing, of course. He'd put it aside, soon to be misplaced, lost,
discarded.

"I was very proud," he said. He glanced up at the clock. Where the
fuck was Meryl, anyway?

They sat in silence as Kerry's eyes scanned the living room. The
house must seem like a museum to her now, he thought. Was he de-
tecting something softer in her countenance suddenly, some sense of
consolation? However much she'd renounced her past, this *was* still
her home, wasn't it? Her cache of memories. Could they all be bad?
Hadn't he taught her a curveball on the side lawn?

"I suppose you're wondering why I'm here," she said. Richard
said nothing. "Tell you the truth, I'm not really sure myself," she continued. "I've kind of bottomed out. It's mortifying to admit, but . . . I
have nowhere to go." She turned her head, as if looking for something, then wrapped her arms around herself. She was cold.

"You want a blanket?" From where he was sitting, Richard could
see the large thermometer on the porch sill. It was just under ninety
degrees.

She held up her hand in refusal, then coughed. "Listen, don't
worry. I'm not here to punish you or anything. Some of the stuff I
did . . ." She shook her head at the memory. "I was a total pain in the
ass. It was very immature."

Richard tried to conceal his surprise and sense of minor triumph.
"I'm sure you had reason to be angry with me."

"No," she said emphatically, "most of it was stupid. There's no
excuse."

Now Richard was overwhelmed. Through all the mayhem, he'd never in his life heard Kerry apologize. Maybe, he thought, just maybe she was human after all.

Then again, this was not the same Kerry, he reminded himself. This was a wounded, limping version of her, hardly the old warhorse. Could her stance be self-preservation? She probably had more drugs in her right now than the local Rite Aid.

"You're so thin," he said. "You haven't been eating."

She murmured something, then closed her eyes, slumping back into the ancient couch.

Richard stood up. He was surprised to find that whatever crippled paternal instincts he'd owned were suddenly asserting themselves. He was worried about her.

"How about a sandwich?" he asked.

But Kerry seemed to have drifted away, and only after a few moments did her attention seem to come floating back.

"Love one," she said suddenly, with a dreamy smile.

Here was the one thing he used to do for her, even during the bad times—make her a sandwich. Such a simple thing. Although he didn't know it, Kerry did, of course, have some fond memories of her Sag Harbor childhood. Summer afternoons usually, sunny days of idleness and protection, the youthful illusion of comfort. The stadium sounds of the ever-present Red Sox game floating through the billowing curtains, her father calling out, *Anybody want a sandwich?* After a summer in Europe and countless New York restaurants, she'd still swear nothing had ever tasted as good.

Richard clapped his hands now, heading for the kitchen.

"One sandwich, comin' up."

Gingerly, Kerry raised herself up. Richard told her to sit, he'd bring it to her, but she shook him off.

She followed him into the kitchen, her steps slow but determined.

She was sick, obviously, perhaps dangerously so, but she wanted to watch him. He understood now; it was more important than the food. She could faint right there on the linoleum, drop dead in his arms—it didn't matter. After everything, she was going to watch her fucking father make her a sandwich.

"Okay, let's see . . ." He began pulling the deli meats from the refrigerator. "Turkey with a little Swiss, am I right?"

She nodded, pleased he remembered.

"Mustard *and* mayo. Though *that* I'll never quite figure out." He gave her a mischievous wink.

As he started to assemble the sandwich, Kerry—languidly, sluggishly—began to talk about what had happened to her. It was not a happy story. In fact, Richard let his mind drift away several times, subconsciously suppressing what he didn't want to hear. Shouldn't they wait for her mother, he'd asked at certain moments, but she was off and running, anxious to tell someone, to get it out.

Basically it was drugs. She was strung out, though not on anything specific. No surprise there, Richard thought, though the knowledge still saddened him. The days of finding a few tabs and a joint in her sock drawer were over now. She liked it all, she said, soup to nuts.

"Cocaine?" he asked, his back to her, pushing down the bread in the toaster.

"Sure, why not?"

He looked back. "Heroin?"

"To snort," she said. "But yeah, sure. Heroin's cool."

Richard spread on the Hellmann's, hands shaking.

The shit hit the fan a month ago when she was evicted from her studio. She'd been living there illegally, but the landlord hadn't cared until the rent stopped coming. There was nowhere to go—all her friends had sworn her off ages ago—and so for the past three weeks or so she'd been living on the streets in Williamsburg.

Richard winced, feeling a crushing sensation around his heart.

"Lettuce?" he asked weakly. He put it on, answering his own question. Then he added some tomato, too, though he thought he remembered her not liking it. "Fresh from the farmstand," he said, packing down the sandwich. "Good for you."

Finally she couldn't take it anymore, she continued. She'd swallowed her pride, hitchhiked out to the Island. A trucker brought her as far as Quogue, then a cop picked her up, bringing her right to the door.

"And here I am," she said.

"I'm glad you're here," her father answered, rather convincingly. He laid a pickle on the plate and brought it over to her. Before he could set it down, Kerry reached up and pulled off half the sandwich, indulging a rapacious first bite.

He turned around and immediately began making her a second.

It was then they heard a noise at the front door, followed by nervous footsteps in the hall.

"Hello," her mother's voice probed anxiously. "Hello?"

"Here," Richard called out.

Meryl gasped as she entered the kitchen, her feet stopping cold as her daughter came into view. She reached a hand out to the counter for support, to steady herself as she viewed Kerry in her entirety: filthy, twenty-five pounds lighter, bag o' bones Kerry.

"*Oh, my darling,*" Meryl whispered in a hushed tone. She turned toward Richard at the sandwich board and cut him with a look of biting disdain. "Look what you've done," she hissed.

Kerry, who was either too tired or too hungry to get up and say hello, sat still and continued to devour the sandwich. Her mother came forward then and clutched her to her breast, turning her back on her husband as if to form a shield between her daughter and her tormentor.

Feeling oddly, though perhaps deservedly, left out, Richard stood idle. He could still see his daughter's eyes peering at him above his wife's shoulder. She was gazing at him intently now, really *looking* at him for the first time since she'd arrived. What was she seeing? he wondered. Of course there were the superficial things: the sagging folds of his neck; the lips, slightly pinched from decades of disappointment; the lachrymose eyes, always melancholy but perhaps more so now. All in all, a botched misfire of a father.

But also she would see the optimism in his eyes, the wisp of guarded expectation. Almost by accident, they had made some connection today, however slight, had danced nimbly around some of the old battlements. Maybe it could continue, he thought. In fact, though her mouth was hidden, he could tell his daughter was smiling at him this very moment, could tell by her eyes, though this left the essence of the smile somewhat ambiguous. What did it say? he wondered. Was it straight, a hope of better things to come? The signal of a truce? Or was it that crooked grin of hers, ironic, twisted in such a way as to warn him not to get his hopes up, that things had not changed, and never could.

Of course, there was no way to know for sure, and try as he might to be encouraged, he could not entirely put out of his head the idea that his daughter had come home to destroy him.

7

August had come in a blaze, noon sun glaring down on the modest softball field off Main Street in East Hampton. It was time, once again, for the annual artists-writers softball game. The lineup sine qua non, the very zenith of American creativity. There's Paul Simon (writer) on the mound, high-arching his pitches to Chevy Chase (artist). We have Billy Joel (writer) digging in at second base, his uniform of dirty blue jeans and denim cap a nod to the Montauk fishermen, his "brothers," whose rights he was still fighting for that summer, and a few of whom had been waving to him ever since the morning warm-ups but were undiscernible through the near-blackout of the $3,600 Serengeti sunglasses perched on the bridge of his nose. Of course there are a few lame ducks on the squad, mere fillers, a few what-are-*you*-doing-heres. There's Kyle Clayton, for example: All–New Jersey pitcher (circa 1979), thirty-sixth most hated New Yorker (current), still lazy after all these years—standing out in right field, a stone on a grave, waiting for one of these wimps to finally get it out of the infield.

Yes, he thinks, exactly. What the *fuck* are you doing here?

Kyle recalled being confronted by the event chairwoman at one of the Whitehursts' parties earlier in the summer. When he failed to immediately volunteer, Maive pulled out her ace in the hole, her *out*-pitch: "Oh, you'll have a great time, Kyle. This year's gonna be packed with celebrities!"

Well, *la-dee-frickin'-da,* Kyle had mumbled to himself, as if the idea of playing catch with Martha Stewart got his panties all in a twirl.

The game would only take a couple of hours, he was assured, but then a writer's momentum is a precarious thing, isn't it? Kyle had thought. Best not to mess with it. He was sober, the pages were flowing; not even the presence of Kerry Whitehurst (or Calamity Kerry, as he secretly called her) could deter him. Why risk upsetting this delicate balance?

No, sorry, Maive. He'd have to pass.

Maive seemed worried for him. "I don't know," she said. "Tom Hanks'll be awfully disappointed."

"My cross to bear, Maive."

"How about a donation at least? Can I put you down for a few hundred?"

Kyle groaned. To be honest, he was never much for organized charities—too anonymous for his taste, and Dorothea's last check was getting thin.

"Sorry, Maive, but I'm a little light right now."

Maive switched into high gear, filling her voice with practiced PTA sanctity: "Oh, please, Mr. Clayton. A big-time famous writer like you? You couldn't part with a few hundred dollars for breast cancer? For shame. Well, I can't tell you how disappointed I—"

"Breast cancer?"

"Yes, the writers are playing for breast cancer," she repeated. "Long Island has been so decimated this last decade. Did you know that in the Five Towns alone one woman in three can expect . . ."

Maive's voice trailed off as the image of his mother came swooping down on Kyle like a dark, looming bird. It was actually leukemia that got her in the end, but it had all started with breast cancer. She'd beaten it three times, but then the bastard kept coming back, year after year, like a perennial weed with attitude. She probably would have kept on beating it too, except the years of chemo treatments finally stripped her blood cells bare. Now all that was left of her was the urn of ashes that stood on his father's bedroom dresser, and the fiery peach pit in his stomach that was often in need of extinguishment.

"Pencil me in, Maive," he suddenly announced. "Right field if you can." He wrote the date down in large letters and posted it above his desk. "I got a pretty good arm, you know."

TOP OF THE THIRD, piercing sun drifting mercifully behind clouds of freshly pulled cotton. One of the Baldwin boys, Benny or Bobby (Kyle could never keep them straight), popped to short, his swing a stiff-armed travesty. To inform the crowd that this was not a typical Baldwin at bat, that he was indeed the hot-blooded progeny of movie fame, the young man took only a few steps to first before he raised the aluminum bat high in the air and brought it down to the turf like a battle-axe at a beheading, the blow delivering a sickening thud that Kyle could hear all the way out in right field.

"Fuck *me*!" Bobby/Benny yelled, a request that brought a cry of volunteers from the female contingent.

Since Hanks was a no-show, the coach decided to put Chevy Chase at bat. As he stepped up to the plate, the right fielder felt the hot rush of vengeance. Wasn't it bad enough that during the pregame introductions the M.C. had presented Kyle like this: "Next, starting in right field and batting sixth, here he is, the Mike Tyson of the word processor, Barnes & Noble's heavyweight champion of the year, *Kyle Clayton*!" And then he'd had to run out to the first-baseline to the sound of one or two clapping hands and a low tide of boos.

Kyle tipped his cap to the crowd, topping it with an exaggerated, kiss-my-ass bow.

Bbbooooooooo.

Then, just as the next introduction was due, when the spectators with their three-second memories were already set to move on and forget him, Chevy had come sprinting out of the "artists'" dugout with a catcher's mask on.

He ran straight up to Kyle and began dancing around him like a boxer. *"Come on, sucka,"* he shouted in his best Ali accent, urging Clayton forward with his fists. "I heard about you. Oh, yeah, I heard about you!" He did a flurry of awkward uppercuts. *"Here we go now!"*

The crowd went berserk. Kyle tried to smile, but then how bad did he want to deck this big goon, send him sprawling backward to kick up a nice puff of crushed limestone in his wake? After a few eternal seconds of this, Chevy indeed flinched as if Kyle had struck him, falling back like a tree onto the soft grass and into the welcoming arms of star-starved hilarity.

So now, as Chevy goofed his way up to the plate, still filling his pockets with chuckles and grins (scratching his balls, pointing to the fence like Babe Ruth—funny, funny stuff), the right fielder pounded his glove, dug his sneakers against the turf, and prayed, fucking *prayed* this guy would get it out of the infield and hit it to him.

You get it anywhere near me, Kyle thought, *anywhere,* and it's mine.

Just the second pitch, and what do you know? Chase drove it to right center, a perfect Clayton wish shot, catchable but still a challenge. *Mine, fucker, mine!* Clayton, former all-state pitcher but also part-time outfielder, on his high horse, long legs eating up sun-scalded acreage, the ball in his crosshairs and falling, the sun behind a cloud, everything perfect. *Mine!*

What he did not see, in this monomaniacal pursuit, was the center fielder, some guy named Ed Burns (movie "writer," Kyle had since been informed, but what did it matter here?), running with equal force toward the same falling orb, a big son of a bitch, big as Kyle even, and then from the crowd a crescendo of warning, and then *Ohhhhhh . . . !* Just as the grapefruit came dropping into his glove, just as Kyle was about to squeeze it, Burns slammed into him, head to chest, knocking them both to the turf.

As he sat up, Kyle could not breathe. Burns can bill me tomorrow for an MRI, he thought, so far had he buried his head into Clayton's midsection. But the dizziness? Ha, dizziness was no distraction to the likes of Kyle Clayton. Until this abstemious stay at the Whitehursts', equilibrium was a luxury to this young man, a momentary curiosity usually experienced only upon waking and rarely then, a state quickly alleviated and even a little creepy, if truth be told—so do not be surprised that Kyle pushed off Burns's limp body and immediately stood up straight, though the field was in vertigo, and upon finding three or four blurry white grapefruits on the turf, managed to reach down and immediately pick up the right one. Practice, as they say, makes perfect.

Meanwhile, Chevy was in full sprint. Kyle could see the four of them as they rounded first, flapping their arms like birds (more side-splitting stuff, can you stand it?), and Clayton with his all-state wing wound and fired a BB, a bazooka launch to second base.

Catch it, Piano Man. Catch it or I'll kill you.

If slow-mo were available, the local hero Billy Joel, or "the contemporary Gershwin," as he was introduced, would have been seen looking a bit tentative as the missile approached. This was not the sort of velocity he remembered from JV baseball, apparently, nor certainly from his pregame tosses with Ben Gazzara. There was a sound that accompanied the throw—that insidiously soft *pphhhfffft*—adding a hint of danger. Joel shuffled back in retreat—but then the ball was already on him, the laces skimming the top of the glove, a butterfly kiss of "genuine" and "patented" leathers, and then onward to the bridge of his nose, the custom-made sunglasses driven into his face and then shattering amid frightened gasps from the crowd's rather large fishing contingent.

Disaster. Though neither injury was serious, both Joel and Burns sat out the rest of the game. Kyle, too, was done for the day, though not by choice. He was simply benched. Not *after* that fateful inning, mind you, when a substitution would have hardly been noticed, but right then and there, as team manager John Grisham informed Kyle that he was "finished." Yes, that was probably true, Kyle replied, but he promised it wouldn't affect his ability to play in today's softball game.

Grisham shook his head. "No, you're done for the day." And that was that.

The rest was a misery of boredom. Arthur Trebelaine, still fit as a fiddle at sixty-two, took Garry Marshall deep for a two-run double—the only runs the writers could muster. Meanwhile, the Baldwin bats came alive. One of the brothers went yard on Mort Zuckerman, then Martha Stewart popped one over a pulled-in outfield for an inside-the-parker, thus opening the flood gates. By the end, the artists had won 9–2.

After the game, while the players shook hands out at the pitcher's mound and reminded one another to be at Billy Joel's postgame bar-becue (still on, everyone was reassured), Kyle paid a quick good-bye to Arthur, then hopped the dugout fence. There he made a beeline toward the parking lot, gaining only a few steps before being accosted from behind by someone with a curt English accent.

"Quite a show, Kyle," the man said. "Bloody typical."

Catching only a quick glimpse of indecorous winter tweed, Kyle put his head down and bulled forward.

"I say, *Kyle.*" The man caught up to Clayton and grabbed him by the back of his jersey. "How *did* you manage to fuck this up?"

Kyle stopped and stared into the man's face. It was shockingly un-familiar, but the voice was not—it was the unforgettable voice of David Trevor.

"Yes, it's me, Kyle. Now shake my hand. Show some manners for once in your life."

Kyle did so, but reluctantly, for the countenance was quite fright-ful. The man was a specter, a ghoul. His skin was so pale as to seem translucent. His face had an unformed quality to it, sunken eyes on a mushy palette where the bones had not fully developed. Taking him in, Kyle wondered suddenly if the voracious ambition he'd heard so much about had actually made sense, was perhaps justified on some level, since nature had greatly shortchanged Mr. David Trevor.

To add insult to this injury of form, Trevor's nose was severely sunburned. It was as if someone had bent him over a simmering pot with the intention of boiling him alive—but was able only to sub-merge his nose. Trevor held a folded *New York Times* over his head, lest his features disintegrate.

"What the hell happened out there today?" he asked. "You almost took out half your own team."

Kyle looked back to the diamond and shrugged. "Fuck them," he said resentfully. Then he resumed his brisk walk to the parking lot. It was two-thirty already; Whitehurst was supposed to be here a half hour ago.

Trevor walked quickly alongside him. "Fuck them? Fuck *you,* my friend. You know what I had to do to get you in this game?"

Kyle abruptly stopped.

"Oh, come on, Kyle, you think they would have invited you if I hadn't told them to? *You* of all people, with *those* folks out there. You're not fit to be the batboy for that crowd."

Kyle frowned and started walking again, his guts in a painful clench. He was screwed, wasn't he? Basically, it came down to this: He owed Trevor's company upward of one hundred thousand dollars *and* a new novel. They had him by the balls. What else could he do but take the publisher's weekly phone calls, allow himself to be threatened, insulted, pushed around? What else but chugalug all the shit this maniac could shovel in a given summer?

"But you know me," the esteemed publisher continued. "I'm always thinking. I heard you were a ballplayer, so I thought it would be good publicity. I thought maybe you'd hit a home run, get your name in the paper, get a little momentum going for the book. I yell and scream and pull rank on people to get you in this game. I even ask Chevy to spice things up a little out there for me. And what do you do? Create a disaster—"

"You *told* him to do that?" Kyle asked incredulously. Disgusted, he threw his mitt down on the hood of a Mercedes.

"It was a favor. He's got a book coming out with us. An autobiography."

"With Brownstone?" Kyle laughed. "Get out of here, Brownstone doesn't do those kind of books."

"Tell our finance department," Trevor rejoined. "Paid a bloody fortune for it."

Finally Richard's Bronco pulled up, though Richard was not at the helm. Calamity Kerry held the wheel, cassette player at a deafening volume.

"Now, who is that?" Trevor whispered excitedly.

"Trouble," Kyle murmured.

He walked up to the Bronco. Kerry lowered the window, and the music leapt out into the parking lot. Kyle winced as if someone had stuck a sharpened pencil in his ear. Finally she turned it off.

"Let's go," she said smiling. "I'm your ride."

Kyle felt a slight chill penetrate him. Just a week ago she'd been bedridden, barely holding down turkey sandwiches in between dry heaves and twenty-three-hour naps. Now she was out cruising around in the family SUV. A rather lax rehab program, he thought.

"Where's your father?"

"Dad? Oh, you know, coughing up blood in the attic. The usual."

Bewitching as ever, thought Kyle.

"Who's the goblin?" she asked, looking past him at Trevor.

"Shhh." Kyle looked back worriedly at his publisher. "That man owns my soul."

"He's frightening," she said. "He's the Count of fucking Darkness."

Kyle turned to David to say good-bye. Trevor grabbed his hand and pulled him closer, whispering in his ear.

"Introduce us, Kyle."

Kyle balked.

"Come now," Trevor said sternly. "Introduce me."

Okay, Kyle thought. It's your funeral.

"Kerry, I want you to meet somebody." He brought Trevor forward, lamb to slaughter. "This is my publisher, David Trevor. David, this is Kerry Whitehurst."

"A Whitehurst? Well, I'm enraptured." He extended a few of his long fingers upward for her to shake.

Kerry sneered, taking them in her hand like you would the tail of a dead skunk.

"I hear your father's a genius," he said. "If you go for that sort of thing."

"You should see him try to mow the lawn," she said.

Trevor didn't get it. He smiled vacantly.

"How about you and I get a drink later," he said to Kerry, coming right out with it. "I'm only in town till tomorrow, so time is short."

Kerry smirked, somewhat incredulously. She looked as if she found this both repulsive and highly entertaining.

"We can drink champagne," added the publisher, "and contemplate the name of our firstborn."

Kerry smiled brightly now, which made Clayton wince—a doozy was on the way, no doubt about it. He had the urge to step away, to get out of the bomb's range.

"I'm really sorry," Kerry said, maintaining her lightbulb grin, "but I only date men with a *full* set of DNA."

Bull's-eye.

A ravaged grin overtook Trevor's mouth. He seemed to rock a bit on his feet, like he was losing his balance.

Meanwhile, Kerry had reloaded. "And as far as a baby goes—"

"*Anyway,*" Clayton intervened, cutting her off with a clap of his hands. He didn't like Trevor one bit, but there was such a thing as mercy. "We should be going," he told her.

Trevor rallied enough to issue Kyle a final order. "We need to talk," he said, eyes still a little glassy. "How about tomorrow?"

What could Kyle say? *By the balls.*

"Fine, where?"

"Bobby Van's. Noon. And bring the manuscript with you. No more honor system here. I want to feel it in my fingers, Kyle. I want to be able to flip those pages like dollar bills."

Clayton grabbed his mitt and climbed in the passenger side. He watched Kerry, her eyes transfixed, staring out at the Count as he strolled menacingly through the parking lot. She'd never seen anything like it.

A car began to honk furiously behind them. It was Chevy Chase in his Benz convertible. Kerry flipped him the bird, then hit the gas.

8

Earlier that day Richard had done Kyle the favor of accepting the first 250 pages of his manuscript to read. "A little rough," Kyle had warned, handing him the stack of paper. Whitehurst was undaunted, eager to dip into the work that he had helped make possible. Richard even cut his own workday in half, so that he could look at the novel with a clear, rested mind. A rare gesture indeed.

The plan had been to read a hundred pages or so and then take a break to pick Kyle up from the softball game—the annual event to which he'd yet to be invited. He would finish the second half that evening or, at the latest, tomorrow morning.

Almost immediately, though, the plan was jettisoned. Problem was, Whitehurst couldn't put it down. It hadn't taken long, about six or seven pages, and then Richard was gone, completely immersed. The new work was so good, in fact, that by page 60 a fit of jealousy overtook him. He started criticizing petty things: a poorly constructed sentence or two, some continuity problems—mistakes easily fixed by an editor. It's okay, he thought, not bad but . . . Then he'd suddenly come across a startling turn of phrase, a burst of invective humor, even pathos—a new one for Clayton—and know all at once that he was wrong. The bastard's done it again, he'd conceded. Only this time it's even better.

At two o'clock Meryl knocked. She didn't dare open the door.

Yes?

Are you going to pick Kyle up? It's getting late.

It's really flowing in here, darling. I'd hate to stop.

I don't hear anything.

I'm writing longhand. I can't type fast enough.

He kept reading even as they spoke.

Well, I'm right in the middle of something in the garden.

Couldn't Kerry do it?

Why should she? He's your guest.

To help out, he said, reading on. *She doesn't do anything else around here.*

Neither do you.

Despite this jab, the subsequent silence told him he had won. He read on, and would keep going straight to the end.

It was a fuller work than *Charmed Life,* had more meat, more muscle. Clayton's descriptive powers, which had been considerable, had become lusher and even more lyrical. And this element of pathos was like a left hook. Never sentimental, never maudlin, catching you unaware and leaving you reeling.

What really put the book over the top for Richard was the aspect of roman à clef, perhaps since it was here the mentor could see his own brush strokes on the canvas. The young man had taken his advice and delivered a whammy to his enemies. There were real people in the book, thinly disguised; some Richard only vaguely recognized, others he knew all too well. Dorothea Clementine, for example, the

PEN benefactor, was a major character, as was Kyle's new rival Devon Schiff, though he had been discreet enough thus far to avoid any reference to their brawl. New York publishing, Wall Street, the mavens of Old Money—all of them lambasted with a brutal, though self-effacing, wit.

Marvelous, Richard thought, but why isn't it *mine*? Of course he had considered such a project many times over the years. A sprawling book, New York at the *fin de siècle*. But doubts had overtaken him. How could he ever hope to write such a book? he'd begun to wonder. What tangible experience could he draw from? He'd spent the last twenty years in a cramped attic trying to make words trickle on the tongue like wine—what did he know of New York anymore? He had cut himself off. No, Kyle was the man for the job now. He was a real part of the metropolis, in a position to observe and in some cases even influence its inner workings.

Whitehurst pushed aside the manuscript and picked up what was completed of his own new work, a novella that was coming forth slowly. His face looked pained as he read it. Compared with Clayton's work, it seemed paltry, without consequence. And yes, God help him, "esoteric." Even from the aspect of craft, things were not going well. His sentences, once hard-crusted, indelible—the cornerstone of his work—now seemed flaccid, transparent. He'd call the new book trash, if only it had half the appeal of trash. It was a strained work, laborious to read. Dead. Absolutely D.O.A.

No, he would have to start all over. From the very first word. Do it again until he got it right.

Of course this hadn't been the greatest summer for working, had it? Initially, Kyle's presence had cheered Richard, but then it had quickly become a distraction. *Will he or won't he have dinner with us tonight? How is Meryl coping with him? Does he prefer Arthur's company to mine?* Then Kerry had shown up, and the writing had all but stopped. Not even Richard Whitehurst could justify working when his daughter had arrived half dead at his doorstep. He'd made time for her that first week, tried to feed her, to get her strength back. They'd gone to the beach together one afternoon, and another night he'd taken her to the theater in Sag Harbor for a play. Before he knew it a week had passed with no writing. Then two. His first sabbatical in nearly thirty years. He'd almost enjoyed it.

But enough was enough, he'd decided. It was time to get back to work, the notion doubly underscored by the excellence of Kyle's novel. In a few months the young man had put together 250 pages! Granted, some of the writing had already been done, the material cannibalized from his drunken days, but nevertheless. Whitehurst had written exactly thirty-four pages. And not a damn one of them was any good. It was time to get going.

As if to mock this assertion, there was a terse rap at the door.

Meryl entered with a tuna fish sandwich and a pitcher of iced tea. She had on her old khaki shorts, the ones that were too tight and ran up sweetly between her buttocks, heeled sandals, and a bikini top. Her skin was a creamy brown from the sun. A rush of desire surged through him like a shot of booze. Discreetly he felt his own crotch, trying to see if the feeling had translated into something corporeal.

No go. *Shit.*

She came up next to him and laid the tray on the desk. She had not showered, and a strong garden scent clung to her. He thought of the name of a flower Meryl favored, *white honesty.* Obviously her smell was an amalgam of various flora, but he'd always loved that name.

"Do you think that's an appropriate outfit, considering we have a guest?" he asked. This was the way they addressed each other these days, their thwarted desire manifesting itself as contentiousness. "I mean, you look absolutely lovely, but—"

"He isn't even here."

"He will be soon."

She pushed some papers aside and removed the dishes from the tray. As she bent over the desk, Richard tilted his head slightly, taking in all the angles, all the swells. "I mean this is rather . . . alluring. Don't you think?"

"I never asked him to come, Richard. I can't worry about what I wear every second."

"So what, then, this is to punish me? You're going to strut around under his nose like this until . . ."

She stepped back and waved a finger at him. "That's your sick imagination, not mine."

"Is it?"

"Oh, please. You always used to fantasize about me with other men, make me tell you all my old stories."

"Mmm, that's right," he murmured, nodding thoughtfully. "And there was no dearth of material, if I remember correctly."

Sometimes in the past, when he was fully aroused, it had actually seemed like a good idea, her being with another man in his view, but the notion always dissolved upon orgasm. Yet the desire had nagged at him his entire life, had been a recurring, albeit hypothetical, motif in their lovemaking. This had never failed to trouble him. Where do these strange sexual tics come from? he'd wondered. Was this some backhanded nod to homosexuality? Or perhaps something else? Foucault had convinced him of a universal masochism; perhaps this was simply the way he liked his served.

"Anyway, you know I would never actually *want* you to be with anyone," he stated.

"That's not what you've said," she answered.

He looked slightly nervous. "Oh, in the heat of the moment, sure, I say things, but—"

"Sometimes after," she said. "We talked quite frankly about this years ago, Richard. We even made plans once, if you remember. We just never followed through."

Plans? Richard remembered the scenario she was referring to, some neighbor back in the New York days, a handsome but rather dull bachelor who lived in the apartment below them. Convinced he was no threat, Richard had hinted to Meryl of some sort of discreet interlude, had talked it up in the form of a joke. Intimating that it would be okay. But there were no *plans*. He waved his hand now in dismissal. "Just talk," he said. "Verbal foreplay."

Meryl pressed her thighs to the edge of the desk. "I was willing," she said.

Richard sipped anxiously at his iced tea, drinking more than he wanted.

"Do you ever wish we had?" he asked.

She shrugged. "It seemed to excite you so much."

"Oh, I see," he began ironically, "so you would have done it for *me*." As usual, he found this talk both highly erotic and extremely worrisome.

"Believe it or not, Richard, there was a time when I would have done just about anything for you."

"But no more."

She paused for a second, furrowing her brow in a tender scold. "Would it matter?" she asked.

Ouch, low blow. Maybe he should take some of those goddamned Chinese herbs still left in the cabinet, guaranteed to give him enough of an erection to fuck that sad smirk off her face.

She poured out some more iced tea for him. "I think that's one of the reasons Kyle's here, if you really want to know," she said.

Richard looked stunned, which only served to annoy her.

"Oh, come on," she said, "you don't see the dynamic here? You're impotent, I'm frustrated as hell, and you bring Henry Miller's grandson here for the summer. It had to be what you wanted. You created the situation yourself."

Richard immediately arched upward in his chair. "So, what then?" he asked excitedly. "You're fucking him? Is that it?"

"Would that be so incredible?" she asked. "You bring this young guy in here for a summer without even asking me. So I have an affair with him. Classic passive-aggressive, though it'd be pretty damned justified if you ask me."

Richard's pulse began to pound. He looked up at her, searching for some hint in her expression. Adulterer or no? Then he suddenly abandoned the search. Strange, he thought, but as much as the idea of an affair frightened him, another part of him almost wished it were true. It was a desire completely devoid of fantasy or eroticism. Rather, it was that some cool, detached part of him longed for change, for some mad drama to enter his life, to strike him at the heart of his complacency. He had taken his wife for granted for too long, he knew. He desperately needed to miss Meryl, for something to *almost* come between them. Secretly he longed for a visceral battle over love, something in which he might prove chivalrous. To feel pain, if that was the only way, but to feel *something*. Anything.

And then this feeling too passed, and the reality of loss struck him flush in the center of his chest.

"It would kill me," Richard said then with quick matter-of-factness. "I mean, literally kill me. I swear it."

"Well, I'm not having an affair with him," Meryl said finally. "Of course I'm not. Don't be ridiculous."

Richard's head seemed to droop a few inches—from relief, from disappointment. He reached out and pulled her in by the waist, resting his head against the smooth curve of her belly. "What's going on here?" he said, with some desperation. "What's *wrong* with us? I love you so much. Don't you know that?"

Her hands went to stroke his head but pulled back.

"I suppose so," she said.

"It's just . . . I don't know what's happening lately. The way we talk to each other. It's terrible."

"I hate it too."

She kissed the top of his head, lightly stroking his gray hair. A warm droplet trickled into her navel.

"I want to make love to you so badly, Meryl, you don't know." His voice was on the edge of cracking. "I don't know what to do, I . . . *you're so beautiful.*"

"It's okay," she said, stroking his head, more maternal than loving.

"The most beautiful thing."

They stayed like this for a few minutes. Richard's tears never quite came. The one in her navel soon evaporated. Finally Meryl announced she had to go. She was going shopping, she said. Before stepping out, though, she pointed to the stack on his desk that was Kyle's novel.

"How is it, by the way?"

Richard flipped the corners of some of the pages. "Painfully good," he said, shaking his head. "Quite amazing, actually. Best book in ten years." He looked up with a crooked smile. "The little fuck."

Meryl tilted her head, regarding him sadly.

"What?" he asked.

"I don't know." She looked around. "It just doesn't seem fair somehow. You know?"

Richard grinned wanly. He knew all right, had thought of it thousands of times himself. How *he*, Whitehurst, should've been the one. How it wasn't fair that he could struggle so long for so little, while some rake comes along, eight years idle, and finally decides to tap a few keys one summer, only to shit a golden egg.

As an opinion, Richard thought, it was overly simple, utterly naïve. And heartbreakingly true.

"Fair's got nothing to do with it," he said.

9

Kerry, meanwhile, was at the helm of the Bronco, singing along with the radio, head bobbing to the beat.

Home was not on the horizon, Kyle could see. They were definitely taking a little detour.

Her strength was back, he noticed. No doubt about it. She was shaking and pulling on the steering wheel, spanking it with her palm, trying to rip it from the column because there were no drugs left in the Hamptons.

"Three days I'm driving around," she said, "and I can't find a fucking aspirin."

Kyle wasn't exactly sure where they were, everything was whipping by him so fast. He guessed it was somewhere just north of East Hampton, possibly in the Springs. The idea, apparently, was to pull into convenience-store parking lots, keeping an eye out for shifty teenagers.

"I wish high school was still in session," she said longingly. "That's where you really clean up."

They pulled up to a general store that looked like a toy model of quaint, then swung around back. What exactly were they looking for? he wanted to know. Burnouts leaning against old cars? Tattooed loafers with goodies in their pockets? Fat chance. All he could see here was a lot full of spiffy SUVs, and horsey women with legs as long as telephone poles clutching bags of sweet corn.

It had changed since she'd gone, she told him. You used to be able to find some snort out here; all the bartenders carried it. A little E from the bouncer. Now it was Hollywood East. Clean and lean. All her old druggy friends were forming Internet companies or trading stocks or working on an "independent" film—or all three at once. And you had to be healthy. They were sick with health, she said. Nobody even got a tan anymore.

"You buncha mummies!" Kerry shouted out the window.

Kyle slid down in his seat.

"C'mon, Clayton. Where're the drugs? You're holdin' out on us, I know it."

"Who, me?" Kyle said. "No way."

"What about your book?" she said, pounding again on the wheel. "The cocaine. The druggy would-be writer."

"That was the other one," he said. "I'm the booze guy."

"Really?" she asked. "*Charmed Life*? Somehow I remember drugs."

"No," he said, "that was *you*."

"Okay, all right," Kerry said. Out of her hip, as if it were a six-shooter, she pulled a pint bottle of blackberry brandy and offered it to Kyle.

How sixth-grade, he thought, waving her off.

"Actually, I'm more of a top-shelf kinda guy myself."

"Well, 'scuse me," she said, taking a plug.

He had met her once before. It was a couple of years ago now, her first exhibition. Kyle had gone simply for the Whitehurst name. The show's preview in the *Voice* never mentioned her father, but he knew Richard's life well enough, knew he had a daughter named Kerry around her age and so on. It was worth a shot. Call it a study in the progeny of genius. He went to see if there would be any of the same magic of her father, any of the same purity and splendor.

In a nutshell, there wasn't. Not to say she wasn't talented, but what he'd been expecting was budding young work in a classical mode. Instead he got Duchamp meets Patti Smith.

It was on a hot night in June. The gallery was in Williamsburg. Warm white wine in paper cups and no air-conditioning. These inconveniences only seemed to highlight the aggressiveness of Kerry's work. Much of her "art," Kyle discovered, was a middle finger to dear old Dad, theoretically speaking. It was political, pugnacious, vaguely psychedelic—everything Richard's work was not. In fact, her aesthetic was such the opposite of her father's that it *had* to be a reaction, a thumbing of the nose. *Look, Dad,* her work seemed to say, *your obsessions are archaic. Art has passed you by. You're a fucking dinosaur!* Another nail into the coffin in which he was already lying.

The only piece that made any direct reference to her father was also the most effective, at least for Kyle's money. It was called *The Writer.* In it, an empty chair was pulled up to a desk with a typewriter. Balls of crumpled-up paper were scattered across the desk and the floor. Also on the floor was a hand towel, looking crusty and stiff, the writer's dirty little secret. Above the desk—approximately where the writer's head would be—hovered an eyedropper attached to a string and a timer. Every twenty minutes or so it would let loose a few drops, the false tears bouncing sprightly off the keys. Pretty brutal, Kyle thought. The only mitigating touch was a piece of paper in the roller, upon which, with close inspection, a viewer could discern one sentence, repeated over and over: *I'm trying, I'm trying, I'm trying . . .*

As they pulled up to a traffic light, Kyle reminded her of the night they'd met.

Kerry crinkled her brow. It didn't seem to ring a bell. "I was a little trashed," she admitted. "What did we talk about?"

"Your work," he said. "I told you how I liked your piece *The Writer*. Then I mentioned your father, about how much I admired him. You told me a story about him."

"Which one? There're so many."

"The one about the note."

"Ah, yes," she said. "The famous note."

The story went that Richard was going into town for a walk and wanted to leave a note for his wife, who'd gone to the beach for the day. Though he sat down to write it, and though there was plenty of paper, and ink in the pen, the note never got written.

Kerry smiled now, remembering. "All he had to do," she said, "was write, 'Going for a walk, be back soon.' But no, of course he had to write the *perfect* note. Apparently he sat there for something close to an hour, revising it, doing different versions, never quite getting it right." She shook her head.

Wonderful, Kyle thought.

"Mom finally came home and found him at the table in this sea of crumpled notebook paper, looking discouraged. By then he'd given up on his walk. It was too late. He just stayed home." She shook her head in amazement. "Now, *that's* sick," she said. She seemed about to get angry with him, to let it get to her all over again, then decided to shrug it off. "Well, what can you do? That's him. That's my father."

The light changed and the Bronco sped through with a screech, only to run into thick traffic a few hundred feet beyond.

"You also told me that you didn't like his work," Kyle said.

Kerry made a sour face. "It's so *austere,* isn't it? So worked over. It's like he's got a cork up his ass."

"Pure," Kyle countered.

"*Pure,*" she repeated. "Pure artifice. So writerly," she added, bridling.

"Who do you like?"

"Miller," she answered. "Genet, his characters smelling their own farts under the sheets. Something real." She reached down and lowered the music, trying to think of more. "Céline, if I'm pissed, and I usually am. Colette on a rainy day. What about you?" she asked him. "What's your idea of a novel?"

He didn't even have to blink. "*Under the Volcano.*"

"Mmm," she said, as if his choice was equally predictable. "Poor Malcolm Lowry. Dad loves him, of course."

"Tragic life. A waste, really."

"Oh, yeah, well, Dad loves that sort of thing. The gestures of failure." She snuck a glance at Kyle. "I'm sure that's what he sees in you," she added.

Kyle bristled in his seat.

"Hey, don't get your back up, tough guy," she said. "That's a good thing. At least where my father's concerned. What're you looking like that for?"

"Well, what're you saying? Are you saying that I'm a failure?"

"Oh, c'mon, you must've heard this before. 'All great literature's about failure.' That's my father. That's the Whitehurst *credo,* for godsakes."

Kyle looked baffled, betrayed. Richard longed for success, couldn't hear enough about it. How could he equate greatness with failure? What the hell was she saying?

"I mean, this is Dad's whole schtick," continued Kerry. "He even has this theory about the novel. It's quite interesting actually. There's this phenomenon, he says, in American writing, whereby every great writer has had a father who was a failure."

Kyle's immediate reaction was that this was absurd. He was ready to laugh it off, call her crazy and be done with it. But then, because it came from Whitehurst, he decided to hear more.

"Go on."

"Well, it's born of the notion that there's this national obsession with success, and that a father's failure is unbearable to a son. So then he makes up for the father's disgrace by getting the biggest prize of all."

"The Great American Novel."

"The so-called. Yes."

Sensing a pith of truth, Kyle felt his head begin to spin. He thought of the names, the lives of the writers he knew so well: Melville, Hemingway, Fitzgerald, O'Neill, Faulkner . . . *Fuck,* he thought. Was there actually something to this?

Benji, Kyle suddenly thought. *Benji Clayton.*

Here it came, the image of his own father. Benjamin Clayton— Benji for short, though Kyle had always hated that, probably because it was so fitting. Insurance man, South Jersey/Pennsylvania circuit. Never a mover, never cut for "success." Perennially middle management, though customer complaints made his knees buckle. Eventually he ran back to sales with the rookies, where he could hide.

Looking back now—an impulse Kyle had stridently avoided—the young man could see in his life all the clichéd trappings of rebellion, all the obvious confluences of nature and nurture. *Of course* Benjamin's son would move to New York, write a terribly smart first novel. A drinker like his father, but strictly "a top-shelf guy," an oenophile at twenty-five. Out in the New York night, a hungry lion, voracious for experience, the inside track.

Benji's kid. Anything but the safe, anything but the provincial.

When he was finally out on his own, the cord to his father was slowly but irreversibly cut, a ten-year project of rejection facilitated by the death of his mother. They spoke rarely, and almost without complaint, the father's expectations of a relationship gradually disappearing. By the end, Benjamin Clayton had been excised like a tumor.

Still, a kind of torch was being carried. Yes, Kyle thought, if my father only knew. When, for example, the son had achieved success for himself—a phenomenal success—he'd trashed it, called it bogus. Success was wicked, corrupt. It had to be; it had rejected the father. Like Devon Schiff had said, all Kyle's heroes were failures.

"What did you mean before when you said it's what he sees in me?" he now asked Kerry. In all his talks with Richard, he'd never discussed his father. Or had Richard just assumed?

They entered the Sag Harbor high school parking lot. Kerry parked diagonally, taking up two spaces, then cut the engine. She looked down at her watch, apparently waiting for someone.

"You play with failure," she began. "You're not afraid to be impulsive, or, may I say, even a little foolish sometimes. You strike it big and then disappear. It intrigues him."

"Maybe I'm just a lazy sack o' shit?"

"Could be. Like I said, it's the gestures that my father admires. There's definitely a superficial quality to this whole thing. He admires the drama that follows you, Kyle, the hostility. To be notorious was always my father's dream." Kerry checked her watch again.

"He admires you. He really does. And on top of everything else, he's incredibly fond of you, though he'd never say it."

Kyle tried to repress the beginnings of a smile.

"He doesn't get what you see in the Trebelaines, though," she continued. "I think he's smarting over that. He doesn't care much for Arthur, deep down."

"I thought they were friends."

She shook her head. "It's more like habit by now, they've known each other so long. Dad likes being around the legend, Arthur likes being around the artist." She took another sip of brandy. "I don't know if you've read any of Trebelaine's work, Kyle, but it's really mediocre. They're movie treatments, those books."

Kerry looked toward the parking-lot entrance, then slapped the steering column in disgust. Somebody was late, Kyle realized. A pharmacist, apparently, one who delivered.

"I wonder why they're both courting me like they do." The question had been gnawing at him recently. "You have any idea?"

"What?"

"Your father and Arthur," he said. "It's like they're fighting over me or something, hammering at me with their advice. I guess I should be flattered, but—I can't figure out what they want."

She stretched out her legs, eyes widening at him with incredulity.

"You don't know?"

Kyle waited.

She punched him lightly on the arm. For his shortsightedness, apparently, his naïveté.

"The *future,* dummy," she said. "These are old men. They want to make you up in their own image, have someone carry on their vision when they're through. You're the big white hope."

A HALF HOUR LATER they were still waiting. Kerry slouched in her seat, her feet up on the dash. For a rebel she didn't seem to mind too much the spaciousness of Daddy-O's car. She began to yawn and leaned her head against Kyle's shoulder. Apparently finding this uncomfortable, she scooted her butt against the driver's-side door and laid her head on his lap.

Oh, no, Kyle thought. No way.

"I'm tired," she cooed.

"Kerry . . ."

"If you see a white Honda, let me know, okay?"

"Kerry, you can't . . . you can't be down there."

"What? I just want to sleep."

She fidgeted, finally resting her ear on the zipper of his shorts. What was she doing? What was she listening for?

"You *can't* sleep. We have to get home. I have to get back to work. I have a fucking *deadline*."

"I'm tired," she said, groggily. "The brandy . . ."

"Why don't you sit up. I'll drive."

"You can't drive," she said.

It was true, they'd taken away his license a while back. Long story.

"Shit," he said.

"Don't be mad."

The clock on the dash said four-thirty. The day was almost done. He still had to touch a few things up for Trevor tomorrow. There was a lot to do, goddamn it.

"I'll tell you a story, how's that?" Kerry said.

Kyle exhaled in disdain.

"It's something you should know, Kyle," she said, her voice drowsy. "Something you'd be interested in."

"All right, fine. Whatever." What the hell choice do I have? he thought.

"Arthur tried to fuck me once."

He looked down at her, wanting to see her face. To see the lie that was in her eyes.

"Bullshit."

"I'm telling you."

"When?"

"I was seventeen."

"Get out of here."

No, he wasn't buying this one. She was probably stoned at the time. The figment of a highly spiked imagination.

"You think I'd lie about this?"

Of course, it wasn't impossible. Such things happened all the time. Still, *Arthur Trebelaine*? The man could have an affair with anybody he wanted. It didn't make sense.

"I went over to swim in their pool. I'd been doing that since I was a kid. I guess this time Patty left after I got there. Anyway, Blockhead eventually comes out and sits on the diving board, just watching me, drinking something and smoking that fat fucking cigar he always smokes. It was creepy. So I'm like, *Gross, time to leave.* Soon as I get out of the pool he just comes up and grabs me, tries to drag me into the pool house. He had me by the hair, that motherfucker."

"So what did you do?"

"What did I do? I kneed him in the balls, that's what I did. I took him *down*, that cocksucker. He fell like a water buffalo. After that I just ran, I took off."

Seventeen years old. Richard's *daughter*. No, it was ridiculous, Kyle thought. Even, dare he say, a fantasy?

"Do you know, even after I'd groined the bastard, he was still smoking that cigar? As I'm leaving I look back to see if he's up, you know, see if he's coming for me, and all I can make out is him on his knees, puffs of smoke all around his fat head. I don't know why, but that really pissed me off more than anything. I mean here the guy tries to rape me, I put his testes up in his throat, and he still manages to keep puffing away like it's teatime."

"Your dad doesn't know?" Kyle asked, just playing along now.

"*No*. And don't you ever mention it." She turned her head, facing up at him from his lap. "I mean, it's not like I'm traumatized or any-thing. I've just about forgotten about it. In fact, no, you know what, it never happened. Forget I ever told you. Promise me."

Kyle said that he would. Easy enough request.

"I wonder why you bothered to mention it."

"He's trying to influence you, that's why," she said, wiggling her head, getting comfortable again. "You probably worship him. A lot of young guys do."

"You're a debunker of myths then, is that it?"

"Look," she said, "why are you out here?"

"To write."

"No, you could do that anywhere. That's only part of it. You're out here looking for *direction*, Kyle. You're trying to figure out what kind of writer you're going to be, what kind of man."

"So forget Arthur then, be more like your father. Is that the mes-sage?"

"Jesus, no," she implored. "No, don't be like either of them." She laughed at the thought. "I'm just trying to level the playing field a lit-tle, that's all. My father's not much on self-promotion."

She turned her head, cheek now resting again on his crotch. Didn't feel too bad, Kyle thought. Man. It had been a long, long time.

Then, perhaps feeling his excitement, she said, without looking at him, "You can fuck me, you know. Actually, I'm a little insulted you haven't tried yet."

No way, Kyle thought; out of the question. He had a rule, one harking back to his teenage years: Never sleep with anyone crazier than yourself. It was a good rule, especially since it had yet to elimi-nate a single sexual partner—until today, that is.

She began to rub him. "Or I can just suck it if you want," she said.

He shimmied in his seat, mostly in embarrassment; he had a full-on erection, this being the first time this summer anyone had touched his poor peter besides himself. He almost didn't believe it was happening. Didn't she know he was a bum, a lout, a loser? Hell, he thought, that was probably the point.

She slipped her hand inside his shorts, pushing aside his underwear.

"Hey, big boy," she said jokingly.

Kyle suppressed a moan, then put his hand down and ended it.

"What's wrong?" she asked.

He shook his head, then looked away. She tried again, and again Kyle put his hand down to stop her. "Kerry," he said dissuadingly.

"What?" She was getting upset. "I can't believe this."

She tried once more, and was rejected for the third time. Propping herself up on her elbows, she complained, "I can't *believe* this. I'm actually getting dick-blocked! Why not, Kyle?" she asked, her face just a few inches from his.

He shrugged. He didn't know why. This wasn't like him, wasn't at all like Kyle Clayton. But his hand kept up its defense.

"Ugh, God, I *hate* this place!" Kerry exclaimed. She let out a bellow of frustration. "I can't get high, I can't get laid, I can't even give a blow job out here, for crying out loud. For *free*!" As she lay back down she slammed her head on Kyle's lap, causing him to wince. "Wake me if my dealer comes. You can at least do that, can't you?"

After a few minutes she fell asleep. Then, finally, a white Honda entered the parking lot and pulled right up alongside the Bronco. Kyle reached over to the driver's-side window and rolled it down.

"Where is she?" the man asked. He had a bandanna over his bald spot and a spotty beard that attempted to obscure a severe case of acne.

Kyle looked down. Kerry was out cold. She looked quite peaceful, actually, in her repose. She hadn't known much tranquility lately, he figured, but she'd found some here, in his lap, under the trees of her old school yard. She looked almost like a little girl again.

"Who?" Kyle asked.

"Kerry," the man said impatiently.

"Kerry?"

"You don't know Kerry?"

The man was looking at the Bronco, trying to see if someone was in back.

"Why'd you roll your window down?" the man asked.

"You drove right up, I thought maybe I knew you." Kyle played indignant. "What do you want?"

They glared at each other. All he heard was Kerry's breathing and the sound of matches being played on the distant tennis courts.

"Shit," the man said finally. He glared at Kyle one last time, then put the car in gear and putted off.

Beneath him, Kerry began to stir. "Wha . . . who'sat?" she said, then mumbled something.

"Shhh, nothing," he said.

Kyle ran a hand through her oily hair, whispering to her that everything was fine, just fine. She laid her head down again and fell back asleep. Then, softly as possible, he eased the seat back, shifting to get comfortable.

It was going to be a while.

10

The next day Kyle arrived at Bobby Van's in Bridgehampton a half hour early. He was hoping Trevor might be early and he could get this meeting out of the way, be back at his desk by one or so. He was so close now. Another three weeks perhaps and he would have a working first draft. But the distractions were closing in. There was Kerry to contend with, Richard's jealousy of Arthur, and now Trevor was out here to bust his balls. Under his arm Kyle carried a copy of his manuscript, as requested. He'd worked through the night to get it ready.

The restaurant was packed. The town was really filling up now that August was here. Bobby Van's had had a facelift a few years ago, and the changes reflected the times. So did the customers. Today, in fact, was quintessential "New" Hamptons. A bustling assortment of pastel- and khaki-clad busybodies, wired for sound, ringing and buzzing and beeping away. It was a symphony of modern electronics. Kyle didn't understand it. Here they were, Sunday afternoon, on arguably the most beautiful spit of land in the Northern Hemisphere, and all they could think to do was conduct business, get a jump on the Monday-morning rush, cell-phone and laptop themselves through their egg-white omelettes and Kahlúa french toast.

How surprised Kyle was to then discover an anomaly in the crowd. He was seated in the back by himself, Sunday *Times* strewn across the table. He wore faded corduroy trousers, ripped canvas boating shoes with no socks, and a plain white dress shirt. Seeing the younger man heading for his table, he raised the *Book Review* in front of him, as if to prove the obvious, the final truth once and for all.

"Kyle, goddamn it, when are you going to write a new novel? Everything's gone to hell." He shook his head disgustedly.

His name was Rollie McIntyre, and Kyle wanted to lean down and kiss him on his wrinkled, liver-spotted forehead. Rollie was the displaced president of Brownstone and Company and, as many believed, one of the last champions of what was once known as literature. This was the man who'd believed in Kyle way back when, who had published *Charmed Life* with blind enthusiasm, who had tendered the young writer an advance of a little over a hundred thousand toward a novel for which Kyle hadn't yet fired a single synapse. Although he had wanted to see another Clayton book as much as anyone, he had assured the young writer that it was fine if he wasn't yet ready to produce (much to Larry Wabzug's dismay) even after the third, fourth, then fifth year had passed. Wait till it comes, he'd said. You're not a factory. Uncanny forbearance from a publisher, obviously, but then Kyle Clayton had that kind of luck, didn't he, had managed to find extraordinary people who would tolerate him, who would take him in and indulge him, not unlike a son.

"Sit down," Rollie said. "Sit down, my boy."

Kyle bent over and gave him a hug. "I've been meaning to call you."

McIntyre shook him off, immediately dismissed the apology, but Kyle was suddenly pierced by guilt. After all his support over the years, the friendship, the loans, Kyle somehow hadn't found five minutes to pick up the phone and commiserate with Rollie McIntyre after he'd been unceremoniously shit-canned eight months ago. Shame on you, Kyle thought to himself now.

"No," Kyle asserted. "There's no excuse."

"Forget it. You were busy. You were writing again!" Seeming genuinely excited, Rollie pointed to the stack of papers under Kyle's arm.

Kyle nodded modestly.

"Good for you, my boy. Good for everyone."

Kyle took a seat. When the waitress approached, he ordered a Virgin Mary—a detail Rollie acknowledged with covert interest.

"I forgot you had a place out here," Kyle said.

"Sure, you know me, the high life." Rollie's bright, disarming smile had changed, Kyle noticed, since he'd last seen him. That boyish grin was a little cracked these days, coming out of the side of his mouth now, as if it had been cut in half. "Actually I got in twenty-five years ago, back when it was still reasonable. But now? Forget it. I can't buy underwear in this goddamned place."

Rollie took a sip of coffee. Kyle noticed he wasn't eating anything. "What are you up to?" he asked.

"Currently unemployed," Rollie answered with forced good cheer. "I may just retire, say the hell with it. I'm sixty-six this year, you know."

"That's still young," Kyle countered, suddenly realizing how ridiculous that sounded. "For books, I mean," he amended. "And anyway, we need you out there."

"Actually, no," Rollie said. "As it turns out, you don't." Kyle seemed about to protest, but Rollie cut him off. "I've inquired, Kyle, believe me. My talents, it seems, are not in demand. But then, hell, I can't really blame anybody. My track record isn't exactly exemplary. Who in their right mind would hire a publisher who's lost money thirty years in a row?" The cracked smile returned.

"But the books you've published," Kyle said. "Your list of authors . . ."

Rollie rolled his eyes with supreme weariness. Clearly he was tired of the argument, the "value" of literature and so on. Attrition had taken its toll. It was sad but true: After decades of conflict and struggle, the bottom line finally began to make sense to Rollie McIntyre.

"Look, I had a nice run," he said, "but it's over now. For years we got away with things at Brownstone that were unprecedented, beyond the pale—all because it was chic to like good books. Even if you didn't read them, books meant something."

"The movies," Kyle said, trying to help. He knew Rollie had always hated the movies.

"Hell yes," said the older man. "You go to a dinner party now and that's all anybody wants to talk about. Movies, movies, movies. God forbid you mention a serious book. People look at you like you're nuts, the practitioner of some arcane obsession. And this is in New York, Kyle. What's happened to our wonderful city?"

Though Kyle had heard this routine a million times, he knew he owed it to the man, to let him rant a little, blow off some steam.

"And then the German buyout didn't help," Clayton offered generously.

Rollie caught the pass midstride and headed toward the end zone.

"That's the problem with foreign acquisitions," he began. "The American stockholders needed Brownstone, to brag to their friends, to look at themselves in the mirror. But the Germans? They could care less. They're too far removed. You think their friends in Bonn care if they're carrying a boutique publishing house back in New York? No, it's over, Kyle. The kind of publishing I used to do is finished."

Rollie waved his hand, dismissing the unseen enemy, then signaled the waitress for more coffee. "But listen to me," he said, "here I am, complaining again, when it just doesn't bother me anymore. It really doesn't. In fact, I don't know what could be more boring."

Kyle didn't believe him for a second.

The waitress poured Rollie some more petrol. As he reached for the cup, Kyle noticed his friend's hands looked a little thin. He had lost weight.

Rollie hoisted his cup toward Kyle's manuscript.

"Very exciting," he said. "Is it finished?"

"Close," Kyle said.

"Well?" Rollie nudged the young man. "How do you feel about it? Do we have a winner here, or what?"

"It's hard to tell." Kyle remained excited about the work, but he considered too much optimism to be bad luck.

"Has anybody looked at it yet?"

"Actually, Richard Whitehurst has taken a peek. He seemed enthusiastic."

"Whitehurst, eh?"

"Yes," Kyle said, proud but simultaneously embarrassed. He was only beginning to realize how unlikely his relationship with Richard appeared to others. The Laurel and Hardy of literature. "We've become friends, strangely enough. I've been invited to his house for the summer."

Rollie looked impressed.

Kyle glanced around, making sure Trevor hadn't arrived yet.

"By the way, you know those loans you gave me?"

"The money?"

"Yes."

"Those weren't loans, Kyle. That was an advance. There's a difference."

Kyle smiled balefully. "Well, yeah, try telling David Trevor that. He's holding them to my head like a gun. Have you met this prick?"

Rollie's eyes moved off at the mention of the name. "Never met him," he said, "but someone did bring me a picture of him my last week at Brownstone." He smiled broadly now, the old, shining McIntyre grin. "We used it as a dartboard," he said with a laugh. "Unfortunate-looking fellow."

Here was perhaps Rollie McIntyre's one vanity, his one true conceit: He had been offhandedly attractive in his day. There were many affairs, whispered rumors in the office. This was insignificant, of course, except to suggest Rollie's charm, such as it had been, many moons ago. That Rollie was homosexual was either forgotten or deemed irrelevant—which, for its time, was rather remarkable. Unless, of course, you'd met him. He'd had dignity, a certain savoir faire. There was nobody like him left.

"Trevor's furious with me," he said with a mischievous glint, "because I haven't cleaned my office out yet. My desk, all my files, everything's just piled up in some corner there, staring at him day after day. I'm sure it's driving him crazy."

"He won't get rid of it?"

"They won't let him! Isn't that a hoot?" Rollie slapped the top of Kyle's hand with genuine mirth. "Some of the old stockholders still have a few shares, you know. Apparently they were uneasy about my firing. They think I'm so busted up I can't bear to take my stuff out, and at the same time they think it's sentimental for me, so they won't let Trevor touch it. Oh, well," he said, with a triumphant shrug. "Noblesse oblige."

Rollie shifted in his seat, resuming a half grin. Kyle wasn't fooled.

If one half of the former publisher's face was smiling, the other half looked on the verge of collapse. He suspected that for all Rollie's show of indifference, a few well-chosen words could easily propel the sentimental man into hysterics. If they were somewhere private, Kyle might have encouraged such a deluge. But not here. This was no place for release, especially since Rollie probably viewed today's patrons as in some way responsible for his undoing.

No, Rollie had his dignity, and he would have to hold on to as much of it as he could. He would be needing it.

"Gentlemen," greeted a slithering voice above them.

It was Trevor, looking down with amber-tinted sunglasses, his scorched nose spearheading the doughy face. He had on a double-breasted suit, pinstriped, with an avocado-colored shirt underneath. He smiled at them, and a baby at a nearby table suddenly began to cry.

Trevor put a hand out to Rollie. With his usual grace, Rollie stood and gave it a strong shake.

"Let me tell you something right off, Clayton," Trevor announced. "This man's a prince, okay? An angel." The firmness of this proclamation was quite astonishing, Kyle thought, given that he and said gentleman had never met. "An absolute bloody saint. Best man in the damned business, hands down."

"Yes," Kyle agreed. "He is."

He watched Trevor's eyebrows rise above the rims of his sunglasses as the manuscript caught his sight. He turned to Rollie.

"Have you read it?" he asked him.

The tone was unassuming, but surely the other two men understood the question's double edge. If Rollie *had* read it, Trevor would want an insight into his opinion, highly regarded as it was. Second, Trevor would want to know *why* the displaced publisher had been allowed to see it first, and to what end, and didn't he have some fucking nerve.

"I haven't yet had the pleasure, but I look forward to reading it with great interest," Rollie said encouragingly. "I'm sure Brownstone will do a wonderful job with it."

Yes, a prince, Kyle thought.

How could you top that? A highly uncomfortable silence ensued, one that Kyle, the axis, did nothing to mitigate. No, he thought, let Trevor eat it awhile—for he assumed the man must be in a state of extreme anxiety, forced as he was to stand before his better. A victim of invidious comparison. *Let him wallow, the bastard.*

Finally, when both men were glaring at him for release, Kyle provided a segue.

"We should get to work," he said to Trevor.

"Yes, yes," the two rivals answered in unison.

"And by the way," Rollie added, standing up to say good-bye, "my apologies for that mess in your office." The Count was silent. "I've been remiss. I'll have it out by the end of the month."

Amazing, Kyle thought. Instead of confrontation, Rollie had opted for gallantry. He must have realized that keeping his things in Trevor's office was picayune, a petty revenge. Trevor hadn't even been the one to fire him, come to think of it; the Germans had taken care of that. Rollie had decided to let it die.

As they walked away, Trevor shook his head.

"He's not much, is he?"

"What? Who?" Kyle asked, looking around, not comprehending who he could be talking about.

"Him," Trevor said, gesturing back to Rollie. "You hear all these stories at Brownstone. Rollie McIntyre this, Rollie McIntyre that. I expected more." He shrugged. "But then, I suppose I am a bit intimidating."

Kyle didn't know what to say. His emotions spasmed out in a sort of choked surprise.

"Maybe he was embarrassed," Trevor said, then added, with a superior titter, "I know I would be."

11

Meryl lay on the cool sheets, her nose filled with the familiar fragrance of pine, cedar, and Atlantic sea salt. She was naked except for a pair of beach sandals and the generous pool of semen that had filled and then overflowed her deep-set navel.

"Want a wipe?"

"No, leave it," Meryl said softly. "I want to feel it." It had been so long.

They were at a modest beachside motel in Montauk. It was late summer, their sixth coupling. Officially, the affair had started three weeks ago, though it had obviously been percolating for some months. After initial trepidation, Meryl was quite surprised to find how quickly her guilt had ebbed. In fact, there had been very little shame at all. After twenty-five years of marriage this was the first time she had ever been unfaithful, yet it didn't feel like a betrayal. The specter of Richard, which she had assumed would haunt her in her adultery, had never arrived. It frightened her how natural it felt. How just.

Ironically, it was this very lack of guilt that had brought her pain, for it was in this that many of the illusions about marriage and love that she had believed in for so long had begun to crumble. These were not sacred things, she felt now, but rather the flimsiest of arrangements, easily subject to whims, lusts, selfishness. The notion that there was tremendous pleasure to be found in adultery, and that there was perhaps no reason to have waited this long, broke off a piece of her heart.

Could this really be so? she wondered. Could fidelity have been the lie?

Strangely enough, she despised her lover. Next to her husband, he was a chump, a counterfeit. That he would do this to Richard, his friend, made her mildly nauseous. Paradoxically, this only intensified her pleasure. In all her youth, in all her rabid, almost obsessive promiscuity, she had never enjoyed so much satisfaction.

We are, she thought, quite despicable creatures. Entirely and completely. Without exception.

"You should leave him, you know." He stood up and walked over to the chair where the towel was. "He treats you like the help."

"He's just selfish," she said. "He loves me."

"Just selfish? Selfish sucks."

"And you're not?" She laughed softly to herself.

"You have to live, Meryl. You have to live your life. You're not getting any younger."

She watched him wipe himself and begin to dress. Was he hinting that they should be together? No, that would be too difficult. Too many feathers would be ruffled, the literary peacocks all astrut. And anyway, he didn't have the mettle to do it the right way.

"It would kill him," she said, "in case you care."

He didn't answer. He dressed quickly, intermittently looking down at his watch. He was suffering over this, she knew; at least there was that. The guilt was much worse for him, though it certainly had not marred his performance. His reputation was right on. He fucked like a world champion.

"We should probably stop this."

"But we won't," she said wearily.

"Better pretend that you don't like me then."

His smile was vile to her, a turd bent upward at the corners.

"I'll try," she answered.

WHEN AT LAST he was gone, she picked up the bottle of Chardonnay from the ice bucket and poured herself another glass. Perhaps as an excuse to perpetuate the minor wine addiction to which she'd lately succumbed, she had begun to consider the alcohol's buzz as medicinal, tending, as it did, to dull the tinnitus that had been aggravated since the start of their affair. He liked to be rough with her, which was perfectly amenable to Meryl. Bedroom humiliations suited her. Afterward, though, there was the sonorous ringing, a lifelong bane that had become almost unbearably acute under her new lover's tutelage.

Slipping on a robe, Meryl stepped out onto the short balcony, setting her wineglass down on the glass tabletop, bottle at her feet. She watched a fishing boat tack across the line of blue, and after another hearty sip she began to think of her father. How banal it was, she thought, how clichéd to know that he'd brought this on, this Sadean bent of hers. You didn't need four years of med school to figure out that her dad's thrashings had had quite an effect. The unprovoked backhands, the books ripped out of the lap and brought down with repetitious fury. Though real estate had made him filthy rich, he was highly uneducated, and her interest in books pissed him off in a way she could never quite explain. He'd make a paddle out of them, chasing her around the study. Or bring the binding down on her head like a hammer, in which case there was no running at all.

How bizarre, Meryl thought now, rubbing her ear, how ironic that she would seek out this same treatment years later. At what point had the pain and humiliation of those years translated themselves to pleasure? What kind of sick fucking life was this anyway?

She sipped the Chardonnay.

Of course she'd triumphed in the end. She'd gotten her revenge. The plan had been for her to go to New York "if she must," play at publishing for a few years, and then marry wisely. Her father's ideal, of course, was someone with deep pockets. Failing that, the gentleman should at least be elegant, someone with social éclat. A man who could offer a wealthy young coquette some incursion into a grand New York life.

Instead, she'd found Richard. A writer, of all things, and an indigent one at that. An *artist,* for godsakes. Her father had nearly delivered twins at the news that they were engaged.

It was no accident, of course. She'd found him because she was looking, she could see that now. She'd taken George Eliot over the head as a girl, and had come back swinging ten years later with Richard Whitehurst. The hopelessly unemployable Richard, complete with patches on his elbows and an immigrant's teeth.

A punishment was induced. Her trust fund, she'd learned, had been cut in half just before their wedding. But Meryl had invested wisely, tripling her father's gelded offering in less than a decade. For a family that had hardly worked a day in their lives, the Whitehursts lived well enough.

Her father had finally died five years ago, at seventy-nine. And with his passing came for Meryl a strange enervation, a sort of resignment. Did she miss her nemesis? She'd spent her life battling him, finding ways to circumvent his wishes. Taking on Richard was the first provocation. (Lazy, her father had said upon meeting him. A life-long project, that one.)

Now there was nobody left to take vengeance on, no one left to retaliate against. The battle was over. She had won.

Exactly where, then, she wondered—using her robe to finally wipe her lover's semen from her navel—did that leave Richard?

12

The hotel, which sat smack-dab in the center of Sag Harbor, had existed as a carriage house during the Revolutionary War. In its rooms lay an archaic mise-en-scène, preserved with unblemished finesse. In winter especially, Richard liked to come here by himself, huddle up with a good scotch, and imagine he was someone else, someone more beloved, more successful. A writer of another time.

Tonight, though, he came as himself, Richard Whitehurst, writer of small renown and dubious popularity, the hotel's restaurant being perhaps the one place in the world where he was actually recognized. In fact, a signed copy of *Sag Harbor Sonata* sat in a lighted bookcase in the lobby, and when Kyle and Richard passed the display as they entered, the younger man took a fresh stab at idolatry by telling Richard how he owned a first edition of every one of the writer's novels.

Whitehurst smiled with his usual weary self-effacement. "How kind you are to say so," he remarked as they hunkered up to the bar,

still half empty at this early hour. "But without dashing your enthusiasm, may I remind you that *all* my novels are first editions, by default.
I have yet in my career to enjoy a second printing."

Kyle flushed, mortified. How could he have been so stupid, he
wondered. Then he saw Richard suddenly break into a hearty chuckle.
He was only kidding, and this increased Kyle's admiration all the
more. Perhaps more than anyone he had ever met, Richard Whitehurst had the ability to see himself as mildly ridiculous, was humble
to a fault.

Kyle too started to laugh, and then things got just plain silly.

It was nearly dusk, one of those days in late August where a few
wisps of fall jump astride the wind. The town was full, and despite the
crowdedness of the stores, the lack of parking, and the general sense
of anxiety directly imported from Manhattan, there was a legitimate
air of excitement on the Island. Even the locals acknowledged it, sub-
mitting to its energy and nourishment. It was the dread of another
ending, the urgency of the last chance. Gone soon would be the lawn
games and Silver Queen corn. Gone the lazy hammock and vaults of
dappled-leaf sky. Another summer had passed. Can't believe it, can
you?

At the bar Richard's laughter seemed to portend a good mood, despite the fact he was feeling somewhat lassoed into this event, organized, as it was, by Arthur Trebelaine, the occasion the completion of
Kyle's novel—though the young man insisted it was merely a first
draft. The party was premature; it wasn't really *done,* he'd complained to Trebelaine, to no avail.

"Well, that's Arthur for you," Richard said. "Never heard of a second draft." The bartender approached, and Whitehurst turned to
Kyle. "Order modestly," he warned. "I have a feeling we're in for a
grand evening of showing off, a cavalcade of vulgar spending. You'll
want to be sober enough to enjoy it."

This happened every once in a while, Richard explained. Some Hollywood money would roll in and Arthur would host a dinner here and nearly clear out the wine cellar. He'd seen dinner bills of ten thousand dollars and more. Although it was quite generous, Whitehurst admitted, it was also a huge ego trip for Arthur, and you were obligated to hail the chieftain upon request.

"So don't feel indebted," Richard advised. "The dinner's really for him. And if he hands you the wine list, by all means, my boy, take him to the cleaners."

This would be a tense night for Kyle, with the triangle of Arthur, Richard, and himself together for the first time in months. Add in Meryl, Calamity Kerry, and, as was rumored, Larry Wabzug, and you had the ingredients for one hell of an evening.

As for Kyle and Richard's relationship, it had settled into a sort of middle ground of compromise and acceptance. Their mutual fascination, the initial spark between them, had ebbed. But their friendship, Whitehurst was pleased to discover, did have some legs. He could see now that Kyle's supposed "defection" to the Trebelaines had been exaggerated. Not much had really changed between them. The young man was still around most nights, conversations as strong as ever, their weekly evening swim never missed.

While Meryl had finally warmed to Kyle's presence, however slowly, Kerry seemed instantly taken with him, though it appeared that Kyle had not abused any trust within their unusual family life. And it was a sort of clan, wasn't it? Or so it felt to Richard on some recent evenings. Kyle and Kerry and Meryl at the table under the grape arbor, candelabra glowing, a Chopin nocturne wafting softly from the living room stereo, the mosquitoes dancing faithfully, the smell of sinsemilla faint on his daughter's breath. Family.

Today was bittersweet for Richard. Kyle would be moving on soon; he would do the revisions back in New York. It had been a good summer, an interesting summer, but it had not quite lived up to White-hurst's somewhat quixotic expectations. What he'd really wanted, he supposed, was for Kyle to have come over to his side entirely, to embrace the myth without exception. The whole Whitehurstian ethos of sublime recalcitrance, the banality of success. That Kyle had resisted this showed a firm resolve, a sturdy character, perhaps even a certain wisdom. But once again, Richard was left with a sense of supreme loneliness. All great writers have their disciples, he believed, their zealots to carry the torch. Young men had leapt to their death with the words of Hart Crane on their lips, or Baudelaire. Hemingway had to beat them off. Where, then, were his? His visions, his dreams, it seemed, were shared by no one. He was, as ever, alone.

These dim reflections were brightened suddenly by the enthusiastic waddle of a familiar figure through the hotel's front door—and smack into the maître d', who affixed the guest with a disapproving eye. The man apologized, repositioned his thick-bonded glasses, and stated his business: "A friend of Richard *White*hurst," he proclaimed with regal emphasis, as if this were a moniker of knee-rattling importance, the very dauphin of Sag Harbor.

His wrinkled Orchard Street suit did not exactly place this customer comfortably in the leitmotif of the room, nor did his aura of an almost comical lack of confidence (the South Claw being *not* the land of uncertainty or equivocation). The maître d' failed to find Mr. Wabzug in violation of any code, and so had no choice but to point him in the direction of the bar.

"You're still alive," Larry said to Richard, stepping back after a hearty embrace. He shook his head with feigned amazement. "You survived a summer with Kyle Clayton!"

The other two men laughed. Now Kyle found himself being stared at with a peculiar intensity.

"Oh, my Lord," Larry said.

"What?" asked Kyle.

Larry leaned in to his face, then backed away, his head zooming in and out. It was unnerving.

"What, Larry?"

"You look terrific!" he erupted. "Have you looked at yourself lately?" He turned to Whitehurst. "Look at this kid, Richard. Will you look at him?"

"I've seen him, Larry. He lives with me."

"Your eyes," Larry continued. "They're so clear. Your whole face. You look like the old Kyle Clayton. Handsome as a goddamned dog!"

Larry's face was electrified.

"Tell me about the kid's book," he said to Whitehurst. "Is it good? No, of course it's good. How good is it? Tell me. Tell me, tell me tell me."

Larry had had a lot of coffee, they could see. He was known to go on an occasional binge, drinking ten, sometimes twelve cups in a day.

Although he'd heard it before, Kyle too waited anxiously for Whitehurst's verdict. He had just handed him the ending a few days ago.

"It's terrific," Richard said. "Start to finish."

Under the bar, Kyle clenched his fist.

"But there's a complication," Whitehurst added.

"Well, Richard, it's always something, isn't it?" Larry murmured. He was speaking so fast he stumbled a bit, as if his lips couldn't catch up to his ideas. Talking just to talk. "Wouldn't be a book if there wasn't a problem. Book equals problems. You gotta problem? You're probably trying to publish a boo—"

"*Larry,*" Richard admonished.

"What?"

"Take it easy." Yes, he explained, there was a problem, a big problem. That's why the three of them were here, for godsakes. After hearing about Kyle's breakfast with Trevor, Richard had immediately contacted Larry, suggesting that the three of them meet an hour early at the bar. They had something big to discuss. A bad turn of events.

"So, all right, tell me," Larry said, in all his caffeined alacrity, "tellme tellme tellme."

Richard told Wabzug to get a drink first.

"A drink," Wabzug said, fixing his glasses. "Yes, yes. Why not, you know? Absolutely. Sure, hell, I worked hard today. Why not? Why not a nice dr—"

"Excuse me," Richard said to the bartender.

The barman approached, and Richard gestured to Wabzug.

"Irish coffee," Larry said.

Richard threw up his hands.

"And, if you don't mind, some pickles."

Kyle's recent meeting with David Trevor had gone as expected—which is to say, badly. Which is to say with his tongue surgically removed, his dignity set afire and then stamped out with turf spikes. With all kindness, support, and generosity seemingly removed from the argot of human companionship.

Here it was, in a nutshell: Kyle's new book (still untitled) was to be the "first of its kind," Trevor had announced. A "never-seen-before, groundbreaking revolutionary event."

"Okay," Kyle had replied, guardedly excited. "In what way?"

"The presentation," Trevor had said. "The *presentation*."

"Great," Kyle had said, expecting the worst. "In what way?"

"Wait, are you ready?" (Here Trevor had made an imaginary headline with his fingers.)

Kyle, lying, had said that he was.

Trevor had paused, allowing the excitement to mount.

"Advertisements!" he had at last exclaimed. (Or, Ad-*verd*-isments, as he pronounced Britishly, trying to give the word a palatable ring.)

"Advertisements?"

"Ad-*verd*-isments!"

"Great," Kyle said. "Where, in the papers? Television? That'll be expensive, but, hey, fuck it, it's your money—"

"No, no. In the book, lad. In the *book*!"

This "revolution," as it turned out, this groundbreaking gift to the publishing universe, was to present in the novel a string of glossy advertisements. *Ads, man!* Not indiscriminately like in a magazine, but clustered together, ever discreetly, in the middle. Full-blown, committee-tested images designed to create optimal anxiety toward ownership of certain key American products: KFC, ABC, DKNY, CNBC, WB, BK, SHIT. This was to be Brownstone's new "presentation," as designed by Trevor, and Kyle's book was to be the launch.

The Germans, apparently, were in a circle jerk of ecstasy. Genius, they'd said. Just ask David Trevor. He'd tell you so himself.

"Did you know, Kyle," the publisher continued, "that movies in Europe have commercials in the middle? They stop the movie halfway through, and there they are. Your novel will be very European in that respect. Very chic."

"But it's not a movie," Kyle said. "It's a book."

"*Ah,*" Trevor said, with impassioned relish. "Not yet."

THE ONLY PICKLES in the hotel's kitchen, as it turned out, were the tiny cornichons that accompanied the country pâté. Richard and Kyle waited patiently as Wabzug speared the infants with a drink stirrer and, with the bartender and a few flummoxed patrons looking on, dipped them into the whiskey-spiked blackness of his Irish coffee.

"A restaurant without decent-sized pickles," Larry said, chomping away unsatisfied. "This is amazing to me. Really, I find this absolutely fascinating."

"So, what do you think?" Kyle asked him. "Does Trevor have any recourse?"

"Oh, don't worry about that." Larry pulled a stray stem off a cornichon. "Launch, my ass. We withhold the manuscript until Trevor agrees to nix the ads. It'll blow over."

"Are you sure?" Kyle asked.

Wabzug looked agitated. "Look, he has no *book* yet. If he had the book, we'd be screwed, but we're okay. There's nothing to publish. We have leverage."

Kyle let forth a sudden *hrrumph*. He lowered his head.

"Kyle?" the agent said.

"He's got the book," the young man murmured at his shoes.

"Who?" Richard asked.

"Trevor. He's got the manuscript."

"No," Larry exclaimed. "No no no noooo."

It was true. Kyle was just supposed to show Trevor the work, to prove to him that it was almost done, but somehow, during that fateful brunch, Trevor had walked off with the manuscript. Had just picked it up and taken off. Of course, the meeting had been so incapacitating to Kyle, he had been in such a state of shock at the said "presentation," he hadn't noticed it was gone until the next day. It was incomplete—minus the ending—but nonetheless *gone*. Kyle was sick about it.

"Trevor said he'd publish it as is," he explained. "I called him the next morning, and that's what he said. I could send him the ending or he'd just publish it the way it was, he didn't care. I have a month, he said."

Larry speared yet another cornichon, bobbing it unmercifully into the Irish coffee. He looked at Richard; Richard looked at him. They'd known each other over thirty years. Larry did something with his eyes and Whitehurst nodded gravely.

"Not good," Richard said.

13

One by one, the Trebelaine guests began to congregate. Meryl arrived first, wearing a lemon sundress, her deep gardener's tan at its late-summer height. Kyle promptly ordered her a Chardonnay. Trey Kittles, a writer with *The Paris Review,* arrived shortly afterward. The magazine was getting ready for some anniversary or another, and as Arthur was to be the featured interview, Kittles had the supreme pleasure of following him, "one of the all-time greats," around for the weekend—an elaboration that knotted Richard's stomach, the *Review* being the one magazine he'd forever longed to appear in, the one in which he'd been conducting impromptu interviews in his head for his entire life.

"Sorry," Kittles said, after Richard had just introduced himself. "Didn't catch your name."

Through clenched teeth, Whitehurst reminded him.

Next came the young director of the movie version of Trebelaine's most recent novel, a one-hundred-million-dollar extravaganza, set to begin shooting next week in Kyoto. Christian was his name, a young man all of twenty-four, who on the basis of a video award had secured a three-picture deal with a major studio. He'd convinced the producers there that Trebelaine's epic love story, set in Japan during the Korean War, was the perfect first project for him, having so enjoyed *Sayonara* on the American Movie Classics cable channel, and himself having dated a Japanese girl once in junior high school.

To Kyle, though, this director was a smart and smashing addition to the party, given that alongside him came the film's supporting actress, an exquisite sparrow of a girl by the name of Tatiana.

Tatiana was Italian and twenty-three—too foreign probably, and a little long in the tooth for the major under-twenty demographic the distributors were hoping to secure. But Christian, ever brave, had urged the studio to take a chance on the aging thespian, citing a strong European following for her two previous films, and pointing out her superhuman nipples ("Tootsie Rolls," he'd called them), which would not only erect on request but were visible even through the thickest-ply army fatigues, which would be her costume as Nurse Maria.

Kyle, for his part, needed no convincing. He thought Italian and twenty-three just fine, thank you very much, and saw her as the perfect actress for the movie *he* had in mind—albeit a low-budget affair, and ready to shoot this very evening in a nearby motel, if she were available.

Greetings were made all around.

"Hiyahiyahiyahiya," Wabzug fired off to each new addition. Kyle offered his bar stool to Tatiana, who accepted with a becoming bashfulness. When she crossed her legs even the maritally pious Wabzug took a deep gulp.

But conversation lagged. Not a surprise, given the many handicaps. Richard and Meryl, for instance, hadn't been speaking to each other for some days. Then there was Wabzug, whose last cup of coffee had turned his lips into a jammed Gatling gun, and the limitations of Tatiana's English (*"How you say?"*), which kept Kyle busy as a dutiful translator.

It was Richard, finally, who broke the awful silence with a parley to the young director. He explained to Christian that he himself happened to be a novelist (a quick glance to the *Paris Review* rep), and not at all a devotee of the modern cinema, but that he did hold an enthusiastic regard for Bernardo Bertolucci's *The Conformist*. A sublime piece of art, Whitehurst admitted, showing a sweeping, almost painterly eye, and ecstatic sensuality. Richard graciously inquired whether a talented young director such as himself might be intimidated by Bertolucci's accomplishment, given that the film was made when Bernardo himself was just in his twenties.

To which the young director scratched his goatee and said, "Who?"

Once again, the Trebelaines were late. It was, of course, an old game, designed to provoke a longing in their guests, to make others feel privy to a company that was, if truth be told, slightly out of one's reach. Trey Kittles tried to assuage the group's silent irritation by explaining that Arthur and his wife had gone sailing for the afternoon with another couple aboard the Trebelaines' yacht, *The Papa*, with Arthur himself at the helm. This fact seemed to greatly impress the interviewer, which, Richard suspected, was exactly why the voyage had occurred.

"Boy, he's larger than life, huh?" beamed Kittles.

Whitehurst rolled his eyes. "He hasn't taken that boat out in two fucking years," he muttered, a comment that earned him a blow on the shin from one of Meryl's sandals, their first communication of the weekend.

Suddenly the volume in the hotel was lowered a notch, almost imperceptibly, and Arthur and Patty Trebelaine made their way to the bar.

In spite of himself, Kyle felt a fluttering in his chest.

Whatever the transparencies so obvious to his mentor, there was still, even by summer's end, much about Arthur Trebelaine that Kyle simply could not shake. Kerry had been right, in a sense: He worshipped Arthur. He was a young writer's wet dream. He seemed to single-handedly embody the panache of a lost era. The way he sipped a drink, the way he held a cigar, a fishing pole—everything was done to perfection. You just couldn't take your eyes off the son of a bitch.

Of course, as even Kyle could tell, Trebelaine was something of an actor. He had a character for every event. This evening he strode up to the bar like he'd won the America's Cup, a deeply tanned face under a frayed baseball cap, eyes blue as the ocean he had just navigated. Actually, he looked bigger than usual today, his forearms pumped up from tying lines and turning cranks. The indiscreet looks from around the room proved his celebrity intact as ever. Without a word, the bartender was already tipping the Gentleman Jack over a glass of ice.

Next to her hyperbolic husband, Patty was pretty and sprightly in her way, but somehow incidental, even innocuous.

"Anybody hear the baseball scores?" Arthur asked with a rather large shit-eating grin.

Kyle saw now that the cap he wore bore the insignia of the New York Yankees.

Obviously, this was an affront to Whitehurst, for disaster had struck that weekend. The Yankees had come into Boston on Friday and proceeded to sweep the entire three-game series, taking over first place from the Red Sox. All of New England—and, of course, Richard Whitehurst—was in great pain. In fact, Richard had a terrible throbbing in his abdomen this afternoon. He thought for sure some kind of ulcer had begun to form with Friday's and Saturday's losses, only to finally burst with today's debacle.

It was true, he thought now, wincing. It was not a joke anymore. The Red Sox were going to kill him.

"Boston Massacre," Arthur said loudly, prompting applause from some of the surrounding patrons. Yankee fever was spreading, now that they were back in first place.

"Season's not over yet," Wabzug said diplomatically.

Kyle looked over at Whitehurst. He was staring at Arthur with a vehemence Kyle had never seen before. He looked ready to go, literally, ready to put up his dukes. Arthur glared right back, silently but deliberately, aggression obvious in his eyes, and now Kyle began to wonder just what kind of party this really was.

THEY SAT at a long table in the front room, by the fireplace, the restaurant's eagerness to show off its charismatic customers surpassed only by Arthur's revelry in being displayed. As the guest of honor, Kyle sat next to the burly host, with Patty to her husband's left. Meryl was to Kyle's right, while Richard delivered himself voluntarily to the opposite end of the table, placing him head-to-head with his rival. Tatiana sat directly across from Kyle.

There was one chair still empty, but not for long, as Calamity Kerry rolled in, nearly an hour and a half late. It was Meryl who pointed out her arrival, then quickly regretted it. Everyone watched as the young woman reached midstride with one hand to take a fistful of pretzels from the bar, quickly shoveling them in her mouth, and then in her other hand snatched a seeded roll from a busboy going by with a stack of dirty plates. Once she was seated, the odor of marijuana engulfed the table like a broken bottle of perfume.

"Hey, kids," she said. "Where's the wine?"

There was the usual nervous chattering as the guests perused the menu, and then Arthur, stating that this was Kyle's night, handed him the wine list, just as Richard had predicted.

"Go crazy," Arthur said.

The book hit Kyle's hands like a cement block. This list had more entries than a New Delhi phone book, and looking through it Kyle could almost feel Richard's hot breath on his neck, pressuring him to take his host "to the cleaners" as he had urged. In this he was torn: He didn't want to seem ungrateful to Arthur (whatever the motives, the dinner was a nice gesture), and on the other hand, he did owe Richard. It was Whitehurst, after all, who had made this whole summer possible, and looking at that sad man's face at the end of the table and considering Arthur's rather churlish remarks about Richard's beloved baseball team, Clayton called over the sommelier and ordered one—"No, actually, make it two," he said—magnums of La Tache, 1976. Burgundy sine qua non. Each a cool $2,700.

"Two," Arthur repeated, coughing dryly into his fist, his forehead suddenly less ruddy than when he had entered.

Down at the other end of the table, in Siberia, Richard clapped his hands, perhaps in imitation of the Yankee rousters at the bar.

"Bravo!" he barked.

Kyle sent a wink in his direction, letting him know that was for him. Many times Richard had mentioned the wine as his favorite, the one he could never afford.

"Well," Arthur said with a counterfeit grin. "This *is* a celebration then, isn't it?"

THE WINE FLOWED. Kyle flirted mightily with Tatiana, making sure her glass was constantly filled with the Burgundy, and successfully subdued his outrage when she asked for hers with ice. Meryl and

Patty cut harsh looks at the Italian beauty and amused themselves with barely whispered aspersions—though with so little English at her disposal, what could be Tatiana's provocation except her youth? Meanwhile, Arthur volleyed between Christian, who was assuring the novelist of the availability of Montecristo cigars in Kyoto, and Trey, who was supposed to be asking questions but was thus far mostly silent, in awe of the subject he had begged to take on. ("Like meeting Achilles in the flesh," he would later write.)

Wabzug, unfortunately, had eschewed the fine wine for more coffee—decaf, at Richard's insistence. Kerry, as ever, had a friendly arm around "Uncle" Larry, whom she had always adored. She was currently wearing his glasses, perhaps hoping the bottle-thick lenses would hide the redness of her eyes.

As for Richard, he was mostly quiet, set off, as he was, at the other end of things. He spent half his time wishing that the THC in his daughter's bloodstream and the caffeine in Larry's could balance each other out somehow. The other half he spent looking across the table at his wife. His magnificent, estranged wife, who for reasons he could not fathom had not spoken to him in three days.

Sadly, he could not remember her ever looking as lovely as she did tonight. Not even that first night at Arthur's, now more than twenty-five years ago. How could this be? Was age itself perpetuating her splendor? Menopause was looming; perhaps her beauty had gathered itself for one last stand, one last hurrah in the name of fertility. Or had her gardening been more vigorous this season? Her tan was exquisite, he had to admit, her legs firmer than they'd been in years. She'd been taking better care of herself this summer. The makeup, the way she dressed. What the hell for? Wasn't it all for naught anyway? Nothing had . . . *come up* in a year and a half. You could put a fork in their sex life, it was *done*. She didn't even bother to try anymore.

And why this weekend's silent treatment? She'd ignored him except for the most functional prattle. And why the new hairstyle, slightly shorter (more independent?), the strands shining like sparklers in the candlelight? Why the giggly, flighty energy over there, on the other side of the table. Away from him.

Why did it seem as if his wife was on a fucking date tonight?

The appetizers came and went, and then Kerry suggested they all play a quick round of The Game before the next course.

Wabzug immediately began shaking his head.

"What game?" asked Trey Kittles.

"*The* Game," said Wabzug gloomily.

The Game, as it was known to the Whitehursts and Trebelaines, could not be easier, Kerry explained. You went around the table once, each person reciting a first line from a novel. The first one to name the book, including the author, got a point. Stump the table and you received two points. The book could be as popular or as esoteric as you wanted. It just had to exist.

The guests shrugged in assent, not exactly chomping at the bit (Richard felt he could see Christian racking his brain for the opening lines of *Green Eggs and Ham*) but not wanting to spoil the fun either. Wabzug thought it was a rotten idea. He had been part of too many rounds of this "game" over the years, seen too many of them descend into arguments and hurt feelings. Make no mistake: This was not a *game* at all. Not with these two families. This was war.

"Okay, Mom, you're up first."

Meryl sat up with a why-me look, but tradition held that, as the perennial champion, she was expected to begin.

"C'mon," Kerry urged. "This way you can keep score afterward." She handed Larry's glasses back. "Is everybody ready? Remember, speed is important. First one in wins."

Meryl took a sip of wine, contemplating. Everyone looked set.

"Okay," she said. She took a deep breath. The words came out hushed, slightly embarrassed: " 'Paint me a railroad station then, ten minutes before dark . . .' "

"*Bullet Park,*" Richard instantly exclaimed.

"Author?" Kerry said.

He glared over at his daughter. "Cheever," he said, slightly annoyed. As ever, Whitehurst hated the details, the protocol of naming title and author. The book was the thing. The *book.*

"Part of the game, Daddy-O," Kerry shot back.

Meryl produced a pen and paper, writing a point for her husband, who was looking over at her. Had there been some secret message in this clue? he asked himself. It was a novel they had read together the moment it had appeared, the year they'd met. Perhaps this was some sort of gift, a secret peace offering.

But then Richard's mind probed further, and he realized this quote could just as easily cut the other way. Cheever. Suburbs. Troubled couples. Infidelity. Divorce. *Shit.*

Meryl did not return his gaze.

"Clayton!" Kerry called out. After their almost-romance, she had taken to calling him by his last name. "You're up, lover boy."

What was amazing, Kyle thought, who'd played twice already this summer, was how difficult The Game really was. You could choose anything, the whole of literature was at your fingertips, and yet you didn't dare choose just *anything.* Being inventive—hell, showing off— was as important as the point tally. And there were other hazards to consider, especially when playing with writers. Ideally, you did not want your quote to be too favorable to any particular player, and you tried to veer away from any specific literary taste. Hemingway, for example, would get him in hot water with Whitehurst, this being Arthur's métier. On the reverse side, anything of Dickens or Nabokov would have Arthur crying foul, since it would play right into Richard's hands. On top of all this, it had to be clever.

"Any day, Clay," Kerry said.

After a moment or two, he recited, " 'The sun shone, having no alternative, on the nothing new.' "

For a few moments there was an electric silence. I've stumped them, Kyle thought excitedly. *Two* points.

Kerry consulted her watch. "Okay, I guess I'm timing this one. Thirty seconds."

At the other end of the table, Arthur bit his lip in consternation, while Tatiana smiled vacantly.

Patty, meanwhile, was desperately trying to look like she could give a damn, like a woman far above such petty frivolity. Truth be told, Meryl was a wizard at The Game, and Patty had always felt it made her look bad by contrast. In fact, though she'd always pretended a great friendship, Patty had never felt entirely comfortable with Meryl. She'd always felt overshadowed by her, and not just in intellectual terms. Sure her I.Q. was formidable, but it was Meryl's breasts that really pissed her off. The woman was blessed. Just ask Arthur: Patty had seen him stealing glances for years. Eventually, she'd assumed, those breasts would fall, and then her own spindly figure would rule the day. But that was fifteen years ago already, and here was Meryl again tonight, the damn things as hoisted and *brimming* as ever. Call it good genes, call it Victoria's Secret, the bitch's tits would just not come down.

She watched now as Meryl closed her eyes, no doubt homing in on the answer, while her husband took in an eyeful of cleavage. Infuriated, Patty tapped her breadstick on her plate to get his attention, then bit off the tip in one crisp chomp.

"*Murphy,*" Richard finally called out.

Kyle nodded and moved his hands in silent applause.

"Author?" Kerry asked.

"Beckett," he said, glaring once again at his exacting daughter.

"Samuel Barclay. Born 1906, Foxrock, Ireland. Will that do, darling?"

Kerry scratched her cheek with her middle finger.

"Damn!" exclaimed Trey Kittles. He flipped his thumb over at Richard. "This guy's unbelievable."

Silently, Arthur burned.

Next it was Patty's turn. In keeping with the tone of boredom she had adopted, she frowned dispassionately. Finally, in her best quoting voice, she let forth her clue: " 'They shot the general at dawn.' "

Quietly, Richard groaned. As the first line of Arthur's second novel, *Titus Drowning,* this quote was an obvious shovel pass from wife to husband. Still, when Arthur hesitated in answering, Richard stifled his own urge to respond. Giving recognition to a quote from this pompous windbag's novel, Whitehurst thought, was a fate far worse than losing a point. So he simply leaned back in his chair, pretending not to know, and waited for Arthur to answer.

What he had forgotten, though, and what poor Patty could never have known, is how strange, how unknown a writer's work can often sound to its author. Especially when read aloud, and out of context. Oh, it sounds familiar enough, and the writer will often swear it is from a book he has just read, or one he took to his heart years ago. In fact Arthur rose a little from his seat in excitement and finally made a rushed, apocryphal guess that was, in many ways, embarrassingly complimentary to himself.

"*One Hundred Years of Solitude,*" he barked victoriously.

Wrong! Richard wanted to call out, but said nothing.

Arthur smacked his hands together in jubilation and returned smiling to his seat. "Yes, García Márquez," he continued. "Gabo, we call him." He leaned over to Trey and added, "He's a friend, you know."

Kerry looked at Patty for confirmation. "Is that right?"

Mrs. Trebelaine looked panicked, not knowing what to do.

"Wait, wait," a voice called out searchingly, "I know this."

It was Trey Kittles, who, having gorged himself on Trebelaine's work in preparation for the interview, was zeroing in on the answer.

"It's Gabo," Arthur said forcefully.

"No," Trey said, shaking his head, having just hit the bull's-eye. "That's *you*, Arthur. That's *Titus Drowning*!"

There were a few embarrassed laughs around the table—even Tatiana chuckled. Whitehurst positively beamed.

"That's *minus* one point for the host," Kerry said, knowing she was making things worse. "You're in the red, Mr. T."

Patty turned to her husband, completely nonplussed. "Darling, I'm sorry," she said. "I thought for sure . . ." She looked deeply at him, her voice trailing off as she suddenly discovered at that moment how badly Arthur wanted to snap her neck like a wishbone.

The wine flowed. The Game went on. Tatiana passed.

"Illegal," Patty hissed, trying to assuage her husband's embarrassment by laying into Tatiana. "She has to say *something*. Can't she say something?"

"Patty, don't be a turd," Kerry remarked, then signaled to Christian.

The young director fidgeted nervously, hemmed and hawed, and then, without any of the requisite sense of shame, actually said, " 'It was the best of times . . .' "

Wabzug scored on this one, he being the least embarrassed to chime in.

"Impressive, Lar," teased Kerry.

Arthur was next. He rolled up his sleeves before he spoke, as if the sight of his corded forearms might intimidate the group into silence and thus garner him a two-point stump.

" 'It was love at first sight,' " he bellowed confidently, seemingly convinced of the line's inscrutability.

"*Catch-22,*" Richard said instantaneously.

Arthur's head fell forward as if from an axe. The table tensed as he bound one of his hands into a tight fist and turned to the wall, as if he might put it through.

Kerry leaned over Wabzug for a high five to her father, which he returned. "*Yeeoh, Daddy-O!*" she said with stoned pride, too excited to ask for the accompanying information.

By now Trebelaine was fuming, and the only way he could think to salve his wound was by regaling the interviewer with the fact that that book's author, Joseph Heller, was yet another "friend."

"A slow writer, Joe," he explained to Trey, "but not nearly as slow as our other honored guest." With this he pointed to Richard, shaking his head in mock disbelief. "You take the cake, my friend."

Richard sat calmly. He could see clearly Arthur's frustration and pique, and wanted to enjoy it. If a confrontation was coming, then Richard was determined to play it smooth. He didn't want another party disaster. Be cool, he thought. For once in your life.

"What was your name again?" Kittles asked Richard for the second time, pen and notebook handy.

This time Richard had had it. "John Holmes," he rejoined.

Kittles wrote it down.

"Yes," Arthur began again, as if he'd heard none of this. "A painstaking writer, our Mr. Whitehurst. Myself, I wrote *Lions in the Sky* in seven weeks. But what do I know?"

"Get out," Christian said, who had never heard of the book.

"But I'm just a scribbler, really," Trebelaine continued. "An entertainer. Mr. Whitehurst's the real artist here." Arthur's tone was ironic and mean. A cornered bear with paws flailing. "Tell us, Richard—you worked today, God knows—tell us how many words you produced. Personally, I got in ten pages this morning. But I'm not an artist like you."

A dirty shot, Richard thought. He had confided in Arthur recently that he was hardly writing at all this summer, that he had accomplished precisely nothing and was suffering over it.

"Tell us, Richard," the host said. "We're curious. This is a sophisticated group of adults here. Offer us a glimpse, if you will, into the artistic process. How many words . . . Wait, I tell you what, let me guess. Yes, I'll bet you wrote just *one* word today. Not four words, not a page. Just *one*."

Arthur topped this off with a chuckle, quickly supported by Christian and, of course, Tatiana, whose mother had taught her to always laugh whenever the man paying the check did.

Richard leaned forward, resting his chin on his fist. He was quite confident, controlled. "Yes, one word, exactly," he said, looking Arthur square in the eye, "but it was the *right* word."

Nobody blinked. Arthur's face turned white.

"You read that somewhere," he said to Richard. His eyes darted to Kittles, his voice betraying desperation. "He stole that line from someone. I know him."

Richard said nothing. Instead of piling on points, he simply sat back, dignified as could be, and took a long sip of Arthur's two-hundred-dollar-a-glass La Tache.

"Game over," Wabzug said.

AMIDST THE WINE, ass kissing, and mot juste insults, Kyle Clayton had a dirty little secret. One he'd held inside for some time now.

A very serious matter, especially considering the company—or

Richard Whitehurst, to be more specific. In fact, the man's proximity made Kyle feel quite filthy all evening, mildly ill, completely unworthy of his affection. Monstrous, considering what he had done lately, what he'd *been* doing. Right here, no less, in front of his face.

Kyle had been considering allowing the ads to run in his book.

Fitzgerald had emphasized the importance of holding two opposing ideas at the same time, the old devil's-advocate trick. If it was good enough for Scott, it's good enough for me, Kyle thought. So he kept asking—and asking and asking, till he came up with the questions that suited him. Such as: Was there really something so terrible about a few ads in the middle of a novel? Would the earth disengage from its axis and slip into the fiery orbit of the sun if Kyle Clayton actually made a few fucking dollars for once in his life? After the shock of the meeting had worn off, Kyle remembered something else Trevor had said that day. How, for instance, the advertisers were willing to kick in an additional four dollars for every copy sold, an amount to be split with the author. What this meant, Clayton was assured, was that upon publication, not only would he be even with his debt to Brownstone and Company, but, with the various incentives and some serious sales, he could earn upward of a quarter-million dollars!

It was all heading in that direction anyway, Trevor had said. "In-book advertising," as he had christened it, was about to become a publishing phenomenon. There was no choice, he explained; too many publishers were losing money. Soon every Brownstone book— every book published by anyone, anytime, anywhere—would be addled with colorful, uplifting ad-*verd*-isments. Simple conduits to happiness, Trevor had said, really nothing evil in it at all. Little more than road signs for all sorts of needful things. Where's the harm, my boy? Where's the harm?

That evening after the meeting, a shaken and highly confused Kyle

Clayton confided in Richard of the publisher's plan. The reaction, of course, was predictable. Whitehurst contended the ads would be an unmitigated travesty. The sky would fall, the four horsemen would arrive in a cloud of dust. He immediately rang up Wabzug for the counterattack. No matter that Kyle might have contradictory feelings on the subject. No matter *whose* damn book it was. As usual, Richard Whitehurst had assumed the sanctity of his perspective, of his romantic, generally unfeasible values. As usual, he had thought only of himself.

And yet Kyle felt guilty tonight. Guilty because Richard had turned his life around for him this summer, had been like a father to him. Guilty because he knew Richard so wanted a zealot to follow him in his loser's march to nobility. Guilty because what Kyle now secretly wanted was to make an obnoxious pile of cash, and Richard would view this as a betrayal, yet another dagger in the heart of his quixotic dreams and ideals.

"I HOPE he doesn't think he's going to fuck her in the house," Meryl was saying.

It was after dessert. The party had begun its postmeal dissipation, the guests changing seats and mingling. Richard had decided he might as well hunker down next to his wife and find out what the hell was going on. Doing this at home would be preferable, of course, but it wasn't getting done at home. God knows he'd tried. Perhaps to corner her here, in public, might yield something. It was time, after all. The whole thing was getting ridiculous.

Meryl had barely twitched when he sat next to her. She seemed focused on the crowded bar, where Kyle and Tatiana were standing nearly chest-to-chest, engaged in a smoky and provocative tête-à-tête.

"Let them go fuck on the beach," she started to say, "or in a car somewhere. I don't want it in my house."

"What do you care?" Richard asked, thinking this an odd opening topic for a couple who hadn't spoken in three days.

"This is exactly what I was afraid of when he moved in here, Richard. The drinking and bimbo girls."

At this he had to laugh. "What're you talking about? He hasn't been drunk once all summer. Or gotten laid, for that matter. At least from what I can tell." He stared hard into his wife's eyes.

She looked back at him directly, revealing nothing.

"Anyway, he's leaving in a week."

"Good," she said, sipping her wine.

"But then this is really just some excuse, isn't it?" he added.

Meryl sighed, making it known how very bored she was. "Now what does that mean?"

"You're looking for some justification to be mad."

Meryl's eyes flashed to him, her face ironic and superior. Highly unattractive, Richard thought. Her tone of voice followed suit: "And *why* would I want that, Richard? Why would anybody *want* to be mad? Except you, maybe. At the world you refuse to participate in."

He sat back in his chair, folding his arms as if to cover a wound. Her voice was like a lance to the heart. She sounded so repulsed by him, so disgusted with the mass of bones and flesh sitting next to her. Meryl couldn't even look into his face now, he noticed, choosing instead to stare straight ahead at the bar, at Kyle and the starlet. Oh, she'd had it with him this time, Richard thought. This one was bad. Worst of all was her disturbing aura of peace, of resignation. It was like she'd decided something, and for the first time in his life it occurred to him that their marriage could actually end.

"What's brought this on?" he asked, trying to smile, trying to play the fool who would take the blame—so that they could move on, go back to the way things were. "What did I do? I've been racking my brain trying to figure it out."

"It's everything," she said, shaking her head decidedly. "Just everything."

"It's always been everything. What's changed now?" he asked, his voice slightly desperate. "What's happened?"

Just then Arthur, showing all the sensitivity of an ox, pulled up a chair and bulled his big shoulders in between them.

"WHERE ARE YOU staying tonight?" Kyle asked boldly.

Tatiana held her Marlboro out for him like a woman who had never lit her own cigarette in her life. An expensive girl, Kyle thought, puffing away on one of Arthur's Havanas.

Asking him to stay still, Tatiana pressed the tip of her cigarette against the lit end of his cigar. The fire was instantaneous.

"Here," she said, taking her first puff. "I stay upstairs."

Kyle felt a surge of propriety as the men around them began to reposition themselves for a better look at Tatiana. A voyeuristic two-step, barely discreet, for a peek over their girlfriend's head, around their wife's broad shoulders.

"What you . . ." She scribbled in the air with an invisible pen.

"What do I write about?" Kyle cocked his head and thought about it. That he could not explain it suddenly troubled him. "Hard to say, I'm afraid."

"Sex?" she asked suggestively. A tress of hair fell down, covering one of her large brown eyes. Kyle brushed it away.

"Well, yes," he said, suddenly brightening. "Especially in my new book." He decided not to add that this avid fictional carnality was probably a substitute for the real thing.

Now it was his turn. He wanted to dispose of the final question, the only possible impediment to tonight's objective.

"Are you . . . Christian's girlfriend?"

She laughed.

"That's funny?" he asked.

She nodded, resting long fingers against her throat, then shook her head. "He is, how you say . . . happy."

"Happy?"

"You know, happy," she repeated. "Happy. *Gay*."

"*Homosexual*," Kyle said finally, and perhaps a touch too excitedly. "Well, that's . . . wonderful!"

"Me too."

"You think so too. Of course."

"No," she said. "*Me* too."

"You too?" he repeated, confused. Then he finally got it. "Oh, you mean you too, homosexual?"

"Sometimes," she said.

At long last, he thought. After the years of wandering. The fruitless pursuits, wasteful nights, shameful dawns. At long last, *love*.

She took his cigar from his mouth, wanting to taste it. When she puffed, Kyle swore he could hear from all around him a collective, ejaculatory moan.

They clinked their wineglasses together in a toast.

Just then a young man about Kyle's age came up to him and tapped him on the shoulder.

"Hey," he said, "you're Kyle Clayton, aren't you? You're the writer guy. I remember you from TV."

"Guilty as charged," Kyle answered, turning to the young man. He was quite pleased by the interruption. Naturally the gentleman would now ask for an autograph, or maybe even a picture. Perfect, he thought. Tatiana didn't stand a chance tonight.

He reached out to shake the man's hand but was rejected.

The stranger suddenly narrowed his eyes. "You're a scumbag," he said, poking a finger into Kyle's chest. "A real lowlife. Why don't you go beat up somebody's grandmother?"

Kyle was silent, quite flummoxed, not to mention petrified. The man's shoulders and arms looked quite powerful.

Great, he thought, another *New York* magazine devotee.

Then, as if too repelled to engage the likes of Kyle Clayton another second, the man moved on.

Kyle turned back to Tatiana. She looked a bit stunned and, as he was relieved to notice, slightly confounded.

"What does he say, this man?"

"He, uh . . ." Kyle puffed his cigar nervously, trying to clear the fear from his throat. "He's angry my new book is taking so long," he whispered.

"Oh, you're a famous writer then, no? A *celebrità*!"

"Oh, yeah," Kyle said. He was gazing over his shoulder now, eyes darting wildly, on the lookout for possible flying objects, sucker punches, the sparkle of the assassin's gun. "I'm quite well known around here."

"I WAS JUST TALKING to Larry," Arthur said.

He folded his arms across the back of the chair, making himself at home. Richard was furious.

"For chrissakes, Arthur, not now."

Arthur didn't budge. As a kicker, he had the longest cigar anyone had ever seen protruding from his mouth. A Lusitania, Arthur had proudly announced. It was so big, in fact, that when he turned to talk to you from a normal distance the burning end was nearly at your nose.

"No," Arthur said, taking the cigar from his mouth and holding it like a pointer, "this is important."

Trebelaine, they could see, was a little loaded. This didn't happen often. Arthur prided himself on his ability to handle his drink. But after Richard's incisive rebuttal he had turned to a few quick belts to drown his embarrassment.

"Larry told me about the ads for Kyle's book."

"We're getting rid of them," Richard said firmly. "Don't worry about it."

"This is what I want to talk to you about."

Meryl seemed relieved by the interruption. Seeing a chance for escape, she stood and headed for the ladies' room. Richard's eyes followed her until she was gone, then turned back to glower at Arthur.

"Fucking shit, Arthur, can't you see how insensitive this is? Don't you have any concept—"

"A certain young man's career is at stake here."

"We're taking *care* of it."

"It's wrong, goddamn it!" Arthur's voice boomed through the dining room. Heads were raised.

Richard rolled his eyes, too annoyed to be intimidated.

"Of course it is," he said, "to *you*. Go with the money—that's the Trebelaine motto. Take it all the way to the bank."

Despite the drinks, Arthur held his cool. "Richard, Kyle has debts. He needs to make a living."

Whitehurst's eyes flickered distractedly about the room. Where was Meryl? Why had she fled so quickly? Where, goddamn it, was his wife?

"You're behind this," Arthur said. "You're influencing him."

"Oh, and you're not? I think he's more impressed with you than he is with me. Big Arthur and his toys. You set him up in your fucking beach house and feed him these stupid cigars." Richard waved at the smoke billowing in front of him. "Would you get that damn thing out of my face?"

Arthur hesitated a moment before leaning back in his seat. Richard grabbed at a nearby glass of wine and took a deep sip, then went back on the attack.

"What is it with you tonight, Arthur?" he said, setting down the glass. "What is it you want from me? Some kind of confrontation? We don't like each other anymore, so what? Friendships end. Let's just stop pretending and leave it at that, what do you say?"

Arthur shook his head, the cigar dancing like a wand. "Let's deal with this first," he said. "Get Kyle over here. I want to hear what he has to say."

"I told you, he and I already agree on this."

Arthur had his hand up, trying to catch Kyle's eye. "I'll bet you never even asked him."

"How do you know?"

"I know *you*, Richard."

"Oh, for chrissakes." Whitehurst turned away in disgust.

"Kyle!" Arthur said, standing up. *"Kyle!"*

Kyle flinched suddenly at the sound of his name. He saw Arthur standing mightily over a highly annoyed-looking Richard. Obviously something was up, he decided. He could tell by the look on their faces. They were *into* it, whatever it was that they'd come here to dispute.

Kyle reluctantly left Tatiana at the bar. Interception was in order, a peacekeeping mission.

Not ten steps from the table and Richard was already talking at him from his chair: "Tell him, already, would you?" he said as Kyle approached. "This stubborn mule here doesn't believe me. Tell him you don't want the ads in the book."

"Whoa, whoa, hold on a second," Arthur tempered. He offered

the younger writer a seat and then joined him as he sat. "This is a big decision here, Kyle. I can't believe it's that simple. It *shouldn't* be that simple."

Kyle still had his cigar. Though he knew Richard hated it, he took a puff. "Actually, it's not," he said.

Arthur raised his eyebrows.

"Well, good, because we want to know what you think about—"

"We've already discussed it," Richard said.

"No," Kyle interjected. "Actually, Richard, we never did."

Whitehurst looked dazed, while Arthur nodded vigorously. "That's what I figured," he murmured.

Sensing some momentum, Arthur continued: "And we're talking a lot of money here, aren't we, Kyle?"

"Yes," he said. "Hell yes."

Kyle snuck a peek back at the bar. Tatiana was talking to an older couple. Harmless, he thought. Nothing to worry about there.

Richard, he saw, was another story. On his face disappointment was pulling at anything it could get hold of. The eyes, the corners of his mouth, the flesh of his cheeks. He looked ten years older than he had this afternoon.

"Look, I mean if it was me, for example," Arthur continued, "if I had a choice between ads and no ads, of course I'd like my book pure. Anybody would. But every man's got to make a living. Everybody except Richard, of course."

Whitehurst turned with a snarl. "My finances are none of your goddamned business."

Arthur ignored him, trudging on with even greater composure. "So it seems our young man here's somewhat confused," he said. "Confused rather than decided. Isn't that a fair assessment, Kyle?"

"Yes," said the young man without hesitation, then hedged a bit as he looked at Richard. "Well, no. I don't know." Come out with it already, he thought. There was really no sense holding back now. He fixed Whitehurst square in the eye.

"Actually, Richard, I've been meaning to tell you this." He took a deep breath, then took a puff from his cigar. "I ... I think I've changed my mind. I think I'm going to let the ads run."

Quietly but audibly, Whitehurst seemed to gasp.

"I'm sorry, Rich—"

"Don't do this," Whitehurst said. "Jesus, Kyle. This is artistic suicide."

"Now hold on," Arthur said, "let the young man make up his own—"

"Shut up," Richard told him, staring at him down the end of the cigar. He turned back to Kyle. "Don't do it, Kyle," he murmured passionately. *"Don't."*

"See now," Arthur reached out and, perhaps unconsciously, grabbed Richard's sleeve, "here you go again."

Almost before he could finish, Richard yanked his arm free of his burly friend and suddenly stood up. Arthur stood too, though he was a little wobbly.

Kyle joined them, making sure to wedge himself in between the two men.

"Look," he said, turning to Whitehurst—he needed to manifest reason here, to end this now and forever—"I have to be realistic. I'm ass deep in debt. I don't think you know how bad—"

"I'll pay it," Richard said.

Kyle shook his head, as if to clear his ears. No, he thought, he must not be hearing correctly.

"I'll pay the debts," Richard repeated.

"What?" Kyle said, almost laughing. "No. No, you won't."

Trebelaine scoffed. "What? You can't do that. You old fool!"

"I could," Richard snapped. "Don't tell me I couldn't."

"No, no," Kyle kept saying.

"What would your wife say?" Trebelaine asked, taking a step around the younger man. "What about Meryl?"

"Don't worry about my wife, Arthur. You hear me? Don't even fucking *think* about her. She can't stand you either, you know. She's told me that a hundred times."

"Guys, guys, guys . . ."

Kyle took another step, again cutting off the two men from each other. There was despair in Richard's eyes now, he noticed. This hurt Kyle deeply. He was putting too much weight on this, Kyle wanted to tell him. He was playing this as if it were the last straw for him, the final indignity. It's just a book, Kyle wanted to scream out. *Just a stupid book!*

"Look, you can't pay my debts, Richard. You can't pay them because I couldn't let you. You've done enough for me already." Despite his rejection of Arthur's touch, he put his hands up on his mentor's shoulders, trying to soothe him, to maintain reason. "That's the point, okay? I could never take it."

Arthur sidestepped Kyle again, finding a spot over his shoulder in which to rankle his old friend. "You can't pay the man's debts," he said mockingly. "It's not *your money* to give, Richard. Remember?"

This pushed Richard over the edge. Dry shards of spit flew from his clenched teeth as he growled, "Will you shut up about my wife!" His head jerked violently toward the larger man, the burning tip of Arthur's Havana finally catching him on the cheek in an eruption of ash.

"Ahhhh!" Richard jerked back, holding his face in pain. "*Fuck*-ing bastard." With a burst of anger he swatted at the cigar, hitting it flush and sending it flying across the room. Kerry and Christian jumped out of the way of the burning baton.

"My Lusitania!" he shouted.

Arthur pushed Richard, who fell back onto the party's table. There was the sound of clanking silverware and a breaking glass. Somebody shrieked. Before Richard could stand back up and defend himself, Larry Wabzug jumped in from nowhere and wrapped his arms around his client like a straitjacket.

This left Kyle in charge of Arthur. He deftly guided the host backward, as far from Richard as he could. "I'll kill him," Arthur growled. "I could kill the son of a bitch." Clayton assured him that yes, of course he could, just not *here.*

A terrible silence ensued as the two men tried to calm themselves, the only sound being that of a busboy trying to clean up the mess Richard's fall had made, and a few astonished voices at the bar. Slowly, cautiously, Larry and Kyle loosened their grip on the combatants.

Richard was wiping off the back of his pants when he noticed his hand was bleeding.

"Wonderful," he said. He held it up in the air like Exhibit A, watching the blood fall in thick droplets. "Great party, Art," he said. "Just splendid."

That was the end of it. Meryl, who'd been absent the whole time, returned to see the table in disarray and the maître d' wrapping a cloth napkin around her husband's bloody hand. What the hell happened? she wondered. She gave Richard a look of loathing from across the room. Their gazes locked.

Yeah, and fuck you too, said Richard's eyes.

Strangely, it was Larry Wabzug who took it the worst. Something about these events seemed to shake the sentimental man to his core. He held fast to his friend's shoulder, looking like a tragedy had just occurred.

Tatiana broke the abashed silence by scurrying up to Kyle from the bar.

"You!" she said angrily.

Kyle took a step back as Arthur moved off toward his wife. He looked to his left, then his right, then behind him—nobody. He was stumped.

"Me?"

"Yes, you!" she said. "You not a nice man. No. No you!"

What did I do now, he wondered.

"They tell me. They tell about you!" She was pointing toward the middle-aged couple at the bar. More "fans," apparently. Jesus, he thought, he couldn't leave a date alone for five fucking minutes without her being inundated with slander. He was doomed.

"You a bad man," she said. "You punch at party. You hit. No good!"

As if to demonstrate this past offense, she slapped him hard on the lapel of his jacket—after which the last chance he would have at sexual relations for who knew how long a time turned and stormed out.

Richard walked past him, he too apparently on the way out. He was slightly hunched over, holding his hand, the blood having soaked through the napkin.

"Richard," Kyle said pleadingly. The man didn't stop. "Please . . . Richard."

With his bloody rag, Whitehurst pointed to Kyle's hand.

"Your cigar's out," he said, without looking up, then kept right on going.

14

Outside, the night was unusually cool. Richard, who'd forgotten his jacket in the mayhem, walked along Main Street like a character from an old horror film, a bleeding Frankenstein gazing in storefront windows and restaurants, looking for sympathy and love. The patrons and pedestrians, however, regarded him with suspicion. One waiter came out of a restaurant he was staring into and shooed him away like an old dog.

He ambled on.

His hand was killing him. He should probably go to the hospital, he knew, but a part of him was enjoying the wound. It gave him that sense of martyrdom that he'd always longed for. That beaten-but-never-defeated feeling he'd found so attractive. Right now it was the only thing he had.

He walked south, heading away from the center of town and down a dark street with huge-trunked trees, many of them older than Sag Harbor itself. He tried to think of somewhere he could go, of a possible refuge, and it saddened him to realize there simply wasn't one. He could probably go back and hook up with Wabzug, but that would be backtracking, wouldn't it? The drama of his exit would be lost.

He knew he wouldn't be welcome at home. There least of all.

Just then the Bronco pulled up alongside him. So soon? Richard thought with a smirk. Meryl was back to beg for forgiveness. Things would be okay after all. He was still in control.

He quickened his pace as the window came down, determined to play hard to get.

"Get in," a voice said. It was not his wife's. He stopped and turned. It was Kerry. She was alone.

"We need to talk," she said. For once in her life she looked earnest, not on the attack. There was a needfulness in her eyes. "That was quite a show you put on back there," she said. "It got me to thinking." She leaned over and opened his door. "There are some things you and *I* need to settle. Once and for all."

This was not exactly what he needed right now, a heart-to-heart with his crazy daughter. What *was* it tonight, anyway, the goddamned *moon*? Everybody wanted a piece of him, to settle all their unfinished business in one evening. The night wasn't getting any warmer. Where the hell else was there to go? Using his good hand, he climbed into the Bronco.

THEY RODE for a while in silence, then parked down by the beach. Because of the cool weather the lot was empty but for a few couples taking a late-summer's stroll by the ocean. Kerry and her father stayed inside, heat pumping low, Kerry wondering how the hell to begin.

"How's your hand?" she asked.

"Hurts." He removed the bloody napkin and took a look at the wound. There was a half-moon slice in the palm, the slit skin already translucent, hanging useless. Probably could use some stitches, she thought.

"Kyle feels terrible, you know. You should have seen his face when you left."

"He'll be all right," Richard said.

"You're angry with him."

Richard scrunched his shoulders. "At myself, mostly," he said. "I was wrong about him, so of course I feel stupid. Turns out he's got the smell of money in his nose, just like everybody else."

She could argue with him, but what would be the use? She watched him sink a little in his seat, relaxed, resigned, as if he finally knew how it was, how it always would be. Whitehurst is disappointed. The Red Sox swoon. Dreams die. *On and on and on.*

"He'll be all right," he repeated. "He's actually quite calculating, as it turns out. Your mother was right about him all along. Your mother . . . ," he repeated, his voice breaking off despondently.

He turned his head to the passenger's window, resting it there and averting his eyes.

"Mom's having an affair," Kerry suddenly announced.

She watched him. Her father didn't move, didn't utter a sound. He reached down and scratched his hand, which had begun to throb.

"I know."

"You do?" Kerry seemed quite surprised.

He turned to her and smiled. "You think I'm very naïve, don't you? Totally oblivious. Well, my darling, I'm not. Not entirely."

"Who is it?" she asked tentatively.

"You mean you don't know?"

"I have a couple of guesses," Kerry said. "What, you're telling me you know for sure?"

Richard went back to his window. His answer was completely forthright, unflinching. "Kyle," he said, glancing over at her again almost triumphantly. "Our very own Kyle."

"That's . . . What? No *way*!" Kerry said. Then she seemed to reconsider. "Are you sure?"

His silence confirmed that he was.

"Wow," she said. She laughed, incredulous. "I mean, holy shit."

"That's right."

"How do you know? Why did you let him stay?"

"I didn't know till tonight."

"He told you?"

"No, your charming mother did."

Kerry looked away, shaking her head. That didn't sound like Mom, she thought. Wasn't her style. If she had been having an affair, she wouldn't just come out and say it, supply him with the who, how, and why. Her mother was not cruel.

"So she just comes out and tells you she's fucking Kyle? That's strange."

"Not explicitly, no."

"Well, then . . ."

He narrowed his eyes at her. "It's Kyle," he said firmly. "Believe me."

With that Richard opened the door and got out.

By the moonlight she watched him walk a few feet, then turn around and come back. He was not crying, she could see, which would have surprised just about anyone but her. Dickens could make him weep, she knew. The Red Sox collapse in the '86 series. But Kerry had never seen "real" life move her father that deeply. In this she had followed suit. Through all the hurt, she'd never cried for him. Not once.

Her father climbed back in the Bronco. "Okay, so what else is on tonight's agenda?" he said with a clap of his hands. His aspect was solid again, collected. "Let me guess, you're going to ask me about the past. Try to get to the bottom of it. You and I, father and daughter. Big talk-show cry fest. Am I getting warm?"

Her father's sudden irreverence was a little disarming, Kerry had to admit. Obviously he was dangerous this evening. A hollowed-out old man with no more illusions, nothing left to protect. He would tell her everything, she knew, divulge all his secrets. Willingly, ruthlessly.

Only question was, did she have the guts to ask him?

"I suppose . . . ," she began nervously. "I guess what I want is . . ." Furious at her apprehension, she took a breath and went on. "What I *need* is, some specifics. So I can move on in my life, or give up, or do whatever the hell it is I'm supposed to do with myself, you know? Put this behind me."

"Mmmm," he murmured, seeming somewhat bored. "So what you really want to know is if I ever loved you. Is that it?"

Now she was truly unnerved. This, after all, had always been *her* forte: the embarrassment of honesty, the willingness to say what no one else had the guts to say. Having it directed back at her was not nearly so inspiring, she'd discovered. A little like looking down the barrel of your own gun.

"Something like that," she forced herself to admit. She noticed that her hand was shaking.

There was a long silence as Kerry watched her father trying to decide just how much of the truth to deliver, for the truth with Richard Whitehurst, she knew, came in different colors and sizes, different levels of magnitude. This, she knew, was *his* specialty. Manipulating the truth was how he survived, for godsakes, how he made it through the day. He pursed his lips, scratched his head. The wait was excruciating.

In the end, he decided to reveal all of it.

"No," he said, clearing his throat for courage. "I'm afraid I never really did. Not in the way you might've hoped." He paused, still looking out the window. "I'm sorry to have to tell you this, but I know that anything but complete honesty is anathema to you."

He turned now, finally, to gauge her reaction. She showed him nothing.

Instead, Kerry looked out into the night. A hand-holding couple emerged over a dune, sea grass rustling beneath their feet. They fell down in the sand, laughing and wrestling playfully. Like all happy lovers, they were an affront.

"Mom wanted a child," she said, looking straight ahead. "I know the story. She forced me on you, it's understandable." She was looking for excuses now, giving him a way out.

"No," he said. "Well, yes. But that's not what prevented me from . . ."

He paused. Kerry watched him run his fingers through his hair.

"My work, you see," he continued. "I never could give myself to anything else. Perhaps if I'd had just one great success along the way, just one triumph I could've pointed to—then maybe, maybe I could've focused on something else—"

"Dad, Christ almighty," she wailed. She was about to tell how he *did* have great success, in his way, but then decided not to give him the satisfaction. He said these things for this very reason, she knew, for the pleasure of hearing others disagree with him.

He waited for her to finish, and when it was clear she would not engage him any further, he went on. "Anyway, it never happened, and everything has suffered. My marriage. Our relationship. My *friend-ships*! Did you know I have no friends anymore? I just realized that tonight. Acquaintances, sure. Colleagues, yes, a few. But no one I can count on. A sixty-four-year-old man with no friends."

Kerry looked impassive, but secretly she thought of lunging at him, grabbing him by the throat. *Who cares about your stupid friends?* she screamed in her head. *Who the fuck gives a shit!* He had just told his daughter he'd never loved her! His wife was getting fucked by a man half his age! How irresponsible, she thought, how outrageous that his mind had suddenly flittered toward the grim prospects of his social calendar.

Kerry took a deep breath. She'd already known what the answer was, long before tonight. Of course he'd never loved her. She was long ago resigned to *that*. Tonight she'd just wanted to find out if he cared enough to lie.

He didn't, and that was okay too, for long ago she'd realized that with her father everything was books. Life, in fact, was really just the novel being written in his head. In this way he'd kept the pain of experience away from him. "Reality" was decidedly *un*real to Richard Whitehurst.

This very exchange was written, of course. The father and daughter scene, having it out once and for all. And like all good writers, he had played the scene for optimal drama, with acute attention to truth. Never mind who it hurt. Let it rip, he would say. *A writer has an obligation . . .*

"Are you still doing drugs?" he asked, ending a long, painful silence.

"A little weed, not much," she answered. And then, in keeping with the night's motif of veracity, she added, "but only because you can't find any in this fucking hellhole."

Richard began to fidget, shimmying himself forward. "Well," he said, "this might seem odd"—he was reaching down with his good hand, feeling under the seat—"but I just might have a little something."

Supporting himself on his elbow to spare his injury, he fished around, not merely beneath the seat but inside it, his hand under the cover and up in the springs and bars of the frame.

What the hell's he looking for? she wondered.

"I hope it's still here," he said. "We both could use a little something right now, don't you think?"

Finally he pulled it out. The little Ziploc bag with the hard gray pebbles and the pipe he'd found on Attorney Street.

"Oh, *Dad,*" she said in whispered wonderment.

He held it aloft, a package he was not sure what to do with but of which he was nevertheless proud.

"A little something I picked up the last time I was in New York," he said. "Some Kubla Khan, if you will."

Kerry realized then how crazy this was, how completely out of character. She was stupefied and simultaneously very excited. They were going all the way tonight, right to the very end.

"What the hell are you doing with this?" she asked, though she didn't really give a damn. It was a loser's drug, of course, never her first choice. But it would do nicely for tonight.

"Never mind," he said. "Do you know how to use it?"

She looked at him like he was crazy.

"Can a chef boil an egg?" she asked, snatching it out of his hand.

She spread the stuff out on the dashboard. At first she tried not to move too fast, reminding herself that this was her *father,* for godsakes—what must he be thinking? All those C's and D's in chemistry over the years and here she was firing up strange, disparate elements like a Nobel scientist. Then she remembered who'd given it to her in the first place, and had the first rocks smoking in under a minute.

Kerry saw her father watching her as she helped herself to the first hit, the car stinking up with a burnt-marshmallow smell. He looked awkward and frightened, she could see, probably more for himself than for her. Experience reminded her how daunting the smell could be to a first-timer. No, this was serious shit, the big time. She handed him the pipe.

What the fuck, Dad? she felt like saying. *What have you left to lose?*

"Is it dangerous?" he asked, peering over at her.

"Probably," she answered. "Yes, as a matter of fact. Most definitely."

Aging novelist smokes rock with drug-addict daughter. A risky plotline, she decided, a real stretch, even for the talented Whitehurst.

She sparked a flame over the open bowl.

"Breathe it all the way in," she said as he sucked tentatively, holding the flame till the pipe's chamber filled with the downy, viscous clouds. "Keep going," she urged, his cheeks dimpling. "That's it, all the way. This ain't no joint, Pops."

He coughed harshly, then waited. For forty-five seconds he felt nothing, though he cringed at the harsh bitterness of the taste, that of charred minerals and stale cigarettes. Maybe it was like what they said about pot, she could see him thinking as he took another quick hit—maybe you don't feel anything the first time, maybe it takes a couple of tries until . . . *Wham!* Then it got him.

"Well, hel-*lo*," he said with a doofy smile. "Whoa . . . Ho *ho*." She watched as his eyes widened and his head rested back in blissful repose.

How stupid he looks, she thought. When all was said and done, a very stubborn, very stupid man.

They kept smoking. Kerry fired up two more sets of rocks, deftly, greedily, until by the third bowl Richard finally declined. He was done. Kerry watched him sit back and close his eyes. He was dreaming, she could see, swimming through the implosion of his subconscious. Suddenly his lids started to flutter, his breath quickening.

Had he smoked too much? she wondered as she watched him quickly open the door to vomit on the macadam, and on his old shoes—a five-hundred-dollar grand-cru spit shine.

This was followed by a deep, ugly crying jag where every sob was like a work-boot kick to the abdomen.

"Ahhhhnnnnnn," he moaned, closing the door. He was rocking back and forth in his seat now. "Ahhhhhhhnnnn."

"Shush," Kerry said. "Shut up." She had her hand on his knee, rubbing him, though he was too numb to feel it.

"*Meryl, darling,*" he whispered. "*Meryl, please . . .*" He stayed like this for a few minutes, half sleeping, then muttering to himself, the feathery glow of the drug fleeing his body like a soul from a cadaver.

Finally, just when he was almost passed out and thought for sure the buzz had dissolved, he felt a faint tickle along his neck, like the dance of butterflies. Then there was a strange mashing of lips, while a searching, slithering mass penetrated his mouth and made contact with his tongue. Whoa, the ride was not over, he thought. This is really some shit. Too high and exhausted to move, he opened his eyes and noticed his daughter's head tilted before him, *on* him, her eyes closed determinedly.

Immediately he tried to move his arms but found he could not, feeling them pinned to his sides, while at the same time his mouth vibrated with the strained, desperate whine coming from his assailant. Gaining some consciousness from the shock, he managed to push her tongue from his mouth with his own and seal his lips, her whine rising to a squeal as she continued to mash her mouth against his and the struggle increased.

"*Ker-ry!*" he managed to yell, turning his mouth away from hers.

Fully roused to consciousness now, he brought up his forearm with the bloody hand, lodging it across her collarbone, and with all his doped-up strength pushed forth, disengaging her. Her head slammed back violently into the sun guard behind her.

Momentarily stunned, she collapsed in her seat.

"Dear God!" he yelled, gasping for breath. Furiously, he wiped his lips on the bloody napkin. "Are you out of your fucking mind?"

"Hit me," she said after a moment.

"What?"

She leaned toward him again, though this time he was ready, stiff-arming her away. She slapped at his elbow and then relaxed, tears filling her eyes.

"You won't hit me?" she asked.

No, he had never hit her, through all she'd done over the years. And he never would. Not even now, when he realized that it was, in a way, what she'd really always wanted. When he realized it could feel like love.

"He won't hit me," she exclaimed, quite amazed. "Not even for this."

She lay back, her body slack from exhaustion, then suddenly punched out at the steering wheel in frustration. That seemed to be the end of it. Limp and defeated, she slid down in her seat.

Richard collected the pipe and what few rocks were left, then threw them into the glove compartment with ultimate disgust.

"Drive," he said. Then he thought better of it. "No, forget it. We'll wait awhile, then I'll drive."

Again he wiped his mouth.

"My God," he said in hushed amazement. "What's happened here? *What has happened?*"

Kerry leaned toward the dashboard, holding her abdomen, as if she'd been gut-shot. She kept leaning until her head rested on the wheel, the horn blowing mournfully, though she seemed not to notice.

Bastard, she thought. *Never seen me cry.*

15

To: K.C@aol.com

From: bigboss@aol.com

Subject: Travesties

I must here alert you that after having just read
your manuscript, the new work is, in my opinion,
an unmitigated DISASTER! I cannot tell you how
disappointed I am in what I have been looking
forward to all summer, and what I now have before
me on my desk.

Read this letter carefully, Kyle, and adhere
to its criticisms, or our project together may be
in jeopardy.

First of all, the roman à clef aspect of the
book is not only offensive to some of the finest
citizens of this city, but also puts our

publishing house in a dangerous litigious
position. The characterizations are far too
accurately drawn. Sure, a few of my editors have
been chuckling at the portraits you've so
obviously based on Zeddy and Dorothea Clementine,
but did you realize that Zeddy is a close friend
to at least four of the five remaining American
investors via the corporate umbrella under which
Brownstone sits? That they in fact share a
Friday-night wine club over which Zeddy presides?
Do you really think Dorothea will sit idly by
when such a caricature of her is manifest in a
major novel? Changes here must and WILL be made!

Secondly, you completely overlook the need for
loyalty to our advertisers. Did it ever occur to
you that your "satiric" image of the grande dame
losing use of her jaw muscles from too many BOTOX
injections could also ruffle the feathers of
Pfizer, an advertiser eager to put money in *your*
pocket? Or your "hero's" (though I shudder to
call him that) romantic observations of "Old" New
York (yawn, yawn), his longing for the
"idiosyncratic stores and shopkeepers of yore"?
How do you think such remarks will fly with the
executives from Coconuts and Sunglass Hut whom
I've already explained to you have signed on as
advertisers? Are you just oblivious, Kyle, to the
machinations of the real world, or do you
purposely try to shoot yourself in the foot?

As you must know, Devon Schiff's book was

published this very week, once again to rave
reviews. I quote: "A *Catcher in the Rye* for the
urban professional set," *Time* magazine; "The *ne
plus ultra* of beach books," *Vanity Fair;* "Schiff
at the height of his powers!" *USA Today.* When and
if you read this fine work—brilliantly titled
Fightnight—make note of Devon's judicious use of
the altercation you two had, and how you have
failed to even *mention* it in your work, for
reasons unfathomable to me. Do I need to remind
you of what a certain scene could mean to you?
($$$$$$$$$!) Schiff's book has debuted at number
nine on the *Times* best-seller list. What kind of
sales performance can we reasonably expect from
your novel, Kyle, without a familiar hook for the
audience? How can I ever hope to get you on
Charlie Rose if you don't play along?

I could go on and on, but I trust you get the
point. I want this fixed, and fast! You have two
weeks. We're already behind schedule.

P.S. On a personal note, I urge you to speak
with your sad old friend Rollie McIntyre, to
please remind him that his mess is—YES!—still
in my office, staring at me even as I dictate this
E-mail. I will give him one week to pick it up.
The next day it goes on the street.

Finally, because your messy book is still in
want of a title, please consider from this list
of four that my staff has personally chosen after
a round-table discussion on the subject.

```
    Punch Drunk

    Brawls and Bras

    Gotham Titty (personal favorite)

    Charmed Life II


    I trust you will find something to your liking

    here. Good luck, Clayton. You'll need it. NOW GET

    TO WORK!
```

Perfect, Kyle thought, closing his laptop. Couldn't be better. The end to the perfect evening.

He actually had a hangover this morning, the first of the summer. A wine hangover, no less, the baddest of the bunch. Still, must get going, he reminded himself. Time to be shoving off. His welcome here was thoroughly worn out. He'd stayed one weekend too long; long enough to enact the Labor Day Fiasco, as he would always remember it.

He felt cheated in a way. In the old days, when he'd ruin everything (a mathematical certainty), he'd at least do it in *style*. Some ill-advised but nevertheless lively sexual miscarriage; some beer-sopped title bout in the name of "honor." Drama—boozy, literary theater! How sad now that this had ended in the name of his piddling little novel and its groveling ad-*verd*-isments. His unctuous, neon-lit, *please-like-me* excuse for a book. Whether it would eventually be a good novel or bad—and he was betting now on the latter—was suddenly no longer of interest to him. Now it was simply a thing to be despised.

He took a last, rueful look around the Whitehursts' bedroom, then zipped up his pack and headed for the door.

He would have left last night, after the mêlée—had tried to, in fact—but the trains and jitneys had stopped running by then. Too bad.

The evening's aftermath was torturous. Everybody looking around, wondering what the hell had happened. Funny how firmly their opinions formed in spite of their ignorance. Trebelaine was unaccountable as usual. A generous soul, the thinking went; why would he ruin his own party? No, Richard must have done it. Ol' Mr. Sourpuss. And Kyle Clayton, of course, as the accomplice. That was a no-brainer.

Kyle had returned from the party to an empty house, and it had remained that way throughout his nearly sleepless night. The vacancy was disconcerting, a feeling confirmed now as he ventured into the creaking hall of the old sea captain's house. The Whitehursts' bedroom was barren, bed neat as a pin. A wave of guilt crashed over him. Was he to blame? Had he inadvertently blown a family wide open from the inside, the grenade in the guest room? Beyond the carnage of people he actually cared for, this presented the problem of predictability. Everyone, absolutely *everyone,* had warned Richard away from the Summer of Clayton, and the young man had wanted to prove them wrong; for if Kyle Clayton stood for anything in this reckless existence of his, it was hatred of the predictable, the obvious, the calibrated. Through all the chaos, all the mayhem and muddle, at least there was *that*. Now this, too, was gone.

And speaking of mayhem, Kyle came downstairs to find Calamity Kerry passed out on the sofa.

"Well, if it isn't Mr. Lover Boy," she said to the ceiling, apparently unable to lift her head from the cushions.

He wondered how he could have missed her arrival, then quickly understood: a lifelong delinquent, she claimed a knack for stealthy entrances. He strode up and laid his pack on the carpet.

"Where is everybody?"

"Everybody, you mean, or just *somebody*?" It was all she could do to roll over enough to take a look at him. "No wonder I couldn't make it with you, Clayton," she said with a sly smile. "You're a busy boy."

What was this now, jealousy of Tatiana? How could she not know their flirtation had ended in disaster?

"Whatever," he said.

She pointed at her ear. "I heard things, Kyle. Little birdies."

"There's a surprise," he said. "Had fun last night, huh? Finally found the real stuff."

She laughed strangely. Then a mask of sadness appeared on her face.

He looked around.

"Where's Richard?"

The question seemed to surprise her. "What?"

"Your father. Where is he?"

"What, you want to torture him some more?"

"I just want to say good-bye."

She cackled like an old witch.

"That bad, huh?" Kyle asked.

"Shithead, what did you expect? You're not exactly on his love list at the moment."

Christ, he thought, is what I've done really that bad? He was actually wondering if they were on the same page here; Kerry was as good as anyone at seeing past her father's unreasonableness—was putting the ads back in the novel so terrible that even *she* was taking her father's side?

Did anyone remember whose fucking book it was anymore?

"So, what am I supposed to do?" he asked.

In what seemed a herculean effort, she finally pulled herself up on one elbow. "Walk away, Kyle, that's what you do." She took a deep breath and began to speak in a tone of surprising earnestness. "Look, we'll pull it together here somehow. We always do. You've sort of done him a favor, in a way. But just go away now, Kyle. Give him a break, for once in his life."

Well, he thought, that was a tone you could hardly argue with. He didn't think he'd ever heard her talk without sarcasm before, and it humbled him. Such solemnity from a world-class ironist really got you in the gut.

There was nothing else to do but pick up his things and walk to the door.

He reached for the knob, then stopped and turned around. So that was it, he thought, this whole thing just ends like this? He suddenly had the urge to set Kerry right by her father, to tell her what a good man he was, regardless of his many faults. He wanted to tell her what a fucking great writer he was, that she had no *idea,* and that the things he'd wanted Kyle to be were indeed heroic and good but that he could not live up to them, that he was just not strong enough. He wanted to tell her that despite what she'd thought, her father loved her very much—had in fact told Kyle as much, just a few days ago—even though he was sure Richard had probably never said it to her face, since he was so cursed (and blessed) with having to question everything, with having to see both sides of every idea, and was such a goddamned stubborn son of a bitch.

Yes, her father loved her, and Kyle had wanted to tell her, but when he looked back he saw Kerry lying flat again with one of the large cushions on her face and one of her hands raised up, signaling in the air with a listless flip, urging him to leave, to please, please go away.

And so he went.

DAYBREAK, in the parking lot at Two Mile Hollow beach. White-hurst awoke to the usual dull melancholy, this morning accompanied by the plop of gull shit on his windshield.

He opened his eyes just as one fell, the droplets exploding like paint bullets. *Ka-ping!* He leaned forward and, peering through the already savaged windshield, he could see that the hood was as splattered as a house painter's tarpaulin. It was not quite six-thirty. The gulls must not be used to visitors this early—he had spoiled their solitude, their sense of aesthetics—and so they had decided to give him a good dousing. The accuracy was impressive, he had to admit. Laying his forehead to the glass, he fixed his eyes upward into the dreary September sky and could see the swirling mass of them, an angry, well-trained dive-bomber squadron, swooping and swirling.

"Little bastards," he grumbled, just as another missile landed squarely between his eyes but for the inch of glass in front of him. The reality of it suddenly hit him. *He was being shit on!* Well, of course, he thought, with a sour chuckle. And won't Meryl be furious! Bird shit was impossible to clean, and wasn't he *always* doing something to the jeep, running over a curb or seizing the engine, never fixing a damn thing.

"Meryl," he whispered. *Oh. Dearest Meryl.*

He had not dared return to the house last night—did not, in fact, have the courage. Instead, he dropped his daughter off at the end of the block and returned here, to the beach parking lot, to sleep off one of the many great disasters of his life. He had not slept much, of course, and his head felt as if it had been filled with cement during the night. His throat and nostrils were the smoldering ruins of an arsoned building. Orange juice seemed at that moment the great elixir of all human life, the only substance that could extinguish the last, smoking embers. He couldn't endure but a few more minutes on earth without some, and so he started up his feces-covered vehicle and headed for the highway.

He arrived at a nearby country market and made a beeline for the fridge full of juice products. Bloody wonderful, he thought. He'd gulp one down right there, before he even paid. But among the entire library of pulpy possibilities, he saw not one orange juice. Not a frig-gin' *one*. Oh, there was orange/cranberry, orange/raspberry, orange/banana (banana?). There was pineapple/orange/grape, black cherry/prune/orange, orange/tangerine/grapefruit/cherry, and so on. But no orange juice. Orange-fuck-ing-juice!

"Hey," he said, approaching the counter. Behind it was an un-happy looking Malaysian woman flipping through *People* magazine's "Sexiest Man Alive" issue. "Do you have any orange juice?"

She scowled, jabbing her finger toward the fridge, then returned to her magazine.

"No. There's none there. It's all this mixed-up shit. I want real or-ange juice."

It was no use, of course. Complaining was not usually Richard's style. Ordinarily he was resigned in the face of modern stupidity. But this morning he would not swallow his frustration, simply refused.

He summoned the clerk to the juice section.

"Orange juice," he said again. He was getting sick of saying it. He raised his bad hand to the rows of shiny bright cartons. "That's all I want. *Orange*-juice-flavored orange juice. Got it?"

The woman frowned and opened the refrigerator door.

Poor thing, he suddenly thought. Like she gives a shit, or should even have to. Five-fifty an hour and a few Charleston Chews on the sly. I'd kill myself, Richard thought, I really would.

From her knees the woman shrugged apologetically—there was no orange juice. Ready to throw a fit, Whitehurst suddenly noticed that the woman was quite pregnant. Oh, Jesus, he thought, and immedi-ately hauled her up by the armpits.

"Forget it, please," he said with a big smile. He was determined to make up for his trouble, to set things right. "It's not your fault. I'm very sorry. Obviously this whole thing is fruitless."

Richard waited, thinking it a rather good pun, but she stared at him blankly. Typical, he thought. Her English was not sufficient for wordplay, a miracle she could understand anything at all. In fact, illiteracy was so rampant these days that . . . Oh, blah blah blah. Shut up, you washed-up old fart, he told himself. You bitter old man.

Then he watched as a glimmer of fright flashed in the woman's eyes. She backed away a step, her mouth contracting in fear, and Richard understood now that from looking closely at him she suspected he was crazy.

What was she seeing? he wondered. Was it really all there in his face, the visage of a man a little off, a little demented by the probable termination of a twenty-five-year marriage, who had smoked cocaine with and then been kissed by his daughter, whose troubles were mostly his own doing? A man with two hours' sleep and a bloodied hand suddenly made hysterical by the absence of the proper kind of orange juice? By God, he thought, she's right. How could it *not* be on my face? In fact, I *am* fucking crazy. Run for your lives!

Not wishing to frighten her any further, Richard decided on orange/pineapple, finishing half the carton before he reached the counter. He also picked up a copy of the *Times*, and being reminded by the masthead that today was, in fact, Monday, Labor Day, he figured that with all the chaos in his life, a little routine might be in order. He paid for the items, trying to look as benign and sane as possible and failing miserably. Then he went out and started up the Bronco.

Weekend from hell or not, holiday be damned, he was going to Montauk.

GRAY MIST, dreary morning drive. Yellow raincoat scissoring a soggy hedge. Roofs of houses sagging like frowns, sick of their renters and contrived gaiety. Glimpses of black ocean. Everything stale, worn, finished.

Needing to urinate, Richard pulled off the highway and into the state park at the west end of Montauk. The jungle gym was empty, the ocean obscured by fog.

It was there he noticed Arthur Trebelaine's Mercedes SL, off in the far corner of the lot.

Suddenly forgetting his bladder, Richard pulled the Bronco in behind the snack-bar kiosk and its adjacent rest rooms, putting himself in a position to survey the Mercedes from a distance. His heart began thumping clamorously. There was something highly provocative about the appearance of Arthur's car here. For surely it was Arthur's car. Didn't the license plate read LION? The car's location was doubly suggestive: at the lot's farthest corner, half buried in the roiling mist. A most suspicious feng shui.

Something illicit was going on in that car. Richard was sure of it.

He had two guesses. The first was extreme intoxication. Last night's mêlée had upset Arthur to the point of drink, he reasoned. He had gone home to drop Patty off and fetch a bottle of whiskey, then had come here to stare at the ocean and booze his way through it. Richard knew that Arthur, though more discreet than most, had a penchant for the all-night bender when things went south. And what better occasion than last night's fracas? Perhaps he had a heart after all.

The other theory was Tatiana. Whitehurst would take hundred-to-one odds that her flirtation with Kyle last night had been a ruse. It was, in fact, Arthur who was giving her the big cannoli. My God, he thought, the things Patty had put up with over the years! Was she a blithering idiot, Richard wondered, or didn't she care? That Tatiana would be less than half his age was of no consequence. This was consistent with Arthur Trebelaine. The older Arthur got, the younger *they* got. Yes, there was a hell of a good chance Tatiana was in that car right now, Arthur feeding his midlife crisis to her, inch by inch.

In fact, looking more closely, Richard could swear he saw the Mercedes slowly undulating in the morning mist. As he did, revenge pulsed in his heart. The urge to embarrass the overbearing goon was irresistible. He turned off the Bronco and stepped down to the slickened blacktop.

Last night's rest had been a mockery of sleep, but the dewy brume invigorated him as he approached the car. The convertible was indeed faintly rocking. His plan was to knock on the window, startle the charming couple, say, Oh, excuse me, folks, just wanted to see if you were all right. So, so sorry. Embarrass the self-important dickhead half out of his skin.

The windows were thickly fogged. They were like a couple of high school kids in there, Richard thought. He tapped firmly on the driver's side, his knuckles splashing up beads of water. Suddenly a small circle began to form, a swirling hand opening a porthole to the outside world, a you-got-some-fucking-nerve point of observation. Richard, in turn, could see inside. The eyes, then the face was clearly visible, the chin jerking slightly upward from posterior assault. Beneath it, the large breasts swayed, somewhat bovinely, clanging together without a sound. Strangely, tragically, Richard had his first erection in eighteen months.

The face was his wife's.

He jumped, startled as if from electrocution, his feet literally leaving the ground. The wind leapt from his lungs; he struggled to breathe. Then a door opened and Arthur emerged from the car. He stood with his belt still loose, the fixtures jangling in the morning air. A sickening sound.

Arthur! *Arthur, Arthur, Arthur . . .*

The big man buckled up and put one hand on the canvas roof, eyes averted, head slightly down. His face expressed not regret, exactly. More like inconvenience. In fact, unless Richard was imagining it, Arthur's look was mostly one of annoyance—a schoolboy caught in an unlamented act, one that now required a show of contrition.

"You bastard," Richard said. "How *could* you? Fucking *bastard* . . ."

Before the litany could begin, Meryl appeared. She rose from the driver's seat buttoning up her blouse. Richard could see her bra still hanging on the rearview mirror. How cute, he thought. What fun the kids'd been having. Her lips looked puffy, the meticulous makeup long worn off. He'd really worked her over, Whitehurst could see.

"Richard," she began, her tone not nearly as apologetic as he might have thought—no, actually rather businesslike. "I'm sorry, but . . . it's good this has finally happened."

He gasped. *"Good?"*

"Yes," she said. "Our marriage is over, Richard, you must know that. It's been over."

He looked stunned.

"Please," she said plaintively, "you must have seen it. You can't go on like this any more than I can." She was looking at him strangely. "Oh, come *on,* Richard, you're telling me you didn't realize it's over?"

It is *now,* he wanted to say, but he knew that would be a lie. He would take her back this very second, without delay. They could go home immediately and forget the whole thing as far as he was concerned. Anything, *anything* but the end.

"I'm sorry you had to see . . . this." She turned her head, not daring to look at Arthur. "This must be terrible for you. Just terrible."

Then came the unkindest cut. In the oppressive silence, Richard noticed that the damp morning air had made Meryl's nipples erect.

Forgetting himself, he lost his eyes there, his long-lost hard-on raging like an adolescent's. Then, noticing her husband's gaze, Meryl folded her arms over her chest, hiding herself. To Richard this was worse than the fucking. He had seen her naked thousands of times, tens of thousands—he was her husband, for fuck's sake!—and here she was hiding her breasts from him. Covering up as if he were a stranger, as if he were nothing to her at all!

He began to weep, his head jerking in taut spasms.

"Oh, shit," Meryl said, reaching out to him. "Oh, darling."

Arthur turned away from the scene, as if for discretion's sake. But then Richard looked up to confront him, only to discover his betrayer secretly checking his watch.

"You son of a bitch," Richard yelled, the sound echoing through the empty lot. "You fucking *fucking* bastard!"

Arthur came around the car toward them, slowly, dutifully, realizing it was his turn to be harangued by his old friend. Richard would scream and yell and insult him, he knew, and he would have to take it. This was the price for his and his lover's boldness, apparently. They had been careless, and now he would have to stand there and let Richard yell at him and act like he gave a shit.

What Arthur wasn't counting on was anything physical. He was sure Richard wouldn't dare confront him on that level. That would be just plain stupid, as he was at least one and a half times the man's size. Plus, he'd always regarded Richard as something of a coward.

Richard waited till he had made it around the trunk, then lunged at him.

His strategy was perhaps not the best, nor the most dignified: He tried to bite Arthur. Clearly outmatched, he felt his only chance was to be crazier than his opponent. Yes, he would bite Arthur like a dog. It was the only thing that he *could* do—to chomp down on him somewhere. To taste his rival's blood.

He was barely near him when Arthur pushed him down to the pavement with scornful ease.

The power of it was daunting. The *force*. Shit, Richard thought.

He got to his feet and lunged again. This time Arthur pinned him down hard.

"Stop," Meryl yelled.

Richard stood up. The knees of his pants had shredded. Blood ran down his shins.

"Enough," Arthur said.

Richard charged again.

This time Arthur grabbed him by his shoulders, stepped aside, and guided him into the driver's-side door with a crash.

"Arthur, god*damn it*!" Meryl was hysterical. She stepped up and punched him harmlessly in his pickle-barrel chest.

"What?" Trebelaine replied with a laugh, throwing up his hands. "He won't stop." He pointed down at her fallen husband. "Look, *look* at him." He laughed again.

Richard was at the man's feet, arms wrapped around Arthur's legs, groping helplessly. Arthur reached down and lifted him up by his shirt collar, easily disengaging him and tossing him back onto his buttocks. The whole thing was sorrowful, just pathetic. Meryl began to cry mournfully into her palms.

Richard made another motion to rise, then sat back again. He was exhausted, thoroughly humiliated. His head hung limply between his knees. Around him the mist thickened.

"Richard, please," his wife said, stepping toward him. Immediately he stood, and as she reached out to him he swung at her, knocking her arm away with a slap. Then he turned his back and began walking toward the Bronco.

"Richard!" she yelled. Behind him he could hear her sobbing. "Rich-*ard!*"

He waved her off. Fuck her, he thought. Fuck *them*. It didn't matter. Nothing mattered. He climbed into the jeep and took out the Kubla Khan. There were two rocks left. He fired them up, just as Kerry had showed him. Looking out the window, he saw Meryl walking quickly toward the Bronco.

One more quick hit and he started the jeep, wheels peeling on the damp macadam.

HE DRIVES ANXIOUSLY, taking less than five minutes to reach his destination. He parks by the chains, as he's done hundreds of times. In the middle hangs the weather-beaten sign: NO TRESPASSING. WILL PROSECUTE. Yeah? Fuck you. I dare you. Pipe in hand, he ducks under the chains and heads down the path of tall reeds.

He has an idea. A definite plan. All is lost but might be regained with one final act, one last historic gesture. The one that could redeem everything. Minds will change, everything will be reevaluated. Everything dull and mediocre will suddenly glisten. Attention will finally be paid.

He takes a hit of the pipe and strengthens his stride.

The path is richer today. How the good pipe stimulates the poetry of the senses, he thinks. My daughter is no fool. The smells! My God, the smells are magnificent. Pine and pepperberries, dogwood and wild savory. A pinch of sea salt on top. To his left, a snake suddenly rustles the reeds. Unafraid, he walks toward it, seeking it, daring a confrontation. "C'mon," he says challengingly, "give me your best shot. Come on! I'm *invincible* now." He grows bolder, hearing it rustle away in retreat. "Ha! You don't have the *balls,* buster."

Onward, through the swaying canopy of reeds, he approaches the rock star's titanic beach house, the lawn dewy and grayly glistening. The owner's dog howls, and then the rocker himself appears, princely in his red robe and flowing locks, followed closely by his princess, an unembarrassed naked Nubian (wife number five?) twice his height, long dark legs shining silver in the odd light. They stand in the glass-enclosed porch, waving to him. Richard replies with a thumbs-up—rock on, dude!—the prince's forehead severely narrowing as his weekly trespasser hoists his pipe, flicks the flame, and takes another hit. Alarmed now, the rocker shouts out to the old man, his first communication in ten years muffled by the glass cage. *Please,* Richard thinks, *like you've never,* tossing the spent pipe behind him before trundling on without reply, all ripped knees and bandaged hand.

A quarter mile more, then the promontory. The cliff is hidden. The abyss is filled this morning with a white, billowing mist as from a waterfall. The sound of the unseen ocean seems muted, unthreatening. Below? A cauldron of delights, he believes. Paradise beckoning. Divine immortality.

He walks to the edge, toes perched for flight, and breathes. How easy, he thinks. How strangely effortless. A sea captain waits below for him—Richard is quite sure of it—one of the old Mystic Whitehursts lingering for him on his skiff. He can see the spires of the masts peering up through the fog, hear the voices calling him down. Real, or pipe magic? he wonders. He cannot say. But all is well.

"One more step," Richard Whitehurst says aloud, or merely thinks, arms outstretched. "Just one more step, and I'm a genius."

16

A few days later, Rollie McIntyre entered the offices of Brownstone and Company at 214 Union Square, under the auspices of picking up, finally, the refuse of thirty-two years in the book business. The trip was not his own idea, of course. In fact, the mere thought of performing the present task was so odious to him that he had become quite masterful in casting it from his mind these last eight months, convincing himself that it was a chore that would be better accomplished next week, next month, next *whenever*. Conversely, he had also watched the matter inflate over time, become something much larger than its mere physical existence: a large desk, three chaotic filing cabinets, and two, possibly three old tweed jackets—that was it. Yet they seemed like all the contents of a world to him now, and the idea of approaching them had become, in his mind, an impossibly Sisyphean undertaking. Not to mention that somehow their presence there kept alive a last vestige of hope, a kind of umbilical cord to his old life. With those items in Brownstone's offices, he still had his foot in the door, in a sense, still had a hand in things. Leaving them there had served him well.

First there'd been the drama of his inaction. The weekly calls from Trevor's secretary, first pleading, then demanding the removal of his belongings. Then there were the supportive messages from the remaining American stockholders, telling him not to worry, to take his time, their guilty sympathy seeping through the receiver like maple syrup.

But then Kyle Clayton had called. Monday, had it been? Perhaps Tuesday—the days all seemed to run together now since his "retirement." The young man had called to ask a favor, as he had many times during the years. Rollie had always treated him like a favorite, though deeply flawed, nephew. A fond relative in need of profound indulgence. There'd been the money, of course, the two advances that Trevor now, ironically, held over his head. Then the years of ridiculous incidents and naughty prep-school behavior that publicly Rollie claimed embarrassed—but secretly knew promoted—the so-called Brownstone tradition, and that also started the publisher as a daily reader of the *New York Post*, Kyle Clayton's "Page Six" antics keeping the older man chuckling in his office many a morning behind closed doors. Finally, there'd been the tardiness ad infinitum of Kyle's second novel, only the promise of which ever arrived on time.

Favors. Years and years of them, except now Kyle was offering something in return. Something so extraordinary, in fact, that it threatened to balance, even surpass, the hugely lopsided debt that he had accrued with his old friend.

"McIntyre," Rollie announced, approaching the woman at the front desk. He was half-surprised to find he did not recognize her. Jeanette was gone, apparently. Twenty-two years she'd sat here. She'd had an acid tongue, and she'd ruled the roost like an armed guard. Gate-crashers were cut to the quick. But now she was gone, another casualty.

"McIntyre?" the new woman said, feigning a large, open smile. "Let's see now . . ." She consulted her appointment book, tapping her pen. Her name plate said simply, MS. CARSON. He disliked her immediately. "McIntyre . . . Mc-In-tyre . . ."

"I called about picking up some things," he said. "I used to work here."

"Oh!" Ms. Carson exclaimed, suddenly excited. "Yes, yes. You're the one with the . . . a . . . with the a . . ."

Rollie sympathized. Yes, how exactly *did* one say it?

"That's me."

She put down her pen and lowered her glasses to get a better look. Rollie McIntyre, in the flesh. The name had undoubtedly been bandied about these last months, its owner a figure of pathos and ridicule.

"Well, sir," she said, returning the glasses to their perch, "I have to remind you Mr. Trevor is out of the office today. Much as he wanted to see you."

"Yes, I remember," Rollie said. "Most unfortunate."

"Shall I call the building porters?" she asked, picking up the phone. "A moving company, perhaps? Mr. Trevor told me to spare no expense, that if you needed any help, *any* help at all . . ."

Rollie shook her off. A fair enough question, he thought, since he had only the canvas bag hanging from his shoulder—obviously not enough to get the job done. A slight panic set in as he scolded himself for overlooking this detail, for not making more of a show of it.

"No, thank you," he said, smiling to comfort Ms. Carson. "First I need to remind myself what's in there. You see, it's . . . well, it's been a long time."

"Hasn't it though?"

"I'll call someone myself. Afterward."

"As you wish," she said, putting down the receiver. She used her glasses to point down the hall. "You'll find Mr. Trevor's office down to your left, just past the second—"

"Yes," Rollie cut in. The woman seemed to have forgotten that the man before her had spent three decades on this floor. His voice was pleasant but firm. "I seem to recall."

IT WAS A STARTLED, tentative Rollie who opened the glass doors leading to the main offices of what was still called Brownstone and Company. In just eight months Trevor had had the place completely transformed. The old steel desks and filing cabinets were out, along with the cigarette-pocked industrial carpet and the pegboards littered with ten-year-old messages and dirty jokes. In fact, the whole tableau of general untidiness—which had been a trademark of the old Brownstone and had always spoken to Rollie as a symbol of his staff's eccentric creativity and sense of purpose—had been replaced. Slashed and burned. Someone had gone through this place with a blowtorch, Rollie told himself, and every vestige of the old Brownstone had been flambéed.

There was Italian tile on the floors now, the furniture a kind of nouveau Mission style. Manual typewriters had been on the run for years but now were apparently banned. It looked like an ad agency, he thought sadly, sleek and mean, and he was surprised to find, as he traversed the deadly silent halls, that the staff was entirely new as well. Not a familiar face in the bunch.

These new faces regarded him with a kind of furtive reverence, unable to resist sneaking a peek at him from their desks. They were on the lookout for bathos, no doubt, some mawkish emotion they could talk about when he'd left. Here was the prodigal father, back to find the children all grown up and insolent in their success. Faster, richer, *better* since he wasn't around. But if it was sentiment they wanted, they could forget it. There was no emotion here, Rollie discovered, nothing familiar to tug at him. He wasn't missing a thing. They could have it.

In Trevor's office he found his desk and filing cabinets tucked awkwardly into a corner; the room was now much larger than when Rollie had occupied it. Looking around he realized that not one but two walls had been knocked down—David's office was triple the size his own had been. The view, though, was essentially the same. Union Square, southeast corner. As if to jilt him, the trees were in their fall crest this afternoon, a triumph of burnt orange, the park awash with the leaf-swept rush of noontime. It was the vantage point of bittersweet memory. Over the years here he'd witnessed protests, delicate rainfalls, the gait of certain attractive men, even a mugging or two. Hours and hours of intense thought, idle dreams. The seasons sliding thoughtlessly one into another.

Forgetting for a moment the urgency of his mission, he went over to the filing cabinets and pulled open a bottom drawer. Over the decades this had been his dumping ground for odds and ends, mementos, things he wanted to save but had no patience to organize. He started to dig through the rubbish. He was in the mood to torture himself.

Things were pulled at random. Here was a graying *Playbill* from 1973, the show incidental, his companion long forgotten. He would go to the theater twice a week back then, he remembered, plays followed by late dinners, endless conversation, sexual stratagems running into the early morning. Here an invitation to a dinner party from a then-unknown writer he had championed. It had been hell to get his first book through; now his name was being whispered about for the

Nobel. Goddamn it, he thought, wasn't I right more often than not? Wasn't I?

He dug deeper. In a manila folder he found a collection of magazine articles written about him, one from the early seventies, a *New York Times Magazine* profile that romanticized him beyond all hope and featured a photo of him that got Rollie more sex for the next five years than he cared to remember. Finally, in the back at the bottom of this paper flotsam, a long-forgotten bottle of Cognac sat idling, still in its box. Now he was blindsided with images of old Christmas parties, the place awash with scotch in Dixie cups and clouds of cigarette smoke, interns being smooched and fondled in abandoned offices. Brownstone, losing money again, but with another Pulitzer under its belt. Still in the center of things, still in its glory. He could almost hear the music echoing down the halls, the raucous laughter.

Enough, he abruptly thought, closing the drawer. My *word*. Enough.

Unconsciously, he plopped down in Trevor's chair as if it were his own, turning to the park below him. Even here—behind his successor's desk, in his ludicrous Paul Bunyan office—he realized suddenly how miserable he'd been these last months. How utterly wretched. Who've I been kidding? he thought. I need to work, to be around people, around books. There isn't anything else for me but books, never has been. Simple as that. Without them, I die.

Remembering his task, he wheeled himself forward to Trevor's desktop, ready to start the dig. All last night he'd gone over in his head the many places where it might be kept. What drawer, he'd tried to imagine, what file? Had it been transferred to disk? Is that how they did it now in the New World?

Over and over he'd brooded on this moment, using his own experience as a compass. *Where would I keep it, if it were mine?* He fretted that it might not be in the office at all, then realized that neither

Trevor nor himself would ever let such a thing leave the premises. No, it was here somewhere.

Then, just as he was about to begin tearing the place upside down, he simply looked at Trevor's maniacally organized desk, his eyes lowering like a homing device right down to the one pile of papers adorning its spare surface. A single manuscript. My word, Rollie thought again, yes, I believe this is it. The simplicity, the ease of this, was somewhat absurd, but then in a way not surprising at all. It was the cornerstone of Brownstone's new vision, Trevor's pride and obsession, front and center. Of *course* it was here.

Looking at it, Rollie's hands began to shake. So obvious, so easy. It should've had a bow on it.

Rollie flipped quickly through the stack, making sure it was the real thing. Three hundred and forty-eight pages, just as Kyle had said. The original copy, marked up a bit now. Even as he read a stray sentence or two the words jumped out at him, sparkling, alive. An unbelievable talent. And Trevor had actually been reading it for himself, he was surprised to see. There was a pencil on the pile and marks in the margins. *Tell me why doesn't he fuck her here?* And then: *Why put on just jeans? Why not put on his Wranglers? $$$$$$* In the middle were the proposed ads, the glossy pages loose and smudged with thumbprints. Trevor had been playing with them like little toys, he could see, moving them around obsessively, looking for just the right mix.

Were there other copies floating around? Unlikely, Kyle had told him. First of all, the manuscript was incomplete, and then Trevor was treating this as strictly top secret.

Without an ounce of regret, Rollie stuffed the manuscript into his bag and headed out of the office. As he moved swiftly toward the elevator, Ms. Carson again lowered her glasses.

"Lunch already, Mr. McIntyre? Why, you've just started."

"Actually, I'm all done."

"I beg your pardon," she said with a shake of the head. Then she smiled, wondering if it might be a polite joke.

"Just have the porters throw it away."

"All of it?" she asked.

"Everything."

He hit the button for the lobby, waiting anxiously.

Ms. Carson was understandably confused. "I'm sorry, I . . ." She blinked, as if straining to comprehend. "You're telling us there's nothing in there that you want? After all these months?"

She illustrated her point by aiming the frame of her glasses. Rollie's eyes followed this direction into the offices, if only to take a last look. To be sure.

"Not a thing," he said finally, swallowing hard. Then the elevator doors opened and he gripped his canvas bag even tighter as the elevator took him away.

17

Sadly but perhaps inevitably, Richard Whitehurst's leap of faith did not have the dramatic impact of which legends are made. He'd meant the act to be the greatest literary swan dive since Hart Crane, to drown himself in the great poetic tradition of Ophelia and *The Awakening*, but in true Whitehurstian fashion, he never quite made the splash. The teeming mist of that fateful morning, which in the moment had seemed like a beckoning elixir to his doom wish, proved only to obscure what poor Richard would certainly have discerned on any other morning: that what lay below him was not the swirling, frothy jaws of the sea, nor the skiff of a Mystic sea captain, but merely a declivity of jagged rock. There he landed after falling only twenty feet, dashed on the side of the bluff. Afterward he lay for many hours, quite alive, his punctured lung slowly filling with blood, intermittently crying, then coughing, then cursing the absurd struggle and general inanity that was human existence.

With a little luck, he could have been saved. If he had been rescued even some five or six hours after, the blood could still have been drained from his lung, the cuts stitched, the broken bones mended. Soon after the fall, Richard himself began to wish for this. The Kubla Khan had worn off and terror had set in. Death was suddenly unwelcome.

"*Hu*lp me," he called out, blood gurgling on his tongue.

He had one good book left, he told himself; he must survive. He would make things right with his wife—by God he would. He loved her. Just as he loved his daughter. How stupid he had been to tell Kerry anything else! Always with the drama, he scolded himself, always saying the unexpected. Of course he loved her. Damn *fool*.

Unfortunately, nobody thought to look for him. Meryl saw nothing unusual in his absence. A jilted husband wasn't exactly due home for dinner, was he? Kerry was distracted, still licking her wounds from the previous night. She lay on the couch throughout the afternoon, inert, already planning her return to the city. Oh, the naughty chemicals that awaited her there! She could taste them now. World records would be set. Dear old Dad could kiss her ass.

Finally, after ten hours of dreadful pain and gargling on his own blood like a mouthwash, Whitehurst died. He was not discovered until late the next morning, sighted on the cliffs as the fog lifted by the members of a bass-fishing vessel named the *Romulus*. Lured close to shore by a copious school of stripers, the boat had gotten stranded for nearly twenty-four hours after the mist had rolled in. Following the discovery, the *Romulus*'s captain admitted to a local news team how lucky he felt that the poor man had not dove from a spot just ten feet north, for he, Captain White, had been on deck almost all the previous morning, and would likely have been injured or even killed.

It took a team of twenty to disengage Richard from the cliff. Rigor mortis had stiffened his body in a tight fetal position, making removal nearly impossible. Then it was discovered that a flock of seagulls had made hors d'oeuvres of his eyeballs and much of his forehead, turning his formerly pleasant, if lachrymose, features into a hideous death mask. An open casket, of course, was out of the question, and so Meryl decided on cremation. The ashes were to be spread at Crooked Pond in Bridgehampton, in a scene reminiscent of Truman Capote's own farewell slightly more than a decade earlier.

THE SERVICE took place the following Friday. The day was suitably gloomy, beautiful in a way Whitehurst himself would have appreciated. A beading rain hissed through the trees, tickling the soft mires and lily pads of the pond, while near the edge of the lone slip silent swans danced a gentle gavotte in Richard's honor. Guests slipped, lurched, and sunk in the boggy earth, but the rain was just as well, allowing everyone to conceal their considerable grief under umbrellas.

Weary after an early-morning train ride from Manhattan, Kyle Clayton emerged from his taxi with a *Times* for an umbrella to find a veritable sea of black lingering on the soggy lawn. For a man who'd thought he had no friends, no acolytes, Richard's death had summoned quite a flock. Moving through the crowd, Kyle noted a rather large contingent of American writers, many of whom Whitehurst had assumed never heard of him, or were unimpressed. There were various family members of course, and a drove of old friends from the New York City days. Kyle spotted a small band of what looked like graduate students or would-be writers, clutching dog-eared copies of *Heart's Crest*, and then there were the few who seemed to have no connection at all, bookish adults who'd loved Richard's work anonymously and felt an inexplicable compulsion to call in sick today and drive out to rainy Bridgehampton.

All in all, it was a scene that would have greatly heartened Richard, had he been around to see it.

Searching for a familiar face, Kyle ran into Kerry Whitehurst, leaning on a car, alone and quite outside the thick of things. She was smoking a cigarette with an exaggerated lassitude, bobbing her head to a music that only she heard.

"Hey, punkass," she said when she saw him.

As Kyle approached the conspicuously unsentimental mourner, he noticed a distinct puffiness under her eyes. As usual, her toughness was a put-on, a performance piece. She was barely together, and probably stoned to the gills for courage. On her head she wore her father's beat-up old Red Sox cap, which Kyle immediately bet would be the morning's most cogent tribute, meaning more to Richard than all the studied homages and hopped-up hosannas that would soon begin.

"I owe you an apology," she said.

"Oh?"

"Yeah," she said, "big time. I got everything all messed up. As usual."

Kyle's curiosity was piqued, but they were suddenly interrupted by Larry Wabzug. Mud up to his ankles, he came waddling through the sod in a blizzard of tears, arms flailing this way and that. He was delirious, nearly out of his mind with woe.

"The poor bastard!" Larry exclaimed in a voice that certainly carried across the pond—even the swans looked up. "The poor son of a bitch!" He flung his arms around both of their necks, lest he fall to the sopping ground from despair.

As Larry buried his head in his goddaughter's breast, Kyle tactfully turned away, keeping a peripheral eye tuned on the stoic Kerry as she melted into Larry's arms. "My dear," Larry wailed into her shoulder, "oh, my dear!" Kerry smiled just a bit, relieved, it seemed—and perhaps even pleased—that finally someone of naked and sincere emotions had arrived through whom she might vicariously mourn.

Even her chin, usually as reliable as a top-notch heavyweight's, slipped briefly into crinkle and spasm.

"Terrible," he said, releasing her at last. "Terrible, terrible, terrible . . . ," letting everyone know he had not been too busted up to stop for coffee on the expressway.

There was a stirring near the pond's edge. A voice, muffled slightly by the rain, asked that all the guests please approach the slip. The service was about to commence. It was at that moment Kyle noticed Meryl Whitehurst for the first time. Her stride was unsteady, heels sinking in the mud, arms hugging the urn of ashes. Above the widow's veiled head hung an umbrella manned by Arthur Trebelaine.

Oddly enough, though they passed within a few feet, neither Kerry nor Wabzug moved to join the procession. Kyle wondered how Arthur had weaseled his way into the position of widow's escort. This was made all the more mysterious when after moving just beyond them, Meryl shifted the urn to one arm and lifted a corner of her veil, clearly trying to make eye contact with Kyle's group. Kerry turned away, stubbing her cigarette underfoot, while Wabzug said nothing, failing to even nod.

"Yeah, I was wrong about you," Kerry murmured to Kyle as her mother's cortège moved away from them. "I thought you were the one. I should have known." She shook her head, eyes following her mother and Arthur as they slowly trudged toward the water.

The crowd's momentum hurried them toward the slip.

Though Richard was a zealous and devout atheist, his wife had summoned a Presbyterian minister for the occasion. This was done, apparently, to give the event some spiritual distinction, and perhaps to assuage the inconsolable guilt Meryl had been experiencing since the discovery of her husband's body. In fact, as the minister began his eulogy, Meryl started to shake uncontrollably, her tears slipping almost instantly into hysterics, her grief becoming so intense that the minister momentarily paused to allow friends to attend to her.

Kyle watched in astonishment as Kerry and Wabzug stood impassive through this, kicking at the mud and whispering to each other. Finally Meryl was subdued to something near calmness, then seated in a lawn chair. The service continued. The minister began by reminding everyone of the fullness of the deceased's sixty-plus years, of the beauty and richness of an artist's "life of the mind"—an assertion Richard had always disagreed with, contending that it had made him miserable and that he wished he'd found something else to do. He cited with pride the presence of a trenchant spirituality in the Whitehurst canon (which the writer had always asserted was "sensual" rather than "spiritual"). And finally, he assured one and all that a soul as beneficent and humane as Mr. Whitehurst's must surely now be residing in the more resplendent quarters of God's heavenly city—to which Richard would've covered his mouth and yawned.

Then an old college friend of Whitehurst's stood up, provoking a small murmur of laughter as he told of Richard's habit of correcting his Dartmouth professors in matters of grammar and history. Another man, now a famous comedy writer, recited anecdotes of their early years on the Lower East Side, of hungry nights and penny-pinching double dates. It was all quite pleasant, and nobody mentioned the word *suicide*.

Finally it was Wabzug's turn. He approached the slip nervously, fidgeting with his notes. He fixed his glasses, blotted outwardly by rain and inside by tears, and stared vacantly out at the assemblage. He was not stagestruck, Kyle guessed, so much as overcome by misery and anguish, by the fierce reality of the occasion he was now to address. It was intolerable, impossible—his dear old friend was dead.

"For over thirty years, Richard Whitehurst was a colleague and a fr—"

He stopped at the word; it was too potent. As if suddenly in physical pain, he grabbed the railing to steady himself, bowing his head. The minister then kindly put his arm around poor Larry, leaning down to comfort and reassure him. Wabzug nodded, trying to gather himself.

He tried again.

"For more than thir-ty . . . years . . ."

Now it was just this simple phrase that was too much. He brought the notes up to cover his face and closed his eyes. Once more the minister stepped forward but did not reach him before Larry had cleared his throat and was bravely going again.

This time as he tried to speak there was nothing, just a jumble of tangled, mournful grunts, and finally Kerry came up to rescue him.

She held Larry by his waist, leading him down from the slip like a broken widower. "Understandable," the minister said consolingly.

Then, out of nowhere, Devon Schiff was introduced. A "fellow writer," said the minister, and "great friend" of Whitehurst, who wished to read a passage from *Sag Harbor Sonata*.

Kyle was flabbergasted, nearly overcome with the urge to laugh out loud, to savagely snicker. He himself had asked Meryl for the privilege of this very task, to read from her husband's work. She, in turn, had left a regretful message, stating that the duty had already been filled. Kyle was disappointed but resigned. So Arthur would read, he assumed. Made sense, despite their recent differences. But Arthur had been conspicuously silent so far—distastefully so, Kyle had felt—and where *was* Patty by the way, and what the fuck was Devon doing up there?

It was ridiculous, he thought, a farce. Schiff had always disliked Whitehurst's work, thought it too pretty, overwritten, regarded the man himself as a kind of literary loser. But here he was somehow, calculating and jejune, closing out the funeral of the "friend" he'd never met.

He had style, though, even Kyle had to admit that. He was dressed in an inky Italian suit that made funerals look sexy, and on his way to the slip he graciously kissed the widow's hand, whispering consolations in her ear. Everything deft, courtly.

"*The forwarding address,*" he began, sneaking a meaningful glance at Meryl, "*of the sea-widow named Darla Betterby . . .*" Even the passage he chose was adroit, Kyle admitted. Evocative of the occasion, though avoiding the maudlin.

Schiff was careful to address the two television cameras as he read. The journalists' pens, stoic until now, suddenly sprang to life, and at his feet, a phalanx of still photographers slipped to one knee, firing like Minutemen. No, Kyle thought, Schiff is perfect. Schiff is the one. Friend or not, Richard would have loved it.

The paparazzi had finally discovered Whitehurst.

18

For those who cared enough to notice, the service had ended on two awkwardly played notes. To the sylvan fancy of Chopin's Berceuse— Richard's all-time favorite piece of music, though produced somewhat incongruously from a boom box—Meryl emptied the urn on the rain-stippled pond. Many mourners gasped when, instead of powdered ash, the urn dispensed large chunks of bone, the widow having to dig out the last bits by hand. When the swans began savagely nipping at one another for the larger pieces, the dismay was audible and the crowd quickly disbanded.

This left Kyle and Kerry alone at last, retiring under the canopy of a lofty elm, where she finished her apology.

Kyle was nearly knocked flat at what he heard. With an insider's panoramic view, Kerry divulged the week's events, the revelations of a summer. He listened raptly as she told him of her mother's affair, her sudden plans for divorce, the great friend's treachery. Mom was on her shit list right now, Kerry said, though her father's death could hardly be blamed on her. And the affair with Arthur was off—they could never be together, Meryl had decided. Despite his role as today's escort, Arthur was to return to Patty, who, no doubt, was waiting breathlessly to take him back.

Of course, Kerry's apology was unnecessary, since Kyle was unaware anything had been going on in the first place, never mind that he'd been accused of it. But she did apologize—for underestimating him, for buying into the image of Clayton as jerk, puke, mug. He probably was, she told him, but he hadn't shown it this summer. This summer he'd done all right.

Then it was time for the good-byes.

"So, what do you do now?" Kyle asked. "Where do you go?"

Around them the rain hissed through the trees, producing a comforting music, though they suffered hardly a drop.

"Back to New York," she answered. "My art, you know. I have a few new ideas."

"And all your favorite substances, of course."

She nodded with some ambivalence, then looked out onto the pond. "I'm thinking maybe I might slow down a bit on that end. Take it easy for a while."

Kyle was about to tell her what a good idea that was, but then thought that was exactly the opposite of what you said to Kerry Whitehurst.

"And sex," she said. "And I need to get *laid*," she said. "You know what I mean?"

Kyle laughed. "Listen," he said, "I'm sorry about that time in the car . . . You and I—"

She shook him off.

"It's all right, Clay," she said, tapping him on the arm with her fist. "You did the right thing."

Kyle blinked, surprised. When was the last time someone had told him that? My, oh, my, he thought, I *am* slipping.

"You're an all right guy," she said with a smile. "I don't care what they say about you."

"And they do."

"Oh, yes," she said, "they do. And they will. But that's good too."

"It is, huh?"

"I think so."

Kyle lifted his newspaper over Kerry's head, guiding her over to one of the cabs that were waiting for them. There he kissed her on the cheek and told her they should get together sometime in the city, maybe have a drink or something. She laughed at him and the cab pulled away.

ENSCONCED IN HIS OWN TAXI, Kyle unfurled the rumpled and soggy *Times*. There, in a two-by-two-inch box adjacent to the cross-word puzzle, he found the tribute to Richard. *In Memory of . . . Aurelian Books* yada yada yada.

Better late than never, he thought.

He knew the story. When Wabzug had called Aurelian two days ago to find out why they hadn't yet printed a memoriam, standard for any deceased author, the publisher apologized profusely, explaining that the imprint was in a dreadful financial state—the same thing he *always* said, Larry reminded himself, when it came to spending money on Richard Whitehurst. Debtors were encroaching, said the man from Aurelian. They were awaiting word from the NEA and PEN, among other potential benefactors, hoping for a miracle.

"Fine, I'll write a check myself," Wabzug said without hesitation. The man was dead two, three days, already, there wasn't time for bullshit. "Just call the *Times* and publish a goddamned memoriam. Can you do that at least?"

Embarrassed but resolute, the publisher then asked what would happen—*by the way*—to the seventy-five hundred dollars they'd advanced Whitehurst for his next book. Larry, who was ready to blow a gasket, said he would take care of that *too,* personally return it in full, and any other dead writers' debts they needed to collect on, and while he was at it, did the publisher's son need any money for *summer fucking camp*!

As the taxi approached Water Mill, Kyle folded up the *Times* and threw it on the empty seat. He'd searched all the papers. There'd been no formal obituary of Whitehurst. Despite his suicide, Richard's death seemed to go unacknowledged.

At first Kyle thought maybe it just needed some time, that the death needed to marinate a bit in the public imagination. But then he thought, No, he is lost forever. Gone.

"HOLY SHIT," the driver said as they climbed the long, winding driveway. Through a thicket of scrub trees it loomed, the Starship *Enterprise*. "I heard about this place," he said. He was looking up, straining his neck to see it. "Wow, it's awful. It's worse than they said."

"Give me five minutes," Kyle said.

The rain had picked up. Down below he could hear the waves booming against the shore, the water tickling the pylons of the guest house that had been his home quite a few nights this summer—a fact that now seemed like a severe error in judgment.

He climbed the steep stairs of the main house and knocked, half hoping Arthur wasn't home. Almost immediately Kyle could hear the footfalls on the floor, feel the pressed wood of the deck shaking perceptibly. Then the door opened, and the hulking mass that was Arthur Trebelaine stood in front of him.

He looked especially large today, Kyle was sorry to observe, a true mountain of a man. Foolishly, Trebelaine seemed pleased to see the young man, naturally assuming, being Arthur, that Kyle had come as an ally. He smiled, which only pissed Kyle off more. Worse, Arthur was sucking lovingly on one of his long cigars. What the hell was this, he wondered, a celebration?

"Hey, Clay!" Arthur said excitedly. "All right, my man! Come on in. Have a drink." Clearly he was a little tanked.

Though the rain was falling hard, Kyle didn't move.

"I didn't know whether or not to say hello to you this afternoon, Clay, you know? Didn't know whose side—"

Kyle wound up and clocked him as hard as he could in the jaw. The blow was perfection. *At last.* After a lifetime of misfires, drunken grazings, the occasional flights of cowardice, Kyle had finally stood strong and landed a flush blow.

Arthur fell backward and then down, taking a coatrack with him. Kyle heard the house quake underneath him as he hit the floor.

"*Yeoooooow,*" Arthur said.

He slid upon landing and now lay stretched out on his back. He pushed the rack and the fallen jackets off his chest. Then Arthur raised himself to his elbows and began massaging his jaw.

"Pretty good, kid," he said, with a fake chuckle. "Pretty fucking good."

Kyle shook out his hand. "That was for Richard," he said.

"Hey, good for you," Arthur rejoined, voice thick with irony. "Give 'em hell."

" 'Don't be intimidated by anyone.' You told me that, remember?"

"Yeah, sure, kid, whatever." He was still smiling. "That's real great." He got up on one knee. "Except now I'm gonna kick your ass."

Fists clenched, Arthur tried to stand up, but he was too wobbly. The blow had destroyed his equilibrium. As he struggled mightily to straighten himself, Kyle gave him another one, this time in the abdomen, burying it down in there good, deep in the soft spot where all the years of high living were kept.

The big man collapsed again in a moaning heap.

"Okay . . . all right," he said, trying to catch his breath. "Now, *that* hurt. I admit it."

"That was for Kerry," Kyle said, somewhat melodramatically. "You know what I mean?"

"What, are we doing the whole family here? Who's next, the half cousin? *Fuck you.*"

He was about to get up again, but Patty had appeared. She came toward them slowly through the hall, her slippered feet sliding sluggishly along the floor. Kyle noticed a ghostly pallor in her face. She held her arms across her breasts self-consciously, yet she was fully covered in a bathrobe. She seemed not at all surprised to see her husband on the floor in a heap.

As she bent down to see if he was all right, she reached out, and Kyle could now discern what she'd been hiding: a massive boob job, the breasts bulging grotesquely against the inside of her robe like a pair of cantaloupes. Meryl's competition had proved too much, apparently. Mrs. Trebelaine had been sliced up and stuffed like a Thanksgiving turkey.

Kyle suddenly felt nauseous. He looked down at Arthur, unable to believe this had once been his hero. All the articles, movies, biographies—it was all horseshit. Everything about Arthur Trebelaine made him sick.

"Go back to bed," Arthur told his wife, once again raising himself to his knees.

"Are you okay?" she said softly.

"Fine," he growled.

She looked up at Kyle. "Should I call the police?"

"*No,*" he said. "Just go. Go back to bed. You need to rest."

She stood up with a wince, then glanced once more at Kyle before shuffling off down the hall.

Arthur looked up contritely. "She had an operation," he said.

"I see."

Kyle watched her walk. From his angle it was the weary shuffle of a seventy-year-old woman.

"Well?" Arthur asked, holding up his hands. "What else? You want another shot? You gonna kick my teeth in?"

"No," Kyle said after a moment. "I guess I'm done."

"Good," Arthur said. He picked up his cigar, which had fallen near him, and sucked on it till it started to smoke again. Energized by this success, he stood up and grinned insolently.

"You're a real fuck, you know that, Arthur?" Kyle said.

"Oh, that's right," answered the big man, brushing off his pants. "I don't embrace failure. I'm a real fuck, a real asshole. Boo hoo hoo."

"You settled. You write books for the movies."

He laughed at this. "Implying what? That I'm a *whore.* How dare you, you fucking sponger. You come here without a penny to your name, stay in my beach house three times a week, eat my food, cigar smoke coming out of your fucking *ears,* then you call *me* a whore?" He waved at the air with the back of his hand. "Now, get outta here, you're full of shit. Get lost."

He tried to close the door, but Kyle jammed his shoulder to prevent him.

"You killed him," he said.

Arthur let the door loose. For the first time his defiance yielded, his eyes showing something like remorse.

"I don't believe that, Kyle."

"You wouldn't."

"He couldn't go on with what he believed in. Nobody could. It's a miracle he lasted as long as he did. The man was a sucker for punishment. Don't ask me why."

"You both believed in the same things once. Way back when."

Arthur's eyes suddenly narrowed.

"What the hell do you know about me? What I believed in?"

"Those early stories of yours. We read those to each other one night, you know."

"Who?"

"Richard and I," Kyle answered. The older man was silenced. "Yeah, we did. Just read them over and over, shaking our heads. Those are classics, Arthur."

Trebelaine just stared at him. He looked more woozy now than when Kyle had clocked him.

"Meaning what?"

Kyle shrugged, looking around. "What the hell happened?"

Just then Patty reappeared at the end of the hall. Something was wrong.

"Arthur?" she called. She was crying softly. *"Arthur?"*

"What?"

She was leaking, she said. There was fluid coming out. Something was terribly wrong. Please come, she pleaded.

Arthur kept looking at Kyle. "In a *minute*," he said sharply.

Kyle stood in the frame of the door, rain chilling the top of his head and back, waiting for what was to come.

"Rumor has it your novel has legs," Arthur said. "Walked right out of Trevor's office."

Kyle was silent, not wanting to admit to anything.

"Big mistake," Arthur said.

"Maybe."

"No, I'm serious. You want to be like him, you want the high road?" He smiled, puffing his cigar. "Okay, you got it, pal." He shook his head, moving in a little closer. "You're in for it, let me tell you. You think you can do whatever you want? They're gonna crucify you out there, Kyle. They're gonna break you."

Kyle nodded—this sounded about right. This had all been figured in.

Patty's voice called again. "Arthur? *Arthur, please.*"

The taxi began to honk. Kyle stepped out and released the door. As he turned to go, Arthur called out to him.

"Hey, Clayton."

Kyle turned back, wiping the rain from his face.

"You're not going to, uh . . ." Arthur's voice dropped to a whisper. "You're not going to tell anybody about this, are you?" He touched his jaw, moving it back and forth.

Kyle looked at him for a second.

"Save it for your memoirs or something, you know what I mean?" Arthur asked. "After I'm gone. I know you don't owe me, but . . . I don't want this getting out."

Clayton was flabbergasted. Of all the damn things.

"I would never say anything," he answered.

Arthur seemed relieved.

"Thanks," he said. "And good luck. You're gonna need it."

Kyle shut the door and, confounded as ever, walked back to the taxi in the rain.

CODA

The wonks have taken over.

Rap rap rap.

Fucking Rose Bowl, Kyle thinks, fucking London goddamned Symphony Orchestra, door to the greenroom suddenly opening like the clash of a thousand cymbals, his head jerking up like a jack-in-the-box. In the rush to normalcy, the show of nothing-untoward-here, there is the painful banging of funny bone, the clank of small bottles, the throat-clearing mumbles.

"You okay?" the P.A. asks.

"*Fine.* Yeah. *Mm-hmm, good.*"

The P.A.—in baseball hat and headset, eyes flushed with the importance of his calling—opens the minibar for a pop inspection, finding it raided, negated, totally decimated.

Kyle sits up, back arched in defense. "Talent can drink," he says plaintively. "That's what they told me, *Talent can drink.*"

It had started as it ever had, with the idea of just one or two, a little something to sand the edges, trim the tassels. He'd wanted to go on the show loose, irreverent. *Make a good showing—for once,* as Wabzug had put it.

Then things had slipped off the rails a little.

Whitehurst's death had been the knell of Kyle's momentary peace of mind. The summer sonata, all poetry and mist, was O-V-E-R. The pressure was on now, he was in a muddle. Still, he was not without his triumphs. The novel (finally titled *Gotham Tragic*) should be hitting the bookstores any day now, compliments of Aurelian Press, Whitehurst's former publisher. In a quid pro quo deal, Kyle had offered the book for a microscopic advance. In return, the work would be edited by a certain former publisher from Brownstone and Company, along with the placing of the man in a substantial editorial position and the granting of his own imprint.

Kyle was quite pleased. It wasn't much money—a mere night on the town, really—but the novel's presentation was suitably dignified, with a simple, attractive cover and nothing inside but plain, boring old *text.* Archaic. A hopeless relic, to be sure.

Then there was the rumor that on Rollie McIntyre's first day of work in almost a year, someone had peered into his new matchbook-sized office and sworn they'd seen a welling in the good man's eyes.

But this was about all on the good-news front. David Trevor had not been in the least bit amused, of course, in watching his most prized project take flight at another house. War had been pronounced. Lawsuits were flying like footballs. They were trying to block Aurelian's publication of *Gotham Tragic* and had already succeeded in causing a considerable delay. Kyle had just about had it; he'd wanted to start working again, but week after week was being wasted with phone calls from Aurelian's lawyers. And then there were Larry's updates, keeping him abreast of the nearly hourly ups and downs. It was ugly; it was mean. It was vintage Trevor.

For the few who cared for such things, the city was indeed abuzz with talk of *Gotham Tragic*—the buzz being strictly of the chainsaw variety. The author's inexhaustible litigious episodes were daily fodder for the papers, the perspective advanced that the two parties— the fascist and the cad—essentially deserved each other. Then, to top it off, a few advance copies of the novel had mysteriously found their way to reviewers; Aurelian, it turned out, was not as commercially inept as it had pretended. *Uncover dogs and lap!* The feast was on.

"BACKSTABBING HYPOCRITICAL SEX MANIAC!" wrote the *Post* with typical Elizabethan poesy. The antipathy of *New York* magazine was a bit subtler, the reviewer entitling her piece "Sophomoric Jinx." Sadly, the new novel didn't stand up to *Charmed Life,* the reviewer wrote, amnesiacally overlooking how viciously she'd panned *that* book eight years ago. *Details,* cornerstone of American artistic principle, proclaimed the roman à clef treatment of various New York notables as "tasteless," its deigning to mention celebrities "vapid," the article including a chart that invited readers to match the novel's characters to their real-life counterparts. On and on it went, a general consensus forming that the young "pugilist" writer had squandered his talent in favor of celebrating the "jet-setting" lifestyle he'd been conducting for the past years. Naughty, naughty boy.

Yet there was a lone wolf at a downtown free paper who must have been writing under an assumed name, or was perhaps perpetrating a hoax, or was most likely mad, for he called *Gotham Tragic* the best novel he'd read in years. The piece took a swing at the recent reviews and their "hamhanded contrivers" who wouldn't know satire if it hit them with "half a million volts." The author, he claimed, was not celebrating his characters but sneering at them. Some of the finest lyrical writing about New York ever, he wrote, the most searing irony since Nathanael West. All of it lost, lamented the reviewer, all of it wasted, apparently, except in the knowledge that at least there was *one* person out there who understood, at least one writer as disgusted as you were. The rest of them, he said, could go to hell.

Kyle kept that one.

"I'M FINE, guys, really." Kyle Clayton clapped his hands. "Let's do it."

The P.A. had returned, this time armed with a cup of Starbucks Sumatra and a hard-eyed producer. Weapons designed to make him sit up, fly right, get with the program.

"I'm good to go," Kyle said. "Seriously." He sipped the coffee to confirm this.

The P.A. and his boss exchanged a look.

"You remember the questions?" one of them asked.

"Oh, yeah, funny stuff."

"You remember the *answers*?" asked the other.

"Sure, sure. Hilarious."

These "live" shows were over before you got on them, Kyle had discovered. Things had changed since he'd last been on the tube. The questions and answers now were long taken care of—no room for error here. In fact, he and the P.A. had spent a good hour when he'd first arrived, the man regaling him with the host's list of queries, one by one, then listening to Kyle's replies, zeroing in on the zingers, the cute retorts.

Live TV. No room for error.

Glug glug glug.

"Five minutes," said the P.A.

Left alone again, Kyle combed his hair, wiped his mouth with a tissue, scratched his balls. Realizing his buzz had been slightly compromised, he took the Tom Thumb–sized Johnnie Red hidden behind the tissue box and dumped it into the coffee. Then, a few final toasts:

I. One for the X. Kyle had discovered in the *Times* recently that she had married. A "prominent securities analyst" at Goldman Sachs. "The couple to reside in Scarsdale, N.Y."

Scarsdale, Kyle thought. Good luck with the poetry.

II. One for Dorothea Clementine. Just a week ago a messenger had buzzed at his door, delivering an envelope. Inside was a letter.

Got your book, old lover, and I declare, I'm just crazy about this Lady Botox. What a cutie! Everyone says it's me. How exciting is that? And how sweet are you to write about lil' ol' me, Honey Kyle. Of course I know I am sorta famous, definitely a somebody, but never dreamed I'd ever be a character in a book! So, anyhow, here's the money you asked for, all those months ago. How silly of me to have quibbled over $$$$, way back when.

Why don'tcha come up and see me sometime.

Feeling something attached, Kyle turned over the letter. Taped to the back was a check for $100,000. "Fuck you" money, literally speaking.

III. Lastly, a big one for Richard Whitehurst. Kyle thought of him every day. The show tonight had him remembering a line of his, the one spoken on the beach during those first weeks, uttered in the hushed, rabid tones, the bitter spittle gathering at the corners of his mouth . . .

Really let 'em have it, Kyle. Let the bastards have it like I never could.

After a minute or so the P.A. came back in and escorted him down a long hallway. There, on the edge of the set, they waited. The lights were blinding, the talk insipid.

This was to be a lynching tonight—that much was clear. The prepped questions were obvious in their hostility, clearly designed to tear him down; the answers fitted for repudiation, for him to laugh at himself, a jocular apology.

I was wrong, they wanted Kyle to admit. Silly me. Won't happen again.

The scream of "Talent" from a loudspeaker. Kyle was quickly ushered to his seat. The host smiled warmly. Water was offered. No thanks, Kyle told him, raising the coffee cup he'd brought from the greenroom.

Ten seconds . . . five . . . The lights were cued *. . . two . . .*

Tomorrow there would be pictures in the paper, headlines. There would be talk on the street, in the offices. Peering into the next cubicle, people would laugh and shake their heads, congratulate themselves on not being crazy like Kyle Clayton.

So be it, he thought. Fine. I'll be the one. Christ, *somebody* had to do it.

I'll be him—their dope, their jerk, their dunce.

Their fool forever.

ABOUT THE TYPE

This book was set in Sabon, a typeface designed by the well-known German typographer Jan Tschichold (1902–74). Sabon's design is based on the original letter-forms of Claude Garamond and was created specifically to be used for three sources: foundry type for hand composition, Linotype, and Monotype. Tschichold named his typeface for the famous Frankfurt typefounder Jacques Sabon, who died in 1580.